OMEN OF DOOM

Varlan of the Scented Waters spoke in a kindly tone. "At least our honor is intact, Ossfil. We cannot help what their alien gadgets tell them."

There was a long pause. "I fear that my honor is not intact." The starship captain closed his ears tight on the top of his head and curled his tail between his first and second pairs of legs. "I fear the monsters may have learned where our home stars are located."

The blows to Varlan's psyche had been very great recently. First had been the shock of capture and the destruction of hope. Now came the news that the information which Salfador of the Eternal Flame had died to protect might be in the possession of humans. Varlan's sudden howl of anguish had supersonic overtones. It was a cry of absolute and total despair.

By Michael McCollum
Published by Ballantine Books:

ANTARES DAWN

ANTARES PASSAGE

A GREATER INFINITY

LIFE PROBE

PROCYON'S PROMISE

ANTARES PASSAGE

Michael McCollum

A Del Rey Book

BALLANTINE BOOKS • NEW YORK

A Del Rey Book
Published by Ballantine Books

Library of Congress Catalog Card Number: 87-91527

ISBN 0-345-32314-9

Manufactured in the United States of America

First Edition: December 1987

Diagram by Shelly Shapiro

Cover Art by Don Dixon

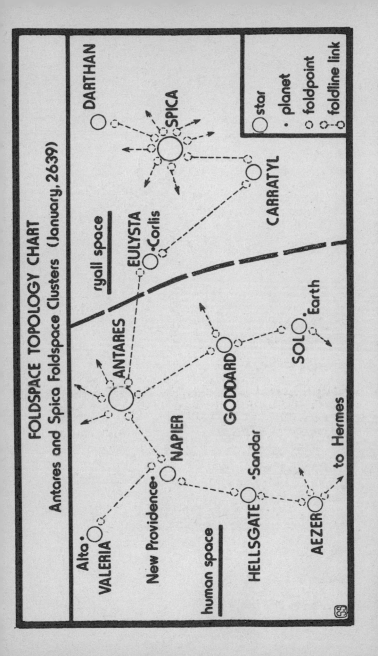

FOLDSPACE TOPOLOGY CHART
Antares and Spica Foldspace Clusters (January, 2639)

human space

ryall space

Alto· VALERIA
New Providence·
NAPIER
·Sandar HELLSGATE
GODDARD
AEZER
to Hermes
SOL Earth
ANTARES
EULYSTA ·Corlis
CARRATYL
SPICA
DARTHAN

star
· planet
○ foldpoint
○--○ foldline link

THE BIRTH AND DEATH OF A STAR

The star was a relative newcomer to the galactic scene. It had begun life as a vast cloud of interstellar hydrogen that over the millennia had collapsed in upon itself, pulled together by gravitational attraction. As the cloud coalesced, the gas at its center grew hotter. After a while, the interior began to glow with a visible light. Then one day, the temperature at the cloud's center reached the level where hydrogen fuses into helium. On that day, a new star blazed forth to illuminate the blackness of the interstellar night.

For millions of years the star shone with a luminosity equal to that of several thousand of its lesser brethren. Indeed, the star's radiance made it a beacon visible across the length of the galaxy. However, such profligacy is not without its costs. Where smaller suns took as long as 10 billion years to consume their available supplies of fusible hydrogen, the giant star managed the same feat in less than a single gigayear. About the time the first apelike prehumans ventured forth onto the savannas of Africa, the star ran low on hydrogen fuel, and as quickly as it had flamed alight, the nuclear fire at its heart was snuffed out.

The end of fusion brought with it a resumption of the

contraction that had molded the primordial cloud. As the core fell inward, its temperature rose precipitously. Within seconds, the temperature at the star's center reached the point where helium fuses into carbon. The nuclear fire flamed anew, this time powered by the helium ash of the previous cycle. Since the new fire was hotter than the old, the star wasted energy even more lavishly than before. It expanded as well, providing a larger surface area from which to radiate the vigorous new energy to surrounding space. Along with the expansion came the cooling of the star's outermost layers and a change in color. Where before the star had radiated a brilliant blue-white light, its visible surface was now a bright yellow-green.

The star continued on the quick-burning helium-carbon cycle until the time when the first agricultural settlements began to appear on Earth. Then, having depleted its supply of helium, the inner fire failed, triggering yet another cycle of contraction and heating. This time it was the turn of the carbon atoms to provide the star's new source of energy. Once again the new fuel produced more energy than previously, forcing the star's surface to expand to provide sufficient area to radiate the heat. By the time the star stabilized at four hundred solar diameters, its hue had shaded down from yellow-green to a deep red-orange.

The star was well into its dotage when the first human telescopes were turned its way. The first starships to arrive at the star made note of this fact a few centuries later when they recorded more neutrinos than expected pouring forth from its fiery interior. It was obvious even then that the star hadn't long to live. Still, a stellar lifetime is a very long time, and no one truly expected the end to come as quickly as it did.

At 1732 hours on 3 August 2512, the star exhausted the last of its carbon fuel. Within seconds the old cycle of contraction and heating began again. This time things were different, however. For now the star's core was rich in iron, and iron cannot be fused to produce energy. Rather, fusing iron nuclei rob energy from their surroundings. With its core hopelessly chilled by iron fusion reactions, the star gave up its ages-old fight with gravity. The core began its final collapse.

As billions upon countless billions of tonnes of matter fell inward, they gave up the potential energy that they had stored through the millennia. This "energy of position" reappeared as heat, causing the temperature at the center of the star to rise rapidly toward infinity. Some of this heat was radiated into the middle layers of the star's atmosphere; these layers, unlike the core, were still rich in unburned hydrogen. A furious thermonuclear reaction resulted. In the blink of an eye, the star began to produce as much energy each second as it had previously radiated away in its entire lifetime.

The end came quickly as the star exploded in the most titanic explosion ever witnessed by human beings.

CHAPTER 1

It was high noon when the commercial shuttle touched down at Homeport Spaceport. Even so, the Antares Nebula was clearly visible in Alta's deep purple sky if one knew where to look. It had been three years since the nova had first burned bright in the Altan heavens, and while Antares was no longer the eye-searing spark it had once been, the supernova's power and its relative proximity assured that it would be visible in daylight for several years to come.

Fleet Captain Richard Arthur Drake unstrapped from his seat and stood to remove his kit bag from the shuttle's overhead baggage compartment. Around him, four dozen fellow passengers did the same. Then each man and woman queued up in the shuttle's center aisle and waited patiently for the landing bridge to be maneuvered across the shuttle's wing and attached to the midships air lock.

Drake was of medium height, with a lean, muscular figure. His hair, which he wore in the close-cropped style of a military spacer, was black with a touch of gray around the edges. A tiny network of worry lines emanated from the corners of his green eyes, and a whitish scar cut one of his eyebrows into two unequal sections.

As he moved slowly down the aisle, he did so with the smooth motion of one who has learned to maneuver under widely varying conditions of acceleration and gravity.

The crowd was slow to disembark. As each passenger reached the storage lockers just forward of the midships air lock, he or she would stop and sort through the carry-on luggage, blocking the aisle in the process. Normally, Drake would have found his patience running short at the continued delay. Not today. After six months spent breathing the reconstituted effluvium that passed for breathing gas aboard a starship, he was more than happy to merely stand and inhale deeply of the virgin air that wafted in through the open air lock.

Eventually, he found himself across the landing bridge and inside the terminal building. He threaded his way through the waiting crowd and was about to board a slidewalk for the main terminal building when a familiar voice called out. "Richard!"

Drake turned at the sound and was nearly overwhelmed by the fragrant bundle of femininity that flew into his embrace. Arms wrapped around his neck, and warm lips pressed hungrily against his mouth. He responded in kind for long seconds before breaking free of his assailant with a grin

"Excuse me, miss, but do I know you?"

"You'd better know me," Bethany Lindquist replied with mock severity. "We've got a date at the altar, remember?"

"Do we?" he asked. "The last time I asked, you said that you didn't want to set a date because—"

"You knew what I meant! Now stop teasing me before I forget that you ever asked me."

"Yes, ma'am, except as I remember, *you* asked *me*."

"Then your memory is faulty, sir. Now then, aren't you happy to see me?"

"You know I am, Beth. Here, stand back and let me look at you." Drake thrust his fiancée out to arm's length and feasted on the sight of her. Bethany was nearly as tall as he was, with a well-proportioned figure and an easy, graceful stance. Her heart-shaped face was framed by shoulder-length auburn hair. Her green eyes had a slight slant that complemented her high cheekbones. She was smiling broadly, which produced dimples in her cheeks. After long seconds of mutual inspection, he pulled her close again and sighed. "My God, you're more beautiful than I remember!"

"Thank you, kind sir. May I say the same about you?"

"You may. How the hell did you know I was coming, anyway?"

"I have my spies."

"I'll bet you do. But seriously, how did you know? I didn't know myself which ship I would be on until a few hours before I left Felicity Base."

"First of all, they're holding a parliamentary briefing concerning the Helldiver Project at the Admiralty tomorrow. I knew you would be attending."

"That's supposed to be a secret."

"Not to me. I'm an invited participant."

"You are?"

She nodded. "I'm the official representative of the terrestrial ambassador, remember?"

"Ah, yes. Now I remember why we can't get married. Something about your duty to your uncle . . ."

"Hmmm, do I detect a hint of annoyance in your tone, m'love?"

"More than a hint," he muttered.

"How sweet!"

"Don't change the subject. How did you know I'd be on this shuttle?"

"My uncle told me."

"How the hell did he know?"

"He has an office on Parliament Hill now. He hears things."

"He could have been wrong, you know. What if I hadn't come through that door just now?"

Bethany shrugged. "Then I would have met every arriving ship for the next month if I'd had to." She snuggled close and kissed him again. "Oh, Richard, it's so good to have you home!"

"Good to be home," he replied with his nose nestled in her fragrant hair. After a long moment in which no one spoke, they released each other by mutual consent. Drake sighed deeply. "Well, shall we go in search of the rest of my luggage?"

"Suits me," Bethany replied.

They avoided the slidewalk, preferring to walk arm in arm down the long concourse. Drake found himself whistling under his breath. As they walked, he became aware of the warmth of her beside him and of the general acuteness of his senses. He watched the bustle around him with newly sharpened vision.

Overhead were several large holoscreens. Some were used to display launching and arrival information, others directed travelers to various destinations within the spaceport, while still others displayed the latest news concerning the recently completed election. Drake ignored the latter. He'd had all the news he cared for on the long flight down from Felicity Base.

They came to the end of the concourse and turned left into the main section of the spaceport terminal building. A large holocube stood at the point where several slidewalks spilled their loads into the cavernous terminal. And inside the cube stood a creature from out of a nightmare.

The basis for interstellar travel was established by Bashir-ben-Sulieman in 2078. Sulieman, an astronomer working out of Farside Observatory, Luna, spent his life measuring the precise positions and proper motions of several thousand stars. After two decades of work, he reluctantly concluded that existing gravitational theories did not adequately explain the placement of various stars within the galactic spiral arm of which Sol is a member. Sulieman became convinced that space is not only curved locally around planetary and stellar masses, as Einstein had maintained, but that it is also folded back upon itself in long lines stretching across thousands of light-years. He theorized that these *foldlines* originate in the massive black hole that occupies the center of the galaxy and that they stream outward in complex patterns along the spiral arms. He further theorized that whenever such a foldline encounters a star, it is focused much as a beam of light is focused by a lens, and that if that focus is sufficiently sharp, a weak spot, or *foldpoint*, appears in the fabric of the space–time continuum.

Twenty years after Sulieman's revelation, scientists positioned a spaceship within one of the two foldpoints known to exist within the Solar system and released copious quantities of energy in a precisely controlled pattern. The energy release caused the ship to be instantaneously transported along the foldline to the system of Luyten's Star, some 12.5 light-years distant from Sol.

There was no holding the human race back after that. Over the next several centuries, the leakage of population into space became a flood. The pattern of the migration was determined almost entirely by the shape of *foldspace*, as the aggregate of foldlines and foldpoints came to be called. While some stars were found to possess only a single foldpoint, others were endowed with two, three, or more. The biggest, most massive stars were found to be especially fertile centers of foldpoint production; therefore, the systems of these stars became the crossroads of interstellar travel. The red-orange supergiant star Antares was the champion foldpoint producer throughout human space. Its six interstellar portals made Antares the linchpin of a network of related star systems known collectively as the Antares Foldspace Cluster.

When Antares exploded on 3 August 2512, the immediate effects were felt far beyond the confines of the Antares system. The release of so concentrated a burst of energy jolted the very fabric of space–time, and with it, the structure of foldspace for hundreds of light-years in every direction. In some systems, foldpoints underwent radical changes of position, while in others, foldpoints appeared where none had previously existed. In still other star systems, preexisting foldpoints disappeared without a trace.

The F8 dwarf star known as Valeria had been doubly unlucky. Situated 125 light-years from Antares, the Val system was what foldspace astronomers called a cul-de-sac system, a star with but a single foldpoint. When Antares exploded, Valeria's foldpoint had simply disappeared. Thus it was that the human colony on Valeria IV—Alta to its inhabitants—had found itself isolated from the rest of human space for a century and a quarter. Then, early in the year 2637 (Universal Calendar), Antares had burned bright in the Altan sky, signaling the arrival of the leading edge of the nova shock wave. Simultaneous with the passage of the nova shock wave, Valeria's foldpoint had reappeared high in the system's northern hemisphere.

"What's this?" Drake asked Bethany, gesturing toward the display.

"Part of the government's 'Know Thy Enemy' campaign," she replied. "They've got them in most public places. Push the button and it will spew out all manner of interesting facts. Here, listen." She stepped forward and pressed a stud that jutted from the base of the holocube. The image came to life and seemed to peer down at them. At the same time, a sonorous voice began to speak.

"The creature you see before you, sir or madam, is a Ryall, and the mortal enemy of all humanity..."

The image in the holocube was that of a creature designed along the lines of a six-legged centaur. The legs were short, less than half a meter in length, and culminated in wide padlike feet. Their shortness was amply compensated for by the creature's forebody—a vertical torso topped by a long, flexible neck that carried the alien's head to the height of a man's. The head was wide at the back, showing considerable cranial bulge, and narrow at the front, where a toothy snout jutted forward some fifteen centimeters. The eyes were set so wide apart that the creature had trouble looking straight ahead. In the hologram, its head was cocked to one side, as though scanning the faces of passersby. The mouth was partially open, showing two rows of conical teeth and a triply forked tongue. On top of the head were two flaps of skin stretched taut by rigid spikelike projections. Of nostrils or any equivalent, there was no sign.

Two heavily muscled arms were attached to the forebody at the same point as the neck. The creature's hands consisted of four slender fingers flanked by two opposable thumbs. At the opposite end of the main body, a meter-long tail dragged the ground. The Ryall's hide was scaled, the scales shading from gray-green on top to light beige beneath.

The lecturing voice continued. "... Although the Ryall bear a passing resemblance to both terrestrial and Altan reptiles, they are neither. Indeed, they don't fit particularly well into any of our normal taxonomic categories. They are warm-blooded, and the females suckle the young—although on a mixture of blood and nutrients rather than milk. In spite of these mammal-like traits, they also lay eggs. Note the vestigial webs between the fingers of each hand, and again between the short digits on the feet. The Ryall evolved as aquatic animals and did not leave the water for the land until quite recently in their past. Experts tell us that they were forced from the water by another sentient race on their home world, a race the Ryall call the swift eaters. It is this incident in their history that we believe makes them so highly territorial that they have attacked us without provocation. That being the case, the only thing left for us to do is . . ."

Drake didn't wait to find out what the narrator had in mind. He nudged Bethany. "Come on, we've better things to do than listen to this."

She glanced at him and smiled slyly. "Maybe we can ask the taxi driver to take a shortcut into town."

The return of their star's foldpoint should have been front-page news throughout the Valeria system. In fact, no one noticed. For a foldpoint is a difficult object to find under the best of circumstances, and after a century and a quarter of isolation, the Altans had stopped looking. Therefore, it came as something of a shock when an unidentified starship materialized high above Val's ecliptic and immediately began thrusting for deep space.

Despite their surprise, the Altans lost no time in dispatching a ship to investigate. What it discovered was a battered warship bearing the markings of the Grand Fleet of Earth and a crew of corpses. Somewhere in its travels, the Earth fleet blastship had been badly mauled in battle and abandoned by its surviving crew members. After that it had jumped blindly from foldpoint to foldpoint under the control of a radiation-damaged autopilot, eventually ending up in the Val system.

With evidence of fighting beyond the foldpoint, the Altans had hurriedly organized an expedition to scout the situation. The expedition's first destination had been the Napier system and the colony world of New Providence, the ancestral home of Alta's first colonists. What the Altan expedition found was a world abandoned by its inhabitants.

The discovery that New Providence was a dead world had saddened but not surprised the Altans. A number of astronomers had warned them that the fifteen light-years separating Napier from Antares was insufficient to protect the system from the full fury of the supernova. What *had* surprised the Altans was the condition in which they found most of New Providence's cities. The steady rain of high-energy photons and charged particles was deadly to all forms of life but should not have materially affected the concrete, stone, and steel of a city. The Altans had expected to find a world of abandoned but pristine municipalities.

What they had found instead were horizon-to-horizon ruins bearing the unmistakable signs of nuclear bombardment. Shocked at the sight of widespread destruction, the Altans had dug through the ruins, searching for clues to what had precipitated the fighting. What they had found had been the biggest surprise of all. For, contrary to the explorers' expectations, the New Providentials had not fallen to fighting among themselves. They had been attacked by a race of centauroid aliens, which the New Providentials had dubbed the Ryall.

Shortly after learning of the aliens' existence, the Altan expedition had departed from the Napier system for the neighboring system of Hellsgate, where New Providence had established a second interstellar colony. According to the records the Altans found in the ruins, it had been to this second colony that New Providence's refugees had fled.

The Altan ships had entered the Hellsgate system and quickly made contact with the inhabitants. They discovered that Sandar, as the modern inhabitants called their planet, had been at war with the Ryall for more than a century. And before the Altans were finished, they had had the opportunity to view the war firsthand!

Richard Drake was jolted awake by a low-pitched hooting from somewhere outside. His first thought was that it was the cry of a night-hunting calu beast. Then, as he came more awake, he remembered that there hadn't been a calu sighted in Homeport in more than a century.

"What is that?" he asked softly in the blackness.

Bethany stirred beside him, stretching as she came awake. After a moment's silence, she said, "I must have fallen asleep. What time is it?"

Drake glanced at the disembodied red numerals that floated in the darkness where he remembered the nightstand to be. "Nearly twenty hundred. What's that noise outside?"

Bethany sat up in bed and listened. "Oh, that's just the space-raid siren. They announced a drill this morning on the news."

"How do you know it isn't a real raid?" he asked.

"Hmmm," she responded. "You don't think the Ryall would have the bad taste to launch an attack during a scheduled drill, do you?"

He laughed. "I'm sure they would if they could. However, they'd have to get past the Sandarians first. Since we haven't heard of any major Ryall successes in the Hellsgate system, I think we're safe for the time being."

"Depolarize the window, Richard. I want to let the night in."

"Where's the control?"

"On the nightstand, beside the clock. The large round knob next to the light switch."

Drake fumbled for the control, found it, and turned it full in the clockwise direction. As he did so, one whole wall of the bedroom disappeared as the floor-to-ceiling window went from 100 percent opaque to fully transparent.

Beyond the window lay a clear, calm night. Across the Tigris River, the lights of Homeport shone brilliantly in subdued colors, while Antares hovered low in the western sky. The nova shed a light the color of a mercury-vapor lamp and suffused the countryside with a pale silver glow. Directly in front of them, nova-light reflected from the surface of the river to produce a broad band of silver across which a small pleasure boat moved upstream in silence.

Bethany rolled onto her stomach and propped her head on a pillow. "Isn't the night beautiful, Richard? Look what the nova's done to the river!"

Drake reached out and let his fingertips trace the soft curves of her spine. "You're the one who is beautiful."

In the distance, the soft ululation of the siren slowly drifted down toward the limits of audibility.

"I guess that's it," she said. "I wonder how much use these drills will be if we're ever raided for real."

"Not much," he replied. "They're mostly to get people in the proper mood. If you are rousted out of bed in the middle of the night to seek shelter, you're more likely to put up with the extra inconveniences a war economy requires."

"I always suspected as much. Not to change the subject, but are you hungry?"

"Famished," he replied.

"Then opaque the window and turn on some lights. I'll make us a snack. We can eat out on the balcony and watch the nova-set."

"If that is your wish, my love."

"It is. Hurry, it will be down in an hour."

They dressed quickly. Bethany busied herself in the kitchen while Drake set the table on her balcony. Fifteen minutes later, they were enjoying a late supper of roast beef, cril greens, and coffee. The coffee was nothing like the bitter Earth original but rather an Altan product that the founders of the colony had decided was the closest local substitute. As they ate, they watched Antares sink toward the western horizon.

They watched in silence for long minutes before Drake turned to Bethany and said, "Will you marry me?"

"It seems to me that I've answered that question more than once," she replied.

"No," he persisted. "I don't mean marry me someday. I mean marry me *now*, this very minute! We'll call up city hall and register our vows, then roust the nearest city magistrate out of bed."

"We shouldn't have to roust anyone out. It's only 2030 hours."

"Even better. We'll have the whole thing over in an hour."

Bethany caressed his cheek with her hand. "I'll do it if you insist, Richard, but I would rather wait. I've had a lot of time to think about it these last six months, and I've decided I want a big church wedding."

He shrugged. "Fine. I'll see if I can't reserve a church for next weekend. Surely the boss will give me the time off if I tell him why I want it. You can invite your uncle and friends, and I'll invite everyone at the Admiralty who has ever spoken to me. We'll even throw in fifty or so strangers to fill out the crowd. I guarantee a minimum attendance of two hundred!"

She laughed. "You don't understand, Richard. I don't want a *big* wedding in a church. I want a wedding in a *big church*!"

"You're right, I don't understand you."

"It's simple really, darling. I've decided that I want to be married in Notre Dame Cathedral. You know, the one in Paris, France."

"You want to be married on Earth?"

She nodded. "I thought it would be a nice touch."

"I'm not sure Notre Dame exists any longer."

She shrugged. "Then Westminster Abbey or St. Peter's Basilica will do just as well. Or even the Little Chapel by the Road. Just as long as we're married on Earth."

"Has it occurred to you that we may never find Earth again?"

"I have confidence, Richard. We'll find it because we must." Bethany got up and stretched. "Now then, if you are through eating, sir, I think it's time we went back to bed."

"What about the nova? There are still fifteen minutes before it sets."

"We can see Antares anytime, and it isn't every night a woman receives a proposal of marriage."

"Or avoids it so skillfully," he said, glancing one last time at the setting star. When he turned his attention back to the table, he discovered that he was speaking to an empty balcony. Lifting a napkin from his lap, he dropped it on the table, stood, and followed her inside.

CHAPTER 2

Except wind stands as never it stood.
It is an ill wind that blows no one good.
                    —Thomas Tusser, 16th-Century Poet

There hadn't been a single inhabitant of Alta—or of the entire Valeria system, for that matter—whose life had not been drastically changed by the Antares Supernova. When the nova first burst bright in the Altan sky, it had transformed the darkness of Alta's night into an eerie daylight as it flooded land and sea with a harsh blue-white radiance. Most Altans had been initially enchanted by the phenomenon, although mothers had often complained that their children refused to sleep with the nova-light peeking around the edges of their curtains.

Then had come word of the restoration of the fold-point. The news had been greeted with universal joy as the pent-up frustrations of the Long Isolation were released. The celebration had gone on for days, and a new spirit of enthusiasm and hope had surged throughout the system. For months it had seemed that Alta was on the verge of a prosperity unknown in its history.

Slowly the nova had faded from its period of maximum brilliance. While it did so, Alta had eagerly awaited the return of its expedition to the Napier and Hellsgate systems. The day had finally come when the first of the expedition's ships returned home, bringing with it news of the Ryall threat. The public mood had shifted almost overnight. Optimism turned suddenly to horror; enthusiasm was quickly transformed into fear. Night after night the news services vied with each other to broadcast the most graphic views of the destruction of New Providence's cities. No longer was the supernova regarded as Alta's personal good-luck charm. For most Altans, Antares had become the visible symbol of an uncertain and dangerous future.

If there was anyone who still had reason to be thankful for the nova in Alta's sky, that man was Clarence Whitlow. Whitlow was the hereditary terrestrial ambassador to Alta, the fifth member of his family to hold that post. It was the job of the hereditary ambassadors to act as though nothing had changed when the supernova had isolated Valeria from the rest of human space. So far as Whitlow and his predecessors were concerned, it was their job to represent Earth's interests on Alta. The fact that they had had no instructions from home in 127 years was a matter not worthy of comment.

To Clarence Whitlow had fallen the lonely task of keeping an important tradition alive. That tradition held that Alta was part of a larger whole, a community of worlds built on the twin principles of tolerance and mutual respect. For thirty years he had lived the fiction that Earth was still a factor in the affairs of Alta. It was a fiction that made him a comical figure to his friends and neighbors. And, as for official Homeport, save for a small yearly stipend voted by Parliament, he had been virtually ignored during his time as terrestrial ambassador.

The coming of the nova had changed all of that. Among the ships trapped in the Val system in 2512 were three heavy battle cruisers of Earth's Grand Fleet. Part of the agreement by which the first terrestrial ambassador had ceded these three ships to the fledgling Altan Navy had been that all succeeding terrestrial ambassadors would have a say in their use beyond the Val system. To enforce the agreement, Whitlow's great-great-grandfather had retained certain security codes needed to operate the cruisers' jump engines. Clarence Whitlow, in turn, had used his possession of those codes to force a promise from Parliament that he would be consulted on all matters of interstellar policy. They had further agreed that Whitlow would have the right to send a personal representative along on any future interstellar expeditions.

For Clarence Whitlow, at least, the Antares Supernova had been an unmixed blessing.

Clarence Whitlow stood behind his oversize, onyx-wood desk and stared out the window that adorned one wall of his office. Whitlow was a frail, white-haired man who walked with a noticeable stoop. The stoop was the result of a progressive bone disease, which the doctors had been able to arrest but not to cure. His bent posture, along with his soft features, had led many an opponent to underestimate him over the past three years. Those who had done so had found that an iron will resided inside the stooped form.

Whitlow let his gaze sweep across the scene in front of him. Across a wide tree-lined boulevard was the black cube that housed the Altan Industrial Council. Next to it, in a structure every bit as imposing, was headquartered the Free Labor Association. On either side of the two were other buildings, each of which held the legions of special pleaders that have congregated around governmental centers since the days of Babylon. If Whitlow looked over the tops of the buildings of Lobbyist Row, he could just make out the ugly pile of stone and mortar that was the home of Alta's parliament.

Not for him this morning were the foreground details of government, however. Instead, he lifted his gaze above the concrete and marble of the government district, past the panorama of Homeport itself, to the azure mountain range that bulked up in the distance. To Whitlow's eyes, the Colgate Mountains were the most beautiful on Main Continent; that, as much as their proximity to the capital, had been the reason he had chosen to make his home in their foothills for most of his life. There had been many times over the past three years when he'd wished he were back in the mountains tending his roses.

Clarence Whitlow was jolted from his reverie by the sudden buzzing of the intercom on his desk. He passed a hand through thinning white hair and returned to his seat. Leaning forward, he keyed the intercom to life.

"Yes, Miss Preston?"

"Your niece is here, Mr. Ambassador."

"Send her in!"

The office door opened almost immediately, and Bethany entered. He could see by the broad smile on her face that her mission to the spaceport the previous day had been successful.

"I take it that you found your young man," he said.

"Yes, Richard came in on the noon shuttle."

"I told you that he would."

"Just how *did* you know?" Bethany asked.

Whitlow shrugged. "I keep my eyes open, and I see things. I listen carefully, and I hear things."

"Have you heard anything about today's conference?"

"Ostensibly, it's to be a classified briefing for newly elected Members of Parliament."

"What does 'ostensibly' mean?" Bethany asked.

"I only note that they've had other parliamentary briefings, and to my knowledge, neither the prime minister, nor Jonathon Carstairs, nor Richard Drake has been in attendance."

"You're implying that it's something more?"

"I hear rumors."

"What rumors?"

"That they may be about ready to make the decision to commit to a launch date. If so, it's about time!"

Bethany nodded. "I understand Jonathon Carstairs has actually developed a nervous tic over what Helldiver has cost to date. It would be embarrassing to explain to the taxpayers how the Navy invested all that money, then wasn't allowed to go."

"I hope you're right, Bethany. The sooner they

launch, the sooner my accumulated dispatches will be delivered to an authorized representative of the Interstellar Council on Earth."

"Have you given any thought to what will happen then?" Bethany asked.

"I suppose I'll retire. Why do you ask?"

"I don't know," she replied. "It's just that we've been working toward this goal for so long, I often wonder what will become of us when we finally succeed. Do you suppose the I.C. will confirm you as ambassador once we've made contact?"

Whitlow's expression flickered through a series of emotions before he answered. "Of course not! What a silly thing to say."

"I don't think so," his niece said. "You've served them faithfully all these years. Why wouldn't they keep you on?"

"Because, my darling child, you and I both know that I've only been playing a role these past three decades. It is the ideal of Earth which I've attempted to safeguard, not the reality. That ideal has been important to us. It's helped our people through the long years of isolation and exerted a moderating influence over our government. So long as the prime minister and Parliament are reminded that they may someday have to answer to a higher authority, they are restrained from some of the excesses which have plagued other governments throughout history.

"But let us not mistake my playacting for reality, Beth. I may possess the title of terrestrial ambassador, but I can never *be* the true representative of Earth. I am no less a colonist at heart than you. If Earth is at war with the Ryall, then they will need one of their own here in Homeport to look after their true interests. Have no illusions about it. They will turn me out to pasture in a moment."

"Then why should we be loyal to them?"

"Because I gave my word to my father on his deathbed. I promised that I would do my very best for Earth. I have followed that credo for thirty years, and I do not propose to stop now." Whitlow stared at his niece's dour expression. "Besides, I'm looking forward to retirement. It will give me a chance to raise my roses.

"Enough of this. What did you and Richard do after you met him at the spaceport?"

Bethany brightened. "First we took a taxi to the Admiralty so Richard could check in with the first admiral. After that, we had a late lunch at the Mandarin Orange down by the river."

"How was the food?"

"Excellent! The alos sprouts were done just the way you like them. You should try it sometime."

"Perhaps you would consent to be my guide someday when you aren't busy."

"Sure."

"Ah . . . was that all?"

Bethany felt her face redden. She and Richard had gone straight from the restaurant to her apartment, where they had made love until nightfall. That she would be intimate with her fiancé after six months of separation should not have surprised anyone. Still, it was uncharacteristic of her uncle to ask such a question. "Richard asked me to marry him again," she said avoiding a direct answer.

"I would have thought once enough."

"We decided that we would have the ceremony on Earth," Bethany replied with a grin. "In a cathedral, if we can arrange it."

Her uncle did not react as Bethany had expected. Instead of congratulating her, he said, "That brings up a point which I've been meaning to discuss with you. I've been considering finding someone else to represent me on the Helldiver Expedition."

"*What?*"

"I've even thought of going myself."

"You can't, Uncle! Your heart would never stand up to the acceleration. Besides, what's wrong with me representing you? I've done it before, and you didn't seem to have any complaints."

"You weren't engaged to Captain Drake before."

"What has that to do with anything?"

"A great deal, Beth. Don't get me wrong. No one was

happier than I when you returned from Sandar and announced your engagement to Richard Drake. He is, if you will pardon my saying so, a distinct improvement over your last fiancé. However, he is also the commander of the Altan contingent to the Helldiver Fleet. That means that he represents the interests of the Altan government. If you are to go along as my representative, then you must represent Earth. Make no mistake about that. Your first duty will be to the Interstellar Council."

"I understand that perfectly."

"I wonder if you do," Whitlow said. "Have you considered that a situation may arise where you will find yourself at odds with your husband to be?"

"I would think, Uncle, that with the Ryall running around loose, the interests of Alta and Earth are the same."

"They probably are. However, you are ducking the question, which is that they may not be. I must know that you will serve Earth first and Richard Drake second. Either that, or I will find someone else to represent me. Can you assure me that you will be my honest advocate?"

Bethany hesitated for an uncomfortably long time. To Whitlow, who had raised her, the inner turmoil was obvious. Finally, she replied. "I think I can do it, Uncle. I hope and pray the situation will never arise, but if it does, I believe I can be sufficiently objective to think of Earth first."

Whitlow nodded. "Good enough for now. However, should today's conference result in a green light for Helldiver, I will expect your absolute pledge of loyalty. Anything less, bad heart or no, I will go in your place."

The Admiralty Building had been built in the earliest days of the Altan colony. It had originally been designed as the central government's embassy and ambassadorial residence on Alta. Granville Whitlow, the terrestrial ambassador at the time of the nova, had ceded the building and grounds to the colonial government at the same time he'd turned over the battle cruisers. For a century and a quarter, the building had housed the headquarters of the Altan Space Navy.

Richard Drake stepped from the taxi that had brought him from Bethany's apartment. He bounded up the steps past the Marine guards who flanked the main entrance and entered through the three-meter-high armor-plated doors at the front entrance. He marched briskly across a marble floor that still bore the stylized outline of Earth in its surface and presented his identification to the Marine sergeant who sat in a glass cage just inside the entrance. When the computer in the subbasement concluded that he was indeed who he said he was, the sergeant directed him toward a bank of public lifts to his right.

"Fleet Captain Drake!"

Drake turned at the hail to find Commodore Douglas Wilson striding toward him. Wilson was the first admiral's adjutant and chief of staff. "Good morning, sir."

"Morning," Wilson replied. "Ready for the big day?"

Drake nodded. "If this is it, I am."

"Should be," Wilson replied. "The prime minister's attending the conference, and you can bet he wouldn't be wasting his time if he weren't ready to give us the go-ahead."

"What about the Conservative Alliance? Are they ready to give us their blessing?"

Wilson nodded. "Their leadership is, finally! Some of their newly elected rank-and-file types have been making troublesome noises. We'll be briefing them. They've heard rumors about Helldiver and now want to see what it's all about."

"Do you think they'll come around after they know the facts?"

Wilson shrugged expansively. "Who can tell with politicians? But enough of this political talk. How go things at Felicity Base?"

"We're in pretty good shape. *Discovery* is in the final phases of checkout, *Dagger* isn't far behind, and *City of Alexandria* should begin systems integration testing sometime tomorrow."

"What about the tankers?"

"They're about on a par with *Alexandria*. All testing

on the new generators should be completed within ten days. We could launch thirty days after that."

"Hmmm," Wilson mused. "I wonder how the Sandarians are doing."

"From what I hear," Drake replied, "they're ahead of us."

The two of them took the lift to the sixth floor, where the Admiralty's main conference room was located. The conference room was some ten meters square. At its center was a rectangular arrangement of tables covered with white tablecloths. The room was windowless. To make up for that, a large holoscreen had been affixed to each wall. At each place around the table was a nameplate, a water glass, three pens, and a pad of yellow writing paper. Pitchers filled with water had been located at strategic locations. The only electronics in evidence were the controls used to operate the holoscreens.

Drake found his nameplate to the left of one bearing the name of First Admiral Dardan. Commodore Wilson took the seat on the admiral's right. Bethany and her uncle were already down the table on the opposite side. Drake smiled at his fiancée and received only the most cursory of smiles in response. He quickly ran through their conversation at breakfast, wondering what he had done or said that might have made her mad. She had been in good spirits when she'd left for her uncle's office that morning. Unable to come up with a cause for her apparent shift in mood, he put the subject from his mind. If he'd done something to offend her, she would let him know soon enough.

Drake let his gaze sweep the table. Opposite him were several Members of Parliament who were unfamiliar to him—which meant that they had been elected since the period four years earlier when he'd served as parliamentary liaison officer for the Navy. On his side of the table were several of the prime minister's aides, including Stanislaw Barrett. Across the table were a number of people from Homeport University.

He had just completed his inventory of the attendees when a voice from behind him spoke. "All rise for the Honorable Gareth Reynolds, Prime Minister of the Altan

Republic; the Honorable Jonathon Carstairs, Leader of the Loyal Opposition; and Admiral Luis Dardan, Commander of the Altan Space Navy."

The three men entered the room single file, then fanned out to take their individual seats. The others present stood respectfully until the prime minister had seated himself. As they returned to their own seats with considerable scraping of chairs, the prime minister waited for the noise to die down, then picked up a wooden gavel and banged it on the table. When the room had drifted into silence, Gareth Reynolds began to speak.

"Good morning, ladies and gentlemen. We are here today because several Members of Parliament have requested a policy review on the program which we all know by the code name 'Project Helldiver.' It is the opinion of these petitioners that we were hasty in our approval of this effort two years ago when we signed the Sandarian Treaty. Since the project is nearing completion of Phase I and will shortly be ready for space, I propose to go beyond the question of policy and make this meeting a full program readiness review. By that, I mean that we will discuss whatever needs discussing to determine whether we launch Helldiver on schedule, delay its departure, or cancel it altogether.

"We will begin with several presentations. I do not expect everyone to agree with everything they hear, nor do I ask anyone to surrender his or her right to voice an objection. However, I do ask you to hold any such remarks until after the speakers have finished. Also, when you rise to speak, please state your name and organization clearly for the record. Finally, I remind you that everything discussed hear today is classified as an Altan state secret. What you hear here, stays here!

"Anyone have any questions? . . . If not, we will begin with Dr. Nathaniel Gordon, who will review our situation with regard to the current structure of foldspace. Dr. Gordon, you have the floor!"

CHAPTER 3

Nathaniel Gordon was a small man with nervous hands and a tendency toward pedantry. He stood at his seat and bowed formally in the direction of the prime minister. "Dr. Nathaniel Gordon, University of Homeport, Department of Foldspace Astronomy and Physics," he said loudly. "May I please have the lights down."

As the conference room sank into gloom, the holoscreens mounted high on each of the four walls lit to show a complex three-dimensional diagram. The figure on the screens was a rough ellipsoid shape composed of two hundred small white spheres connected in a seemingly random pattern by a series of curved red lines. It had the look of a child's construction set or a complex organic molecule model. Close by each of the spheres were small golden triangular markers. Upon closer examination it became apparent that the red connecting lines did not actually touch the spheres but terminated in every case at the golden markers.

"Before one can fully appreciate what the Helldiver Project proposes to accomplish," Gordon began, "it is necessary to understand the effect which the Antares Supernova has had on the structure of foldspace. The figure on the screens is undoubtedly familiar to many of you. It is a somewhat stylized diagram showing the major foldline links within human space—what we astronomers call a foldspace topology chart, or FTC for short. This particular FTC represents the situation prior to the Antares Supernova of 2512. The small white spheres are stars, the red connecting lines are active foldline links, and the gold-colored triangles are charted foldpoints.

"The first thing one notices about this FTC is that fewer than five percent of all the stars in human space are charted. That is because the number of stars which possess foldpoints is less than one in twenty. Another point to note: It is the pattern of foldline connections between the stars, not their actual positions in space, which is important.

"This is sometimes a difficult concept for laymen, so forgive me if I dwell on it a bit. Take the example of our own closest neighbor, the M2 dwarf star Reglati-Sera. Even though Reglati is but three light-years distant from us, no human being has ever visited it. That is because Reglati-Sera belongs to the 95 percent of stars that do not possess foldpoints. Thus, in a very real sense, Valeria's closest neighbor is not Reglati-Sera at all, but, rather, Napier, from whence our ancestors came. The two systems are separated by 110 light-years through normal space, but only by a few billion kilometers via foldline link."

Gordon manipulated the screen control in his hand, and the diagram was replaced by another FTC of considerably less complexity. The stars were far less densely packed, and the scale was such that it was now possible to read the names of individual stars. At the center of the screen was a star around which were clustered six small golden triangles. Floating nearby were a series of green, glowing letters that spelled out the name "Antares."

"It is not my intention to conduct a seminar in foldspace astronomy this morning," Dr. Gordon assured his audience. "Therefore, let us concentrate on the local situation. On the screen is a foldspace topology chart showing part of our own local star group. Specifically, you are looking at the FTC for the Napier sector of the Antares Foldspace Cluster. By the way, please do not confuse the term 'foldspace cluster' with the more common 'star cluster.' A star cluster is a group of gravitationally bound stars, whereas a foldspace cluster is a group of stars intimately linked by foldlines. The individual stars of a foldspace cluster may not be—and indeed, seldom are—in close physical proximity to one another.

"It is a truism that the structure of foldspace determines the economics of all activities which rely on interstellar travel. To understand this point, let us take an imaginary journey. Pretend for a moment that you are a prenova starship captain departing Alta with a cargo for Earth. Since Valeria is a cul-de-sac system, you have no choice as to the first waypoint on your journey. Of necessity, the destination of any starship leaving Val *must* be Napier." Dr. Gordon did something to the screen control, and the faint red line connecting Valeria to Napier turned bright crimson. "Once in the Napier system, however, a prenova ship captain was faced with a choice as to his subsequent route to Earth. For example, he could have chosen to take the Hellsgate–Aezer route, which involves successive transitions from Napier to Hellsgate, Aezer, Hermes, Sacata, Carswell, Vega, and Luyten's Star before finally reaching Sol."

The links between stars brightened on the holoscreens as Gordon called out each name. "That is a total of eight foldspace transitions with intrasystem maneuvering at each star along the way. Or, more sensibly, the same ship captain could have chosen to use one of the Antares routes from Napier to Sol. In that event, he would merely have to jump from Napier to Antares to Goddard to Sol—a total of three foldspace transitions. Obviously, the latter route is the more economical by a considerable margin.

"Now then, let us look at the postnova situation." Dr. Gordon manipulated the screen control once again. The small white globe that represented Antares suddenly expanded to ten times its former size, engulfing the fold-point markers around it. Simultaneously, six red-hued foldlines faded nearly to invisibility, causing the whole center of the foldspace diagram to dim.

"The value of a foldspace cluster lies not in the number of foldpoints it possesses but rather in the increased interconnectivity which that cluster brings to the foldspace topology of human space as a whole. In other words, the supernova not only robbed us of those six trade routes, it also robbed us of the flexibility which they provided to our starships." Dr. Gordon thumbed the holoscreen control, and a third FTC flashed on the screen. He zoomed in on one section of the chart, revealing a string of four stars dangling like a loose strand of beads from the body of human space. The names floating beside the star markers were "Aezer," "Hellsgate," "Napier," and "Valeria."

"Here then," Nathaniel Gordon said, "is what Antares did to us. Where before a starship captain could choose half a dozen routes between Alta and the other systems of human space, now there is but one. Clearly we are poorer and more vulnerable as a result."

When Professor Gordon finished, the prime minister glanced down the table to where Drake sat. "I believe you are up next, Fleet Captain."

"Yes, sir." Drake stood and faced the audience. "My name is Richard Drake. I command the battle cruiser *Discovery*. I was military commander of Interstellar Expedition One and will perform that same function for the Altan contingent to the Helldiver Expedition. I have been asked to review some of the events which led up to the decision to initiate the Helldiver Project. I will try to keep it brief."

Drake paused and gazed at his audience. Except for the dozen or so neophyte legislators present, most looked mildly bored. The newly elected Members of Parliament displayed a less identifiable emotion. Drake had long since decided that they were suffering from ill-concealed impatience. It appeared as though they had already made up their minds and weren't particularly interested in having their opinions swayed by facts. Not for the first time during the meeting he wondered if the decision concerning Helldiver's fate hadn't already been made in some caucus room on Parliament Hill. He hurriedly pushed the thought from his mind and concentrated instead on his prepared text.

"Two years ago, ladies and gentlemen, we had no idea what conditions were like beyond our own fold-point. All we knew was that the remains of a once-powerful warship had fallen into our hands. Since that single ship could easily have defeated our whole navy, we were naturally concerned. It was for that reason that we launched the expedition to New Providence and Sandar.

"As you are all aware, we arrived at New Providence and found that the planet had been extensively bombarded prior to its being abandoned in 2527. We also learned of the existence of the Ryall. After New Providence, I decided to push on to the Hellsgate system to investigate further. There we made contact with the Sandarians, who gave us considerable information regarding the Human/Ryall War.

"Yet when we quizzed the Sandarians about *Conqueror*, they denied ever having seen it. That left us with something of a paradox since, as you can see on the screen, Hellsgate sits astride the only plausible route for *Conqueror* to have taken from Earth. Obviously, if *Conqueror* didn't come via the Hellsgate route, there is only one other possible route it could have used." Drake stabbed his finger at the central star on the diagram. "It had to come straight through the supernova remnant!"

"How is that possible, Captain Drake?" a voice asked from midway down the table.

Drake turned at the interruption. "I beg your pardon, sir. You are?"

"My name is Jasan Pettigrew. I'm the newly elected representative of the New Chalmers District, Paradise Island. Frankly, I've seen the nova with my own eyes and find your suggestion to be utterly preposterous.

How could any ship survive inside the supernova longer than an instant without being vaporized?"

Drake shrugged. "It couldn't, Mr. Pettigrew. Not if the funeral pyre we see in our sky every night were a true picture of the nova. But remember, that light has been in transit for more than a century. What we are seeing is the supernova in its youth. Antares has aged considerably in 127 years." As Drake spoke, he tapped a computer reference into the screen control. Suddenly, the foldspace diagram was gone, to be replaced by a full-color holograph.

The holograph showed a view of the Antares Nebula as seen from the surface of New Providence. More than a century of expansion had transformed the brilliant point of light into a ghostlike nebulosity. The nebula had grown to nearly six light-years in diameter and, when viewed from the relative closeness of the Napier system, covered a staggering 22.5 degrees of arc in the sky. That made it forty times the diameter of Luna as seen from Earth, two hundred times the diameter of Felicity as seen from Alta. At the shell's center burned the corpse of what had once been the second largest star in human space, while nearby a second starlike object was all that remained of Antares' smaller A3 companion.

"That is how the nova looks today. Conditions inside are still pretty hellish by human standards, but compared to the primordial fury of those first few cataclysmic hours, Antares is practically cold!"

Pettigrew shifted uncomfortably in his seat. "Then the rumors we've heard are true! The purpose of the Helldiver Project . . . "

Drake nodded. "Is to penetrate the nebula, retrace *Conqueror*'s route, and find Earth."

There was a long silence in the room. Finally, another Member of Parliament spoke up. "Surely you can't be serious!"

"Why not?" Drake asked.

"Damn it, we've all seen photographs of *Conqueror*. The bow section was practically melted off. Are you telling us that the nova didn't do that?"

Drake shook his head. "I'm telling you that the nova definitely *did* do it. *Conqueror*'s autopilot was damaged but still retained sufficient sanity to use the blastship's bulk as a radiation shield for itself, the engines, and fuel tanks."

"And you're going to send *our* ships into that same hell?" Jasan Pettigrew asked.

"Not without protection, sir. For the past two years, a team of Altan and Sandarian scientists have been developing an antiradiation field of radically new design. It should be able to protect a ship inside the nebula."

"I take it that this project is where all the money has gone?" Pettigrew asked.

Drake nodded. "That was a large part of it. We've also been equipping various ships with antirad generators and making other general improvements."

"What ships?"

"*Discovery, Dagger, City of Alexandria*, various tankers, and support craft."

"My God, you're talking about half our Navy!"

"Not quite half, Jasan," the prime minister replied from where he had been following the debate. "Not when you count our new construction and foldpoint defense program."

"But you *are* sending *Dagger* and *Discovery* out with this expedition!" Pettigrew insisted. "That leaves us only *Dreadnought* to defend Alta!"

"True enough, at least until the first of the new cruisers start coming out of the shipyards," Gareth Reynolds replied.

"What can possibly have possessed you to siphon off so much of our strength for this hare-brained scheme?" Pettigrew asked.

"We had our reasons," the prime minister responded. "Admiral Dardan!"

Admiral Luis Dardan, commander of the Altan Space Navy, rose from his seat and strode to where Drake was standing. He nodded at his subordinate and whispered, "Good job, Captain," before Drake returned to his seat. Dardan waited for the assembled MPs to quiet down before continuing.

"Gentlemen, with the return of Interstellar Expedition One, we Altans found ourselves faced with an outside threat for the first time since the founding of our colony. It was the Navy's job to determine how best to meet the Ryall challenge, and in doing our job, we studied two basic options. These were to help Sandar defend the Hellsgate–Aezer foldpoint against Ryall attack, and to attempt to dislodge the Ryall from the Aezer system altogether. I will address the latter option first.

"By far the best solution to our problem would be to drive the Ryall from the Aezer system. Not only would this put more distance between us and our enemies, it would also allow trade to resume between Alta and the rest of human space. Unfortunately, the military prospects for this option are not good. The reason for this lies in the nature of foldpoints. A foldpoint is what we in the military call a "choke point"—a restricted volume of space through which all attacking forces must be funneled. Since a defender knows precisely where the attack will come, he need not waste his forces in patrolling other sectors. Every ship, every orbital fortress, every weapon he possesses can be concentrated in and around the foldpoint. With the defenders positioned to defend such a limited killing zone, the battle begins the moment an attacker materializes. If the defense possesses a sufficient concentration of firepower, it can annihilate virtually any size attacking force before the aggressor has an opportunity to escape into the system at large. The Sandarians have tried to force the Aezer–Hellsgate foldpoint three times over the past seventeen years. Each attempt has been a bloody failure. In light of this, we concluded that there is little likelihood of our driving the Ryall from Aezer any time soon.

"The other option considered was to assist the Sandarians in defending the Hellsgate–Aezer foldpoint. Not only will this save Sandar, it will also provide Alta with three separate lines of defense." Dardan turned to the foldspace topology diagram. "The Ryall are here in the Aezer system. By fortifying the entrances to the Hellsgate, Napier, and Val systems, we can make them fight for each star system along the way. With such defense in depth, there is a very good chance that we can stop any likely Ryall attack for the indefinite future. Indeed, defense in depth is our primary strategy and the reason why we have embarked on our massive shipbuilding program."

"That doesn't explain why you chose to divert so many resources into the Helldiver Project," Pettigrew responded.

"No, sir, it does not. Normally, I'd agree with you about the inadvisability of diverting such a large fraction of our strength at this time. If anything, I would argue that we should wait until we built up larger reserves before launching this expedition. Unfortunately, the Human/Ryall Institute at Homeport University uncovered a factor that convinced both ourselves and the Sandarian government that it is not in our best interest to wait."

"What factor, Admiral Dardan?"

"During its studies, the institute asked what the long-term effect of our being isolated from the rest of humanity would be. Now, we know from our studies of *Conqueror* and the data we obtained from the Sandarians that Alta has lagged perceptibly in technological development during the Long Isolation. Since the Ryall are more than holding their own against mankind, we can assume that we have lagged behind their technological development as well. What the institute concluded was that we will fall even further behind if our isolation continues and that, as time goes by, the chance of the Ryall developing weapons and techniques capable of countering our defenses increases.

"What form such developments might take, we cannot predict. However, you merely have to observe some of the more advanced devices we discovered aboard *Conqueror* to know that the concern is a real one. By extrapolating the known rate at which we are falling behind, the institute calculated that we can expect the Ryall to defeat the Hellsgate–Aezer foldpoint defenses sometime within the next ten to twenty-five years. Once

Sandar falls, we Altans can expect to be overrun in less than a decade.

"Unless we reestablish contact with Earth immediately, our world has less than thirty-five years to live. That is the motivation behind the Helldiver Project and the reason why it must proceed at the earliest possible moment!"

CHAPTER 4

Bethany Lindquist made her way briskly along the length of the main concourse at Homeport Spaceport. As she did so, she weaved around slower groups of travelers, trying for a maximum of speed with a minimum of tromped feet. She trailed a single suitcase behind her like a dog on a leash, carried a garment bag slung over one shoulder, and clutched another small case with her free hand.

As she walked, she was struck by the paradox inherent in launching the Helldiver Project from Homeport Spaceport. By rights, she should now be moving through the bowels of some top-secret military installation, walking past stoic guards with lasers topped by fixed bayonets. Instead, she found herself fighting a tide of humanity, pushing her way past mothers holding crying babies as she dodged the moving throngs of businessmen with their ever-present briefcase *cum* computers. And while there were military men present, they, like Bethany, were en route to destinations beyond the atmosphere. They showed little interest in her, save for their appreciative glances as she passed.

The problem, she reminded herself, was that Altans had never been a warlike people—a fact that owed more to lack of opportunity than to any inherent righteousness. In the early days of the colony, the Grand Fleet had kept the peace, and Alta had had no need for the paraphernalia of war. Later, with the onset of the Long Isolation, there had been no one to fight. Even the establishment of the Altan Space Navy had been largely a scheme by Bethany's ancestor, Granville Whitlow, to keep the three Grand Fleet battle cruisers in working order until interstellar travel could be resumed. For the century and a quarter that the foldpoint had remained sealed, the Navy had been little more than a police force patrolling the less traveled corners of the Val system.

All that had changed, of course, with the return of Interstellar Expedition One from Sandar. But despite what the newsfaxes were calling "the largest military buildup in Altan history," two years had not been nearly long enough to construct the infrastructure of a true military power. To date, Altan efforts to fortify the various foldpoints leading from Hellsgate had taken precedence over construction of a new military spaceport. And so it was that Helldiver, the most closely guarded secret in the history of the colony, was being launched in broad daylight, at the busiest time of the day, from the largest public spaceport on the planet.

Bethany reached the point where three weeks earlier she had waited for Richard's arrival on the noon shuttle. As she walked briskly past, she remembered the joy of their reunion and the bittersweet sadness of their parting forty hours later. They had spent the time before launch seated in the departure lounge. Bethany had managed to hold back her tears until the moment the loading of Richard's shuttle was announced over the public address system.

"Stop that!" he'd said after kissing her on both eyelids. "We'll be back together before you know it."

"It won't be the same," Bethany had replied. "When next we meet, you will have your job to do and I'll have mine. Neither of us will have a moment alone together until we get to . . ." She had trailed off into silence, afraid to say the word "Earth" lest someone overhear.

He had smiled that quizzical smile of his and chuckled. "You were the one who decided where we should be married, you know."

"I know."

A second announcement from an overhead speaker had caused him to climb to his feet. "Time to go, Beth. I'll see you in three weeks. Don't forget to pack your wedding dress."

"I won't."

Bethany lengthened her stride as the spaceport crowds began to thin out toward the end of the long concourse. As she walked, she shifted the garment bag slightly and heard the rustle of hundred-year-old fabric. She had done as Richard commanded. Inside the garment bag was the wedding dress in which four generations of Whitlow women had been married.

She came to a branching of the public walkway. The main passage turned to the left toward the berths of privately owned ground-to-orbit craft, while a small side passage ran off to the right. Bethany turned into the latter without hesitation. She quickly found herself descending a gentle slope into a brightly lighted tunnel. The tunnel surfaced again a hundred meters farther on. Two armed Marines stood guard at the point of emergence.

"May we help you, ma'am?"

"My name's Lindquist. I'm bound for *Discovery* via *Alexandria*." As she spoke, she pulled a message slip from her pocket. Printed on Navy letterhead, it invited her to appear at Gate 27C, Homeport Spaceport, on or before 1040 hours, 16 Taurus 2639, for transportation to ANC *Discovery*. The message was signed by First Admiral Dardan.

The Marine took the message, punched a code sequence into a hand-held computer terminal, and waited for the machine to emit a quiet beeping tone. When it did, he nodded and handed the orders back to Bethany. "Good to have you aboard, Miss Lindquist. You may proceed to the gate. They'll be boarding in about fifteen minutes."

"Thank you, Corporal."

"You're welcome, ma'am."

* * *

Richard Drake sat in his command chair onboard *Discovery* and watched an apparition on the viewscreen in front of him. The screen showed the blue-white expanse of Alta's limb surmounted by the blackness of space. Val was a bright disk at the upper edge of the screen, while the planet's atmosphere showed as a disconcertingly narrow band of haze above the world's horizon. And, hovering just above the atmosphere line, silhouetted against the star-specked backdrop of open space, was a pattern of blue-white alternating with black, a mirage that changed from one second to the next, a shimmery, ghostlike *something*! The sight brought to mind ancient legends of ghost ships that had entered foldspace and were never seen again.

Drake looked away and chastised himself for letting an overactive imagination get the best of him. In truth, there was a perfectly prosaic explanation for that which lay on the screen in front of him. The "ghost ship" was an optical illusion, an effect that resulted when the hull of a starship was turned into a nearly perfect reflector of electromagnetic radiation. Drake listened to a voice counting down the seconds on *Discovery*'s intercom. "Five...four...three...two...one...zero."

At the word "zero," the apparition dramatically changed appearance. Suddenly, the mirror sheen was gone and a hull of armored steel took its place. The ship thus revealed was a twin of *Discovery*. Its central cylinder jutted from the center of a habitat ring. A total of twelve spokes joined the central cylinder to the ring. A focusing mechanism for the ship's fusion-powered photon engines jutted from the back of the central cylinder, while the business ends of lasers, particle beams, and antimatter projectors jutted from various places on the hull. The outlines of hatches marked the positions of internal cargo spaces and hanger bays in which auxiliary craft were housed.

The Derringer-class heavy battle cruiser was a design that went back nearly two centuries. Designed for speed and acceleration, the ring and cylinder design was a compromise between a good thrust-to-mass ratio and an adequate low-speed spin-gravity capability. The design was ungainly and fragile-looking, but proven in battle. One advantage that cylinder-and-ring ships had over purely cylindrical designs was that if a ship was severely damaged, the habitat ring could be jettisoned, whole or in as many as six separate pieces.

"*Dagger* reports antiradiation shield test complete, Captain."

"Very good, Communicator," Drake said. "Open up a channel to Captain Marston."

"Aye, aye, sir."

Bela Marston had been Drake's executive officer on Interstellar Expedition One. He had since been entrusted with the command of one of the two battle cruisers assigned to Project Helldiver. Marston's image formed on Drake's workscreen.

"Status report, if you please, Bela."

"All systems are nominal, Captain. Our attenuation factor held steady at ten to the minus ninth, and our heat rejection level was good. Both backup systems worked perfectly when we switched them on line manually. Our viewscreen compensators are working fine."

"No problems then?"

"No, sir. I'd say we're as ready as we'll ever be."

"Right," Drake replied. "You may begin preparations to receive passengers."

"We'll be ready for them, Captain."

"Make sure that you are. We're running behind schedule, and we need to make it up. Anything else?"

"No, sir."

"Flagship, out."

"*Dagger*, out."

Drake turned to a member of his bridge crew. "What about it, Finley? Did you note any weak spots in *Dagger*'s field while it was on?"

"No, sir. He didn't even flicker when he switched over from the primary generators. I'd agree with Captain Marston. They're ready."

Drake nodded and put *Dagger* out of his mind, leaving only a million and one other details to be resolved before the Helldiver Fleet left orbit for the foldpoint.

The trip to orbit was an uneventful one. Bethany sat next to Calvan Cooper, one of Stan Barrett's political assistants. Barrett would represent Alta on the coming expedition, as he had done on Interstellar Expedition One. Cooper had been assigned to his staff as political liaison to the Sandarians and to assist in negotiations when contact was reestablished with the rest of the human race. The nervous glance Cooper had given the ground-to-orbit shuttle when he came onboard was all that Bethany had needed to identify her seatmate as a white-knuckle flyer. She had done her best to take his mind off the coming journey while they taxied into position. Even after the boat's fusion engines thrust them into the dark blue Altan atmosphere, she had kept up a running commentary concerning the flight. By the time the first of the giant spherical cryogen tankers of the Helldiver Fleet hove into view, Cooper had relaxed visibly.

"Look there," Bethany said, pointing to where the tanker lay.

Cooper leaned over to look out the boat's viewport. His gaze followed her pointing finger. "Where?"

"There, near that blue star in the Plowman's Foot. See it?"

"That tiny thing?"

"Not so tiny," she replied. "You're looking at a million cubic meters of cryogen. Without it, we might not get back."

"I've always been under the impression that it didn't take much fuel to jump between the stars," Cooper said. "Why all the tankers?"

"Depends on what you consider not much," Bethany replied. "A foldspace transition eats up ten percent of a ship's total fuel supply."

"Then we should have enough for ten transitions," Cooper responded. "More than enough."

Bethany looked perplexed for a moment, then

smiled as she realized his misconception. "You're forgetting the maneuvering between foldpoints, I think. Remember, a foldpoint can occur anywhere in a star system, and multiple foldpoints are often on opposite sides of the system primary. Getting from one to another eats up a lot of fuel. Since we don't know precisely how many transitions will be required before we find Earth, we have to take along an ample supply."

"How do you know so much about it? Surely you aren't a ship's officer!"

Bethany smiled at Cooper's shocked tone. Women were a rarity among Altan spacers, and there were none at all in the Navy. The attitude was a holdover from the original colonists' aversion to allowing women to practice any profession they considered dangerous, which itself was an outgrowth of the founders' need to populate their new world. Even so, there had been half a dozen women—mostly scientists—along on Interstellar Expedition One, and there would be three times that number on the coming voyage. Also, the Sandarian fleet was nearly 20 percent female, the result of Sandar having been at war with the Ryall for more than a century.

Rather than rebuke young Cooper for his unintended slight, Bethany merely said, "I know so much about such things because I was aboard *Discovery* during Interstellar Expedition One."

"Of course," Cooper replied. "I remember you now! You're the hereditary terrestrial ambassador to Alta, aren't you?"

Bethany shook her head. "My uncle is hereditary ambassador. I'm his official representative. I'm a comparative historian by profession, but I've also learned quite a lot about the Ryall over the past two years. I hope to learn more when we get to Earth."

"I hope I didn't offend you with my remark," Cooper said.

"You didn't," Bethany replied.

The first cryogen tanker had fallen behind while they talked. It was quickly replaced with another, then another, and another. Finally, when the last of the big ships had disappeared back along the shuttle's flight path, a large cylindrical vessel appeared.

The passengers watched the new ship grow larger as the boat slowly approached it. Three interorbit freighters hovered near the stationary ship while small boats flitted about. Suddenly, the acceleration alarm sounded, and Bethany and Calvan Cooper were tugged forward against their straps as the boat completed its approach to the spaceliner.

Like most commercial vessels, *City of Alexandria* had been designed on the cylindrical plan so that it could be rotated about its axis to provide spin gravity at times when thrust was absent. The ship's rotation had been halted three days earlier to facilitate the loading of personnel and supplies, leaving the whole vessel in a state of zero gravity. There are few operations more confusing to the untutored eye than the transfer of cargo in weightlessness.

As Bethany entered the passenger liner she was confronted by the sight of hundreds of packing crates floating between deck and overhead. Since it is impossible to pile things in zero gravity, most of the oddly shaped boxes and barrels had been restrained behind large nets until the handlers could move them. A few of the color-coded cartons had escaped restraint, however, and were floating free in the compartment. Other containers were being manhandled toward various open hatchways.

Into this planned confusion trickled the passengers from Homeport. Most had had little or no previous space experience. Confused by the lack of gravity, they clung to the guide rope and stared wide-eyed at their surroundings. Clustered around them were several members of *Alexandria*'s crew. These were the "baby-sitters," spacers who had been unlucky enough to draw escort duty for the groundlings. They were identified by scarlet armbands on their uniforms.

Seeing Bethany emerge from the open air lock, one of the escorts kicked off and arrowed to where she clung to the guide rope. "May I help you, ma'am?"

Bethany nodded. "You can tell me where I can catch the boat to *Discovery*."

"That would be in Hangar Bay Six, port side, just aft of Frame 611. Take Gamma Deck around thirty degrees and head inboard along the main corridor."

"Port side, Frame 611," she repeated, nodding. "Got it!"

"I'll be happy to guide you," the spacer said.

"No, thank you," Bethany replied. "I've been aboard before. I can find my way."

"As you see fit, ma'am."

Bethany pulled herself to Calvan Cooper's side. The young political assistant's face bore the pinched expression of someone on the verge of space sickness.

"Feeling all right?" Bethany asked.

He smiled wanly. "I think I'll live. Where to next?"

"We have to cross to the other side of the ship to get to *Discovery*'s boat."

"You mean this isn't *Discovery*?" he asked, letting his free arm flap in an all-encompassing gesture.

"No, of course not. This is *City of Alexandria*, a converted passenger liner."

"Hmmm, I thought it looked awfully big for a warship," he replied.

"Come on. Keep close."

She led him through the compartment to a hatchway equipped with an emergency pressure door. Once in the corridor beyond, Bethany grabbed hold of one of two guide ropes that ran the length of the corridor. She kicked off and began to make her way toward the main cross-ship corridor. They reached a lower deck to find it alive with activity. It seemed that every spare corner and crevice had been filled with supplies of one sort or another. Especially evident were the blue-coded boxes of foodstuffs. She knew from her previous experience that there would be no showers until *Alexandria*'s passengers and crew managed to eat their way into the 'fresher stalls. Likewise, she guided Cooper past a compartment that had been a ballroom in the days when *Alexandria* had been a passenger liner. The vast space was filled to overflowing with containers whose markings proclaimed their contents to be radiation-resistant gravitational detectors.

They passed another compartment in which spacers sat strapped into chairs in front of electronic consoles.

"Communications center?" Cooper asked as they passed.

"Combat control center, I think."

"Don't you know?"

She shook her head. "It must have been added during the overhaul. *City of Alexandria* didn't use to be armed. Wonder what they put into her."

They continued to the port side of the liner and then moved aft until they came to Frame 611. Bethany led Cooper through an emergency door into a large compartment filled with a number of small spacecraft. Bethany recognized several armed scouts tucked in among a collection of two-man scooters and other ships' boats.

A spacer made his way past the stored ships to where they clung in the hatchway.

"Ah, Miss Lindquist, we've been expecting you!"

She looked at him, vaguely aware that she should know his name.

"Chief Nelson, ma'am. I served aboard *Discovery* last trip."

"I remember you now," Bethany replied. "Good to see you again, Chief."

"We're glad to see you, too, ma'am."

"Who is 'we,' Chief?"

"Practically every spacer in the fleet, ma'am. The captain's been running us ragged these past three weeks. We figured that now you're here, the old man might let up a bit."

Bethany felt her cheeks redden at the implications of Nelson's remark. "Where's the boat?" she asked.

"We're attached to the after personnel lock. We've got one other passenger. As soon as he arrives, we'll be on our way."

"I think you'll find this gentleman is your other passenger."

"Mr. Cooper, sir?"

Cooper nodded. From his look, he was still trying to decide whether weightlessness agreed with him.

The chief grinned, seemingly oblivious to his guest's discomfort. "In that case, if you two will get onboard, we'll be heading out for the flagship immediately."

"Attention, All Ships. It is now T minus ten minutes, and counting!"

Richard Drake sat in his command chair on *Discovery*'s bridge and listened to the announcement on the fleet command frequency. Around him, the cruiser's bridge crew was busy with the myriad last-minute details that always preceded a launch. He watched their quiet professionalism and thought of similar scenes on the seven other ships of the Helldiver Fleet. Two minutes after the "All Ships" announcement, department heads began relaying their status to the ship's executive officer. As Drake eavesdropped on the command circuit, he felt a sudden rush of pride at the caliber of people he had working under him. When the roll call was complete, Commander Rorqual Marchant, his exec, buzzed him on their private circuit.

"All departments report ready for space, Captain."

"Very good, Rorq. Tell Engineering they can start bringing the reactor up to maneuvering power."

"Aye aye, sir."

Drake keyed for the fusion reactor's status screens to be displayed at his command console. The graph showed *Discovery*'s primary power plant well above the level needed for stationkeeping. He waited for the reactor's output to stabilize at intermediate power before keying for the communicator on duty.

"Activate the fleet command circuit, Mr. Haydn."

"Aye aye, sir."

"Report your status, gentlemen," Drake ordered the other captains of the fleet.

"*Dagger* ready for space, Captain," Bela Marston immediately responded.

"*City of Alexandria*, ready for space, sir," replied Rolf Bustamente, commanding officer of the converted liner.

"*Phoenix* is ready, sir."

"Likewise *Tharsis*, Captain."

"*Vellos*?" Drake asked, turning his attention to the C.O. of the largest cryogen tanker in the fleet.

"We're ready, sir."

"*Alcor V* is ready, Captain."

"*Summa Warrior* is straining at the leash, sir," the final starship captain reported.

Drake nodded. "All right, you each know the flight plan. *Discovery* will lead off at precisely 1200 hours, with each successive ship following at one-minute intervals. As soon as you have completed your turn away from the ecliptic, move to your assigned positions in fleet formation. We haven't had as much time for fleet maneuvers as I would like, so let's get in all the practice we can on the trip out. Are there any questions?" There were none. "Good luck to you all."

As soon as his screens were clear, Drake keyed for *Discovery*'s astrogator. "All right, Mr. Cristobal, you have the conn."

"Aye aye, sir."

Having temporarily relinquished command of his ship, Drake pulled tight the straps that would keep him from floating out of his acceleration couch and lay back to observe the departure. As he did so, a graph showing *Discovery*'s proposed orbital track was flashed on the main viewscreen.

Since Valeria's foldpoint was situated high in the system's northern hemisphere, the fleet's departure orbit had the appearance of a bent fishhook. At the appointed time, *Discovery*'s engines would nudge her away from Alta. At first the ship would move along a carefully computed path in the plane of the ecliptic. However, as soon as the cruiser cleared the near-Alta orbital zone and its hundreds of satellites and space installations, it would turn toward the foldpoint.

The astrogator busied himself at his console for a few seconds, then triggered the raucous buzzing of the acceleration alarms.

"Attention, All Hands. T minus one minute! First warning. Prepare for prolonged acceleration. One-half standard gravity in one minute."

An expectant hush fell over the ship as the voices on the intercom tailed off into silence.

"Final warning! One-half standard gravity in thirty seconds. I repeat. Five meters per second squared in thirty seconds.

"Fifteen . . . ten . . . five, four, three, two, one. Boost!"

CHAPTER 5

Admiral Sergei Fallon Gower, Seventh Viscount of Hallen Hall, Fleet Admiral of the Royal Sandarian Navy, and by appointment of His Majesty, John-Phillip Walkirk VI, commander of His Majesty's forces assigned to penetrate the Antares Nebula, sat in his office onboard his flagship and scowled at the viewscreen in front of him. The picture was a view of New Providence relayed from the nose camera of an unmanned scout cruising three hundred meters above the ruins of the planet's onetime capital city. The scene was not a pleasant one. Here a twisted, rusted skeleton showed where a glass and steel tower had once stood; there a pile of blast-marked rubble was all that remained of the concrete walls of a government building; elsewhere stood the blackened sticklike figures of a grove of trees. The colors of the scene were black, gray, tan, and brown. Conspicuously absent was the green of living chlorophyll or any of the other colors of life.

More than a century after the last, catastrophic Ryall raid on New Providence, the surface of the planet remained a barren wasteland. So far as could be seen from orbit, not a single blade of grass grew on the world's landmasses, nor was there evidence of life in the planet's oceans—although the Sandarian ships were ill equipped to probe the most extreme depths and therefore might well have missed seeing a few isolated pockets of proto-plasm.

The Ryall attacks on New Providence had been re-sponsible for vast destruction. They had killed 40 million people and destroyed more than a thousand metropolitan centers around the globe. Yet not even that race of bel-ligerent centaurs could have wrought destruction on so vast a scale. When the black Ryall ships finally broke through New Providence's defenses, they had rained fire on a doomed world. For the true slayer of New Provi-dence—and of all life in the Napier system—had been the Antares Supernova.

The dwellers of New Providence had known some-thing was amiss when they lost contact with their colony in the Valeria system in August 2512. Their concern turned to worry when several ships known to be in tran-sit across the Antares system failed to arrive on sched-ule. Worry turned to fear when the vessels dispatched to check the whereabouts of the missing ships had them-selves failed to return at the appointed time.

The enormity of the disaster had become clear when New Providence's astronomers concluded that only a nearby supernova of unprecedented power could explain what had happened to their universe. And with the real-ization that it had been Antares that had exploded came the knowledge that New Providence was a doomed planet. For throughout the history of the colony, Antares had been the brightest star in the sky. On those nights when the red supergiant was above the horizon, its ocher gleam was nearly bright enough to read by. The fact that their system was physically close to the giant star had always been a source of pride to the inhabitants of New Providence. However, once the astronomers calculated the quantity of radiation that would soon be sleeting through the Napier system, the giant star's proximity be-came a source of despair.

Human nature being what it is, the news had not been well received. At first people refused to believe that they would soon be forced to abandon their homes. Eventually, however, the reality of their predicament began to sink in. An evacuation program was organized. By the end of the first year, the whole of the New Providential industrial complex had been converted to the task of re-settling three billion people to a different star system. Shipyards rushed to build the evacuation fleet while teams of pioneers worked to ready new homes for New Providence's masses on Sandarson's World.

Meanwhile, the New Providential scientists had studied the changes that the nova had wrought on the structure of foldspace. The study began with a survey of the gravitational gradient throughout the Napier system. Upon analyzing their data, the scientists were surprised to discover the presence of a foldpoint where no such had been previously. Further analysis showed the fold-point to be a temporary phenomenon, the result of long-range focusing of a foldline by the expanding nova shock wave. Once the wavefront reached Napier, the new fold-point would disappear.

The scientists were in favor of exploring the new fold-point immediately. Those whose job it was to transplant the population to another star system were not keen on anything that would divert precious resources from the evacuation effort. The scientists were persistent and were eventually given a three-ship armada with which to explore the foldpoint.

Two of the ships had jumped to the system beyond the foldpoint immediately after arrival, while the third remained behind to make precise measurements of the foldpoint's gravitational gradient. Twelve days later, the surveyors who had stayed behind reported a dozen star-ships of unknown type materializing in the nearby fold-point. The report had cut off abruptly as the invaders destroyed the survey ship and then turned for New Providence.

A flotilla of warships and auxiliaries had been dis-patched to New Providence by the Interstellar Council. This flotilla had gone out to meet the invading aliens, the purpose of which was to aid in the evacuation. The battle was joined in deep space, and the human forces were largely successful. Even so, a single alien ship managed to evade destruction long enough to launch a spread of six missiles at New Providence. Six missiles, six cities, and 10 million dead in the ruins!

A second raid followed the first by eighteen months. This time the human defenders were ready, and the invading Ryall ships were destroyed before they could get beyond the foldpoint.

There followed a long period of peace in the Napier system. The years in which no Ryall ship appeared in the new foldpoint lulled the New Providential government into a false sense of security while they wrestled with the problems of evacuation. By the twelfth year following the supernova, they had succeeded in evacuating 80 percent of the population.

The end of the de facto truce with the Ryall had come as a surprise as three dozen starships materialized in the disputed foldpoint. They swept aside the few human guard units and raced for New Providence. The defenders were sluggish to respond. Even so, they managed to throw a respectable number of ships into the path of the oncoming marauders. The battle had been both brutal and short. When it was over, ten of the Ryall attackers were still in shape to deliver their cargo of death to New Providence. What followed became known as "The Great Burning."

Sergei Gower gazed at the ruins and remembered the chilling stories his great-grandfather had told of that last desperate fight for a doomed world. Nor had that been the last of the fighting. Gower stared at the destruction and thought of the millions who had died violently in the century since humans had abandoned New Providence. He thought of his father, killed aboard his ship during the first expedition to wrest control of the Aezer system from the centaurs; of his younger brother, slaughtered a decade past with the second Aezer armada; and of his son, killed only two years before at the Battle of Sandar. He thought of all those he had lost to the centaurs and made a silent vow as he gazed at the ruins of a once-prosperous world.

This time things would be different!

* * *

The sixteen-ship Sandarian contingent to the Hell-diver Fleet had left parking orbit more than a month earlier. The flagship was the Blastship *Royal Avenger*, veteran of a hundred long patrols and two major space battles. With a complement of six hundred, *Royal Avenger* mounted sufficient armament to lay waste an entire world or to win a slugging match with half a dozen lesser warships. She carried in her holds a variety of armed auxiliaries.

In addition to the flagship, the Sandarian fleet included the heavy battle cruisers *Terra* and *Victory*, and His Majesty's Destroyers *Arrow*, *Mace*, and *Scimitar*. Completing the force was His Majesty's Armed Transport *Saskatoon*, onboard which were the men and equipment of the 33rd Regiment, 2nd Battalion, 6th Division, Royal Space Marines. Supporting the warcraft were nine noncombatants—three freighters, five cryogen tankers, and the mother ship for a series of communications relay craft. The latter were small starships with oversize fuel tanks that would be dropped in each foldpoint along the way. It would be their task to relay radio messages between the Helldiver Fleet and Sandar. They would do so by shuttling periodically between the two ends of each active foldline link and passing whatever messages they had accumulated to the next relay craft along the line. All vessels and major auxiliaries had been equipped with the new antiradiation field and were provisioned for a long voyage.

The run from Sandar out to the Hellsgate–Napier foldpoint had taken ten days at one-half gravity of acceleration. The fleet arrived at the foldpoint and underwent foldspace transition without incident. The Sandarian ships had spent the next two weeks traversing the six billion kilometers of vacuum that lay between the foldpoint and New Providence. Once they arrived at the one-time capital planet of the Napier system, the Sandarians had settled into a parking orbit to await the arrival of the Altan contingent.

On the sixth day following the fleet's arrival at New

Providence, Admiral Gower found himself in his sanctum sanctorum situated at the rear of *Royal Avenger*'s combat control center. The office *cum* command center was a glass-walled cubicle with a panoramic view of the CCC, its two dozen weapons consoles, and their operators. Arrayed across the opposite bulkhead were several oversize screens on which all aspects of fleet operations could be displayed. Sergei Gower sat at his command desk and gazed thoughtfully at the activity going on in the compartment below.

One main viewscreen showed a view of New Providence as seen by one of the blastship's hull cameras. White cyclonic patterns of clouds reflected Napier's G8 rays, giving the planet the blue-white marbled look of any terrestrial world. An adjacent screen showed the corresponding electronic map of the planet. A series of green sparks shifted on the planet's surface as Gower watched. These marked the spot where *Saskatoon*'s Marines were engaged in a landing exercise against a simulated Ryall strongpoint. He contemplated the shifting alphanumeric display for long seconds before keying for *Avenger*'s communications center.

"Yes, sir?" the communicator on duty responded.

"Get me Colonel Valdis aboard *Saskatoon*."

"It will take a few moments, Admiral. Colonel Valdis is currently issuing operational orders to one of his landing craft."

"Break in as soon as he is free."

"Yes, sir!"

Nothing in Gower's orders from the Sandarian High Command called for the use of ground forces either before or after the fleet had penetrated the nebula. Even so, a lifetime of fighting the centaurs had taught the admiral caution and had caused him to insist that the expedition have access to ground forces. Having received them, he had no intention of letting pass any opportunity to hone their skills.

"You wanted to speak to me, Admiral?" a gruff-looking man asked from Gower's screen.

"Report status of your exercise, Colonel."

"All ships are now down without mishap. The two

strike forces are converging on the objective as planned. They will link up—" The colonel's eyes flicked toward something beyond the screen camera's field of view. "—in exactly seventeen minutes."

"Are you watching your schedule?"

"Yes, sir. If anything, we're a little ahead of our planned timeline. We should have everything wrapped up and all the men back under radiation shielding at least one hour before local nebula-rise."

Gower nodded. "See that you do. I want the name, service number, and dosimeter reading of the man with the maximum exposure reported directly to me as soon as you get it."

"Will do, Admiral."

Gower cut the connection and turned to other problems. He scanned his workscreen and requested that he be put through to the captain of one of the cryogen tankers. That worthy seemed surprised by the summons.

"What may I do for you, sir?"

"Your morning report shows that you detected a leak in your primary fuel tank, Captain. What have you done about it?"

"Uh, we have men out in suits checking the hull, sir."

"What is your prediction for time to make repairs?"

"Two hours at the outside, Admiral."

"Very well. I want to hear that you have found the leak and have sealed it in no more than three hours' time. If you cannot assure me that your vessel is once again pressuretight by then, I will dispatch a repair crew to assist you. Is that understood?"

"Yes, sir."

The screen went blank, and Gower was about to proceed to the next trouble item on his list when it lit again to show an earnest young ensign in the corridor just beyond Gower's office. The admiral's scowl softened perceptibly as he studied the handsome features peering out of the screen at him. The high cheekbones, aristocratic nose, and square chin were a younger version of the features of His Majesty, John-Phillip Walkirk VI, whose official portrait adorned the bulkhead over Gower's computer terminal.

"Ensign Phillip Walkirk, reporting for scheduled instruction, sir!" the young man said quickly as Gower acknowledged his presence.

"Very well, Ensign," Admiral Gower answered formally. "You have my permission to enter."

The hatch opened, and the crown prince of Sandar strode across the metal deck to stand at attention in front of the admiral's desk.

"Please be seated, Your Highness."

"Thank you, sir," the prince responded.

"Shall I ring for refreshments?"

"No, thank you, sir. I have just come from the officers' mess."

"Very well," Gower replied. "What have you learned since last we spoke, Your Highness?"

"Among other things, sir, that I don't think I care for sitting and waiting when we could be doing something useful."

"Oh?" Gower asked, lifting his right eyebrow in a gesture that would have had any other subordinate in a cold sweat. "Do you have some criticism to offer concerning the way I command this fleet?"

"I meant to imply no such criticism, Admiral."

"Then what did you mean to imply, Ensign?"

The prince hesitated, obviously casting about for the most politic way of explaining himself. Gower gave him no chance.

"Come now, Your Highness. An officer must be quick on his feet, and a future king even more so. You have stated that you are unhappy with the way this expedition is being run. Defend your position, and quickly!"

"Yes, sir. There is a lot of talk in the mess about how we are wasting time. We could be out at the Napier–Antares foldpoint mapping the nebula instead of sitting here in parking orbit waiting for the Altans to arrive."

"Yes, we could," Gower agreed.

"Then why are we orbiting this dead world?"

"You tell me," the admiral responded.

"Because our orders are to do so," the prince replied.

"Correct! And a military man always follows his orders, Your Highness."

Gower noted the studied look of irritation that quickly faded from the young man's features. He leaned back in his chair and regarded the prince with something approaching avuncular pride. For most of the time, Phillip Walkirk was one of *Avenger*'s ensigns, treated no differently than other officers of his rank, save that he was always addressed by his royal honorific. And in the Sandarian Navy, much of an ensign's day was taken up with studying those things which cannot be taught in a naval academy. Such things were best taught by one's immediate superiors. Once each week, though, the admiral took it upon himself to teach the heir to the throne those things that would be useful when he became king.

"Besides," he said, continuing in a less martial vein, "you know enough of the political realities that you should be able to figure out the reason for our orders yourself."

"Well," the prince began, "I suppose our Altan partners might object to being left out of the initial explorations."

Gower nodded. "It would hardly build trust between our two systems if we gave them the idea that we don't need them."

"But we don't need them!" Phillip Walkirk replied.

"That is where you are wrong, Your Highness. We need them badly."

"But why? After more than a century of isolation, they hardly have enough ships to patrol their own system, let alone carry the attack to the Ryall."

"True," the admiral replied. "And by the same token, they haven't been bloodied the way we have. They haven't seen their manpower and treasure poured into futile attempts to break the Ryall blockade of Aezer. They haven't seen their home world under attack. They don't command a people weary unto death of war.

"The truth is, Highness, that we of Sandar are barely holding our own against the centaurs and that we can foresee the day when we will go under if we don't obtain outside aid. Worse, our enemies can foresee that same day. Why else do you think they launched the attack which ended in the Battle of Sandar?"

Two years earlier, when Alta's Interstellar Expedition One had entered the Hellsgate system, Sandar had come under attack from a heavily armed fleet of Ryall warships. The Sandarian Navy, having been decimated by three attempts to break the Aezer blockade, had been unable to prevent a breakout from the fortified Hellsgate–Aezer foldpoint. There had followed a pitched space battle in which the Altan battle cruiser *Discovery* had taken part. Humanity had won the battle that day, but just barely. It gave Gower the shakes to think of how close they had come.

"Obviously, sir," the prince replied, "we need allies. But once we penetrate the nebula, we will have Earth and all the other worlds of human space. We won't need the Altans."

"We will need every ally we can get, Highness. After all, Earth is far away and pressed by the aliens, too. We will need a large production capacity to build the weapons we need. Alta has that capacity. To not court our cousins would be criminally negligent and terribly stupid. As you well know, your father is neither of these. Therefore, we wait until the Altans arrive. Only after we have integrated their forces with our own do we undertake our mission."

"But where are they?"

The admiral shrugged. "The last reports we had were that they were preparing to launch. It is not inconceivable that they have been delayed. We will wait for them."

"How long do we wait, sir?"

"Until they arrive or until I become convinced that they aren't coming," Gower replied smoothly.

Both men were suddenly startled by the hooting of an alarm. Gower looked up to see a flurry of activity taking place in the combat control center. He keyed for the officer on duty. "What's happened, Commander Massey?"

"*Terra* has detected a large number of ships, sir."

"Where?" Gower asked, his every sense suddenly alert.

"In the Napier–Valeria foldpoint, sir."

"How many?"

"I make it a total of eight."

"Identification?"

"Stand by a moment, Admiral. Our computer is crunching the data now. . . . Yes, sir, we have positive identification on two of the craft. They are *Discovery* and *City of Alexandria*. Neutrino and infrared signatures closely match the readings we took when both ships visited Sandar. A third ship seems to be a heavy cruiser of the *Discovery* class."

Gower nodded. "That will be *Dagger*. What of the other five?"

"No identification possible yet, sir. However, they are definitely of human construction."

"No need for further identification," Gower replied. "Please get a message out, Commander. Welcome our allies to the Napier system and ask that they expedite their crossing." Gower glanced at the crown prince, who was watching the exchange with a new excitement in his eyes. "Tell them that we have some young officers onboard who would like to get started with exploring the nebula."

CHAPTER 6

Richard Drake sat in his acceleration couch on the bridge and watched as *Discovery*'s astrogator maneuvered the ship toward the Valeria–Napier foldpoint. The foldpoint was a red-shaded ellipse in the middle of the main bridge viewscreen. Just beyond the boundary to the interstellar gateway, eight tiny gold sparks moved cautiously forward. As Drake watched, the first spark crossed the edge of the ellipse and began to blink rapidly. Within seconds, each of the others did likewise. Drake watched as the last of the ships under his command crossed the boundaries of the foldpoint.

"Mr. Cristobal," Drake said.

"Yes, sir," the astrogator replied.

"When will you be ready for the jump?"

"Anytime, Captain. We're beyond the zone of uncertainty and have entered the foldpoint proper. We've nothing to gain by waiting any longer."

"Very well," Drake replied. "Lock in the preplanned jump sequence."

"Locked in, Captain."

Drake keyed for the general fleet communications circuit. "All captains, link to me."

Drake's screens lit to show the faces of his seven subordinates. He polled them individually and found them eager for the coming jump. Most had never been outside the Val system, and their eagerness brought back memories of his own first interstellar jump. When the last captain had reported his readiness for foldspace transition, Drake nodded.

"All right. You each know the plan. *Discovery* will go first, followed by *Dagger*, *City of Alexandria*, and then the cryogen tankers at intervals of thirty seconds. Once on the other side, immediately report your status and position, then form on the flagship. Any questions?" There were none. "Very well, you may proceed when ready."

As quickly as his screens had cleared, Drake turned back to his astrogator. "You may do likewise, Mr. Cristobal. Proceed when ready."

"Aye aye, sir. One minute to transition. Generators to power, now!"

This last was addressed to the engineering officer whose station was next to Argos Cristobal's. Drake listened to the interplay between the astrogator and the various other departments. At the same time, he punched for a view of Antares on the main viewscreen. The nova was now merely a very bright star.

"Sound your warning, Mr. Cristobal."

"Sounding now, Captain."

There was the raucous sound of alarms, followed by Argos Cristobal's voice on the general annunciator: "Attention, All Hands! This is the astrogator speaking. Prepare for foldspace transition. I repeat, prepare for foldspace transition. You have thirty seconds. T minus thirty seconds, and counting!"

"All hands, report status!" Drake ordered.

Once again there was a roll call, this one for the various department heads onboard *Discovery*. All reported their readiness for foldspace transition.

"Ten seconds, Captain," Cristobal reported.

"Jump when ready, Lieutenant."

"Yes, sir. Five . . . four . . . three . . . two . . . one. Jump!"

No particular sensation accompanied foldspace transition, which was not surprising when theoretically the ship had not "gone" anywhere. For one single instant Drake felt a touch of fear that something had gone wrong, that perhaps the foldspace generators had malfunctioned and *Discovery* still orbited high above Val. Then he glanced at the viewscreen and felt the usual feeling of relief that followed a successful jump. For the object on the screen bore no resemblance to the eyesearing point of violet-white light that had been there just a few seconds earlier.

In the single blink of an eye, Antares had been transformed from a particularly bright star into a vast ball of ghostly light that covered half the sky. At the center of the sphere lay the remnant of the once-mighty red giant. The furiously radiating object that was all that remained of Antares was a vast ball of plasma larger than most stars. Beneath that veil of energetic gas lay a rapidly rotating neutron star. As the invisible neutron star rotated, its magnetic field whipped the expanding cloud of plasma, generating intense synchrotron radiation and considerable radio energy. The quick, "fluttering" call of the Antares pulsar was clearly audible across a wide band of communications frequencies.

Scanning outward from the wrecked star, Drake noted that the nebula turned nearly transparent just beyond the bounds of the central object, allowing several background stars to shine through the gas cloud. The remnants of Antares' A3 companion sun also lay close to the central mass. The gas cloud turned translucent again at approximately one-third the distance to the periphery. The thickening cloud glowed with a deep reddish color. Farther out, the red subtly turned to orange, the orange shaded up to yellow, and the yellow turned to green. At the outer perimeter, the gas thickened until it was nearly opaque and glowing with the blue-white radiance of a fluorescent lamp. Drake's inspection of the nebula took only a matter of seconds. As he gazed at the ghostly apparition, Lieutenant Cristobal's voice could be heard echoing through the ship. "Foldspace transition successfully completed!"

"Communicator," Drake ordered. "Get me a status

report from all department heads. Also, let me know as each ship checks in."

"Aye aye, sir."

Drake reached out and switched his private view-screen to a view of Napier. The system primary was noticeably yellower than was Valeria. Whereas Alta's sun was an F8 dwarf, yellow-white in color and somewhat hotter than Sol, New Providence's sun was a G8 giant, cooler and much larger than humanity's birth star. Its size made for a much larger temperate zone than is normal in systems with terrestrial worlds. Thus, New Providence was planet seven in the Napier system. Napier's size also resulted in foldpoints forming much farther from the system primary than was normal for a dwarf sun.

Drake oriented himself quickly and began picking out guide stars. He let his gaze drift to where New Providence lay. The planet did not show on the viewscreen, nor had he expected it to. The distance between the foldpoint and the onetime capital world of the Napier system was such that a fairly powerful telescope would have been required to make New Providence visible.

"*Dagger* just reported in, Captain," the communicator said over Drake's command circuit. "Its breakout point is three thousand kilometers from us."

"Acknowledged," Drake said. Over the next four minutes, the rest of his fleet materialized around him in the foldpoint. He mentally ticked them off as they came through: *Dagger*, *City of Alexandria*, *Phoenix*, *Tharsis*, *Vellos*, *Alcor V*, and finally, *Summa Warrior*. All checked in as quickly as they arrived. All reported having successfully made the jump from Valeria without difficulty.

"All ships to close on us," Drake ordered when the last cryogen tanker reported in. Because there was no way to predict where in a foldpoint any particular ship would materialize, it was necessary to re-form the fleet after the jump. "Someone get a telescope focused on New Providence."

"Done, Captain," one of the bridge technicians responded. "Channel sixteen."

Drake keyed to switch his screen to the telescopic

view. New Providence showed as a half-moon shape still very small due to the fact that it was five billion kilometers distant. "Any sign of our Sandarian allies?"

"We're analyzing now, Captain. No coherent radiation such as from a message laser, sir. If they're here, they aren't advertising the fact."

Drake watched quietly while the technicians did their work. After a minute's silence, the sensor tech reported. "We've got them, sir! There are several ships in orbit about New Providence. At least a dozen, possibly more. One of them is large, probably blastship class. Shall I pulse them?"

"What's the communications delay at this distance?"

"Five hours each way, sir."

"All right, send them the following message. 'Have arrived in good order. Will proceed to rendezvous as soon as fleet order has been restored. Am anxious to begin explorations. Signed, Drake, Vice Commander."

"Aye aye, sir. All ships have acknowledged your order to rejoin. *Alexandria* is the farthest out. Captain Marsten reports he'll be here in two hours."

"Acknowledged." Drake glanced one last time at the crescent New Providence floating against the black of space. He then keyed for Bethany's cabin. She smiled up at the camera when she saw who it was.

"Well," he said, "we're here."

"So I see. The nebula's more beautiful than I remember it."

He nodded. "I hope we still think so once we've gotten inside."

The ship's boat slipped from behind the curve of *City of Alexandria* and moved out into the blaze of full Napier-light. Ahead lay the backlit sphere of New Providence, its black form turned silvery by nebula-light. A horizon-to-horizon light show was taking place over the night side of the planet as continentwide auroral displays chased one another across the sky. A silver halo along the eastern limb of the planet betrayed the coming of day. Hanging immediately above the advancing terminator was Napier, a perfectly round ball of fire in the sky.

"Hello, *Royal Avenger*, this is *Moliere*. We have departed *City of Alexandria* and are en route to your position."

"I have you on my screen, *Moliere*. You are cleared for approach to Landing Bay Seven. Please report the outer marker."

"Will do, *Avenger*. *Moliere* out."

"*Avenger*, out."

Ensign Grant Nals, *Moliere*'s pilot, turned to Richard Drake. "We're in the groove, Captain. I estimate rendezvous in ten minutes."

"How long after that to achieve a hard dock?" Drake asked.

"Another five to ten minutes, sir. We're cleared for the central axis entry into the hangar bay. That should speed matters up considerably."

"Excellent! What margin of safety have you programmed into our trajectory?"

"We're set up for a miss distance of one hundred meters, Captain, if that meets with your approval."

"You're the pilot in command, son," Drake said. "You don't need my approval when it comes to flying your ship. Now, if you're asking my advice . . ."

"Yes, sir."

"Then I would say that a margin of one hundred meters is entirely adequate. It's close enough to impress them with your ability as a pilot but far enough to make sure that we don't plaster ourselves across *Avenger*'s hull. Needless to say, smashing into the flagship would hardly endear us to our new boss."

"No, sir," Nals replied. "I'm sure Commander Marchant would have something to say about it, too."

Drake nodded. "I believe he would. Please buzz the passenger cabin as soon as you report the outer marker."

"Yes, sir."

Drake turned, floated to the exit hatchway, braced himself against the zero-gravity environment of the boat, and opened the hatch. The quiet chatter of the outside radiation detectors, which had been the only background sound on the flight deck, was suddenly drowned out by the buzz of many voices. He pulled through the hatch and closed it behind him before turning to face his fellow passengers. In addition to Drake, *Moliere* was carrying Stan Barrett, Bethany Lindquist, Captain Bela Marston of *Dagger*, Captain Rolf Bustamente of *Alexandria*, and several of the expedition's senior scientists.

Drake pulled himself to the empty couch beside Bethany, pivoted once more in midair, and pulled himself down into the seat. He turned to her and smiled. "Have I complimented you on how beautiful you are today?"

She smiled back, displaying two prominent dimples. "I believe you've mentioned it once or twice." Bethany was wearing a powder-blue pants suit, black space boots, and the scarlet sash traditionally worn by terrestrial diplomats. She had piled her hair on top of her head in a formal zero-gravity style for the occasion. The effect was stunning. "Did the pilot mention how long it would be before we arrive?"

"Not long," he replied. "*Avenger* is only about thirty kilometers ahead of us in orbit. We should be aboard within twenty minutes."

"Will we be able to see *Avenger* during the approach?"

"Better than you may like. We'll be coming up astern and will transit its whole length at a distance of one hundred meters before we match velocities."

Bethany slipped her hand into Drake's. "Are you nervous?"

He smiled wanly. "A little."

She gave his hand a reassuring squeeze. "No need to be. You'll do fine."

"I hope so," he replied. "Otherwise, I may find myself swabbing decks for the Sandarian Navy..."

It had taken the Altans two weeks to cross from the Napier–Val foldpoint to New Providence. Much of that time Drake had spent in long-distance communication with Admiral Gower. The subject of their exchanges had been how best to integrate the Altan and Sandarian fleets into a well-functioning whole.

The gross details regarding how the expedition was to be organized had been established two years earlier by the Altan–Sandarian mutual defense treaty. One of the things the treaty stipulated was that the military commander of the Helldiver Expedition must be a Sandarian, while the post of vice commander must be filled by an Altan. The treaty gave the military commander overall responsibility for the safety of the men, women, and ships under him. It also required that he listen to the advice of a triumvirate of civilian advisers.

Drake knew of no one who had been totally happy with the arrangements mandated by the treaty. Parliament had not liked being forced to accept a Sandarian in overall command, nor had the two militaries involved enjoyed having civilians looking over their shoulders. Despite the dissatisfactions, however, both governments had worked diligently to implement the provisions of the treaty. Despite all the preplanning, Drake and Gower had discovered numerous organizational details that required their personal attention. By the time the Altan fleet had closed the range to where two-way screen communication became possible, Drake had developed considerable respect for his new boss. He hoped the feeling was mutual.

Ten minutes after departing *City of Alexandria*, Landing Boat *Moliere* drew abreast of His Majesty's Blastship *Royal Avenger*. The view through the starboard viewports was awesome. At the blastship's stern were the focusing rings and field generators of three large photon engines. Even quiescent, the engines that drove the flagship gave the impression of unlimited power. Just in front of the engine exhausts were the radiators and other piping associated with the ship's four massive fusion generators. In front of the generators were the blastship's fuel tanks, heavily armored and insulated to keep the deuterium-enriched hydrogen fuel as close to absolute zero as possible.

Drake let his gaze move forward along the blastship's flank. The cylindrical hull was pierced in places by large hangar doors through which armed auxiliaries could sortie into battle. Forward of these were the snouts of a dozen antimatter projectors, *Royal Avenger*'s primary antiship weapons. The business ends of other weapon systems also jutted from the heavily armored hull. Interspersed with the weaponry was all manner of sensor gear.

As the landing boat slipped past the blastship's flanks, they were rewarded with ever-changing vistas, since *Avenger* was rotating about its axis at the rate of several revolutions per minute. So close was landing boat to blastship that it was easy to imagine oneself in a small aircraft flying over an endless plain. The optical illusion came to an abrupt end when the landing boat passed abeam of the blastship's prow.

As with most starships, little or no effort had gone into streamlining *Avenger*. In fact, the prow was actually slightly concave, and its surface was covered with arrays of electronic and electromagnetic sensors. A hangar door outwardly identical to those which dotted the blastship's flanks was set flush with the hull at the giant ship's axis of rotation.

As quickly as the bow portal came into view, *Moliere*'s pilot fired the attitude control thrusters to halt the landing boat's forward speed. Once *Moliere* had halted in space, he began firing his side thrusters to align the landing boat with the central portal. A popping noise echoed through the passenger cabin each time the thrusters fired. When *Moliere* was lined up with *Royal Avenger*'s axis portal, the thrusters fired twice more to match the flagship's rate of rotation. The hangar door retracted, and *Moliere*'s pilot nudged his boat toward the lighted opening. Within seconds, the boat passed into a spacious cavern lighted by million-candlepower polyarc lamps. There followed a series of bumping and scraping noises and a gentle tug of deceleration as the landing boat's forward velocity was halted. After that there came a long span of silence interrupted by the sudden sound of air swirling outside the hull.

Moliere had arrived.

CHAPTER 7

Richard Drake was the first to leave the confines of the landing boat for the brightly lit steel cavern that was *Royal Avenger*'s forward hangar bay. He stepped over the air lock coaming onto a raised platform some two meters above the level of the main deck. He paused for a moment to take in his surroundings. From the springiness in his step he estimated the local gravity field to be approximately one-third standard, which jibed well with what he knew of *Avenger*'s rate of spin and his own location with respect to the blastship's central axis. A wisp of exhalation fog swirled around his shoulders as he breathed deeply of the frigid air. The atmosphere had a dry metallic taste that was common to spacecraft environmental control systems and especially noticeable immediately after a compartment exposed to vacuum had been repressurized. Drake found the combination of low gravity and cold air exhilarating. He craned his neck to scan the interior of the hangar bay.

Royal Avenger's forward hangar bay was a cylindrical cavern some thirty meters in diameter by thirty meters long. The forward bulkhead was a complex hatch mechanism built on the principle of an observatory weather dome, save that each dome segment was hinged at its base to allow it to swing back and out of the way, opening the bay totally to space. The aft bulkhead was flat and pierced by a passageway some ten meters in diameter. At the moment the passageway was sealed by a series of airtight doors that could be opened to allow access to the blastship's interior spaces and aft hangar bays. Had it been empty, the bay's twenty thousand cubic meters of enclosed space would have been daunting. As it was, there was barely sufficient room for *Moliere* on the crowded cylindrical deck.

Drake scanned the dozen or so auxiliary craft housed in the bay. Directly overhead were four small armed scouts of a type similar to those carried aboard *Discovery*. These were vacuum craft, as shown by their complete lack of aerodynamic symmetry. Beside them were two large winged lifting body shapes, landing boats designed to transport men and materiel to and from the surface of a terrestrial world. Beyond *Moliere*'s wing tip, several small two- and four-man orbital workboats lay strapped to the deck. Beside them, a series of empty cradles showed where other craft were normally stowed. Whether they were out working with the fleet or had merely been moved to make way for the Altan landing boat, Drake had no way of knowing. Impressed by the number and variety of the Sandarian equipment, Drake turned his attention to the Sandarians themselves.

A reception committee consisting of a double row of naval officers and a single civilian dignitary stood at the foot of the embarkation stairs. Drake recognized Admiral Gower in the front rank. Two places beyond the admiral was a young man in the uniform of an ensign. Drake had met Phillip Walkirk during his visit to Sandar two years earlier. Even had he not recognized the crown prince, however, the young man's inclusion in the front rank of such a distinguished gathering would have been all the clue needed. Behind the high-ranking officers was a second rank of middle-grade officers. Opposite the welcoming party stood a

rank of Sandarian Royal Marines. Their crimson uniforms, mirrored helmets, and matching boots were resplendent under the glow of the polyarcs. Each Marine
stood rigidly at attention with an electromagnetic rifle
thrust out before him.

Drake moved to the ladder and carefully descended to
the deck. He walked the two paces to where Admiral
Gower stood, snapped to attention, and saluted.

"Fleet Captain Richard Arthur Drake, Altan Space
Navy, reporting for duty, sir!"

Gower returned his salute with millimetric precision,
then held out his hand to Drake.

"I have been looking forward to meeting the hero of
the Battle of Sandar in the flesh, Fleet Captain," Gower
said. "My king asked me to express his undying gratitude
for what you did in stopping the Ryall attack on our
world."

"A lot of people were heroes that day, Admiral,"
Drake responded. "The victory belonged to them, especially those who died during the defense."

Gower nodded. "We are well aware of the sacrifices
which Alta made on our behalf. I can assure you that all
of your casualties have had their names inscribed in our
roll of honored dead."

Drake smiled. "With your permission, sir, I will have
an announcement to that effect posted in every Altan
ship."

"Permission granted," the admiral replied. "But
enough talk of the past. The time has come when we
must carry out our own obligations. Are your people
ready to tackle the nebula?"

"Ready and eager, sir. You have but to give the
order."

"I will do so, but not until I am sure that our two
fleets can work properly together. To that end, we begin
a two-week-long fleet exercise tomorrow at 0800."

"We'll be ready, sir."

"In the meantime, I have scheduled a small banquet
for our respective staffs. I'm afraid the food isn't very
fancy, but the cuisine's shortcomings should be more
than made up for by the comradeship."

"I'm sure the food will be fine, Admiral."

Gower turned to the officer beside him. "Fleet Captain Drake, I have the honor to present Senior Commander Valor Rossmore, First Knight of Rossmore and my chief of staff."

"Commander."

"Fleet Captain."

Taking Drake by the elbow, Gower guided him down the receiving line. "His Highness, Ensign Phillip Walkirk, Crown Prince of Sandar, Duke of Cragston, and Hereditary Game Warden of the Alsenan Life Preserve."

"Your Highness," Drake replied, inclining his head in a quick bow.

"At your service, sir," Ensign Walkirk responded.

"Count Victor Husanic, senior member of the Council of Royal Advisers and His Majesty's personal representative on this expedition."

Count Husanic was a tall white-haired man with a heavily lined face and a stooped posture. Drake estimated that the count's age was at least sixty standard years and was frankly surprised that the Sandarians would risk such a man to the stresses that warships were sometimes forced to endure. He nodded in the nobleman's direction. "Count Husanic."

"Fleet Captain Drake," Husanic replied. "I, too, want to express my appreciation for what you did during the Battle of Sandar. You took a considerable risk for the sake of my world, a risk that you could easily have avoided."

"It seemed that we had no other choice at the time, sir."

There was a quiet throat-clearing noise from Admiral Gower. Drake turned to look at him.

"Count Husanic's son was with Commodore Bardak's blocking force, Captain," the admiral said softly.

"Oh?" Drake asked. "What ship?"

"*Warwind*, second wave," Husanic replied.

Drake blinked as understanding overtook him. The force that had gone out to stop the invading Ryall fleet had been divided into three attack waves. The first and third waves had taken heavy casualties during the battle. The second had been wiped out to the last ship.

"My condolences on your loss," Drake said in a low voice.

Husanic nodded gravely. "Thank you for your sentiment, Captain. I'm afraid that the past century has visited far too many such losses on Sandar. Perhaps this expedition will change that."

"I hope so, sir."

"Now then, Captain Drake," Admiral Gower said. "I think it time that we met your people."

Introducing his fellow Altans to the Sandarians took another ten minutes. After Bethany Lindquist and Stan Barrett had been presented to the admiral, the crown prince, and Count Husanic, the introductions became something of a ritual. As each Altan officer descended the ladder from the landing boat, his Sandarian counterpart was called forward to meet him. The two would then exchange a few courtesies before the admiral suggested that the Sandarian officer guide his guest around the blastship. Each pair or quartet would then move through a pressuretight door in the aft bulkhead, and the process would begin anew. When the last of his people had been through the ritual, Drake discovered that his party had dwindled to three: himself, Bethany, and Stan Barrett. Save for the rigid line of Royal Marines, the number of Sandarians had also shrunk. Admiral Gower's party consisted of himself, the crown prince, and Count Husanic.

"I thought we six would take a tour of the flag bridge, Captain," Gower announced, "following which we will adjourn to my flight cabin for a few drinks before dinner. His Majesty was kind enough to stock *Royal Avenger* with wine from his private cellars. I think you will find it quite good."

"I am willing to entertain the two ambassadors if you and Captain Drake wish to review policy, Sergei," Count Husanic offered.

"There will be plenty of time for that later, Victor," the admiral replied. "Besides, you, Miss Lindquist, and

Mr. Barrett are the real power behind the throne on this expedition, are you not?"

"I sometimes wonder," the older man replied. "It is my experience that you Navy people would just as soon we civilians kept our opinions to ourselves."

"Please, Victor, you are going to shock our guests with such cynicism. I'm sure that Captain Drake is no advocate of military supremacy."

"No, sir. We Altans are brought up to believe in the ancient tradition of civilian control of the military."

"Are you, now?" Husanic asked with a half smile. "You might be surprised to learn just how recent a development that tradition is."

"You speak like a historian, Count Husanic," Bethany said.

"In a small way, milady, I am."

"So am I!"

"Really?" the Sandarian representative said, his expression changing to one of total pleasure. "What is your specialty?"

"Earth history, sir."

"Excellent! That is my own vice, although I must confess that I have little enough time to follow it these days. Would you do an old man a favor and sit with me at the banquet tonight? It isn't very often that I get a chance to speak of my hobby with a professional."

"I would be honored, sir."

Husanic offered his arm to Bethany and led her through the airtight door into the blastship proper. The four men followed them. Drake found himself paired with Admiral Gower, while Stan Barrett walked along in company with the crown prince.

As quickly as they had entered the inhabited areas of the blastship, Richard Drake found something to disquiet him. Quick glances into a few of the compartments that opened onto the passageway suggested that *Royal Avenger* was an older ship than he had realized. Everywhere he looked, there was evidence of extensive and recent modifications, of equipment ripped out and other equipment installed in its place. The impression was that of a ship that had seen better days.

Not that *Avenger* wasn't clean inside. It was clean enough to eat off the decks, he noted. Every surface seemed to have received a recent coat of paint, all the brightwork had been polished, and even the ventilator air filters were free of telltale traces of dust. But the equipment was old, and much of it seemed out of place. In some places, the scars of welding torches were still visible under the fresh coat of paint. Even the steel decks bore the marks of years of use.

"How old is *Royal Avenger*, Admiral?" Drake asked as they walked down a long corridor broken every ten meters or so by an airtight door.

"She was launched sixty-five standard years ago," Gower replied. "For the past thirty years, *Avenger* has been in orbital storage. We brought her out specifically for this expedition. Don't worry, Captain. She's old, but she can still fight."

"Yes, sir," Drake responded, surprised at the dismay he felt upon having his suspicions confirmed. After all, his own ship had a proud history going back nearly 150 years. Who was he to criticize a vessel constructed any time during the past century? Still, it worried him that the Sandarians were so strapped for ships that they'd been forced to resurrect this relic.

Avenger's combat control center was one compartment that showed no sign of age. Every piece of equipment in it appeared to be brand-new. Most were more modern than anything Alta possessed, a visible reminder of the technological obsolescence Alta had suffered during the Long Isolation. Drake gazed down upon the rows of workstations from the admiral's glass-enclosed flag bridge and watched the activities of the console operators with interest. As he did so, he listened with half an ear to Admiral Gower's explanation to Bethany and Stan Barrett.

"... the console operators monitor every aspect of a space battle. The consoles themselves are run by six large computers. They take sensor readings and convert them into meaningful data, operate on those data, and come up with short-term predictions of an enemy's probable strategy. These predictions are passed on to my battle staff, which assimilates the data and advises me in real time. I follow the course of the battle here . . ." He pointed to a holocube that measured two meters to a side. "And order corrections in strategy as I feel they are needed."

"By the way, Drake, I will want six of your best officers to begin training for positions on my battle staff."

"I'll go over my rosters and have the names to you by this time tomorrow," Drake replied.

"Excellent!" Gower responded. "I will, of course, provide you with six of my own officers to take their places."

"Admiral," Stan Barrett said.

"Yes, Mr. Barrett?"

"You sound as though you expect the Ryall to attack us sometime during the course of this expedition."

"No, Mr. Barrett, I do not. However, I propose to be ready for such an attack should one come."

"But surely we'll be safe once we're inside the nebula."

"Why do you say that?"

"It stands to reason," the Altan ambassador replied. "It's only by the wildlest stroke of luck that we discovered that the nebula is navigable. Unless the Ryall have had their own version of the *Conqueror* incident, they should have no reason to question the possibility."

"Have you ever considered that they may have seen *Conqueror* jump into the nebula in the first place?"

"Then they will think it destroyed."

"What if some Ryall ship captain or astrogator was sufficiently intrigued that he ran a few simple calculations to see what happens to a ship that dives into the nebula?"

"Why," Barrett replied, "I suppose he might realize that an improved antirad field would allow a ship to survive inside the nebula."

"In which case," Gower answered, "we'll be ready for them."

The welcoming banquet was held in the officers' mess on the outermost deck of the ship. *Royal Avenger*'s rate of spin was such that spin gravity at the outer hull was 0.95 standard—the precise value for Sandar's surface gravitation. Like all the inhabited spaces aboard the cylindrical ship, the mess compartment was designed for frequent conversion from the "out is down" orientation of spin gravity to the "aft is down" of powered flight. Two long metal tables were bolted to the curved deck and arranged parallel to each other. Fittings on the aft bulkhead showed where they were bolted down when the ship transitioned to powered boost.

Admiral Gower and his party arrived at the officers' mess two minutes prior to 2000 hours. They found the compartment already filled with Altan and Sandarian officers, many of whom were engaged in animated conversation with one another. A few of the Sandarian officers were women. Without exception, these were the center of the largest groupings. Drake caught bits of talk as he moved to his position at the center of the head table and was pleased at how well the two groups seemed to be getting along. The buzz of conversation subsided. The assembled officers sorted themselves out and found their assigned seats at the two mess tables. As they did so, white-coated Royal Marine stewards moved among them, filling wineglasses and placing appetizers on the white linen tablecloths. After a few minutes, Admiral Gower rose at his seat and gently tapped a wineglass with a spoon.

"May I have your attention, please." The compartment became instantly silent as Gower scanned his listeners' faces. After a few seconds, he nodded in satisfaction and continued. "Ladies and gentlemen. For those of you who are Altan, I say welcome. I hope that you have seen something of the flagship since your arrival and that you will see more before you return to your own ships. If you have questions, please don't hesitate to ask them. That is the only way you will learn about us.

"Now then, a general comment. Each and every one of you is to be complimented. You have earned your place on the rolls of this expedition by being the best our respective peoples and worlds have to offer. You *must* be the best, because we have a herculean task before us. That task comes in many parts and will require the unstinting efforts of all of us.

"Our first duty will be to weld our separate fleets into a single fleet. This should not be difficult. After all, both our peoples are descended from good New Providential stock. We share a common bloodline, history, and tradition. We share something else as well. We are fighting the same implacable enemy. Shared danger has always proved a powerful cement, and I expect no difference this time.

"However, it would be foolish for us to close our eyes to the fact that our two peoples have grown apart this past century and a quarter. We Sandarians are warhardened royalists, and you Altans will probably find us too authoritarian, callous, and cynical for your tastes. If you wish to understand the key to our personalities, you must remember that no Sandarian now alive has ever known anything but battle. You Altans are parliamentary democrats who have never known warfare of any kind. It is likely that we will find you lacking in certain things we consider to be military virtues.

"That there will be friction between us is inevitable. When it happens, I ask that each of you give the other the benefit of the doubt. Remember that our only safety lies in working well with one another." Gower paused to let his message sink in. "Now, I believe your vice commander has something to say to you."

Drake stood and spoke of Earth and of the vast fleets that the Interstellar Council would send to aid the two colonies once contact was reestablished. He spoke of clearing the Aezer system once and for all of Ryall ships and of driving them forever from human space. "To those of us in this compartment has fallen the task of reuniting the human race," he concluded. "Let us not fail in our duty."

Admiral Gower lifted his wineglass and signaled for the others in the mess to do the same. "Ladies and gentlemen, I give you His Majesty, the king, and His Honor, the prime minister. May God grant them wisdom, long life, and victory!"

When the first toast had been completed, Drake raised his own glass and said, "To Earth!" The compartment reverberated as two dozen voices echoed his sentiment.

CHAPTER 8

Twenty-two starships floated motionless in the infinite vacuum of deep space, their hulls illuminated by the subdued yellow of a shrunken Napier and the soft blue-white of the Antares Nebula. The interplay of light and shadow across the ships' hulls created an effect rarely seen outside a surrealistic painting. It was an effect largely wasted on the three thousand spacers, scientists, and politicians who manned the ships. To the naked eye it appeared as though each ship floated alone in a universe populated only by the far stars. Even *Royal Avenger*, the largest ship in the fleet, was too far from its nearest neighbors to be visible. However, the impression of isolation was misleading. Onboard each vessel were sensing devices far more acute than the human eye. To those who continually monitored screens displaying the output from such devices, the true size and disposition of the Helldiver Fleet was readily apparent.

The screens showed twenty-two bright golden sparks arrayed in a vast globe around the pale, indistinct ellipse that defined the Napier–Antares foldpoint. Sometimes there was movement on the status displays as auxiliary craft transported personnel, spare parts, and supplies from one starship to another. At much greater intervals, pairs of starships could be seen to break formation, enter the foldpoint itself, and disappear into hard vacuum. It was not unusual for various alarms to sound a few minutes after starship pairs jumped from the Napier–Antares foldpoint into the heart of the nebula. Such alarms were triggered by the return of other ships from the nebula. Returning ships invariably glowed all over with the blue-white intensity of an electric spark. These glows faded rapidly as antiradiation fields reradiated absorbed energy to surrounding space, but while they lasted, they made the returning ships conspicuous objects indeed.

It had been three months since the Altan and Sandarian fleets had joined forces. One of those months had been devoted to fleet exercises ranging from battle maneuvers to abandon-ship drills. In the process of integrating the two fleets into one, Richard Drake had learned that Admiral Gower was an officer who drove himself and his subordinates to their utmost limits. Even though a hard taskmaster, the admiral somehow managed to avoid the role of martinet while building esprit de corps throughout the fleet. It was a display of professionalism that Drake found reason to study with interest.

After a month of sustained effort, the admiral grudgingly conceded that the fleet was sufficiently integrated that they could get on with their mission. Before giving the order to space for the Napier–Antares foldpoint, however, Gower had one final innovation to implement. He ordered each Altan ship to exchange one officer with a Sandarian counterpart. The purpose of the order was to continue the process of breaking down the barriers erected by a century of isolation. It was a plan that Drake heartily agreed with—that is, until the moment when he discovered the identity of the Sandarian the admiral had assigned to *Discovery*.

"Your exchange officer is to be Ensign Phillip Walkirk, Captain," Gower had deadpanned from Drake's screen a few days before the fleet was due to move out for the foldpoint.

"The crown prince, sir? You must be joking!"

"I never joke about orders, Captain. Have you some personal animosity toward this officer? Am I to assume that you do not wish him to serve under you?"

"You know damned well what my objection is, sir," Drake had replied. "I can't take the responsibility. Damn it, he's the heir to the Sandarian throne! What if he were injured or killed while serving aboard an Altan naval vessel?"

"He is as safe aboard *Discovery* as *Royal Avenger*, Captain."

"But if anything should happen to him, it could rupture Altan–Sandarian relations for decades!"

"I don't think you know us very well," the admiral had replied. "We are a warrior people. Our king is a warrior king. Every Sandarian parent knows that one day his or her children will be called upon to serve. John-Phillip Walkirk is no different in that respect from any other Sandarian. Were he to attempt to shield his own offspring from danger while asking the rest of us to risk our children, he would not remain our monarch for very long. No, the crown prince must take his chances like everyone else."

"Well then, what of the disruption to routine? Most of my people are uncomfortable around royalty. They don't know how to act and won't take kindly to bowing and scraping."

"You are to treat Ensign Walkirk exactly as you would any other officer of comparable rank. In fact, since you are not his subjects, there is no need for you to address him as 'Your Royal Highness.' "

"I still don't like it," Drake said in one final attempt to get the order revoked. "Whose brilliant idea was this, anyway?"

"His Highness made the initial suggestion," Gower replied. "After some thought, I agreed with him. It will be valuable experience for a future king of Sandar to live and work among people other than his own. Any further objections, Captain Drake?"

"No, sir." Fifteen years in the military had taught Drake the futility of arguing when a superior had his mind set on something. "We'll welcome him with open arms."

"Excellent, Captain. His Highness will be pleased!"

Ensign Walkirk had come aboard later that same watch. If he had any knowledge of Drake's conversation with Admiral Gower, he showed no sign of it. The same boat that delivered Phillip Walkirk had taken Stan Barrett and Calvan Cooper back to the flagship, where they could coordinate more closely with their Sandarian counterparts.

Two days later, the fleet had departed New Providence for the Napier–Antares foldpoint.

It had taken three weeks at an acceleration of one-half gravity for the Helldiver Fleet to recross the Napier system to where the Napier–Antares foldpoint lay high in the northern sky. For a week after their arrival, the scientists onboard *City of Alexandria* had painstakingly charted the portal's structure and location. Once that task was completed, it was time to test the new antiradiation fields under realistic conditions. To do that, a ship would have to enter the maelstrom of the nebula.

Ever since leaving New Providence, various starship captains had waged a friendly battle over the question of who would be first into the nebula. Admiral Gower had put an end to the contest by choosing His Majesty's Armed Destroyer *Scimitar*. Virtually everyone in the fleet found a reason to be in front of a viewscreen as the destroyer broke formation and made for the foldpoint's interior. After maneuvering his ship to the center of the foldpoint and killing all forward velocity, *Scimitar*'s captain took a few minutes to double-check his systems before switching on his ship's antiradiation field. Moments after the ship's hull turned totally reflective, the destroyer slipped into the heart of the cosmic catastrophe that dominated Napier's northern sky.

There had followed half an hour of rising tension in the ships of the Helldiver Fleet as chronometers slowly ticked off the passing minutes. That tension reached its peak as the appointed time for *Scimitar*'s reappearance approached. The act of breathing virtually stopped throughout the fleet as the countdown clocks reached 00:00:00, then resumed in a collective sigh of relief as the destroyer once again appeared on the fleet's screens. *Scimitar*'s captain lost no time in reporting that the antiradiation field had worked perfectly. If anything, conditions inside the nebula were less stressful than the engineers had predicted they would be.

The next ships to enter the nebula had been *Mace* and *Victory*. To these two had fallen the task of mapping the Antares end of the foldline link. It was a task that was not particularly easy under the best of conditions, and conditions inside the nebula were among the worst imaginable. The nebula was filled with electrostatic repulsions, powerful pulses of radio energy, strong and shifting magnetic fields. Compared to these background conditions, the subtle variations in gravitational constant by which foldpoints are normally detected were nearly imperceptible.

When first presented with the problem of mapping foldspace in the midst of so much cosmic fury, the Altan and Sandarian scientific communities had despaired of ever finding a solution. Only the fact that a badly damaged *Conqueror* had somehow managed to find its way through the nebula kept them looking. Eventually they hit upon a promising approach and constructed more than fifty thousand specially designed, instrumented probes. The only problem was that there had been no opportunity to test the probes in the laboratory. The first they would know whether the design was successful would be when *Victory* tried to measure the curvature of space around the Antares–Napier foldpoint.

Over a period of ten days, the two ships had quartered and requartered the volume of space around their emergence point. Slowly the scientists onboard the Sandarian cruiser had filtered out the worst of the noise, computer-enhanced whatever signal remained, and then subjected the resulting data to a battery of sophisticated algorithms designed to extract the essential gravitational data from a sea of white noise. To their great relief, they found that when all the signal processing was complete, a small nugget of information remained. They used each bit of hard-won data to construct a three-dimensional map of the local structure of foldspace. By the fifth day, the clumping of isogravity lines that denote a foldpoint became obvious. By the tenth day, the scientists had collected sufficient data to be able to define with confidence the foldpoint's boundaries. *Victory*'s captain used that information to post navigational beacons around the foldpoint. His mission accomplished, he ordered his small task force back to the Napier system.

The next ships to enter the nebula were *Dagger* and *Terra*. With them had gone virtually the expedition's entire complement of foldspace astronomers and multidimensional physicists. This second task force's mission was similar to that of *Victory* and *Mace*, but with a significant difference. Where the previous entrants had stayed close by the Antares–Napier exit point, *Dagger* and *Terra* had orders to penetrate deeply into the nebula. Their goal was to obtain gravitational data from as wide an area as possible. By doing so, the scientists hoped to gain insight into the location of other foldpoints within the nebula.

Richard Drake sat in his command chair on *Discovery*'s bridge and glanced at the chronometer in front of him. "They're late!"

"Only by a few minutes," Bethany replied from the observer's seat beside him. "And they were fine when *Mace* contacted them last week."

Drake nodded. Helldiver Mission rules called for the number of ships inside the nebula to be minimized during the initial foldspace survey. Later, when the hazards to be found within the nebula were better understood, the entire fleet would enter. In order to maintain contact with the two cruisers, the three Sandarian destroyers had been assigned the job of periodically entering the nebula and establishing a communications link. Contact was via laser beam, since all other forms of long-range communications were effectively jammed. Once contact was complete, the destroyer would jump back to Napier and relay the two cruisers' reports to Admiral Gower.

Suddenly, alarms began to ring all over the bridge.

"Breakout!" one of the sensor technicians in *Discovery*'s combat control center called out over the command circuit. "We have breakout on two targets. The first bears 73 mark 165, range 8000 kilometers. Target Two bears 65 mark 155, range 5000."

"Identification?" Drake asked.

"They're ours, Captain," the technician replied. "At least, they're blipping today's transponder codes."

"Mr. Haydn! Please make a signal to Captain Marston onboard *Dagger*. Tell him, 'Welcome Home!' and ask him to report at his convenience."

"Aye aye, sir."

Thirty seconds later, Drake's screen lit to reveal Bela Marston's chunky features. *Dagger*'s captain broke into a broad grin as soon as he caught sight of Drake.

"The nebula-mapping expedition has returned, sir. Request permission to rejoin the fleet."

"Permission granted, Captain," Drake replied formally. "Have you anything to report?"

"Yes, sir," Marston replied. "Pursuant to orders, my ship and the Sandarian battle cruiser *Terra* entered the Antares Nebula. We mapped the gravitational constant over as wide a volume of space as we were able to reach while remaining within the time constraints allotted to our mission. We also observed the structure of the nebula and the Antares pulsar."

"Were you able to ascertain the overall pattern of foldspace within the nebula, then?" Drake asked.

"Yes, sir," Marston responded, grinning. "Also, sir, I believe we may have discovered a second foldpoint!"

Bethany Lindquist stretched sleepily and rolled over in bed. As she did so, her head came in contact with something sharp. Swearing under her breath, she came fully awake to discover herself in a strange bunk. It took a few moments to remember where she was and how she had gotten there.

Following the return of *Dagger* and *Terra* from their survey expedition, rumors had gone through the fleet like a flash fire in an atmosphere of pure oxygen. Most had at their core the facts of Captain Marston's official report, namely, that the surveyors had found a second foldpoint inside the nebula. The interesting thing had been that so many variations on the same theme could be developed so quickly. Some had the foldpoint winking out of existence even as the scientists had confirmed its existence. Others were sure that Earth itself lay just beyond and that the expedition commanders were having second thoughts about ordering that contact be made.

The discovery sparked an official reaction as well. Admiral Gower had ordered all data regarding the new discovery refined immediately. He had scheduled a full-scale review for the next week. Upon hearing of the deadline, the scientists had objected. The astronomers in particular had been especially caustic in their comments. They pointed out that the volume of data was such that it would take years to analyze it all. Furthermore, they argued, there were only a handful of specialists along who had the necessary skill, and they had to sleep sometime. Considering the available resources, the chief astronomer had explained, even the most preliminary of reports would take a hard month of effort.

The admiral had not been sympathetic. He'd informed Dr. Grayson, the expedition's senior Sandarian scientist, that the king would hear of it if he wasn't ready with a report in seven days. As for the plea of insufficient resources, Gower agreed to temporarily provide the astronomy section with every expedition member skilled in the required computer correlation techniques. Because of her background as a historian —a profession that was almost totally a matter of computer correlation—Bethany found herself temporarily transferred to *City of Alexandria*.

"Good morning," Bethany's roommate said from across the tiny cabin. Sara Crofton was a woman of about thirty standard years, an expert in nova phenomena and one of the dozen and a half Altan women along on the expedition. She had been the only woman with a private cabin when Bethany came onboard and had been gracious about doubling up for the duration.

"Morning," Bethany replied, still rubbing her head where she had hit it on the corner of her bunk. "Ready for the big conference today?"

"If you mean, 'Did I get enough sleep last night?' the answer is no! I'll be glad when these twenty-hour days are over!"

"Me, too," Bethany replied, swinging her legs over the edge of her bunk and putting them on the carpeted deck. The past six days had been a blur of activity as the scientists had worked overtime to squeeze all they could from the data before the admiral's deadline. Nor was the effort isolated to the multidimensional physicists and foldspace astronomers. Other astronomers concentrated on learning all they could about the nebula.

Bethany washed her face in the cabin's basin while Sara busied herself in the tiny head adjoining the cabin. They then traded places. When Bethany returned, she found her roommate making both bunks.

"You don't have to do that," she said. "I can make my own."

The red-haired astronomer glanced up with a smile. "I don't mind. You get dressed and we'll go down to breakfast."

"Thanks, then. I'll do the same for you tomorrow." Bethany slipped into a clean shipsuit, combed her hair, put on a minimum of makeup, then reached into her overnight bag and brought out a tiny bottle of perfume. Opening it, she dabbed a drop behind each ear.

Sara raised her eyebrows in an unspoken question. In the week they had shared a cabin, it was the first time she had seen Bethany wear perfume.

Glancing up, Bethany saw her roommate's quizzical expression in the mirror. She smiled. "Richard will be at the conference today. I want to look and smell my best for him."

CHAPTER 9

The scientific conference was held in what had once been *City of Alexandria*'s main ballroom. Situated on the outermost deck, the compartment was large enough for the surface underfoot to show a perceptible curve. Tables were arrayed around three sides of a rectangle, with the open side occupied by a dais, lectern, and holo-screen.

Bethany arrived early to help set up the conference. The first attendees began streaming in fifteen minutes before the scheduled starting time, and the compartment quickly filled with people. When Bethany finally sought her own place at the table, she found Stan Barrett and Calvan Cooper seated to her right and Count Husanic and Phillip Walkirk to her left.

"Good afternoon, Miss Lindquist," Husanic said as he leaned forward to kiss her hand. "I'm told that you had a great deal to do with what we will be hearing today."

"I merely did the drudge work so the real brains could devote their time to thinking." Bethany was cut off by the sudden sound of chairs scraping across the deck. She turned to see Admiral Gower enter the compartment with Richard Drake in tow. She hurriedly climbed to her

feet, as did those around her. Drake followed the admiral
to the center of the table directly opposite the holoscreen. As he did so, his gaze swept the compartment
until he found Bethany. She answered his wink with a
beaming smile.

"Good afternoon, ladies and gentlemen," Admiral
Gower said after waiting a few seconds for everyone to
be reseated. "These past six weeks have been a busy
time for all of us. I thought it time we reviewed what
we've learned since our ships first entered the nebula.
Since this is primarily a scientific meeting, I will turn it
over to Dr. Fel Grayson, Senior Scientist."

Grayson, a tall, bony Sandarian, moved to stand behind the lectern. "Ladies and gentlemen, what you will
hear today are *preliminary* findings. We will undoubtedly modify our views of things as we learn more.
Therefore, I urge you to read the weekly reports which
we put on the fleet data base. It's especially important
for those of you in command positions to keep current
with the latest scientific thinking, since you will be
making decisions based on that thinking. With those
words of introduction, I will now call on Sara Crofton,
Professor of Astronomy, Homeport University. Professor Crofton will discuss the findings of the stellar astronomy team."

Sara Crofton mounted the dais with a sheaf of notes in
one hand and a screen control in the other. She moved to
take Dr. Grayson's place at the lectern and spent a few
seconds arranging her notes before launching into her
statement.

"Ladies, gentlemen, colleagues. It was the task of the
stellar astronomy team to study the Antares Nebula. In
this we had a distinct advantage over our multidimensional brethren. The object of our interest is clearly visible out any viewport. It wasn't necessary that we dive
into the nebula to study its structure."

The lights dimmed, and the holoscreen lit to show
an old-style 2-D color photograph. The photograph
showed two closely linked stars surrounded by an ir-
regular shell of faintly glowing gas. The brighter of the
stars glared red-orange, while its smaller companion's

color was greenish white. Sara Crofton continued her discussion. "This is a view of Antares taken by the Palomar Observatory on Earth late in the twentieth century. At that time, Antares was an M0 red-orange supergiant with a mass sixteen times that of Sol and a diameter four hundred times as great. The star was slightly variable and, like all M-class stars, rich in heavy metals, particularly titanium. The other star in the photograph is Antares' much less massive A3 companion."

She manipulated the screen control, and the scene changed. The center of the screen was dominated by a single point of violet-white light so bright that it washed out every other star in the picture. "This is Antares as it looked in the first minutes following the arrival of the nova shock wave in the Napier system. The view was taken by one of the last ships out of the system in 2027 and comes to us courtesy of the Royal Sandarian Archives."

Again the scene flickered. The exploding star was replaced by a great bubblelike cloud. At the center of the cloud, a single starlike object burned with the light of an electric spark. "This, of course, is Antares as we see it today. One hundred twenty-seven years after the initial explosion, the nova cloud has expanded to a diameter of six light-years, with a concomitant degree of dilution and cooling. Even so, conditions inside remain very hazardous for starships."

The view changed again, this time showing a closeup of the nebula's central star. "What you are looking at now is the remnant at the center of the nebula. When Antares went supernova, virtually the whole stellar atmosphere was blown away into space, leaving the central core exposed. The pressures exerted by that explosion were sufficient to collapse Antares' innermost layers. The result was a neutron star deep inside the body of the postnova star. Since angular momentum was conserved during the collapse, the neutron star rotates at a speed of six hundred revolutions per second. It is this rotation which powers everything in the nebula and which represents the greatest danger to our ships.

"When Antares' core collapsed into the highly dense neutron star, the star's magnetic field collapsed with it. The field is now several billion times more concentrated than it was. More importantly, it rotates in sync with the neutron star. Thus, the rotating magnetic field has the effect of turning Antares into a giant particle accelerator. As the field rotates, it whips the electrically charged plasma into motion, accelerating it until individual ions are moving at nearly the speed of light. This white-hot plasma gives off a hellishly strong spectrum of emissions —everything from synchrotron radiation, to hard and soft X-rays, to gamma rays, to high-speed charged particles. If this weren't bad enough, these energetic radiations encounter gas particles as they move through the nebula, producing all manner of secondary radiation phenomena."

Sara Crofton manipulated the screen control once more. A schematic diagram of the Antares Nebula flashed on the screen. The diagram divided the nebula into a series of concentric layers. Each layer was labeled with a hazard factor.

"You will find this diagram in your handouts. What it shows is the degree of risk you face at any point within the nebula. Obviously, the closer one approaches the central star, the worse things get. Nothing mysterious about that. It is simply the inverse-square law working against us. As indicated by the diagram, any ship which approaches within 400 million kilometers of the neutron star is very likely to suffer an overloaded antiradiation field. The risk is tolerable for short periods between 400 million and 800 million kilometers. Beyond 800 million, your antirad fields should be able to withstand the flux indefinitely.

"I will leave it to Academician Loren St. Cyr, the next speaker, to relate these danger zones to foldpoint positions within the nebula."

Loren St. Cyr was the Sandarian multidimensional astronomer who had headed the foldspace mapping effort. St. Cyr was a pudgy man in his late forties whose deeply lined face and shock of white hair made him appear older. He stepped to the podium, glanced at the screen of a pocket computer/notebook, and began to speak in the tones of one who wrongly believes himself a gifted orator.

"Foldlines!" he began thunderously. "Virtually everything depends on foldlines. Yet how many people truly understand what a foldline is or how such a thing could possibly have been affected by the Antares Supernova? Since much of what I have to say depends upon such understanding, I will begin with a digression."

The diagram of the Antares Nebula left over from Sara Crofton's presentation disappeared from the screen. What appeared in its place was an abstract figure composed of thousands of separate line segments arranged in a double spiral pattern. "Astronomers have long known that a massive black hole occupies the center of our galaxy and that billions upon billions of foldlines emanate from it. These foldlines sweep outward along the spiral arms in a complex, interwoven pattern. Whenever a foldline encounters a star, it is focused by that star's mass much as a lens focuses a ray of light. If the focus is sharp enough, a weak spot, or foldpoint, develops in the fabric of the space–time continuum.

"It has long been known that the larger a star, the more likely it is to attract a foldline and thereby form a foldpoint. Since prenova Antares was one of the largest stars in human space, the early explorers were not surprised to discover that it possessed six foldpoints, the largest number yet discovered in a single system."

The diagram changed to show a stylized view of the Antares system prior to 2512. At the center of the screen were the red-giant Antares and its green-dwarf companion, Antares' twelve planets, and the gold-yellow symbols showing the star's foldpoints.

"Obviously, a star's size and mass are exceedingly important in determining the number and distribution of foldpoints within a system. As Professor Crofton noted during her talk, Antares' original mass was sixteen solar masses. However, its diameter—some four hundred times that of Sol—gave the star a very low overall density. Actually, prenova Antares possessed two distinct regions within the boundaries of its photosphere. The star's interior was dominated by a highly dense stellar core, while the outer region was a relatively diffuse stellar atmosphere. This dual density resulted in two different classes of foldpoints being formed within the prenova Antares system.

"Note that there are four foldpoints which are quite distant from the system primary. These four—leading to Napier, Grundlestar, Faraway, and Saracen—range from eight to twelve billion kilometers distant from Antares. These 'long-focus' foldpoints, then, are the result of focusing by the star's atmosphere. Two other foldpoints—leading to the Goddard and Braxton systems —are 'short-focus' foldpoints, and the result of focusing by the star's core. These two were 900 million and 1.8 billion kilometers distant, respectively."

Professor St. Cyr manipulated the screen control to replace the schematic diagram with one similar to that used by Sara Crofton. "Obviously, Antares' physical properties underwent drastic changes when the star went supernova. What was once the star's atmosphere is now a gas cloud six light-years across. Even though the mass is still there, the density is now far too low to focus foldlines. What this means is that those four outer foldpoints cannot possibly be where they were in prenova times. Similarly, the collapse of Antares' core into a hidden neutron star has changed the focusing powers of the core and, therefore, changed the location of the short-focus foldpoints. Understand that the *foldlines* are still there, but their positions have changed in ways we cannot yet predict.

"We do know that one of the 'long-focus' foldpoints has survived, however. That is the Antares–Napier foldpoint through which our ships are able to enter the nebula. Antares–Napier is now three hundred million kilometers distant from its prenova position. Presumably, the other foldpoints have shifted like amounts from their former locations.

"It was this sort of data which we set out to obtain

when we began our surveys inside the nebula. It's a big star system and one in which conditions make it difficult to obtain the data we need to isolate foldpoint positions. Indeed, we could spend our lives crisscrossing the nebula without ever finding another foldpoint. However, the gods appear to have smiled on us. During its sweep across the system, *Dagger* detected the clumping of isogravity lines which mark the location of a second foldpoint within the nebula."

Professor St. Cyr pointed to the second of two foldpoint symbols on the screen. "The new foldpoint is roughly here, some eight hundred million kilometers from Antares and a mere two hundred million distant from the Antares–Napier foldpoint. We haven't enough information to isolate it precisely, of course, but we do know that it exists. Nor is there sufficient correlation between the position of this new foldpoint and that of any prenova portal for us to make a positive determination as to where it might lead. Nevertheless, it *is* a foldpoint and, as such, well worth exploring!"

Following St. Cyr's presentaton, the meeting quickly devolved into discussions as to how best to exploit the new discovery. The arguments continued until Gower ordered a halt to the proceedings to give all those present an opportunity to think about what they'd learned.

The conference reconvened the next morning without the presence of the fleet commander or vice commander. Rather than listen to the endless hairsplitting that is the essence of scientific discourse, Drake and Gower met to review fleet operations. After discussing recent expeditions inside the nebula, the admiral changed the subject to the overall level of fleet preparedness.

"It's been six weeks since our last general inspection, Drake. Time we found out who has let their guard down, don't you think?"

"My reports indicate that things are still relatively shipshape, Admiral."

"Reports can be wrong, Captain. I've seen it happen

before on orbital duty. Anytime the main engines aren't operating, the crews seem to think there's no reason to be vigilant. No, I think we'd best have some surprise inspections."

"I'll put out the order to all commanding officers immediately."

"Don't *order* it, Captain. *Do* it!"

"Sir?"

"I want you to handle the inspections yourself. The captains will work that much harder if the fleet vice commander finds a problem they should have caught themselves. Also, you want to see how they respond when you and your team show up unannounced. Don't give them any warning."

"I'll begin immediately."

"Good. Try to hit at least four combatants over the next seventy-two hours. That should be a sufficient sample to judge how the men are holding up. After that, word will be all over the fleet and your element of surprise will be gone."

"And when I've completed these inspections, Admiral?"

"Report to me aboard the flagship."

"What about the conference recommendations regarding this new foldpoint, sir?"

"They'll be arguing about that for days. We can't very well let our force fall apart while the scientists contemplate the whichness of what, now, can we?"

"No, sir."

As ordered, Drake spent the next three days moving from ship to ship, conducting surprise inspections with the aid of six trusty subordinates. On the third day, he took a landing boat to *Royal Avenger* to report the results to Gower.

"Welcome," the admiral said. "You look haggard."

"Nothing wrong with me that twelve hours' sleep wouldn't cure, sir."

"How did things go?"

"On the whole, very well. We hit *Dagger, Terra, Victory, Saskatoon,* and *Mace.* We found a few things wrong, but no major complaints. You'll have my report in the morning."

"Which ships are ready for operations inside the nebula?"

"All of them, sir."

Gower nodded. "All right. I've decided to send an expedition to check out this new foldpoint. Would you care to lead it?"

"Yes, sir!"

"Then the job's yours. The battle staff has studied the problem and has a number of recommendations concerning the composition of the task force." Gower glanced down at a computer printout lying on his desk. "They suggest *Discovery*, *Terra*, the three destroyers, and *Saskatoon*."

"The regimental transport, sir? I'd rather have *Alexandria*. We're a lot more likely to need scientists than Marines."

"You'll have scientists aboard *Discovery* and *Terra*. Since we don't know what's on the other side of that foldpoint, we don't know what you'll need in the way of forces. Think of the Marines as an insurance policy."

"What about tankers?"

"You will be taking three into the nebula with you. They'll stay there. After topping off your ships, they will act as communications relays. Any other questions?"

"No, sir."

"Very well. You may begin your preparations. Good luck to you."

"Thank you, sir."

CHAPTER 10

Richard Drake sat in his command chair on *Discovery*'s bridge and gazed at the image of the Antares pulsar relayed from *Discovery*'s largest telescope. In addition to having been magnified, the image was electronically enhanced to show both the star's surface features and the surrounding—and normally invisible —corona. Every minute or so, a dark-tinged wave would pass across Antares' face almost too quickly to see. As it passed, the star would be wracked by a violent explosion. Torrents of white-hot plasma would arch into the sky. Before they could properly form, the geysers were wrenched into great glowing rivers that spiraled continuously away from the star's surface— mute testimony to the power of the pulsar's rapidly rotating magnetic field.

Drake lowered his gaze to an auxiliary screen where the same view was displayed at a lesser magnification. On the smaller screen Antares' corpse was a tiny ball of scintillating fire surrounded by an endless sea of fluorescent fog. Concurrent with each explosion, a series of light rings would race away from the star like waves escaping a pebble tossed into a pond. The most powerful of these traveling waves of radiance would persist for

long minutes and climb nearly to the edge of the screen
before dissipating into the background glow of the nebula.

"Captain, *Phoenix* reports that they have us in sight,"
Discovery's communicator said.

The comment brought Drake back to the business at
hand. In the month since *Discovery* had entered the nebula, the cruiser's fuel stocks had reached the critical
point. It was time to tackle the tricky task of refueling in
the radiation storm that was the nebula's interior, an
operation that was fraught with danger for both the ships
involved.

"All right, Communicator. Tell them that they are
cleared for approach and tell the chief engineer that he
may begin taking the spin off the ship."

"Aye aye, Captain."

Half a minute later, the voice of the chief engineer cut
into the general intercom circuit: "Attention, All Hands!
Make all preparations for refueling operations. Despinning begins now! Zero gravity in five minutes. I repeat,
the ship will be in zero-gravity conditions in five minutes. Secure all loose equipment and personnel. Take all
necessary precautions."

As the announcement echoed around him, Richard
Drake ordered the main viewscreen switched to one of
the hull cameras in position to view the cryogen
tanker's approach. The seething Antares pulsar was replaced by the rosy glow of the surrounding nebula.
Drake searched the fog for the tiny shape of the cryogen tanker. He searched in vain for nearly a minute
before his eye caught a single white sparkle. The sparkle grew and quickly turned into a tiny pearl that
glowed with an internal white light. Silhouetted as it
was against the red hue of the nebula, the glow had an
almost supernatural beauty to it. In reality, of course,
there was a much more prosaic explanation for the
phenomenon.

Prior to their jump from Napier to Antares, each
starship captain had ordered his ship's antirad generators activated. Instantly, the eight ships' hulls had
taken on a mirrorlike sheen. But Napier is not Antares,

and the fields were not perfect. A few billion kilometers from Napier, the quantity of energy that leaked into the field was insignificant. In the raging storm of the nebula, however, even a few tenths percent leakage would quickly be fatal. The engineers who had designed the field had known this and had taken steps to transform energy leakage into visible light, which was then radiated back into space. The result was that each of the task force's starships glowed with white radiance.

The image of the tanker continued to grow until it filled the screen. *Phoenix* halted its approach when it was a few hundred meters from *Discovery*. At nearly the same moment, the cruiser's rate of rotation slowed to a halt. There followed several minutes of careful consultation before the tanker fired its attitude jets and slowly moved to place its bulk between *Discovery* and the Antares pulsar. The purpose of the maneuver was not to shield the cruiser but rather to shield the refueling line that would soon stretch between the two ships. Even at their current distance from the central star, the energy flux was such that the most heavily armored fuel transfer line would melt within minutes of leaving the protection of *Phoenix*'s shielding.

As Drake watched, the teleoperated line suddenly appeared from out of the featureless pearl-white surface of the tanker and made its way toward the battle cruiser. It quickly passed out of the hull camera's field of view and under the rim of the cruiser's habitat ring. Thirty seconds later, the ship echoed with the report that *Phoenix* was ready to begin the fuel transfer.

"Tell Captain Stuart that he may begin when ready," Drake replied to the report. He listened as the communicator passed on his order. Then, on the screen, the fuel transfer line stiffened as deuterium-enriched liquid hydrogen began flowing into *Discovery*'s tanks.

Bethany Lindquist ate a late breakfast in the officers' mess on the morning *Discovery* was scheduled for refueling. She had slept late, having been up categorizing isogravity data for the astronomy team well into the late watch the previous evening. She had just finished half a raja fruit when the overhead speaker blared out: "Attention, All Hands! Make all preparations for refueling operations..." She sighed and reached for the hold-down straps on her chair. As she did so, someone slid a covered tray into the table restraints across from her.

"Mind if I anchor here for a bit, Bethany?"

She glanced up to see the young, smiling face of Phillip Walkirk hovering over her. "It would be my pleasure, Your Highness."

Walkirk grimaced. "Please, I'm trying to camouflage myself as a good democrat. On this ship, I'm just Ensign Walkirk, or Phillip to my friends."

"In that case, I would be honored to have you sit next to me...Phillip."

The Sandarian prince strapped himself down just as unpleasant sensations in Bethany's inner ear told her that the despinning process had begun.

"Work late last evening?" Phillip asked as he sipped coffee from a low-gravity container.

Bethany nodded and told him of her late bout with the ship's computer. It had been two weeks since *Discovery* and the other ships of the task force had reached the region where *Dagger* had noted a distinct clumping of the isogravity lines. They had spent the time crisscrossing the region, refining the data in order to pinpoint the new foldpoint's exact position. The quantity of data had proved too much for the half dozen astronomers onboard, so Bethany had volunteered to assist the analysis effort.

They ate together in silence as gravity slowly disappeared around them. Finally, Bethany asked, "How is your sister?" Princess Lara Walkirk had been Bethany's guide on Sandar.

"I imagine she's busy just now," Phillip replied. "Preparations for the wedding, you know."

"What wedding?"

"Lara is to be married next glacier melt."

"Really? When did she become engaged?"

"Oh, about fifteen years ago," Phillip replied.

"You're kidding!"

"Not at all," Phillip said. "Lara has been betrothed since age six. Didn't she tell you?"

"I guess the subject never came up."

"I'm surprised. The official date was established some five years ago at a full meeting of the Council of Royal Advisers."

"Didn't Lara have something to say about it?"

"No, of course not. Why should she?"

"The couple involved should have the final say in such matters."

"Not if one of them is a Sandarian royal princess, Bethany. Such weddings are a matter of state policy."

"Who is the lucky man?"

"The principal suitor is the Count of Claremore."

"*Principal* suitor?"

Phillip paused, thinking how best to explain the Sandarian marriage custom. Finally, he said, "There are many reasons for us to plan royal marriages a decade or so in advance. Such an alliance is always the subject of difficult political negotiations, and it is best to get it over early. Also, there is the need to provide the populace with a sense of stability, to give them time to get used to the idea. And, most important, it is vital that the prospective bride or bridegroom be evaluated over a long span of time to ensure that he or she is suitable for the task of ruling."

Bethany nodded. "Many Terran cultures practiced child betrothals for much the same reasons."

"We Sandarians, however, have a rather unique problem," Phillip continued. "We have been at war with the Ryall for the whole of our history, and it is our custom to send the children of our ruling class out to serve with the fleet. This means that there is a nontrivial probability that a prospective bride or bridegroom may be killed in battle. That would upset the stability which we strive for. To avoid such disruptions, we name a primary suitor for a royal princess and at least one backup suitor. Lara's backup is the Earl of Rodeston. If anything were to happen to Claremore, Rodeston would marry Lara."

Bethany thought about how she would feel if she

were auctioned off to the highest bidder like some
prized cow and, after having gotten used to the idea,
had her mate switched on her at the last minute. She
shivered at the thought and then was struck by another. She glanced at Phillip, who was just finishing off
his coffee. "I just realized, Phillip, that you must also
be betrothed!"

He nodded. "Since I was three. Would you like to see
her photograph?"

"Very much."

The prince pulled a small hologram out of his pocket
and passed it over to her. Bethany took it and studied it
for long seconds. In it, a young blond woman was making a face at the camera. Despite that, the woman's
beauty was clearly evident. "The Lady Donna Elisabeth
Carendale, my future queen. I took this on a picnic some
three years ago. She keeps asking me to destroy it, but I
find it more real than all the official portraits ever taken
of her."

"She's lovely," Bethany said. "I assume that she also
has a backup."

"Two," Phillip replied. He smiled. "Although I doubt
if I will be needing them."

"When is the big day?"

"Sometime after we get back from this expedition.
How would you like to come to the wedding?"

Bethany smiled. "I would be honored, Phillip."

"In that case, consider yourself invited."

"Perhaps you will return the favor for me, then,"
Bethany replied. She found herself explaining her and
Richard Drake's plans to be married on Earth.

"That's marvelous," Phillip replied. "How come I
haven't heard of this before?"

"We didn't want it to get around the fleet," she cautioned. "We don't want people to make a fuss over us."

"Then they won't hear it from me," he responded. He
made a sign in the air with his fingers, a sign Bethany
didn't recognize. When he finished, he said, "I understand you've become quite an expert on our enemies
since you visited Sandar."

Bethany nodded. "Alta needed Ryall experts, and it

seemed a natural extension of my job as a comparative historian."

"Have you read Buckman's *Guide to Ryall Social Behavior*, and Adamson's *Ryall Mores and Manners*?"

Bethany nodded. "Although I'm not sure I followed Buckman's reasoning. In fact, all my studies have left me with the feeling that we may not understand the Ryall as well as we think we do."

"You aren't alone in that feeling," Phillip replied. "I know men who have spent their lives studying the centaurs who wonder the same thing."

"I suppose the thing that strikes me as most odd is the mythology the Ryall have invented concerning novas. In all other respects they appear to be completely rational, yet when it comes to exploding stars, they're as superstitious as the ancient Gypsies."

"Considering their history," Phillip replied, "can you blame them?"

In the century of war since the New Providential refugees had first settled Sandar, there had been dozens of major clashes and hundreds of individual battles with the Ryall. Usually when a ship was struck in the course of such battles, it was destroyed outright. Occasionally, however, ships escaped destruction but were sufficiently damaged that they could not make it back to base. In such cases, both sides went to considerable trouble to rescue the surviving crew. For in a war between alien species, prisoners were worth their weight in platinum.

Over the years, the Sandarians had managed to collect a few hundred prisoners in this way. They had also taken the bodies of foes from the wreckage of slain ships. From the dead, they had gained a considerable understanding of Ryall physiology. From their prisoners, they had attempted to learn the workings of the Ryall mind, with significantly less success.

One of the first things the Sandarians had discovered was that the Ryall, like humans, were a culturally variegated race. The outlook of any individual Ryall was largely dependent on where he was raised. For instance, prisoners from Avadon, as the humans had code-named one of the major worlds of the Ryall hegemony, would not eat certain meats, while those from Belaston would eat nothing else. Prisoners from Caarel built shelters of reeds when given nothing better, while those from Darthan preferred to dig burrows in the ground. But no matter where the prisoner was from, all Ryall agreed on one thing: the Legend of the Swift Eaters.

Some thirty thousand years earlier, humanity and the Ryall had been about on a par with one another. At a time when most humans lived in family villages and were hunter/gatherers, the Ryall had also lived in small family groupings. They had preferred the banks of rivers or the shores of shallow seas for their settlements. They were simple fisher folk who spent their time in the water harvesting other forms of marine life. The streams and seas of the Ryall home world were sufficiently bountiful that it was unusual for a fisherman to go hungry. And while Ryall villages might occasionally war with one another over a particularly rich fishing ground, the Ryall were, by and large, peaceful and happy.

This tranquil way of life had come to an abrupt end about the time humans learned to carve stone and ivory and long before the era of agriculture began on Earth. The cause had been a single star that suddenly burned bright in the home world sky. The primitive Ryall had not known what to make of the new star, which was bright enough to be seen even in daylight. Like most primitives, they saw any change in the sky as an evil omen and fled to their witch doctors and shamans to seek advice. These worthies advised them to cower in their burrows until the star passed. And pass it did. After a few years, the new star faded back into the obscurity whence it had come. Indeed, it would have quickly been forgotten except that the daily lives of the Ryall began to change rapidly about the time the new star disappeared.

Like the Antares Supernova of thirty millennia later, the nearby nova had showered the Ryall home world with radiation. The levels were not high enough to sterilize the Ryall worlds, but they were bad enough. The rain of primary and secondary radiations had wreaked havoc with the genetic reservoirs of life, causing the mutation rate to rise precipitously. With each new generation of hatchlings had come grotesque new shapes and abilities. Most of these had been harmful and mercifully killed their owners while still in the egg. Others were of limited utility and were quickly weeded out by either natural selection or the elders of the tribe. Some mutations, however, proved beneficial and were incorporated into the quickly evolving race.

Nor were the Ryall the only race evolving. Some five thousand years after the nova first burned bright in the sky, there came into existence on the Ryall home world another intelligent species. The Ryall prisoners had various names for these beings. The most common translated as "the swift eaters."

The swifts were amphibians descended from a nonsentient carnivore that inhabited the oceans of the Ryall world. They were fast, cunning, and voracious. They attacked the Ryall breeding grounds and gorged themselves on Ryall eggs. As a result, the Ryall population plummeted. There was even a time when the swifts threatened the existence of the older species.

After generations of trying, the Ryall finally devised a successful defense against the depredations of the swifts. They withdrew completely from the water and became full-time land animals living in groups far enough inland to avoid attack. They learned to lay their eggs in artificial pools fed by streams and to hunt and herd other land animals. They learned to farm to provide fodder for their herds. They learned to use fire and metals. Eventually, they developed cities and a true civilization. Sometime during their Bronze Age, the Ryall had also learned to hunt the swift eaters. It was a long hunt, lasting some fifteen thousand years. As generation followed generation, the Ryall learned to hate the swifts. Eventually, that hate became instinct.

When the hunt was finally over, the Ryall found that they had learned a valuable lesson. History had taught them that there is but one possible response to any potential competitor species—to seek that species' extinction. Thus it was that when a new nova blazed forth just beyond the Ryall realm, the Ryall discovered a new, even deadlier threat to their species. This threat was a species of warm-blooded bipeds who came in a variety of odd colors. They were spacefarers whose ships showed a certain flair for the technical arts. So far as the Ryall were concerned, no hatchling would be safe while a single member of this strange new race was left alive anywhere in the galaxy!

Bethany sipped from her zero-gravity coffee cup and contemplated Phillip Walkirk's comments about Ryall history. Or, rather, what human beings thought Ryall history was, she reminded herself.

"I've often wondered whether the Legend of the Swift Eaters is oral history or merely a legend," Bethany said. "Do you think the swifts really existed?"

Phillip shrugged. "I don't know that we have any hard evidence one way or the other. It doesn't really matter, though. So long as the Ryall believe in the swifts and continue to act on that belief, then the question is moot."

"Are you sure they *do* believe in them?"

"Oh, most definitely! That is the primary reason why the Ryall psyche leans so heavily toward xenophobia. So long as they want us dead, what difference the reason?"

"But if they truly want us dead, how can we ever hope to negotiate a peace with them?" Bethany asked.

Phillip Walkirk blinked in surprise at Bethany's question. He paused for long seconds, as though he were having trouble wringing meaning from the words. Finally, he said, "There can never be peace between us until we drive them back to their home worlds. As for negotiation, how does one negotiate with a mad dog?"

"I'm not sure I'm ready to concede that they *are* mad dogs, Phillip."

"That is your privilege. We Sandarians have had a century to study our adversaries. We can hardly expect you Altans to come around to our way of thinking in only two years."

Bethany sensed the tension that lay behind Phillip's words and decided to change the subject. Slowly they drifted into telling each other stories about their homes. They were in the midst of comparing notes on hobbies when an overhead speaker blared out the news that refueling was complete and that spin gravity would be restored in five minutes.

Quick on the heels of the announcement, Commander Marchant, the executive officer, floated through the wardroom hatch. "Ah, there you two are!" he exclaimed.

Phillip Walkirk glanced up. "Have you been looking for us, sir?"

Marchant nodded. "The captain's called a meeting of all officers. You're to come too, Miss Lindquist."

"What's up?" Bethany asked.

"Professor St. Cyr has just reported that they've isolated the foldpoint!" Marchant replied. "The captain has given the order to prepare the ship for foldspace transition. It looks like we're going to jump!"

CHAPTER 11

Bethany Lindquist sat in the observer's seat next to Richard Drake's command console on *Discovery*'s bridge. She watched wide-eyed while all around her the control-room crew prepared the cruiser for battle or flight, whichever proved more appropriate in the coming hours. Two images graced the main viewscreen, which Bethany had been watching off and on for the past twenty minutes. The left side of the screen showed the five oddly shaped bubbles of brilliant white light that would shortly enter the system beyond the foldpoint. They floated in an endless mist of pale red. The right side of the screen showed three equally bright spheres silhouetted against the mist. These were the task force's cryogen tankers, which would be staying behind to relay reports back to *Royal Avenger* and the rest of the fleet.

"Do you think we'll find Earth on the first try, Richard?" Bethany asked.

"We know that fully half of Antares' original foldpoints led eventually to Sol," Drake replied. "Maybe this is one of those."

"And if it isn't?"

"Then we try again."

109

Drake reached out to clasp Bethany's hand briefly, then keyed for the communicator on duty. "Set up an 'All Ships' circuit, Mr. Haydn. Commanding officers' conference."

"Yes, sir!"

Within a minute, Drake found himself staring at the features of the five starship captains under his command. He searched out the round face of Captain-Lieutenant Lord Harl Quaid of His Majesty's Destroyer *Mace* and the mustachioed visage of Captain-Lieutenant Sir Carter Ashton Rostock of *Mace*'s sister ship, *Arrow*.

"Gentlemen, are your ships ready?"

"Yes, sir," Quaid replied. He was echoed immediately by Rostock.

"Very well, Captain Quaid. You will be in command. You will immediately take star readings and initiate a passive sensor sweep on breakout. Look for any evidence of inhabited planets, military installations, or space traffic. If you find any, both ships will return immediately. Otherwise, *Mace* stays to guard the foldpoint while *Arrow* jumps back here to report. Is that understood?"

"Yes, sir. And if we're attacked?"

"Then your first duty will be to see that one of you survives long enough to get back here and report."

Drake's gaze moved to the screen next to the one Quaid was displayed on. "What is *Terra*'s status, Captain Dreyer?"

"All personnel are at battle stations, sir," the Sandarian cruiser captain replied.

"Captain Stiles?"

"*Scimitar* is ready."

"Captain Eberhart?"

"All personnel are in acceleration tanks, sir. Give the word and *Saskatoon* will be out of here like a snow lizard skating across glazed ice."

"Very well, gentlemen. *Mace* and *Arrow* will begin all preparations for foldspace transition. This conference is ended."

One by one the faces on Drake's auxiliary screens

winked out. He keyed for his executive officer in *Discovery*'s combat control center. "Status, Commander Marchant."

"All sensors alive and seeing, Captain. All primary and secondary batteries are manned and operating. All antimatter projectors at power and ready to shoot. We have full firepower capability out to one hundred thousand kilometers."

"All right," Drake replied. "Keep your eyes peeled for unfriendly visitors."

There followed five minutes of increasing tension as the two destroyer captains checked and rechecked their ships. Despite the calm voices that filled the command circuit, Drake and everyone onboard the two destroyers knew that the job of being first through the foldpoint was a dangerous one.

Until the Antares Supernova, there had never been a confirmed case of an active foldline link terminating in the interior of a star. However, if that had changed and the foldpoint on the other end of this foldline link had formed deep inside a star, then *Arrow* and *Mace* would never know it. Worse, if neither destroyer survived to return and report, Drake would not be free to search for them. Losing both destroyers would be prima facie evidence that conditions on the other side of the foldpoint were lethal. It would be difficult to send another ship and crew to near-certain death on the slight chance that whatever had destroyed *Arrow* and *Mace* would spare them.

More likely than the possibility of coming out inside a star was the prospect that the two destroyers would materialize inside a defended foldpoint. If they did, the sudden appearance of two glowing apparitions of unknown origin would undoubtedly set the defenders to shooting. It would matter little whether the defenders were Ryall or human.

"Permission to begin countdown, sir," *Mace*'s captain said over the audio command circuit.

"Permission granted," Drake replied.

"Attention, All Ships! Foldspace transition in sixty seconds. I repeat, foldspace transition in sixty seconds!"

There was a sudden flurry of good-luck messages over the ship-to-ship circuits and then total silence, save for the voice of *Mace*'s astrogator counting down the seconds remaining to transition. Drake glanced up at the main viewscreen and searched for the two tiny cylindrical shapes that were the Sandarian destroyers.

"Ten...nine...eight..."

He ordered the screen magnification raised to maximum. The two ships expanded on the screen. Details were still indistinct because of the surrounding antiradiation fields.

"Five...four...three..."

Drake felt his fingers grip the edge of his acceleration couch and was vaguely aware that he had been holding his breath.

"Two...one...jump!"

On the screen, two cylindrical bubbles of light winked out as one. *Mace* and *Arrow* were gone.

Nearly an hour later, the scene on *Discovery*'s bridge had not changed noticeably. Drake sat in his command chair, his eyes sweeping restlessly back and forth across his auxiliary screens. Beside him, Bethany chewed her lower lip while devoting her full attention to the main viewscreen. Around them, console operators sat rigidly at their stations, fingers poised for action over keyboards.

"How long has it been?" Drake asked no one in particular.

"Fifty-seven minutes, sixteen seconds, sir," one of the technicians replied over the command circuit.

"Less than three minutes to go," Drake muttered.

Suddenly, a single mirrored form materialized five thousand kilometers in front of *Discovery* and alarms began to clang all over the ship. Orders were snapped out over comm links, and weapons operators scrambled to obey. Within seconds, the cruiser's heavy laser and antimatter projector batteries had been brought to bear on the intruder. Almost as quickly, reports came in from *Terra* and *Scimitar*. They too had the newcomer in their sights.

"Combat Control, identify new arrival!" Drake snapped.

"It's *Arrow*, Captain," was the immediate answer. "She appears undamaged."

Drake sighed quietly and made a conscious effort to release the tension that had been building for the past hour. "Get me Captain Rostock, then tell *Terra* and *Scimitar* to stand down."

"Captain Rostock is on your number three screen, sir."

One of Drake's screens cleared to show the features of *Arrow*'s captain.

"Report, Mr. Rostock!" Drake ordered.

"Mission accomplished, sir! The system beyond the foldpoint is situated approximately two hundred light-years from here, midway between Antares and Spica. The system primary is a G7 dwarf with at least five planets. Two of these are typical inner-system worlds. One has an oxygen atmosphere and shows definite traces of chlorophyll. The other is a hothouse planet unsuited for human habitation. The other three worlds we spotted were all outer-system gas giants."

"Any sign of civilization?"

Rostock shook his head. "We scanned for everything from high-frequency electromagnetic waves to low-frequency gravity waves. Nothing, sir."

Drake frowned. An uninhabited G7 star in the direction of Spica was not what they had been looking for. To Drake's knowledge, the entire region of space around Spica had never been explored. It was one sector of the galaxy that had remained closed to humanity because of a lack of active foldline links. The fact that *Mace* and *Arrow* had penetrated two hundred light-years in that direction proved yet again that the local structure of foldspace had been drastically altered by the Antares Supernova. Drake said as much to Rostock.

"Yes, sir. That was the conclusion Captain Quaid and I reached."

"Anything else I should know, Captain?"

"We have star studies and other recorded observations, Captain. They may prove valuable to the scientists."

"Very well. Transmit them to us, and also to the cryogen tankers for relay to Admiral Gower. Then stand by while we prepare the task force for foldspace transition."

"Yes, sir!"

Drake keyed for *Discovery*'s communicator on duty. "Put me on the 'All Ships' circuit, Mr. Haydn."

"You're on, sir."

"Attention, All Ships and crews. This is the task force commander speaking. I have just received *Arrow*'s report concerning the system on the other side of this foldpoint. It appears not to be inhabited, nor to have been previously explored. We will therefore enter the system and map it for additional foldpoints."

Half an hour later, the small fleet had positioned itself in a roughly spherical formation at the center of the foldpoint. Drake watched *Discovery*'s preparations for the upcoming jump on his screens. In truth, the cruiser had been ready to jump since before *Arrow* and *Mace* had disappeared into hard vacuum. Still, it never hurt to double-check things, and the cruiser's crew did so with an enthusiasm born of the knowledge that their lives depended on it.

The countdown clock was within five minutes of jump time when Drake said, "Mr. Haydn, get me the chief engineer, please."

"Yes, sir."

The face of Gavin Arnam, *Discovery*'s chief engineer, appeared on Drake's screen. "Are we ready to jump, Chief?"

"Ready, captain. Mass converters are holding steady. Antirad fields are nominal, jump computers are online. Engine boost is a steady zero point five gees."

"Very good, Engineer. Hold her together for a few more minutes and we'll be out of this plasma soup. Commander Marchant?"

Arnam's features were quickly replaced by those of the executive officer.

"Status, please!"

"Combat Control is ready for anything, sir. All battle

stations are manned. All offensive weapons systems are ready."

"Mr. Cristobal?"

"Foldspace generators are energized, Captain. I confirm the chief engineer's report that the jump computer is online and functioning."

"Very well. All departments stand by."

Drake surveyed his ship captains. One by one they announced that they were ready for the long jump. Satisfied, he gave them their orders. *Discovery* would go first, followed at ten-second intervals by *Terra*, *Arrow*, and *Scimitar*. *Saskatoon* would bring up the rear. With that duty finished, Drake leaned back in his acceleration couch and watched the countdown chronometer's red numerals march inexorably toward 00:00:00.

From his station on the bridge, Argos Cristobal counted down the seconds to jump time. Drake barely heard him. His gaze was riveted on the red haze that filled the viewscreen instead. Cristobal's clear voice suddenly cried, "Zero!" and the haze was gone, replaced in an instant by a starfield of white stars silhouetted against black sky.

"Get me a view of Antares, Mr. Cristobal."

"Aye aye, sir."

The screen changed to show a red-orange star with a greenish-white companion tucked in close beside it. The sight brought memories of long-ago winter camping trips with his father flooding into Drake's consciousness. Whatever star system this was, the nova shock wave would not arrive for another seventy years or so.

Drake found his reminiscences cut short by the sudden blaring of an alarm. The raucous noise was abruptly cut off, and Commander Marchant's voice issued from an overhead speaker.

"Captain! *Mace* is under power. It has left the foldpoint and is accelerating at six gravities in the direction of the inner system. Range is fifty thousand kilometers."

"Where the hell does Quaid think he is going?"

"Unknown, Captain. Stand by. Sensors have just picked up another ship!"

"Where, Number One?"

"It appears to be just departing the second planet, sir. *Mace* is in pursuit."

"Identify that second craft!" Drake ordered.

There were another few seconds of silence. Then the answer came. "Drive flare spectrum indicates the other craft is Ryall, Captain. I repeat. The craft is definitely Ryall!"

Several things happened at once following Marchant's identification of the Ryall ship. Drake put through a call to *Mace* at the same moment one of the sensor operators reported *Terra*'s arrival in the system. There were a few seconds of confusion while Drake issued orders that each newly arrived ship be brought up to date as it materialized. By the time he had finished that, Captain-Lieutenant Harl Quaid was on his screen. The Sandarian nobleman's features were stretched tight across his skull in the dead man's grimace that is the mark of high acceleration.

"Report!" Drake ordered.

The words poured forth, each one laboriously delivered against a gravity field six times normal. "Our detectors picked up a drive flare departing the second planet just after *Arrow* left the system, sir."

"How the hell did you miss it on your initial survey?" Drake asked.

"It must have been in close parking orbit about the planet and emitting too little energy for detection. Speed-of-light delay between here and the second planet is twenty minutes. They must have detected our arrival, spent some time deciding what to do about us, and then lit out. Light from the flare then took twenty mintues to get back to us. We tracked him long enough to make sure that our instruments weren't acting up. I then ordered *Mace* to pursue."

Drake nodded. "Good man! We can't allow them to leave the system. They must know we came out of the nebula."

"That was my thought, too, sir!"

"Save your strength, Captain," Drake advised. "I'll get back to you as soon as we're organized here."

Drake switched the communications screen off and cursed the bad luck that made a Ryall starship a witness to their arrival. He then put such thoughts from his mind. There would be plenty of time for recriminations later. What was needed now was to stop that ship from reaching wherever it was going.

Drake thought for a moment, then frowned as he wondered if the quarry was a warcraft, and if so, how large it was. *Mace* might not be big enough to take on the fleeing ship. A Ryall victory over the Sandarian destroyer would leave their quarry to spread the alarm across the Ryall hegemony. What had a single ship been doing orbiting an uninhabited world, anyway? Indeed, *was* it a single ship? For all Drake knew, an entire Ryall battle fleet could be lurking out of sight behind the G7 star's second world.

And what of the world itself? Even if there were no fleet, there was the fact that the planet might well be inhabited after all. If this were a Ryall colony, then the fact that neither *Arrow* nor *Mace* had detected energy emissions meant little. Humanity's ships had entered the system a mere ninety minutes earlier, too little time in which to survey an entire world. The Ryall could have substantial ground installations, even cities, on the far side, where their emissions would be hidden by the planet's mass.

A chill wave of fear ran down Drake's spine. He had a sudden vision of a million or more centaurs listening avidly to news reports that human ships had been seen exiting the Antares Nebula. It was one of the prime rules of the Helldiver Expedition that no Ryall must ever learn that the nebula was navigable. For if the Ryall ever learned that the nebula could be penetrated, they would use that knowledge to attack human space. Some of the proposed remedies to prevent the centaurs from learning the secret were draconian.

Drake glanced up and momentarily locked eyes with

Bethany. She read the expression on his face. A look of horror slowly diffused her features.

"Oh, Richard! You wouldn't destroy a whole planet to keep our secret, would you?"

"I may have no alternative," he replied gruffly.

"But that would be genocide!"

He didn't answer, keying angrily for Communicator Haydn instead. "Captains' conference!" he snapped.

The three remaining ships of the task force had arrived during the time Drake had spent placing his thoughts in order. Within seconds his screens lit up to show the faces of his subordinate commanders. He quickly summarized his analysis of the situation for them.

"Considering everything we don't know about this system, I've decided to split the force. I will take *Discovery* and follow *Mace* in pursuit of the Ryall ship. Captain Dreyer, you will take *Terra*, *Arrow*, and *Saskatoon* and engage the planet. Captain Stiles, *Scimitar* will return to the nebula and relay what has happened to Admiral Gower. Once you have made contact with the rest of the fleet, you will return here and stand by in the foldpoint. Any questions, gentlemen?" There were none. "In that case, good luck to you all."

Drake switched off and turned to his astrogator. "I want a full-performance intercept plotted for that Ryall ship, Mr. Cristobal."

"Plotted and engaged, Captain."

"Good man! 'All Hands' circuit, Mr. Haydn."

"You have it, sir."

Drake paused a moment, licked dry lips, then began to speak. "Attention, All Hands! Prepare for prolonged and heavy acceleration . . ."

CHAPTER 12

Varlan of the Scented Waters Clan lay in front of her computer console on a cured herbos hide and watched the dots that reported the current period's production scroll rightward across the screen. Occasionally, she would run her grasping digits over the ten-centimeter-wide control sphere, causing other patterns of dots to appear on the screen. As she read, she alternately raised and lowered her earflaps in irritation.

The mineral extraction facility on Corlis had been operating for an entire twelve period, yet production still lagged far behind computer projections. It had been bad enough in previous periods when they had barely managed to fill the ore carriers that called infrequently at the frontier world. Now *Space Swimmer* orbited overhead, and there was only enough extract in the storage bins to fill eight-twelfths of the ore carrier's capacious holds. The continuing shortfall in production could no longer be hidden.

Varlan knew that she had failed in her responsibilities, and it angered her. What made the failure doubly irksome was the fact that it was not entirely her fault. Rather, there had been an unexpected spate of equipment breakdowns and a freak storm that had toppled a

119

number of power pylons. The pipeline that carried water from the upstream diversion dam to the laser drill cooling jackets had also been late going into operation. Without an adequate supply of cooling water, the drills had had to be operated at less than maximum power. And if that weren't enough, the laborers were forever coming down with diseases the philosophers had never seen before. Still, the safety of the race depended on a continuous flow of power metals, and Varlan knew that Those Who Rule would pay scant attention to her excuses.

"May the laborers precede me to the Evil Star!" Varlan cursed as she finished the production report and wondered how long it would be before the manager's caste found someone else to run the Corlis facility.

The hexagonal walls of her cell/office reverberated with the soft hooting cry of a windsniffer. Varlan turned her long supple neck to face the curtained entryway and called permission to enter to the unknown who had triggered the signal. As she had half expected, the visitor was Salfador, Corlis Complex's chief philosopher/priest. Varlan watched the priest flow gracefully across the carpet of new-mown rushes to stand before her. Salfador was a strong male whose scales were a healthy gray-green, whose six legs rippled with strength, and whose grasping digits had the dexterity and skill of a first-class surgeon. Varlan had long considered asking him to be her mate during the next copulation season but had not yet broached the subject for fear that it would lessen her authority over him.

"Greetings, Salfador of the Eternal Fire!" she said, bowing her neck as custom required.

"Greetings to you, Varlan of the Scented Waters," he replied before going on in a more conversational tone. "I see that you are doing your ledgers. Have I arrived at a bad time?"

"There are no good times when we cannot even fill the holds of one old ore carrier," she replied. "I fear that you will have a new manager to counsel shortly, Salfador. I expect to be recalled before the next period is over."

"You are too unforgiving of yourself, Varlan," he said,

slipping effortlessly into his role as confidant. "You have done as well as anyone could, considering the handicaps under which you are forced to labor. How were you to know that the local microorganisms would find Ryall flesh tasty and thereby have half of your labor force under my care at any given moment?"

"Those Who Rule do not listen to excuses," Varlan replied, repeating the warning she had given herself only a few dozen heartbeats earlier.

"Nor do they remove managers who produce at the best rate the situation warrants. Besides, with the drilling of Shaft Number Six, we are bound to improve our output in the future. All will be forgiven if you perform well next period."

"I hope so," Varlan replied. "What may I do for you, O Spiritual One?"

Salfador's mouth opened, and his tongue flicked out from between two rows of conical teeth. "I had hoped to relieve your burden of command by inviting you to bathe with me."

There was a quick whistling noise as Varlan drew air in between her own slightly open teeth, in the Ryall equivalent of a sigh. "I would enjoy that greatly. Unfortunately, there is the loading of *Space Swimmer* to worry about, and the sending of dispatches."

"Let your subordinates do it."

Varlan hissed her anger at the suggestion. "Never let it be said that a member of the Clan of the Scented Waters allowed others to do her duty!"

Salfador shrugged. "As you will have it, Varlan. I go now."

The priest had just circled to move back toward the entrance when the communications gear at the manager's workstation began to squawk. He turned his head to look directly backward along his dorsal spine while Varlan answered the call.

"Space Leader Ossfil of *Space Swimmer*," the communicator hissed. "Greetings, Varlan of the Scented Waters."

"Greetings to you Ossfil of *Space Swimmer*. Speak."

"We have detected two vessels of unknown type materializing in the gateway from the Evil Star."

Varlan slid nictitating membranes over her eyes, then opened them again to signify her shock. "Are you sure?"

Ossfil bobbed his head rapidly from side to side. "No doubt at all. I have reviewed the records. They appeared together some twelve-cubed heartbeats ago. They were very bright and attracted the immediate attention of our automatic sentinels. They faded over a period of several heartbeats until they were no longer visible."

"But how could any ship survive inside the Evil Star?"

"I know not," Ossfil replied.

"What of their origin? Could they be of the Race?"

Ossfil's answer was a curt negative finger movement. "Unlikely. If they were of the Race, they would have arrived by the normal gateway. Not so?"

"Agreed," Varlan replied. "That means they must be ships of the two-legged monsters!"

"It would seem logical," the ship leader replied. "I await your orders, Varlan of the Scented Waters."

Ossfil's last comment made Varlan blink again. True, she was manager of the Corlis Mineral Extraction Complex and, as such, outranked a mere shipmaster by several degrees. Still, what did she know of fighting the monsters? That was for the warrior castes. Yet there were none such on Corlis. No one had thought them necessary this deep inside the hegemony. What to do? Military expert or no, Varlan recognized that the arrival of monster starships via the gateway from the Evil Star was a matter of overriding importance. It meant that the two-legged beasts had developed a new capability, one that might be unknown to Those Who Rule. She considered her priorities and concluded that warning the hegemony would have to take precedence over the smooth operation of the Corlis Complex. It was a decision that would have been difficult for any member of the Ryall managerial caste to make.

"You must carry the word to the hegemony," Varlan told Ossfil.

"Your command shall be heeded," the starship commander replied. "What of you on the surface?"

"We will defend ourselves as best we can. Launch *Space Swimmer* as quickly as you have jettisoned your cargo."

"But we are half filled!" Ossfil protested. "And the power metals are sorely needed."

"It is more important that your ship attain its maximum acceleration. If those are truly monster warships, they will undoubtedly have many times your thrust-to-weight ratio," Varlan replied. "The cargo can remain in orbit until you return with warriors."

Ossfil bowed his head. "Your words shall be heeded."

"May the Great Hunter protect you . . ." Varlan said.

". . . and the swift eaters ever be slain," Ossfil replied, finishing the ancient formula.

Richard Drake grimaced under the burden of four gravities of acceleration and watched his screens. *Discovery* had been under high gees for more than eighty hours, and their quarry was very nearly in range. As he watched the symbol that represented the Ryall ship on his screen, he reviewed the events of the past three days and wondered what mistakes he had made.

During the first twenty hours of the chase, *Discovery*'s sensor operators had noted a number of peculiarities in the Ryall starship's behavior. The most important was the leisurely three-quarters of a standard gravity with which the Ryall ship had pulled away from the second planet. A suspicious man would have thought the Ryall ship was a ruse. However, ruse or no, *Discovery* and *Mace* had no choice but to take the bait. Failing to give chase would allow their quarry to escape and report their presence in the Ryall-held system.

Hour piled upon hour, and Drake began to discount the possibility that he was diving headlong into a trap. Among other reassuring developments, sensors reported that the quarry's rate of acceleration had slowly increased from 0.75 to 0.93 gravity over a period of some forty hours. Such an increase was to be expected from a ship straining everything to escape its pursuers. As it burned off fuel, its thrust-to-weight ratio would slowly increase, and so would its rate of acceleration. On the other hand, a warship intentionally pulling them into a trap would more likely maintain a constant rate of acceleration until it turned on its pursuers.

Having become convinced that their quarry was the Ryall equivalent of a commercial starship, Drake put through a call to Captain Quaid onboard *Mace*. "Our quarry doesn't seem to be acting much like a warcraft."

Quaid's features were haggard as he nodded. "Agreed, sir. I've seen better legs under tramp interplanetary craft."

"You have experience with Ryall ships, Quaid. What kind of armament would they mount on a merchantman?"

"Only short-range stuff, sir. They wouldn't have any reason to mount larger weapons, and any such would detract from their cargo-carrying ability. Remember, the Ryall are subject to the same laws of economics that we are."

Drake nodded. "I thought so. A change of strategy is in order, I think."

"Change, sir?"

"Instead of blowing our quarry out of the sky, Captain, I think we'll try to capture it."

The Sandarian nobleman said nothing, but his expression reminded Drake of someone who has just bitten into an underripe grava fruit.

"You don't agree?"

"Surely you are aware of the difficulties inherent in boarding a hostile spacecraft, sir—especially one under acceleration!"

"I'm also aware that *Terra* is preparing an attack on the second planet and that we have no idea what they're facing. We need detailed information on the planetary defenses. For that we need prisoners."

"Yes, sir."

"Get me Ensign Walkirk aboard *Barracuda*," Drake ordered. While he waited, he watched the smeared splotch of light centered on the main viewscreen. The

splotch was the drive flare of the Ryall ship some one
hundred thousand kilometers in front of *Discovery*. The
Altan battle cruiser had matched velocities with the
Ryall ship two hours earlier and was now shadowing it.
One hundred thousand kilometers beyond the target,
Mace had also matched the Ryall ship's pace, effectively
bracketing it between its two human pursuers.

"Ensign Walkirk on screen four, Captain."

Drake turned to see the Sandarian crown prince staring out of the screen at him.

"You wanted to speak to me, Captain?"

"Are your men ready, Mr. Walkirk?"

"Yes, sir. The first squad is here with me in *Barracuda*, the second is in *Malachi*. We're ready and spoiling
for a fight."

"I want no heroics, Ensign. You are to take no unnec-
essary risks. If you find that ship heavily defended, back
off immediately. We'll finish them with our main batteries."

"Understood, sir. We'll be cautious as a Sandarian
snow chicken."

"You'd better! If anything happens to you . . ."

The prince's smile was evident even through the face-
plate of his vacsuit helmet. "Don't worry, sir. We Wal-
kirks have always been lucky."

Drake signed off and spent the next dozen seconds
cursing the day he'd sought to keep the Sandarian prince
out of trouble by assigning him the job of company commander of *Discovery*'s Marine detachment. It had
seemed a good idea at the time. Had he foreseen that he
would be sending Marines to force their way into a ship
filled with hostile aliens, however, Drake would have
shuffled the assignments of virtually every officer aboard
to avoid risking Phillip Walkirk's life. He had considered
sending another officer with the boarding party but had
rejected the idea. To do so would have been a gross in-
sult to the prince, to his father, and to every Sandarian
alive. So Drake had assigned the task of capturing the
Ryall starship to the Sandarian prince and prayed that he
would come through the operation unscathed.

Drake scowled, made a conscious effort to stop worrying, and issued the order to launch *Discovery*'s scout ships. Within seconds, four winged shapes cleared the cruiser's habitat ring and spread out for the long run in toward the target. One of Drake's screens relayed a view from one of *Mace*'s hull cameras. On it, two additional shapes streaked away from the destroyer and disappeared into the blackness of space.

"He's jinking, sir!" came the immediate report from one of *Discovery*'s sensor operators.

Drake glanced up at the main viewscreen. Sure enough, having seen that his pursuers had launched auxiliary craft, the Ryall captain had begun evasive maneuvering.

"Launch camera probe!"

A squat cylindrical device departed the habitat ring and moved toward the Ryall ship at an acceleration no manned vessel could match.

For the next three hours, Drake watched the ballet of lights that marched across the tactical displays. The Ryall ship was a bright red diamond, which data showed to be thrusting at right angles to its velocity vector. Six amber arrows steadily closed on the target, effortlessly matching its futile attempts at evasion. Much closer to the Ryall vessel than any of the scout ships was a yellow-green sunburst shape that represented the camera probe. It too matched the movements of the Ryall quarry as it bored in for a fast flyby.

"Put the view from the probe up on the screen," Drake ordered when the yellow-green symbol had nearly merged with the red diamond shape.

The tactical display was replaced by a starfield against which a small fuzzy blob of violet-white light was centered. The patch of luminescence quickly swelled to fill half the screen as the camera probe closed the distance. Centered on the screen, silhouetted by the violet glow of its own drive flare, was the Ryall ship. Drake's first glance told him that the Ryall craft was no warship. Rather, it was some sort of bulk carrier with a spherical hull, oversize access hatches, and a drive system that was woefully inadequate for its bulk. The ship expanded to fill the viewscreen as the probe reached minimum distance. There followed a moment of blurring, then a bright starlike light as the probe whipped past the Ryall ship and sped into the blackness of space. Drake signaled for his executive officer.

"Can you identify the class, Mr. Marchant?"

"Negative, sir. The computer doesn't seem to be able to match it."

"Any attempt to attack the probe?"

"None that we could detect, Captain. He may have been holding his fire until the scouts are in range."

Drake shook his head. "The probe looks enough like a missile that he would have tried to destroy it if he could. The fact that he didn't probably means that he lacks ship-to-ship armaments."

"Yes, sir."

"Transmit copies of those views to the scouts and follow up with computer enhancements as soon as you have them."

"On their way now, Captain."

"Very well. Mr. Haydn. Transmit the following to Ensign Walkirk aboard *Barracuda*: 'You may begin your attack when ready!'"

Varlan of the Scented Waters stood on the hilltop and gazed wistfully out over the valley in which the Corlis Mineral Complex was located. She often climbed that particular hill when faced with a problem, or to observe the progress of a construction project, or merely to be alone to think. In the past her observations had been tinged with more than a little pride at the accomplishments of her race.

When the first boatloads of Ryall workers had arrived on Corlis, they had found a mineral-rich valley choked by blue-green vegetation and inhabited by a few odd-looking quadripedal animals. Gone were the rampant native growths, burned and rooted out when the valley had been scraped clear of soil to expose the underlying bedrock. Gone were the native species, killed or driven off to keep them out of the automated machinery. Gone was the stream that had carved the valley from the planet's crust, dammed upstream to provide cooling water for the lasers.

The transformed valley was now filled with vast domelike buildings and longhouses. The former housed the delicate extraction and refining mechanisms, while workers lived in the latter. It had taken a full ten revolutions of Corlis about its star to transform this valley into a working mine and smelter complex. Now the two-legged monsters might well turn the whole effort into radioactive dust in less time than it took to slide a nictitating membrane over a vision ocular.

Varlan shivered and turned her attention to the reason she had climbed the hill. Down in the valley, giant rock cutters were carving trenches and throwing the detritus to the outside. Varlan had no experience or training in military matters, yet it seemed to her that such a construct would serve to hold off any ground assault the monsters might attempt. The problem was that Corlis Complex was largely automated, leaving her with a total work force of twelve twelves of laborers, a single twelve of technicians, and another of administration personnel. Also, there were no real weapons to be found in the complex. They had nothing with which to fight even had her staff known anything about fighting.

It was Salfador who had solved the problem of weapons. The philosopher/priest had suggested converting mining machinery to serve as weapons, particularly the heavy laser drills. Varlan had little hope that such a thing was possible but had set the artisans to work as a means of keeping up morale. To her surprise, the converted drills made fairly efficient military lasers. The artisans were now converting ore cars into fighting machines. Despite the artisans' progress, Varlan couldn't help worrying as she gazed down at the barrier construction. It wasn't necessary for one to be hatched a warrior to see that there was too much perimeter and not enough workers to defend it properly.

Varlan was pondering her dilemma when her personal communicator signaled for attention. She answered it to discover the technician in charge of communications staring out of the tiny screen at her.

The underling made the gesture of respect. "I have a message for you from Ossfil of *Space Swimmer*."

"Proceed with the message."

"'The monsters have me surrounded, and I am unable to reach the gateway. I am taking action but will not be able to escape. Request instructions. Ossfil, commanding *Space Swimmer*.'"

Varlan muttered a few deep imprecations to the Evil Star before replying. "Transmit the following: 'From Varlan of the Scented Waters to Ossfil of *Space Swimmer*. As a minimum, you will destroy your astrogation computer and trigger the amnesia of your astrogator. After that is done, you may act on your own initiative.'"

When the communications tech had acknowledged the message, Varlan returned to her private thoughts, now more depressed than ever. *Space Swimmer* had been their only hope. Had it reached the gateway to Carratyl, ships of warriors would have been winging to the rescue within a few thousand heartbeats of *Space Swimmer*'s call. As it was, no one in the hegemony would learn the fate of the Corlis Complex for another half planetary year at least, not until the next scheduled ore carrier arrived to load power metals. No, she corrected herself, that wasn't so. *Space Swimmer* would be missed. Undoubtedly the hegemony would send a ship to search for the ore carrier when it failed to arrive at the processing center on Pasotil. The rescue force could well arrive within the span of a single production period!

Much buoyed by the thought, Varlan turned and ambled down the hill. As she walked, she began to imitate the sound of a leather-winged sasbo to signal her new confidence in the future. What matter if four shiploads of monsters were bearing down on her even as she whistled? The race had always succeeded in the past and would do so in the future. In the meantime, she had defenses to prepare and monsters to slay!

CHAPTER 13

Ensign Phillip David Eusabio Walkirk, Duke of Cragston, Defender of the Foldpoints, offspring of warrior-kings, and would-be slayer of the Ryall foe, lay in his acceleration couch, encased in a vacsuit, and breathed in the cloying stink of his own fear. Around him, similarly encased in airtight armor, a dozen members of *Discovery*'s contingent of Altan Space Marines also lay strapped into acceleration couches.

"Ten minutes to go, Ensign," the gruff voice of Sergeant Willem Barthol said over Phillip's earphones. "We'd best be preparing them for disembarkation."

"Right," the prince answered as he began to unstrap from his couch.

The plan was simple if somewhat dangerous for those who were to carry it out. The camera probe had provided detailed photographs of the Ryall craft's exterior and had confirmed its apparent lack of heavy weaponry. The next ships to approach the Ryall bulk carrier would be the scout boats *Questor* and *Calico*. It would be their job to disable the Ryall ship's engines and burn away all the sensor pickups on its hull. Once the quarry was immobilized and blinded, Scout Boats *Barracuda* and *Horned Devil* would close to within ten meters of the Ryall ship and offload their twenty-five-man boarding party. The two scouts, along with *Questor* and *Calico* and the two scout vessels from *Mace*, would then surround the Ryall ship and provide cover while the Marines blasted their way through the hull at two widely separated points. Once inside, it would be the Marines' job to capture the quarry.

"We're ready to disembark," Phillip Walkirk radioed to the scout boat's pilot.

"Stand by, Ensign," the pilot replied. "We'll be shutting down boost in another ten seconds."

Phillip watched the tiny chronometer display in his helmet. True to the pilot's word, the pressure on his chest died away ten seconds later. Simultaneously, the pilot's voice could be heard over the general circuit: "All Hands! We will be in zero gravity for another 8.6 minutes and then will go to two gravities. Make sure that you are well anchored before that time! Good luck, Marines!"

Ever since leaving *Discovery*, the scout boat had been slowly closing the gap by backing toward the Ryall ship on a tail of fire. Paradoxically, with the Ryall ship still decelerating for a foldpoint it would never reach, once *Barracuda* shut down its engines, they would close the gap even more quickly than before.

"All right, Marines!" Phillip Walkirk said over the general circuit. "Odd files, by the numbers, prepare to disembark!"

Six Marines lifted themselves from their couches and moved to line up in the scout boat's too-narrow center aisle. They moved awkwardly in the cramped passenger cabin toward the bow air lock. As quickly as the first group had cleared the aisle, Phillip Walkirk ordered the even-number files out of their couches. The starboard side passengers quickly followed suit. At the air lock, the scout boat's crew chief, also suited up, stood with his hand on the valve that would spill air from *Barracuda*'s passenger cabin to space.

"Ready to depressurize when you are, Ensign," the chief said.

Phillip Walkirk ordered a suit check made. There followed two minutes of mutual inspection and a quick, precise countdown of acknowledgments that suit checks were complete.

"Anchor yourselves, Marines. We're about to depressurize."

The sudden tugging of a gentle wind and the keening of air being vented suddenly filled the small cabin. The sound quickly died away as the air that carried it drained out into space. Concurrent with the sudden silence, Phillip Walkirk's vacuum armor puffed up and stiffened at the joints, as did that of every man aboard. As quickly as the air was gone, the crew chief reached out and cycled both air lock doors open, leaving Phillip a clear view of the infinite black outside.

"Follow me!" he ordered.

A scout boat was a small, heavily armed auxiliary capable of interplanetary, but not interstellar, flight. It was the normal task of such warcraft to scout an enemy prior to battle and to harry him while he engaged the mother ship. Scouts were also used to ferry passengers and cargo between ships and down to the surface of a planet. They were not, however, designed to deliver ground troops to the scene of battle.

Since *Barracuda* was not a proper assault boat, there being none such aboard the Altan cruiser, engineers had been forced to improvise. They had done so by welding a pair of rails to the upper surfaces of *Barracuda*'s two stubby delta wings. The plan called for the Marine boarding party to exit the cabin, pull themselves along the wings via the safety rails, and anchor themselves for the final approach to the Ryall starship. Being out on the wings would allow a much quicker assault, even though it exposed the boarding party to whatever furies the Ryall captain had at his disposal.

Phillip Walkirk snapped the end of a safety line to the rail leading toward the port side of the scout and stepped out into nothingness. He pulled himself hand over hand toward the far left position on the wing. Once there, he carefully snapped other lines to padeyes bonded to the wing for just that purpose. The new lines each had a small explosive charge at the points where they attached to Phillip's armor. At a signal from him, the charges would shear the lines, freeing him from his temporary bonds. In the meantime, however, the four-point attachment assured that he would remain fastened to his perch no matter how violently the scout maneuvered during its approach.

He looked back toward the air lock to see his six companions similarly positioned along the surface of the wing. He then watched other figures exit the air lock. Sergeant Barthol led the even-number files up and over the fuselage to the attach points on the starboard wing. Phillip watched them move out of sight, then turned to view that V-shaped section of black sky framed between his armored boots. As he watched, a bright flare of light lit the black sky, then another and another.

"What the hell was that?" a voice asked in his earphones. He recognized the thick accent of Alta's western continent and identified the voice as that of Corporal Kevin Sayers, immediately to his right on the wing.

"That will be *Questor* and *Calico* burning out his eyes and crippling his engines," Phillip replied.

"Hope the centaurs don't decide to suicide on us," the corporal muttered.

That makes two of us, Phillip thought to himself. Out loud he said, "If they were going to blow themselves up, they would have done so before now."

Phillip watched the Ryall starship grow in size as the scout boat bore down on it. It had started out as a mere pinpoint and had grown to the size of a half-crown piece when the pilot's voice echoed in his earphones.

"Acceleration in ten seconds! Hold on tight out there."

A sudden violet nimbus sprang into existence below Phillip Walkirk's feet. At the same time, a sudden surge of acceleration threatened to pull him into his boots. He slid downward inside his armor, reaching bottom with an audible *oof* as *Barracuda*'s pilot fought to bleed off the high closing rate that had developed between the two ships. Out of the corner of his eye, Phillip noted another violet-white star spring forth in the firmament. That, he knew, would be *Horned Devil* delivering the other half of the boarding party.

Suddenly, the pressure was gone and the scout boat hung motionless a mere ten meters from the Ryall ship.

"Cut yourselves loose, now!" As Phillip said it, he thumbed the switch that would detonate his own separation charges. There was a muffled *whump*, and he was free. "Engage maneuvering units! Jump for that ship!"

Varlan of the Scented Waters lay in front of a large holotank and watched the monster starships close in on *Space Swimmer*. The tank, which was normally used for mapping variations in the underground strata, had been jury-rigged by the technicians to display a more or less up-to-date view of the situation in space. In its depths, Corlis' yellow star, Eulysta, was a tiny glowing jewel. High above it, near the upper edge of the display, lay the gateway to the Evil Star. The gateway to Carratyl was much lower, about on a level with the blue-green point of light that denoted Corlis itself. Three other close-in planets also showed in the image space, as did their orbital paths around the star.

There were other faint lines of light in the tank, lines that moved at nearly right angles to the concentric circles that marked the plane of Eulysta's ecliptic. The orbital tracks of the ships that pursued *Space Swimmer* were dimly etched in an emerald hue. Next to the course lines, several time and vector notations gave mute testimony to the speed with which the two-legged devils had crossed the system in pursuit of the fleeing ore carrier.

Varlan's gaze was drawn to a second group of alien warships. These, too, trailed dimly lit green threads behind them. They were not, however, in pursuit of *Space Swimmer*. Rather, these enemies were bound directly for Corlis and would arrive in only three revolutions of the planet. Varlan cursed the fact that there would not be more time to ready her defenses, although objectively she knew that a thousand years would be insufficient if the monsters really wished to take Corlis Complex.

Putting her own problems momentarily out of mind, she turned her attention back to *Space Swimmer*'s fate. Raising the pitch of her voice to the frequency range guarded by the computer that operated the holotank, she said, "Move focus to *Space Swimmer*. Increase magnification to maximum."

The overall view of the Eulysta system faded away, to be replaced by another. The central region of the tank was now inhabited by a swarm of ships. At the center lay the rose-colored dot of *Space Swimmer*. Around it swarmed purple-green enemy craft. Out of each point of light emanated small violet lines, the direction and length of which denoted that particular vessel's velocity and acceleration vectors. Varlan was no expert, but the fact that the closest monster ships had velocities and accelerations nearly identical to those of the Ryall ore carrier indicated that the end was near for Ossfil and *Space Swimmer*.

"What is the basis for this display?" Varlan asked.

"The information is the most probable projection of the observations which *Space Swimmer* provided in its last communication," the computer responded.

"How long ago?"

"The span of time has been twelve-cubed heartbeats."

Varlan signified her pleasure at the relative currency of the information. There had been a time when she would have taken for granted an uninterrupted flow of information concerning the soon-to-be-fought battle. The past several planetary days had educated her considerably in such matters.

"Varlan of the Scented Waters!"

Her concentration regarding the display was so great that Varlan had not heard the rustle of dried rushes behind her. Startled, she snapped her neck 180 degrees about to observe Salfador standing behind her. Such was her mood that the philosopher/priest's call, which had been delivered at minimal volume, had seemed a shout.

"You should be named Salfador the Silent, Philosopher!"

"My apologies if I caused you distress, Varlan. I have completed the tasks which you set for me. The medical facility has been moved to Shaft Number One and prepared to receive wounded. Also, I have trained two of your laborers to operate several of the healing machines."

Varlan signaled her appreciation, then moved her head to stare intently with one eye at the philosopher/priest's downcast features.

"What is wrong, Salfador?"

The priest indicated the screen. "How goes the battle for *Space Swimmer*?"

Varlan's response had no equivalent among humans. The closest a man could have come to translating the sound would have been a snort of disdain coupled with cynical laughter. "The *battle* is more a fish drive than a contest between warriors. I fear the monsters will have Ossfil in another few hundred heartbeats."

"Will they not merely destroy him?"

"It would appear not. I am no expert in matters of piloting, but it seems that either of the larger monster starships could have done so before now. Instead, Ossfil reports they have launched daughter craft. Apparently, they will try to capture *Space Swimmer*."

"What of the astronomical data in his computer?"

"I have given the order that he destroy his computer and trigger his astrogator's amnesia. Failing that, of course, he will destroy his ship."

The normally facile philosopher/priest allowed his triforked tongue to flick between open teeth as he hesitated for an uncharacteristically long time. When he finally spoke, it was in a voice nearly too quiet to hear. Varlan shifted her earflaps to catch his words more clearly.

"I have come to you, Varlan, because I need the advice of one wiser than I."

"Surely there are none such here, Salfador."

"You underestimate yourself, my manager. And in any event, it is a poor physician who diagnoses his own illness."

"Proceed, then."

"I have never told you the story of my youth and how I became a healer."

"That is true," Varlan agreed. "It has never been a matter of concern between us."

"We have never suffered invasion by monsters before."

"True."

"The priesthood and healing were not my original vocation. I was a gifted pupil, and my teachers thought me capable of studying natural philosophy. I trained as a seeker after astronomical understanding, a stargazer if you will."

"I long ago noticed your interest in such matters and remarked to myself that it is unusual in a medical technician," Varlan replied.

Salfador signaled wry humor. "Agreed. My colleagues are not renowned for their love of galactic structure or of the differences between the great stars. You do well to get them to look up into the sky at night."

"Your point?"

"Unfortunately, I found that I did not have the aptitude which my teachers believed. I could have been a good natural philosopher, but not a great one. I therefore chose my current path. I have had no reason for regrets in this choice . . . none until now, that is."

"I do not understand."

"It is regrettable, Varlan of the Scented Waters, but I still have considerable astronomical data in my brain, including knowledge of the positions of many of the gateways throughout the hegemony."

Varlan blinked in horror at Salfador's revelation. Like all Ryall, she had an abiding pride in the works of her race. She had been barely out of the egg when she had been taught the names of the worlds which the Race controlled, and only slightly older when she knew each of their histories in detail. But one thing she *had not* learned was the method by which starships traveled from one to another. Such data were the domain of astronomers and astrogators, information unneeded by the average Ryall. Indeed, it had only been since

she ascended to the managership of Corlis Complex
that she had learned the secret of the gateways between the stars.

"You must have been fitted with an amnesia spell.
Give me your trigger code and I will excise the knowledge from your brain," she said.

The miserable look on Salfador's features was all the
answer she needed. "I'm afraid that I was never fitted
with such. I had not intended to be an astrogator on a
starship and therefore had no need."

Varlan stared closely at her adviser and confidant,
trying to divine some way out of the predicament. She
thought of ordering him to take to the jungle to hide
until the monsters left, then rejected the idea for the
same reason that she had rejected having the complex's staff do the same. The local biochemistry was
sufficiently close to Ryall norms to cause illness, but
lacked several essential ingredients. To ask a philosopher to camp in the woods like a barbarian was unthinkable. Even more unthinkable, however, was
allowing Salfador to fall into the grasp of the monsters.

"You know what you must do, of course," she said
finally.

Salfador signaled his agreement. "I have already done
so. There are many poisons in the medical kits. I injected
myself with one before coming here. Do not fear. My
death will be quite painless."

"Then your purpose in coming here . . ."

"Was to take my leave of you. I ask that you tell my
clan of my death should you return one day to the hegemony."

"I will do so. How long until the poison takes effect?"

"My vision is already affected. That is the first symp-
tom. I will be dead in another thousand heartbeats."

Varlan moved to Salfador and hugged him in a very
human gesture of affection. "Farewell then, Salfador of
the Eternal Fire. I will miss you."

"And I you, Varlan of the Scented Waters."

* * *

Phillip jumped for the vast spherical hull of the Ryall starship and grounded expertly between two of the large access hatches. As he did so, reaction jets began to fire around the ship's waist. At first he thought the Ryall captain was using them in the hope of catching one or more attackers in their white-hot flame. When the jets continued to fire, however, Phillip guessed their real purpose. "Anchor yourselves!" he ordered. "Quickly! They're rotating the ship in the hope of throwing us off."

There followed a flurry of Marines anchoring themselves to the hull with magnetic clamps. The point where the boarding party had landed was midway between equator and pole, and the rotation did not affect them greatly. Phillip felt a light tugging at his feet as his body rotated outward. Around him, the Marines hung like spiders from their webs. The only figure in sight not anchored was Corporal Sayers, who was using his maneuvering jets to compensate for the slow spin and move toward the spherical ship's too-close horizon. Sayers was *Barracuda*'s sapper. He carried a large explosive charge strapped to his chest. He disappeared from sight. Half a minute later, he was back, jetting for Phillip's position at high speed. He had just grounded expertly next to the prince, when the hull plates shivered beneath his boots. Phillip felt a sharp tug on his safety line just as something large and flat spun away into space from somewhere beyond the horizon.

"I planted the entry charge against one of those medium-size doors a quarter of the way around the circumference, sir."

Phillip nodded, forgetting in his excitement that no one could see the gesture. He unlimbered his weapon, a projectile device that fired anesthetic darts. The darts were heavy enough to punch through vacuum armor and contained a dose of anesthetic that would knock a Ryall down in a matter of seconds. He unhooked from his perch and jetted in the direction of the explosion. "Follow me! And remember, we're after prisoners!"

Through pure luck, Sayers had found a hatch that led directly into the crew quarters and not into the capacious holds. Phillip jetted through the jagged hole and moved immediately to take cover in a jumble of what had been equipment lockers. One by one, twelve other shapes entered the darkness from the brilliantly lit hull outside.

"Hope them centaurs had sense enough to get into suits before we blew their hull," one of the enlisted men commented. Phillip hoped the same thing, since they had destroyed the ship's pressure integrity with their charge. They would also blow any pressure doors they encountered. If the Ryall weren't protected by vacuum suits, the whole mission would be in vain.

Another sudden hammer blow caused the deck to jump. "That will be the *Horned Devil* force," Phillip said. "Watch out who you shoot. Sergeant Barthol, lead out!"

Phillip watched as a large figure with chevrons on his suit ambled through the nearly weightless corridor to a cross passage farther on. Barthol glanced first one way down the passage, then the other, before taking cover in the junction. He signaled for the rest of the squad to leapfrog him. They continued for ten minutes in this way, meeting no opposition.

Phillip Walkirk was beginning to wonder if there were any Ryall left aboard when Private Traconen pushed open a bulkhead hatch and was suddenly thrown back across the passageway in a shower of small explosions. Traconen recoiled from a glancing blow against the bulkhead, his punctured suit spewing red mist as he tumbled head over heels down the passageway.

"Carter, go after Traconen!" Phillip ordered. "The rest of you lay down covering fire."

Not all of the boarding party carried anesthetic projectile throwers. Some carried explosive rifles and heavy riot guns. Two Marines braced themselves against handy stanchions and began to spray automatic fire through the open hatchway. The weapons fired in an eerie silence, and a sporadic wind flowed down the corridor as their muzzle gasses expanded into vacuum. Sergeant Barthol hugged the near bulkhead as he moved to the hatchway. He unclipped a small egg-shaped object from his equipment belt.

"Better stand back," he cautioned. The two Marines who had enfiladed the compartment moved back along the corridor. Barthol armed the grenade and launched it in the awkward sidearmed throw of a man in space armor, then hurriedly backed off.

The ensuing explosion was far from silent. It buffeted Phillip Walkirk, jarring his teeth even inside the armor. A moment later, his helmet rang with a sudden clanging noise as a bit of debris bounced off of it. He was surprised to find a small star break in his helmet visor in front of his left eye. Gulping down bile, he ordered a scouting party into the compartment from which Traconen had been felled. Thirty seconds after slipping through the deadly door, the scouts reported that all was clear.

Phillip trotted forward to see the Ryall defenders with his own eyes. What he saw was sufficient to turn his stomach. Two Ryall encased in their own versions of vacuum suits had lain in wait inside the compartment behind a barrier of furniture. Weapons ready, they had shot the first human face to poke its way through the door. Their weapon, Phillip Walkirk was surprised to see, was a crude gun that appeared to have been manufactured in the ship's machine shop.

Phillip left the compartment and moved to where Sergeant Barthol stooped over Private Traconen.

"How is he?"

"I'm afraid he's dead, sir."

"Leave him, then, Sergeant. We'll pick him up after we've secured the ship."

"Yes, sir."

The rest of the capture was relatively uneventful. It had taken ten minutes more for Phillip Walkirk's forces to link up with the second Marine boarding force. Together they had swept through the ship, collecting prisoners. There were eight in all. Seven of the centaurs gave up peacefully, each spreading his arms in a gesture of submission. One chose to resist.

Half an hour after their entry into the Ryall ship, Corporal Sayers returned to the assembly point with an unconscious Ryall in tow.

"What happened to you?" Sergeant Barthol asked upon seeing the gingerly way he moved.

"Damned centaur near broke my arm with a big crowbar, Sarge."

Barthol looked down at the limp alien that Sayers had in tow. "Did you kill him?"

"Naw. Shot him with a dart. He'll be all right, 'cept that he's crazy as a high plateau jumper."

"How so?"

"I found him amidships in one of the equipment rooms. He had this big bar he'd ripped out of some machinery and was using it to beat holy hell out of some access panel. Looked to me like he wanted to get through it and into the machinery beyond. Anyway, I flashed my light in his face. He turned and attacked me with this damned thing!" Sayers said, holding up the bar. "I was so surprised that I didn't do more than get my arm up to ward off the blow. Anyway, he hauled back for another swing, and I shot him. He got in two more licks before he keeled over."

Barthol nudged the limp Ryall with the toe of his boot. The transparent fabric of the Ryall's vacsuit dented in under the pressure and then sprang back. "I guess we'll find out what it was all about when he wakes up."

Phillip Walkirk, who had listened to the conversation over his suit radio, moved over to where the sergeant and corporal were standing. In this part of the ship there was just enough gravity from the spin to keep his boots on the deck. "What did you say just now, Corporal?" he asked.

"I said this damned crazy centaur attacked me, sir."

"No, about his trying to smash a machine. What machine?"

"'Fraid I don't recognize this alien machinery too good, sir."

"Take me to it."

Sayers led the way, followed by Phillip Walkirk and Sergeant Barthol. They moved through gloomy corridors until they reached a small compartment almost at the very center of the spherical ship.

"Yonder machine over there, sir!" Sayers said, playing the beam from his handlamp over a dented access panel.

Phillip gazed at the panel, blinked, and then emitted a low whistle.

"This thing important, sir?" Barthol asked.

"You might say that," Phillip replied. "What Corporal Sayers refers to as 'yonder machine' is their astrogation computer. The fact that he was trying to beat it to death may mean that their normal destruct mechanism failed to operate properly."

"That good, sir?"

Phillip Walkirk's sudden laughter startled the two noncoms. "That box, Sergeant, may well contain information vital to the conduct of the war."

"What information, sir?"

"If we've been very, *very* lucky, we may just dredge up a foldspace topology chart for the whole damned Ryall hegemony!"

CHAPTER 14

The rays of the unnamed yellow star cascaded over the small fleet, causing ships to glow in the surrealistic half-light, half-dark pattern so familiar to those who space. In the center of the fleet floated a battered, over-size sphere. On one side of the sphere, a series of sheared-off pylons marked the locations where long-range sensing and communications gear had once been mounted. At the other side, the delicate mechanisms that once drove the ship from foldpoint to planet and back again had been converted to scrap by a single disabling stroke. In between, the points at which the two boarding parties had forced entry remained as silent reminders of the battle fought onboard.

Discovery and *Mace* hung in space less than a kilometer from the Ryall starship as various landing craft and interorbit shuttles moved back and forth between the three vessels. The scout boats that had aided in the Ryall ship's capture stood well out from the main fleet. They had taken up outrider postions after the battle, insurance against other Ryall craft entering the system through the local—and as yet unidentified—foldpoint.

"Technician Scarlotti on Channel Six, Captain," Moriet Haydn reported to Richard Drake on *Discovery*'s bridge.

Drake had spent the morning going over inventory reports with his executive officer and was glad for the interruption. He activated the communications channel. "Drake here. Go ahead."

The face of *Mace*'s senior computer specialist gazed out of the screen at him. "I've finished my inspection of the Ryall computer, Captain."

"And?"

"Whoever it was that took a wrecking bar to this thing succeeded in making it unusable. Half the input/output circuits are mangled beyond repair."

"And the memory banks?"

"They appear to be undamaged, sir. Whatever this computer knew before the attack, it still knows. Had any blow fallen two centimeters to the right, however, it would have been a different story."

"What about the destruct mechanism? Why didn't it go off?"

Scarlotti held up a hexagonal box of alien construction from which a thick cable protruded. "The damned thing's corroded, sir. When they activated it, the pulse shorted out in the power leads. It looks like it was installed years ago and then degraded to the point where it failed when they tried to use it."

Drake nodded. He wasn't particularly surprised by the news. The entire Ryall starship had the air of a tramp about it. "Can you extract the data in the computer?"

"Already have, sir. I did that before I started poking around inside. Didn't want to trigger an automatic memory wipe."

"Did you get it all?"

"I think so, sir. I dumped using three different techniques, then compared each data set with the other two. All three are identical down to the least significant bit. If anything else is in there, it's hidden too deep for me to pry out."

"Can you read it?"

"No, sir. My specialty is Ryall hardware. You'll need a damned good software technician to interpret the crap.

Frankly, I don't know of any that good this side of the main fleet."

"How much data is there?"

Scarlotti glanced down and read a number from a computer printout. "About two trillion bytes, Captain."

"How long to transmit it to *Arrow* back at the Antares foldpoint?"

"All of it, sir?"

Drake nodded. "Unless you know of some way of extracting only the data we're interested in."

The tech was quiet for a moment, his lips moving as he performed a quick calculation in his head. "I'd say a day and a half for the initial squirt, followed by two days to check for transmission errors and resend any suspicious blocks."

"Very well, Mr. Scarlotti," Drake responded. "Duplicate your recordings. Bring one copy here to *Discovery* and send the other to *Mace*. As soon as you're aboard, prepare the data for transmission to *Arrow*."

"Aye aye, Captain."

Drake turned to Commander Marchant after the computer technician had signed off. "That's damned good news, Rorq. Now if only we've been lucky and their astrogation data is still intact."

The exec nodded. "It would be quite a letdown if all we've got is the Ryall captain's laundry list."

"I don't think he was trying to beat his laundry list to death with that wrecking bar."

"No, sir. Neither do I."

"Is he still sticking to his story?"

The exec nodded. "He says the Ryall presence on the second planet is limited to a mining and smelting operation. His ship was a bulk ore carrier sent to pick up the mine's output. It's a regular run."

"When is the next ship scheduled to arrive?"

"Not for six months at least, sir. Maybe longer."

"Where was he headed when we caught up with him?"

"He doesn't know, sir."

"You mean he won't tell."

"No, sir. I mean he doesn't know! The interrogators

had him hooked up to a whole battery of sensors when they questioned him. He showed no physiological changes at all when asked his destination. Something or someone has completely wiped his mind of all astrogation data. He even looks blank when they mention foldpoints to him."

"What about the astrogator?"

"I'm afraid, Captain, that the astrogator was one of the two centaurs killed after Private Traconen got it."

"All right. Get a summary of everything we've learned about the planet's defenses off to *Saskatoon*. Perhaps it will help Colonel Valdis plan his assault."

"Yes, sir. What about the Ryall ship?"

"We'll give the salvage crew another three days before we destroy it. After that, we'll see if we can't find this mysterious foldpoint Ossfil doesn't remember being out here."

The attack against the planet took place forty-eight hours later. Drake spent three continuous watches in his command chair monitoring the assault via relayed tactical displays and reports. He needn't have bothered. The Ryall defenders proved no match for the Sandarian Marines.

Saskatoon's assault boats had entered the planet's atmosphere in the hemisphere opposite the Ryall mine and smelter. Once safely down, they flew around the globe to positions just below the horizon from the Ryall installation. Two hundred Sandarian Marines in full battle armor had then disembarked and moved into position for a dawn assault.

The Ryall defenders fought bravely but unskillfully. Many of them began firing their makeshift weapons wildly at the first sign of attack and quickly ran out of ammunition. Some chose to defend positions better abandoned, while others had appeared confused when overrun, as though they didn't understand what they were supposed to be doing. Still others refused to surrender at all and had to be shot down.

The most difficult part of the assault involved taking the kilometer-deep mine shafts, several of which had been heavily fortified. For a time it looked as though the shafts would have to be sealed by bombardment. However, the stalemate was broken when a squad of Marines probing the outlying areas of the complex found an unguarded shaft and made their way through cross tunnels to positions behind the Ryall positions. Once the defenders discovered humans behind them, they quickly surrendered.

Even before the last tunnel was pacified, the Marines had spread out and begun a thorough search of the mine complex. When they were finished, they were in possession of twenty live prisoners and eighteen enemy corpses. Marine casualties for the battle included seven dead, twelve wounded.

With the planet in human hands, Drake ordered salvage operations aboard the Ryall starship concluded. The last work party to board the ore carrier left a nuclear explosive charge in the main cargo hold. When the human ships had pulled back to a safe distance, Drake ordered the charge detonated. The resulting ball of plasma was visible on the screens for a dozen minutes and to the instruments for several hours longer.

Following the ore carrier's destruction, the small armada shifted operations to the point in space where the Ryall ship had appeared headed. *Discovery* launched a series of probes to measure the local gravitational constant and, after a week of careful measurement and calculation, confirmed the presence of a nearby foldpoint.

Drake ordered *Mace* to take up position within the newly discovered foldpoint to guard against any further intrusions by Ryall starships. Having thus secured his flank, he ordered *Discovery* to begin boosting for the nameless star's second planet.

Bethany Lindquist walked down the corridor in a swish of light blue fabric and a cloud of perfume. Her dress was a formal evening gown of a style popular with Homeport trendsetters; her auburn hair was piled high atop her head; her face was shaded subtly to accentuate her high cheekbones. A gold necklace that had come originally from Earth completed the picture. The reactions from the few grinning spacers she encountered told her that the hours she'd spent in front of a mirror had not been wasted.

Bethany walked a quarter of the distance around the habitat ring to Richard Drake's cabin. She knocked lightly and waited for the door to open. Richard was resplendent in the full-dress uniform of the Altan Navy. He extended his hand to draw her across the threshold.

"You're beautiful!" he exclaimed, letting his eyes roam up and down her form.

"Thank you, kind sir," she said, curtseying slightly. "The invitation did specify a *formal* dinner party, did it not?"

"It did."

Bethany's gaze swept the room. She was not surprised to note the presence of only two place settings at the table.

"Aren't you afraid the rest of the crew will be jealous?" she asked.

"Let them. I'm tired of not being able to pay proper court to my lady. Besides, if you are going down to the surface tomorrow, this may well be our last chance to have dinner together for quite some time."

Bethany laughed. "If I'd known accepting Professor Alvarez's offer would bring this response, I would have brought him to see you sooner."

"I'm just glad you brought him when you did," Drake replied.

Bethany had been eating lunch in *Discovery*'s wardroom the previous day when Professor Boris Alvarez, Fellow of the Royal Sandarian Academy, had taken the seat next to hers and struck up a conversation.

After fifteen minutes in which it became obvious that he had something more on his mind than merely passing the time with the only woman aboard ship, Bethany had asked him, "May I help you with something, Professor?"

"Well...ah, I mean...well, yes, now that you mention it, Miss Lindquist, you can. I would like to speak to you about a matter of some importance."

"I'm listening."

"Ah, you are aware that I have made something of

a specialty in the study of Ryall technology, particularly information systems, are you not?"

"I know that you are the closest thing to an expert we have aboard this ship, Professor."

"Have you also heard that the Marines have captured a large Ryall computer down on the planet's surface?"

Bethany had nodded. "I understand they're planning to suck this one dry of data, too."

"In my opinion, Miss Lindquist, that would be counterproductive."

"Why?"

"Look," Alvarez replied, suddenly becoming more animated. "We took a great deal of information out of that ore carrier's computer, only we have no way of deciphering precisely what it says. Like us, the centaurs store data in a form which makes sense to their machines but not necessarily to themselves. That starship information consists of all manner of computer programs mixed in with subsidiary data. Even were we able to segregate the programs from the data, we would need to understand the operation of the programs to read the data. Do you understand what I am saying?"

Bethany nodded. "No one said that it would be easy."

"True. But that is no reason for us to make it more difficult than it need be."

"I don't understand, Professor."

Alvarez hunched forward earnestly. "It seems to me that we may be able to install the ore carrier's information in the computer which the Marines have captured and possibly get the programs running. All Ryall computers use more or less the same operating system, you know."

Bethany had frowned. "To what purpose?"

"Simply this," Alvarez had replied. "If we can get the programs running, there will be no need to decipher the whole mass of information in order to extract the data that interest us. Rather, we have merely to ask the computer what we wish to know. If we've done our job right, it will tell us!"

Bethany was pensive for a moment. "Have you talked to Captain Drake about this?"

Alvarez shook his head. "No. I'm afraid that I don't explain things well to people. You know a lot about Ryall information systems. You can help me explain the concept to him. Afterward, I will also need an assistant down on the surface."

"Are you offering me the job, Professor?"

"Yes, if you would like it."

"I accept. Brief me on the mechanics of what we are talking about, and then we'll ask for an appointment to see the boss."

Upon hearing Alvarez's proposal, Drake had ordered its immediate implementation. The three of them had spent an hour discussing what would be needed for the project to proceed, then Bethany and Alvarez had returned to their respective cabins to begin packing. Thirty minutes later, Bethany had been interrupted by a spacer who had presented her with a sealed envelope. Opening it, she'd found the dinner invitation from Richard.

Drake took Bethany's wrap and guided her to the leather couch. They were served drinks by a white-coated steward who otherwise remained in the background. They spoke of Alvarez's plan and of various other minor matters until dinner was ready. Transferring to the table in the center of the cabin, Drake held Bethany's chair as she seated herself, then moved to the side opposite. The steward had previously lighted three candles in the center of the table. As soon as they were seated, he dimmed the overhead lights to their night settings. Watching the perfect manners of the steward, Bethany found it difficult to remember that this same man had helped storm the Ryall starship only ten days earlier.

Eventually, dessert was served and Drake dismissed the steward, who left the cabin without a word, trundling a cart piled high with the ship's finest silver service. Bethany finished off the last of a piece of pie with ice cream and lifted a coffee cup to her lips. Gazing over the rim of the cup, she said, "You didn't have to do this, you know!"

"Do what?" Drake asked.

"Put on this fancy spread for me. I've been ready to

sneak into your bed nightly for the past three months. A sandwich of cold lunch meat and day-old ribolf salad would have been more than adequate."

"But this is so much more romantic," he replied, letting his arm sweep across the table in a gallant gesture. He then went on in a more normal tone. "Besides, I'm afraid I had an ulterior motive when I planned this dinner."

"Oh?" she asked in mock surprise.

"What I should have said is that I have *another* ulterior motive. Do you remember a conversation we had just after returning from Sandar? You expressed concern that the prisoners we'd talked to might have been telling us what the Sandarians wanted us to hear."

She nodded. "I thought they might have been coerced into parroting Sandarian propaganda."

"Do you still feel that way?"

"No," Bethany replied. "I've learned enough since to know that data obtained from prisoner interviews is meticulously controlled. However, I do wonder whether such data isn't misapplied at times."

"How so?"

"Obviously, Richard, since most prisoners are members of the Ryall military caste, our views of the Ryall species are strongly influenced by the military caste outlook. How do we know that outlook is shared by the managerial caste that runs the hegemony, or by the other castes, for that matter?"

"Would you like an opportunity to find out?"

"How?"

"We captured the manager of the Corlis mine and smelter along with nineteen other Ryall. I would like you to interview her for us when you're down on the surface."

"Why me, Richard?"

"Because the Sandarians have been conditioned to think of the Ryall as humanity's implacable enemy. If we rely solely on Colonel Valdis' interrogators, everything we learn will be colored by that attitude. You, on the other hand, are relatively open-minded when it comes to the Ryall. You possess a specialized knowledge of both

Ryall psychology and physiology. You have studied the centaurs enough so that you should have some feeling as to whether you are being told the truth. In summary, my love, you are the perfect person for the job. How about it?"

Rather than answering him directly, Bethany said, "Do you know, Richard, that my uncle almost refused to let me come on this expedition?"

"For God's sake, why?"

"He was worried that my love for you would blind me to the fact that my primary duty lies with Earth."

"What has that to do with what we are talking about?"

Bethany shrugged. "Perhaps nothing. Still, we both know that prisoner interview data is normally classified at least 'confidential' and sometimes much higher. It is also a well-known fact that interrogators aren't supposed to talk about their work."

"So?"

"So I want it understood in advance that I am free to share anything I learn with the Interstellar Council the moment we reach Earth."

"I see no problem with that, Bethany."

She smiled. "In that case, I consider it an honor to interview this prisoner for you, Richard. In fact, I would never have forgiven you if you'd given the job to anyone else. I've dreamed of getting my hands on a member of the managerial caste ever since I knew there was such a thing. I have some theories I'd like to see tested out."

"Good! Now that that's settled, let's talk about something else," he said, taking her hands in his own. "You are looking particularly ravishing tonight, my love . . ."

CHAPTER 15

The polyarcs in *Discovery*'s main hangar bay gave Landing Boat *Moliere* a bright, blue-white sheen as Boris Alvarez and Bethany Lindquist arrived the next morning for the one-and-a-half-hour flight down to Corlis. Bethany was slightly hung over and sleepy but otherwise content. After dinner, she and Drake had made love into the small hours of the morning, parting only when she had to return to her own cabin to finish packing. She was definitely logy, however, as she followed Professor Alvarez onboard the landing boat. It was all she could do to strap herself into one of the acceleration couches before she drifted off to sleep.

She woke some time later to a jolting sensation and the high-pitched keening of hypersonic wind rushing past the hull outside. Opening her eyes with a start, she turned toward Alvarez, who was watching the play of plasma streams outside the viewport.

"How long have I been asleep?" she asked.

"Forty minutes," he replied. "We're just entering atmosphere now."

She considered going back to sleep but then thought better of it. Instead, the two of them watched in silence as the boat sliced through the night air a hundred kilome-

ters above the surface of the virgin planet below. Save
for a few wildfires burning in the distance and the widespread sparks of lightning flashes, the planetary disk was
black. Half an hour later, they crossed the terminator
into daylight and the landscape turned a dull tan and orange color.

"Pretty big desert," Alvarez observed.

Bethany nodded. Their speed was such that the desert
quickly fell astern, to be replaced by a wide sea. For ten
minutes they flew above the azure blue of deep water
before once again making landfall. This time the land
was covered by a dense forest of blue-green vegetation.
Bethany watched in fascination as ever greater detail appeared to boil up out of the land below, an optical illusion brought about by the landing boat's swift descent.

Finally, they were over their destination. Bethany had
only the briefest glimpse of the Ryall installation before the
boat transitioned to a low hover and dust kicked up by the
underjets rose to throw a curtain over everything beyond
the viewport. Even so, the momentary view had left her
with an impression of domelike buildings scattered among
the open frameworks of alien machinery.

The boat had barely touched down when the dozen
passengers began unstrapping and dragging their luggage
out of the overhead bins. Bethany inserted herself between Professor Alvarez and the broad back of a corporal of the Sandarian Marines. As she did so, she
caught sight of the activity taking place on the other side
of the crude landing field.

"What's going on?" she wondered aloud. "Why all the
landing craft?"

The corporal turned and stooped to look through the
viewport. "Those are *Saskatoon*'s boats, ma'am. We've
got orders to ship our assault vehicles and heavy
weapons back to orbit as quickly as possible. Scuttlebutt
has it that we may have to abandon this world in a hurry
if a Ryall ship pops through that second foldpoint."

"Makes sense," Bethany said, nodding. Her original
question had been largely rhetorical. If she had thought
about it, she would have known that *Saskatoon*'s boats

would be loading about now. She'd been present at the meeting where Richard Drake had decided to order *Saskatoon*'s commander to get the Marines' heavy equipment back onboard their ship.

"Yeah, *that* makes sense, ma'am. But what about the other orders?"

She attempted with partial success to stifle a yawn. "What other orders, Corporal?"

"The orders to clean this damned place up, ma'am. Silliest damned thing I ever heard. They want us to pack up everything we brought down with us, and I mean *everything*! Garbage, ration tins, spent cartridge cases, used-up power packs. Why, they've even got teams out obliterating our vehicle tracks and footprints back in the bush! For chrissake, you'd think the king hisself was coming for Sunday morning inspection! Does that make any sense to you?"

"That's the Army for you, Corporal," Bethany replied.

"Damned right it is!"

Actually, the cleanup orders had their origin in the same meeting where it had been decided to begin the reembarkation process. The hope onboard *Discovery* was that they could erase all traces of human presence from the planet. If they were successful, and if the fleet subsequently managed to get clear of the system before the next Ryall starship arrived, they would leave the centaurs with a mystery to solve but no hard evidence that humans had penetrated this deep into Ryall space.

Bethany's ears popped as the boat's internal pressure was equalized with that of the outside atmosphere. In the front part of the passenger cabin, the air lock door swung slowly inward, accompanied by a puff of dust-laden air.

Upon disembarking, Bethany and Professor Alvarez found a Sandarian lieutenant waiting to escort them to Marine headquarters. The three walked along a pathway that had been cut from native rock. Their goal was a large, dome-shaped building. Once inside, the lieutenant led them to an arched doorway curtained by an animal skin. Beside it, a hand-drawn sign had been hung:

COLONEL O. Z. VALDIS, K.O.S., O.B.V.

COMMANDING OFFICER
33RD REGIMENT, 2ND BATTALION, 6TH DIVISION
SANDARIAN ROYAL SPACE MARINES

KNOCK BEFORE ENTERING

The lieutenant rapped twice on the door frame next to the sign, waited for permission, then lifted the animal skin to allow them to enter.

Colonel Valdis was a tall gray-haired man with the trim body of a professional warrior and an impressive set of facial scars. He rose from the makeshift desk he'd been using with a portable command console and crossed the room to where Bethany and Professor Alvarez were standing.

He leaned forward and kissed Bethany's outstretched hand. "Good to have you with us, Miss Lindquist."

"Good to be here, Colonel. I'd just about given up hope of getting my feet back on solid ground until we reach Earth."

The colonel guffawed. "Spoken like a true Marine! I hope we can make your stay here a memorable one." He then turned to Professor Alvarez and saluted him. "Welcome, Sir Boris. If there is anything that I can do for you, please don't hesitate to ask."

"All I require, Colonel, is for someone to show me to this computer you captured."

"And you, Miss Lindquist?" Valdis asked, turning his attention back to Bethany.

"Did Captain Drake advise you that I was to interview one of the prisoners?"

"Yes, ma'am, although I can't think of why you would want to."

"I've made the Ryall my special field of study ever since we discovered their existence," Bethany said. "Yet I've never actually seen one."

"It will take some time to arrange the interview, Miss Lindquist. My own interrogators are using the equipment at the moment, and it's important that we get the individual stories on tape before they have time to agree on a lie."

"I'm in no hurry, Colonel. Just sometime before we head back up to the ship."

"Very well. Lieutenant Harreck!"

The lieutenant who had guided them from the landing area immediately appeared.

"Please show our guests to their work area and instruct them in the regulations governing our occupation."

"Yes, sir."

"It was good to meet you, Miss Lindquist. You too, Sir Boris. Harreck here will show you to your work area and will arrange quarters for you."

"You are most kind, Colonel."

"My pleasure, Sir Boris. Now, if you will excuse me, I have an evacuation to run."

The captured Ryall computer turned out to be a fairly typical example of centaur information-processing technology. Even so, and despite Professor Alvarez's cavalier assumption that loading the astrogation data base would be relatively straightforward, they ran into difficulties almost immediately. The first problem involved incompatible storage media. The data that had been taken from the starship had been recorded in standard holographic data cubes—standard, that is, for human beings. Unfortunately, the Ryall equivalent was designed to use thin, translucent strips. The captured computer included several strip readers but, of course, no cube readers.

It had taken nearly an entire thirty-hour day for Alvarez to adapt the cube reader out of a Marine fire-control computer to interface with the Ryall machine. Then he and Bethany had slept six hours before another long session to load the starship data into the captured machine.

Then had come the problem of activating the various starship programs. To Bethany's surprise, Boris Alvarez turned out to be a skilled translator of the dot patterns that made up the Ryall script. For two days he scanned the computer operations manual, translating those sections which he thought would be of some use. He kept Bethany busy transcribing notes and putting them into an easily retrievable form.

Finally, when Alvarez felt confident enough to begin manipulating the computer directly, he seated himself in front of the readout screen and ran his hands over the slightly slippery surface of the input/output sphere. The machine responded by scrolling a distinctive pattern of dots right to left across the face of the screen.

"It looks as though you know what you are doing," Bethany said, observing the ease with which he manipulated the alien artifact.

Alvarez nodded, obviously pleased by the compliment. "I could do a lot better if I had an extra thumb like the Ryall. Still, it isn't difficult once you get the hang of it."

"Shall I set up the recorders?"

"Yes. We should be ready to begin exploring our data base any time now."

"I'll get started right away. At least the hard part is over!"

Alvarez looked at her as an adult looks at a child. "The *preliminaries* are over, Miss Lindquist. The hard part is about to begin!"

A crisp, cool wind blew down the valley and wafted Bethany's hair into her eyes as she stepped from the protection of the headquarters building. She stopped to stretch and work out the kinks of too many hours spent in front of a computer screen. As she did so, she breathed deeply of Corlis' virgin air and noted that the smell of rain had been added to the normal cinnamon and orange blossom scent. Overhead, the scudding white clouds of late morning had turned to dark, towering thunderheads just as the meteorologists had predicted they would. Bethany didn't mind. After months of being cooped up in *Discovery*, a bit of violent weather was a welcome diversion.

Having worked the largest of the knots from her muscles, she moved quickly away from the dome-shaped headquarters building, being careful to keep to the hard-surfaced pathway. Her destination was the Quonset-style structure in which the Ryall prisoners were housed. As she walked, her gaze was drawn to the hills on each side of the valley and to the line of blue-green vegetation that marked the farthest extent of the Ryall excavations. From a distance, the growth looked like a typical forest of the Altan highlands, although the trees appeared more stunted and gnarled than those at home.

Bethany let her gaze follow the forest line to the large earthen dam that the Ryall had constructed upstream of their complex. Marines who had scouted that far reported a large lake behind the dam, one that grew perceptibly larger with each afternoon thunderstorm. At the dam's base was a white box of a structure from which a dozen large-diameter pipes emanated. The pipes split into two groups just below the valve house and ran ten kilometers down each side of the valley. They disappeared into the ground just prior to reaching the first of the vertical shafts that the Ryall had drilled into bedrock.

Rising in the distance beyond the dam, their flanks softened by atmospheric scattering, were several large snow-capped mountains. The mountain range reminded Bethany of the Colgate Mountains east of Homeport and it made her a little sad that this beautiful world would soon have to be abandoned.

She was still staring off into the distance and thinking of what humankind could do with a world like Corlis when she reached the prisoners' barracks. Forcing her attention back to the job at hand, she checked through the Marine guard post at the only opening in a hastily erected electric fence. She was escorted to an interview room. Inside, she found a single metal folding chair, a matching table, and a translator computer. The translator's pickup microphones had been affixed to the walls and ceiling. The room had solid doors—a temporary improvement to the barracks.

"They're bringing Varlan now, ma'am," the sergeant who had escorted her from the guard station said.

Bethany thanked him and turned to face the door opposite the one through which she had entered. Less than a minute later, the door opened and two Marines armed with riot guns escorted a Ryall into the interview room.

The Ryall was gray-green on top and shaded to tan below. Its cranial bulge was prominent, but the snout seemed shorter than the photographs that Bethany had seen. The body was also sleeker than the drone warrior types that made up the bulk of humanity's prisoners. The tail was longer, and the pads at the ends of the feet were larger. The head on the long neck twisted in a slow traverse as the Ryall surveyed its surroundings.

"Miss Bethany Lindquist," the sergeant said formally. "May I present Varlan of the Scented Waters, manager of the Corlis Mineral Extraction Complex. Varlan, I have the honor to present Bethany Lindquist, a great leader among my people."

Bethany found herself the object of intense scrutiny by a single jet-black eye. Varlan's mouth was open, revealing a double row of razor-sharp teeth and a tri-forked tongue. Bethany knew from her studies that the Ryall breathed through their mouths, which accounted for the resemblance to a panting dog.

"Hello, Varlan," Bethany said.

There followed a noise something like the sound of a flute; then the speaker on the table translated. "Greetings, Bethany of the Lindquists. How may this one assist you?"

Bethany glanced up at the three Marines who had taken up stations around the room, their riot guns at the ready. "Thank you, Sergeant. Will you and your men please wait outside."

"I wouldn't advise that, ma'am. Those teeth are sharp, and they can swing those tails of theirs with a vengeance. One of the defenders nearly took my head clean off, and me wearing battle armor at the time!"

"I'm sure I will be safe, Sergeant. Varlan isn't going to harm me knowing that you are outside."

"Okay, ma'am. It's your funeral."

The Ryall watched the Marines file out of the room, tilting her head in order to follow their progress with her right eye while keeping Bethany in constant view of her left. When the door closed behind them, she shifted her entire attention to Bethany.

"It is my understanding that you are female, Varlan of the Scented Waters," Bethany began.

"I am," the Ryall replied.

"So am I," Bethany responded. "I am curious as to whether we females think alike."

"How can we?" Varlan asked. "We are of different species."

"But there must be similarities. We are the sex which brings forth new life, are we not?"

"We are," Varlan replied.

"Then surely our outlooks must overlap somewhat."

"What an odd thought."

"Shall we attempt to find common ground on which to base our discussions, then?"

Varlan made a gesture that Bethany didn't recognize. It consisted of emitting a hissing sound at the same time that she flapped her ear membranes. "Among my race we would say, 'Shall we attempt to swim the river of consensus?'"

"Shall we?"

"A prisoner does well to humor her jailers," the Ryall replied. "Also, the concept is an interesting one."

Bethany started the discussion by describing the human reproductive cycle and the fact that human young are born alive. She continued by explaining the effect this simple fact of nature had on human attitudes. The Ryall, she soon learned, had somewhat analogous attitudes, although, since they had no way to know which hatchlings were their own, their affection tended to be generalized. This in turn made it easy for the Ryall to grasp the concept of group loyalty and, ultimately, loyalty to the entire species.

"See," Bethany said after they had been talking for more than an hour, "there appears to be nothing which our two races cannot discuss rationally with one another."

"That would appear to be true."

"Then why do you Ryall hate and fear us so?"

"We do not hate you, Bethany of the Lindquists. Nor do we fear you."

"Yet you attacked us without provocation and refuse all of our attempts at negotiating an end to this war between us."

"Your very existence is provocation enough," Varlan replied.

"That is not an answer. Surely the universe is big enough for both of us. Why must we fight one another when there are so many stars to be claimed?"

Varlan moved her head to gaze at the single window in the interview room. "Look there, Bethany of the Lindquists," she said, gesturing with one six-fingered hand. "What do you see?"

Bethany followed the Ryall's gesture. "I see the other side of the valley, the forest, and the mountains beyond."

"Do you find this scene attractive?"

Bethany nodded. "I do indeed. This is a lovely world. It reminds me of home."

"Then we agree on something else," Varlan replied. "I, too, can gaze at the mountains in the distance and think of my home among the stars."

"One more reason why we should be friends."

The Ryall hissed. "All the more reason why we must be enemies! History teaches that two intelligent species cannot share a single habitat. Both must expand their range until one day they will find themselves in conflict."

"Even if that were true," Bethany replied, "it will be thousands of years before we run out of living room on the planets we now hold. Why fight now?"

"Would you have us place the burden of ridding the universe of you humans on future generations?"

"I would try to avoid fighting altogether," Bethany replied with a sigh. "However, I appreciate your honesty. A human in your position would probably have told me what he thought I wanted to hear."

"To what avail?" Varlan asked. "When the logic of a situation is plain for all to see, where lies the advantage in proving oneself a liar or deluded?"

CHAPTER 16

"Decontamination complete, milady! You may step through into the next cubicle and get dressed."

Bethany watched the last of the vile-smelling decontamination fluid gurgle down the drain at her feet, then glanced up at the overhead speaker from which the unseen operator's voice had emanated. As she did so, she wondered if he could see her.

"What about my clothing?" she asked, shivering slightly in the sudden cold draft of the chamber.

"Undergoing fumigation, milady. You will find a new shipsuit in the cubicle."

"Thank you!"

"You are most welcome."

Bethany pressed the control that opened the airtight door leading from the chamber to the changing cubicle beyond. True to the operator's word, the plastic bag into which she had sealed the clothing she had worn on Corlis was gone. In its place was a neatly folded replacement outfit. She dried herself, then carefully slipped into new underwear, shipsuit, and soft boots. She brushed her hair using a brush from the tiny personal effects kit that had accompanied the clothing, then studied the result in the full-length mirror that hung on the inside of the cubicle door. Other than temporarily looking like a drowned rodent and smelling of disinfectant, she decided that she was none the worse for wear. She slipped the packet of personal effects into a pocket of the shipsuit, opened the cubicle door, and stepped into the corridor beyond.

"Welcome aboard *Terra*," a voice said from somewhere behind her.

She turned to find Captain Lord Rheinhardt Dreyer, the Sandarian cruiser's captain, waiting for her. The captain was a tall man with a lean figure, close-cropped sandy hair, and pale blue eyes. He wore the undress uniform of the Royal Sandarian Navy.

"Captain Dreyer! There was no need for you to come down to meet me."

The Sandarian officer chuckled. "Oh, but there was. Captain Drake would have my ears if you weren't treated properly while aboard my ship. I'm sorry that you couldn't have been routed directly to *Discovery*, but the regulations concerning decontamination after a visit to an alien biosphere are extremely stringent."

"As they should be," Bethany replied. "I understand from Varlan that the Ryall had a number of laborers come down with unknown diseases on Corlis. I'm no expert, but it seems to me that any microorganism which can feed off Ryall biochemistry might do as well on human."

"Varlan?" The Sandarian captain looked blank for a moment, then nodded. He struggled to keep a tone of disapproval from his voice and very nearly succeeded. "Ah, yes, that is one of the Ryall prisoners, is it not? Colonel Valdis reported that you had quite a number of interviews with the prisoners while you were on Corlis."

"I interviewed Varlan, the manager of the Corlis mine, three times. After two years of studying the Ryall from books and printouts, I found it refreshing to finally meet one in the flesh."

"And did he match your expectations?"

"She."

"Beg your pardon."

"Varlan's female. And yes, it was definitely educational. Ever talk to one of them?"

The Sandarian shook his head. "In my business, milady, we seldom get close enough to the enemy to hold a conversation. No, our 'communicating' is done with missiles and antimatter projectors. As for prisoner interrogations, I leave those to specialists."

"You are probably wise. The Ryall seem to have their own logic for looking at the universe."

Dreyer nodded. "My people have been trying to understand the centaurs without success for the better part of a century."

"Now that I've talked to a Ryall, I think I understand the problem better."

"Where is Sir Boris, milady?"

"He stayed behind to check out some last-minute information. He's scheduled up on the morning shuttle."

"Speaking of which," Dreyer said, "I'm afraid that you just missed the scheduled boat for *Discovery*. Shall I arrange a special ferry?"

"No need. I can wait for the scheduled run in the morning."

Dreyer grinned. "I was hoping you would say that. I have taken the liberty of having your luggage sent to Cabin 173 on Gamma Deck. I would be honored if you will be my guest at dinner this evening."

"Thank you, Captain. I accept."

"Excellent! Dinner is at 2000 hours."

After a late evening of Sandarian hospitality, Bethany was up early to catch the interorbit ferry for *Discovery*. With four ships in orbit about Corlis, the task force had established its own scheduled spaceline, with two flights daily between the orbiting warships. From *Terra* to *Discovery* was a twenty-minute voyage. Bethany spent the time with her nose pressed to the viewport, watching the beauty of Corlis stream by below.

Richard Drake was waiting in *Discovery*'s main hangar bay when she disembarked. Seeing him at the foot of the ladder, Bethany literally flew into his arms in the microgravity of the hangar bay. It was all that he could do to keep his grip on the stanchion he had used to anchor himself.

"Welcome home," he said as he enfolded her in a one-armed embrace. They kissed and then clung to each other while ordinary spacers either grinned or studiously ignored them.

"It's good to be home, Richard," she said, breathless, after their lips finally parted. She glanced at the bay around them. "Nothing's changed, I see."

He turned his head to follow her gaze and noted the sudden increase in activity among the spacers whose job it was to offload cargo from the ferry craft. "You've only been gone ten days. Here, these are for you."

She struggled from his arms to discover a bouquet of red and white roses in the hand he'd been using to steady himself.

"They're beautiful!"

"Not nearly as beautiful as you."

"You flatter me, sir . . . and I love it!"

"It's the plain truth."

"I still love it."

"How was your trip?" he asked.

"Both interesting and educational. How were things while I was gone?"

"Nerve-wracking," he replied. "Every day I expected *Mace* to report that a Ryall ship had popped out of that second foldpoint. I understand you and Alvarez hit the jackpot!"

Bethany nodded. "The man's a virtuoso when it comes to playing a Ryall input/output sphere, Richard. You should have seen him. It was uncanny."

"So I gathered. He's requested that I arrange a conference to go over your discoveries."

"When?"

"This afternoon. Care to give me a preview?"

"Borlis asked me not to. I hope you don't mind, Richard. He did most of the work, so it's only fair that he get the credit."

Drake shrugged. "I suppose I can wait."

"That's why I love you so, Richard. You are the most understanding martinet I've ever known."

Having left the hangar bay, they pulled themselves hand over hand along the main Alpha Deck circumferential corridor. Drake led the way to his cabin, which was up two decks and a quarter of the way around the habitat ring. When they arrived, Drake guided Bethany to the guest chair in front of his desk.

"When will gravity be restored?" she asked as she fumbled for the chair's restraint belt.

He glanced at the chronometer on the far bulkhead. "Another ten minutes. As soon as they launch the ferry, they'll put some spin on. Care to report on your discussions with the Ryall manager?"

"Yes, as long as I have time to clean up before the conference. I showered once last night and again this morning, and my hair still smells of that damned bug spray."

"On you, my dear, even bug spray smells good."

Bethany laughed. "Love isn't only blind, it also lacks a sense of smell!"

Drake leaned forward and switched on his recorder. He spoke for more than a minute, reciting for the record the circumstances under which Bethany had gone down to Corlis and his instructions to her. With a final glance at the sound-level readout, he nodded to Bethany. "Proceed with your report."

Bethany began by describing her initial meeting with Colonel Valdis.

"What was Colonel Valdis' reaction to your request to interview the prisoner?"

Bethany shook her head. "He was gracious, although I think he may have been annoyed, too. He hid it well, but I got the impression that he would have preferred if I hadn't been such a bother."

"Any trouble with scheduling the interview?"

"It took a few days, but then, we *were* awfully busy with the computer. I received word one morning that Varlan would be available late in the afternoon. They had everything ready for me when I reached the prisoner barracks."

"How did you approach the question of a negotiated end to the war?"

"I don't remember exactly, but it seemed a natural question to ask at the time."

"And Varlan's response?"

Bethany sighed. "The same as every other Ryall prisoner I've ever heard of. So far as she's concerned, there isn't enough room in the universe for both our species."

"What was her mood when she told you that? Angry, nervous, distraught?"

"None of those. That's what makes it so discouraging. She could just as easily have been discussing the first law of thermodynamics. As far as the Ryall are concerned, the extermination of one intelligent species by another is just an unfortunate fact of life."

Drake leaned back in his chair and gazed at Bethany through steepled fingertips. "That is essentially the same story we've gotten from Ossfil and his crew. If high-level Ryall managers and merchant starship captains aren't able to see the futility of carrying on this war, then there probably isn't a single Ryall alive who can. Damn the swift eaters!"

"Which reminds me," Bethany said. "Varlan and I discussed the legend of the swifts during our second interview."

"And?"

"And they're no legend. The Ryall have swift skeletons in their museums. They use them to indoctrinate the hatchlings."

"Then the Sandarians are right? The only way to win this war is to blow the Ryall back to their home worlds?"

"I'm not so sure of that," Bethany replied, her brow furrowed in concentration. "I think maybe both we and the Sandarians are giving up too easily. After all, I've only had eight hours or so to talk to Varlan about things which must be very alien to her."

"What are you suggesting?"

"That she be brought here to *Discovery*, where I can continue to work on her. Perhaps I can bring her around to our way of thinking. If I succeed, at least it will prove that they can be swayed by logic."

"And if you don't?"

Bethany shrugged. "Then I guess we do unto others before they have a chance to do unto us!"

* * *

Drake accompanied Bethany to the afternoon conference. "I see you've had some time to pull yourself together," he said when she opened her cabin door for him.

"Like it?" she asked, pirouetting for his inspection. The shipsuit and the plain hairstyle of that morning were gone. Instead she wore a semiformal pants suit with a moderately plunging bodice and an asymmetric hairstyle. "I thought I would get dressed up. After all, this *is* something of an occasion."

The wardroom was full to capacity when they arrived. Bethany and Drake weaved their way through the crowd to the front of the compartment, where a lectern and holoscreen had been set up. Their destination was the clump of scientists and Sandarian military officers who had congregated around Boris Alvarez. Drake pushed his way through and extended his hand to the Sandarian scientist.

"Good to have you back, Sir Boris."

"Thank you, Captain," Alvarez replied. The scientist had dark bags under his eyes and sunken cheeks that Drake didn't remember having been there before. Still, his eyes shone with an unnatural brightness, and his handshake was firm and resolute.

There followed five minutes in which everyone found a seat, and Alvarez conferred in urgent whispers with Bethany. Eventually, Bethany sat down next to Drake; she let her hand steal into his as soon as the lights faded to the dim blue radiance normally used to simulate night.

"Greetings, Captain Drake, Captain Dreyer, officers of *Discovery* and *Terra*, and colleagues," Alvarez began in a loud, strong voice. "As you know, ten days ago, Miss Lindquist and I went down to Corlis. Our task there was to see if we could extract the astrogation data we captured with the Ryall ore carrier. I am pleased to announce that we were successful!"

Alvarez manipulated the screen control and caused the holoscreen to light up. Near the bottom of the screen were two star symbols. The larger was labeled "ANTARES NEBULA"; the smaller, "EULYSTA/CORLIS." Between the two symbols was the dotted line marking an active fold-line link.

"Here you have the path by which we entered this system. The link between Antares and Eulysta is quite recent. It was originally formed when Antares exploded. Because the Eulysta–Antares foldpoint leads directly into the heart of the nebula, the Ryall apparently consider it impassable."

Alvarez touched the control, and a third star suddenly materialized in the depths of the screen. "This is Carratyl. It is the next system in from Eulysta." Alvarez paused and looked up from his notes. "I hope everyone realizes that these names are translations of Ryall originals. The original of 'Carratyl' sounds like someone clearing his throat.

"It was Carratyl toward which the Ryall ore carrier was fleeing when we caught up with it. Unlike Eulysta, which is basically uninhabited, Carratyl is a bona fide system of the Ryall hegemony. It possesses a single inhabited world, Kalatin, which has a population of approximately one billion. Kalatin is an agricultural world. The pilot's ephemeris from which we obtained these data indicates that there is a small naval base on the largest of its three moons.

"Which brings us to the next system of interest," Alvarez said as he caused a fourth star symbol to appear on the screen. "I won't trouble you with the Ryall name, for we humans have known this star since ancient times. I give you *Spica!*"

There was a sudden silence throughout the wardroom, followed by a low muttering from the astronomers present. Drake gazed with amazement at the flock of symbols that had suddenly appeared on the screen. From somewhere nearby, a voice muttered in surprise. "My God!" someone exclaimed. "Six . . . seven . . . eight foldpoints!"

Up on the podium, it was obvious that Boris Alvarez was enjoying their reaction to his sudden revelation. He grinned. "As most of you have already noticed, Spica possesses a total of eight foldpoints. This makes it the hub star of the largest foldspace cluster ever discovered.

More importantly, however, Spica is the premier system of the Ryall hegemony, as you will shortly see."

Alvarez manipulated his control, and the other stars of Ryall space began appearing. Even before the full diagram was completed, the pattern was clear to those who knew how to read a foldspace topology chart. Drake scanned the diagram in growing disbelief. The individual star systems of the Ryall hegemony were tied to one another by short strings and branches of foldlines. Here three stars were strung together, there two others branched away from a third. In another case, four stars were connected in a rare closed ring pattern. As he searched the diagram, however, Drake could find no telltale line connecting any two of the small groupings save through the central hub system of Spica. Alvarez confirmed his growing suspicions a few seconds later.

"There are twenty-two separate systems in the Ryall hegemony. *Every single one of them belongs to the Spica Foldspace Cluster!*"

CHAPTER 17

TO: ALL SHIP CAPTAINS AND GROUND FORCE COMMANDERS

FROM: DRAKE, R. A., TASK FORCE COMMANDER

DATE: 11 SEPTEMBER 2639 (U.C.)
TIME: 2000 HOURS (U.T.)

SUBJECT: ORDERS

1. FINAL PREPARATIONS FOR THE ABANDONMENT OF CORLIS WILL BEGIN IMMEDIATELY. ALL PERSONNEL SHALL ADHERE TO THE FOLLOWING TIMETABLE:

   1.1 RYALL PRISONERS WILL BE TRANSFERRED TO ORBIT BEGINNING 0900 HOURS, 12 SEPTEMBER 2639.

   1.2 FINAL INSPECTIONS OF CORLIS MINING COMPLEX WILL BE COMPLETED BY 0900 HOURS, 13 SEPTEMBER 2639.

   1.3 THE LAST LANDING BOAT WILL LIFT

FROM CORLIS NO LATER THAN 1800
HOURS, 13 SEPTEMBER 2639.

2. THE FLEET WILL DEPART CORLIS PARK-
ING ORBIT AT 2400 HOURS, 13 SEP-
TEMBER 2639, AND WILL ARRIVE AT THE
EULYSTA—ANTARES FOLDPOINT AT 1200
HOURS ON 18 SEPTEMBER 2639.

3. SANDARIAN SPACE NAVY DESTROYER
MACE WILL COORDINATE ITS DEPARTURE
FROM THE EULYSTA—CARRATYL FOLD-
POINT IN ORDER TO ARRIVE AT THE
EULYSTA—ANTARES FOLDPOINT SIMUL-
TANEOUSLY WITH THE REST OF THE
FLEET.

(SIGNED)
RIGHARD DRAKE
FLEET CAPTAIN
ALTAN SPACE NAVY

Drake sat in his command chair and watched Landing
Boat *Moliere* disappear into *Discovery*'s open landing
bay. As quickly as the winged arrow had vanished into
the curve of the habitat ring, the cruiser's senior ship
handler reported via ship's intercom.

"Landing boat successfully retrieved, Captain."

"Very good, Mr. Salmonson," Drake replied. "Secure
the bay."

"Securing now."

"That does it, sir," one of the bridge technicians reported to Drake. "All boats are now back in their cradles."

"Have you confirmation of *Moliere*'s passenger list?"

"Yes, sir. All task force personnel are accounted for."

"And the prisoners?"

"All secure, Captain."

"Excellent, Mr. Davis. Mr. Marchant!"

"I'm on the circuit, sir," Drake's executive officer
said from his station in the combat control center.

"How are we doing on time?"

"The Ryall mining complex should be coming over the horizon in about two minutes, Captain. All telemetry signals are strong and clear."

"Stand by to detonate on my order, Commander."

"Standing by."

"Mr. Haydn. Put the planet on the main viewscreen, please."

"Going up now, sir."

The blue and white limb of the planet as seen through one of the telescopes mounted on *Discovery*'s central cylinder flashed on the screen. The view scanned right, then grew larger as the telescope's magnification was increased.

Drake watched the scenery slip across the screen as *Discovery*'s orbital speed took it ever closer to the target area. After a minute, the Ryall mine and smelter complex came into view. The valley in which the centaurs had established their settlement was a buff-colored slash clearly visible amid the greenery of the surrounding forest. A large patch of blue marked the position of the lake that supplied the mine with water. The buildings and frameworks of the Ryall mine cast shadows across the bare countryside.

"More magnification if you can, Mr. Haydn."

"Going to full mag, Captain."

The image enlarged once again, causing the valley to overflow the edges of the screen.

"Not quite that much," Drake ordered. The view backed off until the ends of the valley were once again visible.

"Are you ready, Mr. Marchant?"

"Ready, Captain."

"Detonate!"

At first nothing appeared to happen. Then puffs of orange-yellow smoke rose all around the white cube of the valve house at the base of the dam. The valve house tilted, rolled down a short slope, then disappeared from view as a dark stain began to fill the valley below. The stain developed a leading edge of white froth that moved with astonishing swiftness. The earthen dam collapsed completely as its base was chewed away by rushing water. A tidal wave broke through and raced downstream, easily overtaking the first surge of boiling foam.

Drake watched the wave gobble up the lengths of pipe on each side of the valley. Three minutes later, the wall of water washed over the buildings and framework structures of the mine complex. The roiling flood submerged white domes and longhouses alike, splintering them into hundreds of pieces of debris. The initial bits of wreckage were dashed against rocks, splintering them further until they disappeared completely from the telescopes and cameras orbiting two hundred kilometers overhead.

"So that was your plan!" a voice muttered beside Drake. "Blow the dam and cover the evidence under a blanket of mud!"

Drake glanced up to see Bethany maneuvering herself into the observer's seat beside him.

"That was it," he replied. "Now, when the Ryall come looking for their lost starship, they'll find their settlement wiped out by what appears to be a natural disaster."

"Surely they will expect survivors!"

"Not necessarily. They could all have been caught down in the mines." Drake gestured to the section of viewscreen where large whirlpools had developed in the rushing river as millions of cubic meters of water poured into open mine shafts. "And even if there were survivors, it's logical that they would have been evacuated on the ore carrier."

"And then been lost with the ship!"

Drake nodded.

"Do you think they'll buy it?"

"It doesn't matter whether they buy the disaster story or not so long as they don't associate *us* with it."

Varlan of the Scented Waters had been awakened in the prison barracks early on the previous day and herded into a room where shackles had been affixed to her legs. She and her fellow prisoners had been loaded onto the back of a transport and driven to the area the

humans used for their landing field. There they had
been placed five to a cage, loaded into the cargo hold
of a landing boat, and ferried to orbit. Varlan had used
her status to claim the corner of the cage closest to a
viewport. Thus she was able to watch the planet fall
away below as the blue sky turned slowly black.

The other four prisoners in her cage were laborers.
They had squealed in panic as the boat lifted away from
Corlis. Only Varlan's sense of dignity kept her from join-
ing their cries with her own. For while they had remained prisoners in Corlis Complex, it had been possible
to hope that Those Who Rule would learn of their fate
and send warriors to rescue them. Once aboard the
humans' ships, there could be no possibility of rescue.
The best that could be hoped for was a quick death when
warriors of the Race caught and destroyed the inter-
lopers.

Varlan and her party had been taken to a great cylindrical warship in Corlis parking orbit. There they
had been subjected to a terrible spray of foul-smelling
liquid. At first it had seemed that the humans were
trying to poison them, but Varlan's judgment had
quickly overcome her terror. Had the humans wished
their prisoners dead, she reasoned, they would not
have gone to the trouble of hauling them to their orbiting ships. The deed could easily have been done in the
confines of the prison barracks. No, Varlan decided,
rather than poison, the humans were dousing them
with some kind of disinfectant, much as the medics did
when they treated someone suffering from parasites.

Following the ordeal of the noxious spray, Varlan and
her four companions were herded into a closed compartment. Save for the sanitation facilities—poor copies of
ground-based plumbing rather than the zero-gravity
adaptations used in Ryall starships—and a series of tie-
down straps, the compartment was unfurnished. Varlan
and her companions had settled down to await developments. They had been in their new prison for a thousand
heartbeats when they were joined by a second party of
five prisoners. The same ritual occurred twice more until

all the centaurs captured on Corlis were once again together.

Nothing else of significance happened for what Varlan
judged to be an entire day. They were fed regularly, and
the compartment was supplied with fresh water for
drinking. Several times during their stay, alarms sounded
throughout the ship and overhead speakers warned that
a condition of null gravity would shortly be experienced.
At these times, the Ryall moved to tie themselves down
with the straps attached to the floor. A number of laborers lost the contents of their first stomachs during
these periods, causing considerable discomfort for all
concerned.

After a sleep period in which Varlan managed to
doze only fitfully, the single hatch opened and one of
the humans equipped with a translating machine called
out her name. She briefly considered refusing to answer but decided against it. Maltreatment was not to
be courted without purpose or hope of future gain.
Also, should the humans truly want her, they would
not find it difficult to sort her out from the other prisoners.

She moved forward and meekly allowed the humans
to shackle her again. They led her to the large hangar
through which they had entered the human starship.
There she was placed aboard one of the winged landing
craft and transferred to a second ship, this one a toroid
and central cylinder design. She had been escorted to a
prison compartment aboard the second ship. This one
contained Ossfil and the seven surviving members of
Space Swimmer's crew.

"Greetings, Varlan of the Scented Waters," Ossfil had
said after making the gesture of respect.

"Greetings, Ossfil, once of *Space Swimmer*. How
fare you at the hands of our captors?"

"Well enough. They feed us regularly from our own
ship's stores. The fare is monotonous but filling. How is
it with you and Corlis Complex?"

Varlan told of the brief attempt at defending the mine
and smelter and of their ignominious capture by the
human warriors. She had just finished when a human

voice emanated from an overhead speaker and made some sort of announcement.

"What now?" Varlan asked.

"They are warning everyone to secure themselves. They are about to energize the ship's main drive engines," Ossfil said.

"Do you speak the language, Ossfil, late of *Space Swimmer*?"

Ossfil gave the sign that signifies a minor accomplishment. "A few words only. That long sound pattern that sounds like someone gargling can best be translated 'acceleration.'"

"Where do you suppose they are taking us?"

The answer when it came was almost too low to hear. "I fear we are bound for the Evil Star."

Varlan stiffened. Like most upper-caste Ryall, she had learned enough astronomy to know what a supernova was and how such were triggered. Even so, such events had been considered evil omens throughout the history of the race. The thought that she was on a ship bound for the interior of such a cataclysm brought the fears of a thousand generations to mind.

"How is that possible? Surely to enter the Evil Star is to be instantly destroyed!"

"One would think so," Ossfil replied. "However, I myself have seen their starships appear in the portal leading out of the Evil Star. One must believe one's own oculars. Therefore, we must assume that the monsters possess knowledge which we do not."

Varlan noted Ossfil's use of the term "monsters" and was surprised that she no longer thought of their captors as such. Instead, she had begun to think of them by the name they themselves used. It was a curious transformation in attitude and one that she resolved to study at greater length when she had time. Now it was necessary to learn all she could from Ossfil concerning his captivity.

"When you were taken prisoner, did they question you?"

Ossfil signaled an affirmative. "I and all of these survivors from my crew. They asked about Corlis Complex and whether we were aware of any other ships in the Eulysta system."

"Did you answer their questions?"

Before questioning, they attached sensors to various parts of my body and hooked them into a box of some kind. After each question they would look at the readouts. It was as though they knew what I would say before I spoke."

Varlan nodded. She too had been subjected to something of the sort when questioned. Mostly they had asked about the roster of workers then on Corlis and whether any had escaped.

"At least our honor is intact, Ossfil," she said in a kindly tone. "We cannot help what their alien gadgets tell them."

There was a long pause before the starship captain responded. "I fear that my honor is not intact, Varlan of the Scented Waters."

"How so, Ossfil, late of *Space Swimmer*?"

Ossfil closed his ears tight on top of his head and curled his tail between his first and second pair of legs. It was a gesture of one in the throes of extreme shame.

"The destruct mechanism on *Space Swimmer*'s computer malfunctioned. I fear the monsters have learned where our home stars are located."

The blows to Varlan's psyche had been very great recently. First there had come the shock of capture. Then there had been the destruction of hope when she realized that they were to be taken off Corlis. Now came the news that the information that Salfador of the Eternal Flame had died to protect might be in the possession of humans. The sudden howl of anguish that Varlan emitted had supersonic overtones. It was a cry of absolute and total despair.

ALPHA VIRGINIS
(SPICA)

POSITION: 132511.5 R.A.,-110900 DEC, 274
L—Y (Solcentric)

SYSTEM TYPE: BINARY

SYSTEM DESCRIPTION:

As viewed from Sol, Alpha Virginis is an eclipsing variable binary system (0.91–1.01 absolute magnitude) with a period of 4 days. The two stars are very closely coupled and are not resolvable by ground-based telescopes on terrestrial worlds. The binary nature of the Alpha Virginis system was originally discovered using spectrographic techniques.

Alpha Virginis-A is a Spectral Class B1.5, Luminosity Class V, giant star. Diameter: 6.2 Sol. Mass: 16.0 Sol.

Alpha Virginis-B is a Spectral Class B3.0, Luminosity Class V, dwarf star. Diameter and mass are not well determined.

REMARKS:

The Alpha Virginis system has never been visited, since no foldline leading to it has yet been discovered. Multidimensional astronomers consider this fact unusual since the larger of the system's two stars is sufficiently massive to produce optimum conditions for foldpoint formation. Many astronomers have predicted that a foldspace transition sequence leading to the system will eventually be found.

Alpha Virginis is the brightest star in the zodiacal constellation of Virgo and one of the 15 brightest stars in the terrestrial sky. The name "Spica" is Latin and means "Head of Grain."

—Excerpt from *The Pilot's Almanac*, 2510 Edition.

Richard Drake sat in front of the workscreen in his cabin and gazed at the two-dimensional photograph in which a single brilliant blue-white star lay centered

against a field of black. As he did so, he slowly read
the almanac entry that accompanied the picture.
"...no foldline leading to it has yet been discovered
...sufficiently massive to produce optimum conditions
for foldspace formation...transition sequence leading
to the system will eventually be found..." He wondered what the long-dead author of those words would
have said had he known that Spica was even then the
central star of an alien civilization.

After long minutes spent staring at the blue-white
star, Drake cleared the screen and brought up another
view. This time the screen was filled with more than a
hundred stars. Having discovered that he couldn't
sleep after a long, eventful day that had included the
fleet's departure from Corlis, Drake had put his insom-
nia to good use. He had plotted the positions of the
twenty-two stars that Boris Alvarez had identified as
being part of the Ryall hegemony and then color-coded
them a bright crimson for easy identification.

After studying the shape of Ryall space for a moment,
he had called up *Discovery*'s astrogation data base and
input the same data for the nearly eighty inhabited stars
that comprised human space. He'd colored the human
stars green and then merged them with the Ryall star
map. Finally, he had reduced the scale of the display to
the point where he could take in the two realms at a
single glance.

For five hundred years, the human race had expanded
out along the foldlines, eventually occupying an ellip-
soid-shaped region of space some five hundred light-
years long by two hundred light-years in diameter. The
Ryall had been expanding as well, occupying their own
region of the galaxy. Ryall space was approximately one-
third the volume of human space and nearly a perfect
sphere. The two realms shared a common boundary and
actually interpenetrated in the region around Antares.
Displayed as they were on the same screen, it was obvious why humanity was slowly losing its war with the
centaurs.

The long history of warfare on Earth had taught
generations of generals the value of seeking favorable

terrain on which to fight a battle. From Waterloo to Little Round Top to the Battle of Prudhoe Bay, the victors owed their success more to the lay of the land than to their military superiority over the vanquished. What the star map did for Drake was prove that the same could well be true of humanity's war with the Ryall.

Ryall space, localized as it was within the Spica Foldspace Cluster, was blessed with short internal lines of communication and a high degree of interconnectivity. No system in the hegemony lay more than six foldspace transitions from any other system. Human space, on the other hand, was strung out along the axis of the galactic spiral arm. The distance between the two farthest human systems was fifteen transitions.

The tactical and strategic value to the Ryall of their foldspace cluster was substantial. If attacked, they could spread the alarm and rush reinforcements anywhere in their realm much more quickly than could *Homo sapiens* in similar circumstances. And once mustered, their forces could also shift rapidly from trouble spot to trouble spot, allowing each ship to do the work of two or more human craft.

Drake stared at the star chart for long minutes and considered the implications. He was still doing so when his screen beeped for attention. He reached out and accepted the call.

"Sorry to bother you so late, Captain," Phillip Walkirk said. The Sandarian prince was officer of the deck.

"No problem, Mr. Walkirk. I've been doing some doodling with the computer. What's up?"

"Sensor operators have just detected a ship materializing in the Eulysta–Antares foldpoint, sir. They think it's *Arrow*."

"Have the communicator confirm the identification and report to Captain Rostock the fact that we are on our way to the foldpoint. He is to hold there until we arrive."

"Aye aye, Captain."

Phillip Walkirk signed off, and Drake returned to his ruminations. Fifteen minutes later, the Sandarian prince was once again on his screen.

"Communications have been established, sir. *Arrow* is transmitting a message from Admiral Gower."

"What do they say?"

"Admiral Gower is ordering us to abandon this system and return immediately to the nebula, sir."

"Does he give any reason?"

"Yes, sir. The fleet has located another of Antares' foldpoints. The admiral wants us to rejoin before they send anyone through to see what is on the other side."

CHAPTER 18

While Richard Drake's task force explored the Eulysta system, the scientists onboard *City of Alexandria* had worked round the clock to update their mathematical model describing the structure of foldspace within the Antares Nebula. The job had proved more difficult than anticipated. Since foldlines were focused by gravitational curvature—so-called gravity lens effect—the quantity and arrangement of matter within a system was the major factor affecting foldpoint formation. In most star systems, the overwhelming majority of mass was in the stars themselves. That fact made it relatively easy to predict foldpoint formation once the involved foldline had been identified.

The Antares Nebula was far more complex than the average star system, however. The innermost element tending to focus foldlines was the neutron star at the heart of the pulsar. The tiny star's high rate of rotation and small size tended to distort those few foldlines that passed directly through the star's heart. As for those foldlines with a small offset, they avoided the neutron star's influence altogether. Surrounding the neutron star was a several-million-kilometer-thick layer of highly charged plasma. Energy transferred from the star's rapidly rotating magnetic field tended to keep the plasma energized and thereby minimized the density variations. This relatively homogeneous layer of plasma tended to strongly focus foldlines that passed anywhere within the boundaries of the Antares remnant.

Beyond the central mass lay the nebula. Diffuse to the point of being a very good vacuum, it nevertheless contained a full 30 percent of giant Antares' prenova mass. Foldlines entering that six-light-year-thick globe of gas could not help but be affected by it. And beyond the gas and dust lay the leading edge of the supernova shock wave, now some 127 light-years distant. It had been the shock wave that had caused Alta's long isolation, and the passage of the shock wave beyond the Valeria system that had ended it. Thus, no model intended to predict foldpoint formation inside the nebula could ignore the effect of that far-off discontinuity in the interstellar medium.

It was the job of the astronomers aboard *City of Alexandria* to take each of these factors into account, incorporate them into a series of simultaneous equations, and determine the influence each focusing element exerted at every point within the nebula. That work was both subtle and exasperating, yet the scientists eventually produced a foldspace map that accounted for the foldpoints leading to both Eulysta and Napier. And with the known foldpoints finally in the right place, the scientists used the model to ask where else in the system such interstellar portals might be found. The computer predicted additional foldpoints at four new locations and assigned probabilities to its guesses.

While waiting for Drake's task force to return from their explorations, Admiral Gower ordered the two most probable locations for new foldpoints investigated. The first mapping expedition was led by the Sandarian cruiser *Victory* to a point in space more than a billion kilometers from the Eulysta foldpoint. The second expedition was led by the Altan cruiser *Dagger*, which was assigned a foldpoint some two billion kilometers distant. The *Victory* expedition arrived first and combed its assigned search area diligently but found nothing. The *Dagger* expedition did the same and quickly detected the characteristic clumping of iso-gravity lines.

It had been *Dagger*'s report, along with *Arrow*'s delivery of the Sandarian astrogation data, that had caused Gower to order the Corlis expedition to return to the nebula.

"Honor party, *ten-hut*!"

The double rank of Altan Space Marines, resplendent in black and silver, their boots locked into the deck cleats underfoot to keep them from floating away in the zero gee of the hangar bay, snapped to attention at Phillip Walkirk's command. Before them, an interorbit transfer craft from His Majesty's Blastship *Royal Avenger* lay secured in the dock. The transfer vehicle's air lock opened, and a single figure floated into the bay.

"Honor party, present arms!"

Twelve rifles snapped into position as Admiral Gower maneuvered to the base of the disembarkation ladder where Richard Drake and Phillip Walkirk waited. Like the Marines, they had inserted the toes of their ship boots into deck cleats to free both hands. Drake and Walkirk saluted as the admiral reached them. Gower, one hand on the safety line, returned the salute.

"Good to have you back, Fleet Captain," the admiral said.

"Good to be back, sir."

Gower turned toward the prince. "I have just read the report of your action against the Ryall ore carrier, Your Highness. The king will be pleased when he hears of it."

"I had a good team with me, sir. In fact, the honor party consists entirely of veterans of that boarding."

The admiral turned around and gazed up and down the rows of rigid Marines.

"Gentlemen, you have my heartfelt gratitude, that of His Majesty, John-Phillip Walkirk, and of all the Sandarian people. Thank you for protecting our prince."

A dozen voices shouted, "You're welcome, sir!" in unison.

Gower turned to Drake. "Now, Captain, if you will lead me to your cabin, we can get on with the reason for my visit."

"Yes, sir. Follow me, please."

Drake led the admiral out into the main circumferential corridor. By the time they reached Drake's door, sufficient spin weight had been restored to allow the two men to skate down the corridor rather than pull themselves hand over hand.

"May I offer you refreshments, Admiral?" Drake asked as Gower made himself comfortable on the leather couch in Drake's cabin.

"Thank you, Captain. A glass of that marvelous brandy Mr. Barrett brought with him when he boarded *Avenger* would be welcome."

"Yes, sir," Drake replied. He slid back the wooden panel that hid a small but well-stocked liquor cabinet and a supply of low-gravity glasses. Drake poured two glasses of brandy and handed one to the admiral.

Gower took a sip, then slipped the base of the glass into a low-gravity holder on the table at the end of the couch. "I've just read your report of the Corlis operation, Captain. My compliments on a job well done."

"Thank you, sir."

"That astrogation data alone is worth a dozen blastships!"

"Have your experts made any progress in deciphering the raw computer data which *Arrow* delivered to you?" Drake asked.

Gower shook his head. "It's still much too early for results."

"At least we have Professor Alvarez's data."

"I only wish it weren't quite so distressing, Drake." It hadn't taken long for Gower to recognize the problems associated with fighting an enemy whose home territory was contained entirely in a close-coupled fold-space cluster. "My battle staff estimates the force multiplier effect of their internal lines of communication to be at least two, and possibly as high as three."

"Yes, sir. That was my conclusion as well."

"No wonder we've barely held them at bay all these years. God help us if they ever learn to penetrate the nebula. Which brings me to my next question. How sure are you that you got away from Eulysta clean?"

"Very sure, sir," Drake replied. "*Mace* guarded the second foldpoint virtually the whole time we were there. And even after Captain Quaid abandoned his station to rejoin the fleet, we kept a close watch on the Carratyl foldpoint until we jumped. Nothing entered or left the system while we had it under observation."

"What about Corlis?"

"We spent a lot of effort cleaning up every trace of human activity, sir. Hopefully, anything we missed was wiped away by the flood."

"Any chance that there were Ryall survivors you didn't know about? Any refugees hiding out in the woods?"

"The interrogators quizzed the prisoners quite extensively on that, sir. Everyone seems to be accounted for."

"Where are these prisoners now?"

"The survivors from the ore carrier and the manager of the Corlis mine are housed on Gamma Deck, sir. *Terra* has the other Corlis survivors."

"How are conditions in those cells?"

"Crowded, sir. I'm afraid we couldn't spare very much room for the holding pens."

"We have both the space and facilities for them aboard *Avenger*. I'll arrange to take them off your hands as soon as I get back to my ship."

"With your permission, sir, I'd like to keep the manager of the Corlis mine here on *Discovery*."

"Why, Captain?"

"Miss Lindquist is currently studying that particular prisoner, sir."

"What does she hope to learn from these studies, Drake?"

"She is trying to quantify the differences between the way the Ryall managerial and warrior castes react to humans."

"What makes her think there *are* any differences, Drake?"

"She doesn't know, Admiral. That's the reason for the study."

Admiral Gower pursed his lips, then nodded his agreement. "Very well. It's certainly God's own truth that we've lacked managers to study over the years. Tell her that I will expect weekly reports of her progress."

"Yes, sir."

Gower picked up his glass and took a sip of brandy with obvious relish. He carefully returned the glass to its holder, then turned to regard Drake with a fixed stare.

"I liked your work in the Eulysta system, Drake. You got in, obtained valuable information, covered your tracks, and got out without getting caught."

"I appreciate your confidence, Admiral."

"You've earned it. Now, how would you like to lead the expedition to explore the new foldpoint?"

"Will I be allowed to pick my own ships?"

"What's the matter? Didn't you like the fleet I provided to explore Eulysa?"

"It was more than adequate, sir. However, there are one or two changes I would have made."

"Very well. When can you be ready to leave?"

"Will seventy-two hours be soon enough?"

"That will be fine, Captain."

Bethany arranged for Varlan to be placed in a cabin of her own at the same time the other Ryall prisoners were transferred to the flagship. The cabin had been modified to reflect the living quarters that they had found on Corlis. It was also equipped with an entertainment screen and a copious supply of recordings. To further relax the Ryall and make her more susceptible to cajolery, the security arrangements were kept as discreet as possible. They included a video surveillance system, a door that opened only from the outside, and an armed Marine guard in the corridor outside.

"What do you think of your quarters?" Bethany asked the Ryall the day after the transfer.

Varlan ducked her long neck in an imitation of a human nod. "They are much more in keeping with my station. However, I confess that I do not understand why you have done this." The Ryall's words emanated from the portable translator that she wore on a chain around her neck.

"My purpose is the same as it was on Corlis," Bethany replied. "Just because your people and mine are competitors is no reason why we two have to be enemies."

Varlan considered Bethany's comment for a moment before replying. "Were you another Ryall, I would think this an attempt to suborn me into treason against my caste and clan."

"I don't ask you to betray your race, Varlan. I merely ask that you attempt to understand mine."

"To what purpose?"

"In the hope that we can find a mutually acceptable way of ending this war."

"I have noted this curious blind spot in your character before, Bethany of the Lindquists. Why are you unable to face the fact that we are competitors and must remain so? How can you hold to this delusion that all intelligent beings are spawn-mates when it is obviously not so? Is this an attitude common to your race or merely a personal idiosyncrasy?"

"I leave that for you to judge, Varlan, when you know us better."

"Very well," the Ryall replied. "I will study you at the same time you are studying me. It can do no harm, and it will make my imprisonment pass all the more quickly."

Richard Drake found himself a popular man following Admiral Gower's announcement that he would lead the expedition to explore the new foldpoint. Within two hours of the order going out, he'd spoken to the commanding officer of every destroyer and cruiser in the fleet. Drake had assured each petitioner that tactical considerations would be the sole determinant regarding which ships were chosen to make up the new task force. One particularly insistent officer was Bela

Marston, *Dagger*'s commander, whose ship was just back from its journey of exploration.

"You just *have* to tap *Dagger*, Richard," Marston had pleaded. "After all, we found the damn thing!"

Drake had nodded his head. "I grant you that you have a good claim, Bela, but first I need to see what sort of resources I'll be needing. If your ship fits into the plan, you're in. If not, then I can't use you."

"Damn it, Richard. My crew is still grousing that they didn't get in on the Eulysta expedition."

"As I said, *Captain*," Drake replied, emphasizing Marston's title in order to signal that he was treading far too close to the line between duty and friendship, "I will let you know."

Marston's face froze into an expressionless mask. "Yes, sir. Thank you for considering us. Have I your permission to sign off?"

Drake had sighed. "Don't go away mad. Damn it, I'll try to work you in if it makes any sense at all tactically."

"Thank you, sir!"

Drake had gone to work immediately planning a reconnaissance in force. As before, the initial entry would be made by two of the Sandarian destroyers, and for the same reason. Even if attacked immediately upon breakout, there was a good chance one or both would be able to return to the nebula to report. If, on the other hand, no one was waiting to ambush arriving starships, then one destroyer would stay to guard the foldpoint while the other returned to Antares to report.

Drake's first decision concerning force composition was a relatively easy one. Figuring that local naval superiority would be of more immediate use than a ground force, he decided to leave *Saskatoon* behind. If a ground target presented itself as it had at Corlis, then there would be plenty of time to call in the Marines once enemy space forces were defeated.

Drake selected his team after a long night spent in front of his computer console. The task force would be essentially the same as had explored the Eulysta system, with the single exception that *Dagger* would substitute for *Saskatoon*. It was with a sense of some satisfaction that Drake transmitted his selections to Admiral Gower:

> Request assignment of Cruisers *Discovery*, *Terra*,
> *Dagger*, Destroyers *Arrow*, *Mace*, *Scimitar*, and
> three cryogen tankers, your choice, to explore
> Foldpoint No. 3.
>
> Drake, Task Force Commander

It was with even greater satisfaction that he received the admiral's official reply an hour later:

> Assignments approved. Tankers *Phoenix*, *Tharsis*,
> and *Sandarian Soldier* are assigned to your force.
> Launch when ready.
>
> Gower, Fleet Admiral

Upon his arrival in the vicinity of the newly discovered foldpoint, Drake ordered each of his ships topped off from the cryogen tankers and then had the tankers pull back to a safe distance. He ordered the three battle cruisers and the destroyer *Mace* to draw up in defensive formation and ordered *Arrow* and *Scimitar* to make all preparations for foldspace transition.

Just as at Eulysta, he listened to the two destroyer captains make their final prejump checks prior to beginning their dual countdown; felt his own tension build with each passing second; and, finally, watched two glowing antiradiation fields disappear from *Discovery*'s viewscreen. Just as it had at Eulysta, time dragged on interminably while Drake waited for one of the destroyers to reappear and report.

"We have a breakout, Captain!" came the welcome cry from *Discovery*'s combat control center at the end of a tense half hour.

"What ship?"

"*Arrow*, sir."

"Get me Captain Rostock," Drake ordered the communicator on duty.

"Yes, sir."

It took another thirty seconds for Carter Rostock's

flushed features to appear on Drake's screen. Drake would have sworn it was longer.

"Report, Mr. Rostock," he ordered.

"All clear on the other side, Captain."

"Do you recognize the system?"

"Yes, sir. It's Goddard!"

"Are you sure about that?"

"Absolutely positive, sir."

Drake felt suddenly light-headed. Goddard was one of the first systems ever colonized by human beings. And beyond Goddard lay Sol!

CHAPTER 19

GODDARD—STAR:

BASIC DATA: F8 spectral class dwarf star.
Abs. Mag.: +4.5.

Position (Sol Rel.): 1627.1 RA,-2207.4 DEC, 114 L-Y.
Number of Foldpoints: 3
Foldspace Transition Sequences:
Primary: Sol, Goddard
Secondary: Antares, Goddard
Tertiary: Vega, Tsiolkovsky, Goddard

The system contains twelve planets, 82 moons, and a scattering of small asteroids. Planet IV, Goddard, and Planet V, Felicity, are Earth-type worlds with indigenous lifeforms. The planets, in order of their distance from the system primary, include...

HISTORY: First explored in 2130 by ships of the First Foldspace Survey, the system was named for Robert H. Goddard, a pioneer in the development of rockets. The fourth planet is habitable over much of its land surface, although the equatorial regions exceed 70 deg. C during summer. The fifth planet is also inhabited. Temperatures at the highest latitudes of Goddard V drop to the freezing point of carbon dioxide during the winter. (See separate entry for GODDARD —PLANET and FELICITY.) The colony on Goddard IV was established in 2135; Goddard V, 2148. Both colonies were established by the Community of Nations, which controlled the system until independence in 2208.

THE PEOPLE: The population of the Goddard system was 4,527,650,000 during the 2500 census. Because of the diversity of the original colonists, the principal languages spoken in the system are . . .

— Excerpted from *A Spacers Guide to Human Space, Ninety-seventh Edition*, Copyright 2510 by Hallan Publications, Ltd., Greater New York, Earth.

"Foldspace transition complete! All departments, report damage or injuries! Sensor technicians, begin full ambient sweep and report."

Richard Drake listened to the postjump announcement echo throughout the bridge, then punched for Argos Cristobal, *Discovery*'s astrogator.

"Put Goddard up on the screen, Mr. Cristobal."

"Aye aye, sir."

The main viewscreen cleared to display a black starfield with a single yellow-white point of light at the center. Drake felt a sudden touch of homesickness at the sight. Goddard could have been Valeria's twin. He quickly scanned the screen, looking for dots of light that showed the not-quite-dimensionless shapes that would betray the presence of planetary bodies. If there were such, he didn't notice them.

"Any radio traffic, Mr. Slater?"

"Yes, sir," the communicator reported. "I've got both inhabited worlds spotted, as well as a large number of discreet points scattered across deep space. The place is crawling with ships!"

"Human, I hope."

"Yes, sir."

"Are your recorders running?"

"They are, Captain."

"Mr. Cristobal, show us Antares!" Drake ordered. The request had become a tradition aboard *Discovery*. More than anything else, Antares' transformations from baleful red-orange sun, to blazing nova, to distant ring nebula, to endless red fog helped drive home the point that each time *Discovery* underwent a foldspace transition, it crossed an unthinkably broad gulf of interstellar space.

In the center of the screen, Antares was once again the red-orange beacon that had graced the Altan sky for centuries. The Goddard system was situated outside the expanding nova shock wave and therefore would be spared the electric blue-white of Antares dawnlight for another century.

"Switch over to Sol, astrogator."

"Yes, sir."

This time the viewscreen cleared to show a dim yellow star. It would have been difficult to spot at all except that it was marked by a set of electronic cross hairs.

"Is that it?" Bethany asked from her usual place beside Drake.

"That's it," he answered.

"It isn't very impressive."

"It isn't an intrinsically impressive star. At this distance Sol is just barely on the edge of visibility for naked-eye viewing. At home, you need a good-size telescope and a better knowledge of astronomy than most people possess."

Bethany nodded. "My uncle once took me up into the Colgate range to try and show it to me when I was a little girl. He spent the night fiddling with a borrowed telescope and was never really sure which star was Sol."

After a long minute spent looking at the pale light on the screen, Drake keyed for his executive officer in *Discovery*'s combat control center. "What's the status on the rest of the fleet, Mr. Marchant?"

"Everyone seems to have arrived safely, Captain. *Dagger* is ten thousand kilometers off our beam, *Terra* is five thousand astern. The destroyers are scattered at similar distances around us."

"Have the rest of the fleet close on us. Then put your intercepts up on the screen."

"Yes, sir."

Almost immediately a schematic diagram of the Goddard system appeared on the screen. On it were symbols denoting where sources of artificial electromagnetic radiation had been detected. The two brightest radio stars were the system's two inhabited planets. The inner world, Goddard, rode the inner edge of the temperate zone, while the outer world, Felicity, did the same in the region where water turns to ice. A sprinkling of smaller specks marked the apparent positions of hundreds of ships in transit across the system. Most appeared clustered in a broad band between the points where prenova astrogation charts placed the system's other two foldpoints. A second stream of ships were obviously en route between Planets IV and V.

Half an hour later, the number of contacts identified as ships or orbital installations had risen to more than a thousand. In addition, *Discovery*'s sensor operators had mapped the surfaces of the two inhabited worlds from afar and discovered them to be covered with electrical grids. The scientists were attempting to estimate the system's industrial potential when their instruments were overwhelmed by a high-power pulse from the inner system.

"We were just scanned by some sort of high-energy search radar!" the communicator reported.

"Didn't take them long to spot us, did it?" Rorqual Marchant asked over the intercom.

Drake shrugged. "Not surprising when you consider how much energy our antirad field dumps on breakout."

"Shall we tell them who we are?" the executive officer asked.

"Not quite yet," Drake replied. "Let's see how they react toward us first."

An hour later, sensor operators began reporting several ships headed in their direction.

"How many, Mr. Marchant?"

"I make it an even dozen, Captain," Marchant replied, watching his readouts. "No, another just lit off and two more appear to be powering up. Fifteen, sir. The computer is tentatively identifying three of them as capital ships."

"They're sending the whole damn fleet out after us!"

"Can you blame them, Captain?"

"I don't *blame* them, Rorq. I just hope we can convince them of our identity before they pull within firing range."

Gregory Oldfield, first secretary to the terrestrial embassy on Goddard, roused slowly from his slumber as he became ever more aware of the raucous noise emanating from his nightstand. Rolling over, he groped for the communicator, intent on silencing its emergency tone before it woke the young woman beside him. His hand contacted the rounded screen housing, then groped its way through the dark to the handset. Maneuvering the receiver to his ear, he moaned, "Go ahead."

"Is that you, Mr. Oldfield?" Byron Caldwell III, the night duty officer at the embassy, asked. "Why can't I see you?"

"Because I have the visual pickup turned off," Oldfield muttered as he opened one eye to gaze at the assistant third secretary's peach fuzz cheeks silhouetted in the soft fluorescence of the screen. "What is it that you want, Caldwell?"

"The old man says for you to get your posterior down here right away, Mr. Oldfield!"

Suddenly, Oldfield was wide awake. He lifted his head from the pillow and craned his neck to glance at the chronometer on the nightstand. The green digits displayed 0316. "It's three o'clock in the morning, Caldwell. The ambassador isn't at the embassy, is he?"

The face on the screen nodded. "Yes, sir, he is. He rolled in all excited about twenty minutes ago. He says that Admiral Ryerson got him out of bed."

"Ryerson? When did he get back?"

"Get back from where, sir?"

"Last I heard, he was out with the fleet."

"Uh, yes, sir. He is. He called the ambassador from orbit. Seems we've been getting reports of a number of unidentified ships coming out of the nebula."

Oldfield sat straight up in bed despite the pounding headache left over from the previous evening's partying. "Are you sure?"

"No, sir," the newly hatched assistant third undersecretary said. "I'm not sure of anything. That's why we need you here."

"I'm on my way!"

Oldfield commanded the bedroom lights to full radiance. As he did so, the beautiful young woman on the other side of the bed stirred, covering her eyes for a moment against the sudden light.

"What is it, Greggy?"

"Something's come up at the embassy. I have to go down there and straighten it out. Go back to sleep. If I'm not back by morning, make yourself breakfast and call a cab."

"Do you *have* to go?"

"Duty calls, love." He leaned forward to kiss her on the forehead. She smiled, turned over, and fell back to sleep. Five minutes later, Greg Oldfield commanded the illumination off as he left the bedroom on his way to the front door. It wasn't until he had reached the underground garage where he parked his sportster that he realized that he couldn't remember his companion's name.

The embassy was ablaze with lights when Oldfield pulled into his parking space under the building. He grabbed his briefcase from the back seat and hurried to the lift that would take him to the highest level in the building. He found Ambassador Elliot at his desk reading communications.

"What's up, sir?" He asked as he plopped down in the big easy chair the ambassador kept for important visitors. Ambassador Elliot looked up, causing light from the desk lamp to reflect off his old-style glasses.

"Where have you been?"

"I was at home in bed, sir. I got here as soon as I could. What's up?"

Elliot handed him the printout he'd been reading. Oldfield started to skim it, blinked, then went back to read it slowly line by line. The further he read, the more incredulous he became.

```
****MOST SECRET****MOST SECRET****
         ****MOST SECRET****
```

DATE: 17 OCTOBER 2639 (U.C.)
16:22:48.6 (U.T.)

FROM: RYERSON, R. T.
FLEET ADMIRAL
TSNS *TEDDY ROOSEVELT*

TO: (1) ALL SHIPS AND STATIONS, GRAND FLEET, GODDARD

(2) AMBASSADOR, TERRESTRIAL EMBASSY, GODDARD

(3) RELAY VIA FAST COURIER TO HOME FLEET, SOLSYS

SUBJECT: CONTACT IN GODDARD/ ANTARES FOLDPOINT

1. AT 15:12:15 HOURS STANDARD, 17 OCTOBER 2639, TWO OBJECTS WERE DETECTED MATERIALIZING IN GODDARD—ANTARES FOLDPOINT. IMMEDIATELY FOLLOWING BREAKOUT, OBJECTS WERE OBSERVED TO GLOW WITH MULTI-SPECTRAL LIGHT. THIS GLOW FADED

OVER A PERIOD OF FIFTEEN SECONDS UNTIL THE OBJECTS WERE NO LONGER VISIBLE.

2. AT 15:50:33 HOURS STANDARD, 17 OCTOBER 2639, AN ADDITIONAL FIVE OBJECTS WERE DETECTED MATERIALIZING IN GODDARD—ANTARES FOLDPOINT. SHORT-LIVED LUMINESCENCE OBSERVED.

3. DIFFERENCES IN POSITION OF OBJECTS IS TYPICAL OF STANDARD BREAKOUT SCATTER FOR VESSELS ARRIVING IN A FOLDPOINT.

4. OBJECTS ARE BELIEVED TO BE UNIDENTIFIED FLEET OF STARSHIPS FROM INSIDE ANTARES SUPERNOVA REMNANT.

5. ALL AVAILABLE COMBATANTS HAVE BEEN ORDERED TO THE FOLDPOINT TO DEFEND AND INVESTIGATE.

R. T. RYERSON
FLEET ADMIRAL, COMMANDING
SQUADRON 1712
TERRESTRIAL SPACE NAVY

****MOST SECRET****MOST SECRET****
****MOST SECRET****

When he had finished reading, Greg Oldfield glanced up. "Is this for real?"

The ambassador nodded. "Confirmed by Admiral Ryerson to me personally not more than one hour ago."

"Are they Ryall?"

"That is the suspicion. I don't know how they managed it, but the centaurs have somehow succeeded in penetrating the supernova remnant. There's going to be hell to pay over this." Elliot opened his mouth to say something else but was interrupted by the quiet buzzing of his desk communicator. He reached over, lifted the receiver, and listened intently. Oldfield couldn't hear the words, but from the rapid-fire delivery of whoever was on the other end, he concluded that something was up. The ambassador listened for long seconds in silence, then said, "Thank you," and hung up.

"What's the matter?" Greg Oldfield asked, noting his boss's dazed look.

"That was communications. Admiral Ryerson just sent out another general broadcast. Seems he's made contact with the mystery ships."

"And?" the first secretary asked.

"They claim to be colonists from the Valeria and Hellsgate systems!"

Oldfield frowned. "I've heard of Hellsgate, of course. That was the system cut off when the Ryall grabbed Aezer some fifteen, no, seventeen, years ago. But what is this Valeria?"

"Good question." The ambassador keyed the workscreen on his desk and soon had lines of amber characters scrolling up its face at fast reading speed. He scanned the information. "Says here that the Valeria system was one of the smaller colonies in the Antares Cluster. All contact between Valeria and the rest of human space was lost the moment Antares exploded."

"Failed foldpoint?" Oldfield asked.

"Apparently." The ambassador scowled as he continued to read. A minute later, he cleared the screen and leaned back in his chair. "Well, this puts a different light on things, doesn't it?"

"How so?" Oldfield asked.

"Didn't you hear? They aren't centaurs. That makes it a diplomatic problem rather than a military one. And since we're the diplomats on the scene, we'll have to handle it."

"Handle it how?"

Elliot's face split into the broad grin that usually meant that someone was about to be assigned to latrine duty. "I suppose one of us will have to get out there to take charge of the negotiations."

"What negotiations?"

"You surprise me, Oldfield. You've been a career diplomat long enough to know that there are *always* negotiations."

"I don't suppose you are volunteering, Mr. Ambassador?"

"I'd love to, Mr. First Secretary. However, I can't break away just now. Goddard Founders' Day coming up, you know. You'll have to go in my place."

Oldfield groaned. "Somehow I thought that was what you were getting at."

A week after their arrival in the Goddard system, Richard Drake stood in the small control room that looked out over *Discovery*'s main hangar bay and watched as a small interorbit ferry floated through the open hangar doors. The ferry bore the markings of the Terrestrial Space Navy's Grand Fleet and had the name of its parent ship, TSNS *Teddy Roosevelt*, stenciled across its prow. As quickly as the craft cleared the doors, the petty officer in charge of docking operations ordered the bay sealed and pressurized. A minute later the subdued roar of escaping air reverberated through the armor-glass window that separated the control room from the bay, and a storm of expansion fog hid the newly arrived shuttle in its swirling embrace.

The petty officer watched his gauges, then nodded to Drake. "Safe to go in now, sir."

"Thanks, Chief. That was a good, crisp approach and docking. My compliments."

"Thank you, sir."

Drake pulled himself hand over hand to the air lock that provided access to the bay. He entered the bay and used a guide rope to traverse the oversize compartment to where the rest of the welcoming party had already taken their places. Bethany Lindquist, Phillip Walkirk, and six Marines had anchored themselves to the meshwork deck underfoot. Drake joined them.

"Isn't it exciting, Richard? We finally get to meet people from Earth!" Bethany said.

"What about those two lieutenants who looked us over yesterday?"

"They don't count since you wouldn't let me ask them any questions."

Drake shrugged. "They had other work to do."

The fleet that had put out to meet them had arrived twenty hours earlier. After an initial conference held in deep space aboard landing boats, the terrestrial admiral had ordered two of his junior lieutenants to inspect the Helldiver Fleet to ensure they were who they said. The two had poked through *Discovery*'s various spaces and had then gone on to inspect the other five ships of the fleet. The inspection had taken eight hours, and in the end, the two terrestrial officers had pronounced themselves satisfied.

Drake's attention was caught by the sudden movement of the outer door of the ferry's air lock. Phillip Walkirk called his Marines to attention as a tall man in a black and gold uniform stepped out onto the landing stage. Overhead, "Ad Astra," the unofficial anthem of human space, began to play. The admiral stopped and held himself in place via a guide rail until the anthem finished, then used the same rail to pull himself toward the waiting colonists. Several other terrestrials followed him out of the air lock. The second man in line wore the formal dress of a diplomat, while those who followed him were garbed in the uniform of the Terrestrial Space Navy. The admiral stopped when he reached Drake.

"Captain Drake? I am Fleet Admiral Ryerson."

"Good to meet you, Admiral," Drake replied as he saluted.

Ryerson returned the salute before turning to the man in the diplomatic sash. "May I present First Secretary Gregory Oldfield from the embassy on Goddard?"

"Welcome aboard, Mr. Oldfield," Drake said, shaking the diplomat's hand. He introduced Phillip Walkirk and Bethany Lindquist.

The two terrestrials introduced the officers with them, all of whom were members of Ryerson's staff. Following the introductions, the admiral gazed around, his eyes taking in the details of *Discovery*'s hangar bay. "This is an old Dragon-class heavy battle cruiser, isn't it?"

"Yes, sir. We inherited three of them from the Grand Fleet when the nova destroyed our foldpoint."

"Looks like you've taken good care of her."

"We've done our best, Admiral."

"I would say that your best is damned good, Captain, from the look of this hangar bay."

Drake gestured to the air lock leading back into the habitat portion of the ship. "Now then, if you gentlemen would follow me, we'll make you as comfortable as we can and try to restore some spin to the ship."

Drake led the party toward the wardroom. Their progress was slowed as the terrestrial officers asked questions concerning the ship and its history. Like the admiral, most remarked on their surprise at how good a condition the 150-year-old cruiser was in. By the time they reached their destination, full spin gravity had nearly been restored to the ship.

Once inside the wardroom, Drake introduced the terrestrials to Rorqual Marchant, Professors Alvarez and St. Cyr, and six other senior scientists. As soon as the introductions were concluded, everyone took a place around the wardroom table. First Secretary Oldfield began the discussions.

"I can't help but notice that there are no political people here, Captain Drake," he commented. "Why is that?"

"The official representatives of both the Altan and Sandarian governments are with our flagship, which is still inside the nebula, Mr. Oldfield. I'm afraid that what you see here is merely a scouting party."

"Some scouting party," Ryerson, sitting beside Oldfield, said. "Three cruisers and three destroyers! What did you expect to meet on this side of the foldpoint?"

"We didn't know what to expect, Admiral. That is why we came in force."

"Excuse me, Admiral," Bethany said. "Has Earth been notified of our presence yet?"

Ryerson nodded. "Indeed, young lady. A fast courier was dispatched as quickly as he learned your identity."

"And when can we expect a response?"

"Any time now," Ryerson said before turning his attention to Drake. "Captain, this is your meeting, and you can run it any way you wish. However, it would be useful if you would explain how it is that you arrived in this system in the manner you did. News of ships coming out of the supernova remnant created quite a stir!"

"I can imagine, Admiral," Drake replied with a laugh. "We had a similar experience in my home system a few years ago." Drake went on to quickly sketch the history of the Altan colony from the time of the Antares Supernova, through the Long Isolation, to the moment when *Conqueror* had suddenly appeared in their sky.

"What ship did you say that was?" Ryerson asked.

"TSNS *Conqueror*, Admiral."

The terrestrials exchanged knowing looks, and there were several nods around the table. Ryerson was one of those who nodded. "*Conqueror* was lost three years ago at the Second Battle of Klamath, Captain. I know. I was there."

"We have often speculated as to what happened, Admiral," Bethany said. "If you wouldn't mind telling us..."

"Not at all, Miss Lindquist. The plan was to drive the Ryall from the Klamath system, which you may or may not know is one of three where human and Ryall space come together. We assembled more than a hundred ships for the operation. Fleet Admiral Carnaby was in overall command. *Conqueror* was his flagship. My own *Teddy Roosevelt* led one of the subfleets assigned to the operation.

"The battle began very well for our side. We caught a small Ryall fleet just outside the orbit of Klamath III and engaged it. They were fewer than twenty ships while we were more than a hundred, so they had no choice but to fall back toward the planet in the hope of using it for cover. Naturally, we pressed the attack. The battle quickly found itself just beyond the atmosphere line of Klamath III and, in some cases, had dipped down into the planet's stratosphere.

"It was then that we learned we had fallen into a Ryall trap. You see, the whole of the Ryall fleet was at Klamath III. Except for the twenty ships that had baited us in, they were hovering low on the far side of the planet, out of sight of our sensors. One moment we were on the verge of wiping out an outnumbered enemy, and the next the sky was full of centaur warships. They came boiling around the planet's limb and hit us in the flank.

"To his credit, Admiral Carnaby recognized what was happening instantly and ordered everyone to disengage before the flankers could get behind us. While the rest of us boosted at eight gravities to get clear, Carnaby ordered *Conqueror* to attack the Ryall fleet head on. It was a magnificent gesture, but of course, he didn't have a chance against the combined strength of eighty Ryall ships of the line. *Conqueror* was savaged as the Ryall got hit after hit on her. Yet she still kept firing until the rest of us had put enough delta V between ourselves and the Ryall. Only then did Admiral Carnaby give the order to abandon ship.

"I'm afraid we aren't sure what happened after that since Carnaby wasn't one of those we picked up after the battle. Still, we surmise that he ordered the blastship's autopilot to seek the nearest foldpoint as a diversion to allow his lifeboats to escape. We tracked *Conqueror* until she reached the Klamath–Antares foldpoint and jumped. We have always assumed that she was vaporized the instant she entered the supernova." Ryerson paused to sweep his gaze across the assembled colonists. "Obviously, we assumed wrong."

"You weren't alone in that, Admiral," Drake replied. "We too found it difficult to believe any ship could penetrate the nebula and survive. We found it so difficult, in fact, that we didn't even consider the possibility until we'd exhausted all other possibilities."

"How *do* your ships manage to survive inside the nebula, Captain?" one of Ryerson's staff officers asked.

"Antiradiation shielding," Drake replied.

"Would the design of this shielding be for sale?" Ryerson asked.

"We're ready to give you the design, Admiral," Drake replied.

"In return for what?" First Secretary Oldfield asked.

"Your assistance in dislodging the Ryall from the Aezer system," Phillip Walkirk replied from where he sat at the far end of the table.

"I hope you understand, Your Highness, that you will have to take that matter up with Government Central on Earth. We poor hinterland diplomats lack the power to commit the Grand Fleet to battle, I'm afraid."

"When can we go through to Earth, Mr. Oldfield?" Bethany asked.

"Very soon, Miss Lindquist. In fact, Admiral Ryerson will assign suitable escort just as soon as you choose the vessel which you want to make the trip."

"I don't understand," Drake said. "The entire Helldiver Fleet will be making the trip."

Oldfield looked surprised, then smiled sheepishly. "Silly of me, Captain. You are strangers here, so, of course, you aren't familiar with the regulations."

"What regulations?"

"Why, those that govern the entry of warships into the Solar system. With modern warships capable of so much destruction, we are quite sensitive about allowing them close to the home world. Surely you can understand our caution. You will be allowed one ship for the trip to Earth, and that ship will have to be escorted by at least one of our own."

"And the rest of the Helldiver Fleet?"

"They will, of course, have to remain here in the Goddard system until you return."

CHAPTER 20

"What do you mean they won't allow *Royal Avenger* to travel to Earth?" Admiral Gower asked, his angry features glowering out of Drake's screen. It had been two weeks since the first meeting aboard *Discovery* between the colonists and representatives of the central government and barely an hour since *Royal Avenger* had materialized in the Goddard–Antares foldpoint.

"They won't allow it, sir," Drake replied. "They claim they have no way of knowing the capabilities of a foreign-built blastship. Therefore, they cannot allow *Avenger* anywhere near Earth."

There followed a string of oaths. "And so they chose *Discovery*?"

"Yes, sir. They know the type well and doubt we could endanger the planet before the planetary defense centers destroyed us. I was given the choice of *Discovery* or *Dagger* for our embassy ship. I chose *Discovery*."

"And how do you propose squeezing our entire embassy into a single battle cruiser?"

"I don't, Admiral. The regulations don't apply to unarmed transports. As soon as I discovered that, I offered to disable *City of Alexandria*'s fire-control system and dismount her antimatter projectors. Admiral Ryerson agreed to my proposal."

"I'm surprised he didn't insist on the liner going alone."

"He suggested it, sir. I told him that we weren't about to go into a strange system *completely* helpless."

"And what did he say to that?"

"He said that he understood."

There was a long pause as Admiral Gower digested what Drake had told him. At the end of it, his brows were knit by equal mixtures of anger and worry. "Is this beam secure, Captain?"

Drake punched up the readout that told him the status of the communications channel between *Discovery* and *Royal Avenger*. The glowing numbers declared the beam to be tightly focused and highly scrambled. "Secure, sir."

"How do these people strike you?"

"Beg your pardon, sir?"

"Are they friendly?"

"They're friendly, Admiral, although a bit distant."

"In what way?"

"We tell them our troubles, they listen politely, but make no commitments. It happened the first time when we offered to trade the antiradiation field for their help in driving the Ryall out of Aezer. They told us we would have to take it up with the home office. It has happened two or three times since. I think Oldfield is under orders not to make any promises that might prove bothersome later. Admiral Ryerson, on the other hand, appears to want the antirad field badly."

"Don't put too much faith in that, Captain," Gower replied. "Now that they know the field exists, they should have no trouble developing it for themselves. No, if we require bargaining leverage, we'll need something stronger."

"What else have we got, sir?"

"Quite a lot—maybe. Have you or anyone else told them about Eulysta and what happened there?"

"No, sir."

"You're sure?"

"Quite sure, Admiral. We haven't said so directly, but we've left them with the impression that we came straight from Napier."

"Excellent! Pass the word. The subject of Eulysta is classified, and I'll space the first man who even hints at the existence of the Ryall astrogation data." He paused. "What's the matter, Captain? You look like you just bit into something sour."

Drake frowned. "Uh, we may have a problem there, sir."

"Problem, Drake?"

"Miss Lindquist, sir. She may not agree to keep quiet."

"Why should we need her agreement?"

"She *is* the representative of the terrestrial ambassador to Alta, Admiral."

"I'd forgotten that," Gower said. "Any chance of you convincing her to keep quiet?"

"I'll try, of course."

"Perhaps I should talk to her, Captain. You may be a bit too close to the problem."

"That won't be necessary, sir. I'll handle it."

"I think not, Captain. Please ask Miss Lindquist to report here aboard *Royal Avenger* tomorrow. I need to ask her advice on several matters pertaining to Earth anyway, and we'll use the opportunity to discuss this other matter."

"Yes, sir. I'll deliver your message immediately."

Bethany Lindquist had been aboard the flagship only once previously. On that occasion she had been impressed by the oversize compartments and the seemingly endless corridors. Nor was the flagship's size the only difference between it and the Altan cruisers she was used to. Whenever she encountered crewmen aboard *Discovery*, they would invariably acknowledge her presence with a smile or a quick greeting. Not so aboard *Royal Avenger*. The Sandarian male and female crew members she encountered were always in a hurry. Bethany found their studied humorlessness disconcerting.

"We're here, milady," her guide, a fuzzy-cheeked ensign, said in a lilting Sandarian accent.

"Where is 'here,' Ensign?"

"My Lord Admiral's cabin, milady." The ensign tapped a code into a bulkhead-mounted keypad. A moment passed before the pressure door slid back into its recess. Bethany stepped over the raised coaming, and the door closed silently behind her.

Admiral Gower was seated behind a massive desk, his finger still on the door control. He rose and moved to where Bethany stood. "Good morning, Miss Lindquist. How was the flight?"

"Fine," Bethany replied. "It wasn't really necessary for you to send a special shuttle. I could have waited for the regularly scheduled run."

"Nonsense. If I must interrupt someone's busy schedule, the least I can do is provide proper transportation. Care for a drink?"

"Yes, thank you."

"How about Sandarian vodka?"

"I'm afraid I'm not familiar with it, Admiral."

Gower's eyebrows went up in a look of surprise. "Really? Surely we introduced you to our planetary drink while you were on Sandar."

"Not that I remember."

"Well, then you have to try it," he said as he moved to a small bar clamped to one of the bulkheads.

While the admiral poured drinks, Bethany let her gaze sweep her surroundings. The first thing she noticed was the life-size portrait of John-Phillip Walkirk VI hanging behind Gower's desk. The monarch was clad in the uniform of admiral-general of the Sandarian armed services and seemed to be looking directly at her. The cabin was otherwise devoid of decoration save for a large Sandarian flag, tattered and singed around the edges, that hung inside a glass case on the bulkhead opposite the king's portrait. Gower noted Bethany's interest as he returned with her drink.

"That flag came from my father's destroyer. His ship was holed during a fight with the Ryall. One of the survivors risked his life to salvage that flag and present it to my mother."

"How old were you at the time?"

"Sixteen standard years. It was my fourth year at the naval academy."

"Do all Sandarian children begin their military training so young?"

Gower nodded. "Those who show an aptitude for it."

"What a terrible shame it is to have to draft twelve-year-olds into the Navy!"

Gower shrugged. "It has been our way for so long that it seems natural to us." There followed an awkward silence in which Gower sipped from his glass. Bethany did the same and then grimaced slightly as the alcohol burned its way across her tongue and down her throat.

The admiral noticed her discomfort. "Shall I get you something else?"

Bethany fanned her lips. "I'll be fine. I just didn't expect it to be this strong."

"We come from a cold world, Miss Lindquist. This," he said, gesturing with his glass, "is a drink for cold worlds. It warms the blood and makes one forget the bite of the wind."

Carefully, Bethany took another sip. The burning seemed less this time, as though her mouth had been injected with a local anesthetic.

"I understand that you are a historian and an expert on Earth history."

Bethany nodded. "I'm a comparative historian, Admiral."

"What is that?"

"We study history looking for situations which are analogous to some current problem. We then study how our ancestors handled, or failed to handle, the similar situation and use that knowledge to advise the Altan government."

"And have you studied the Human/Ryall War? Is there any period in Earth history that is similar?"

"If you mean has there ever been a war in which our enemies were intelligent aliens, obviously not! However, if you consider the centaurs' rigid attitude regarding our right to exist, you can find close analogs in any number of religious wars that have been fought down through history. 'Christ and No Quarter!' would not be a difficult concept for the Ryall."

"And how were these religious wars resolved?"

Bethany shrugged. "Mostly, they weren't! Most didn't end until one or both sides had fought to exhaustion."

"Is that to be our fate as well?"

"I hope not. That is one of the reasons why I'm studying Varlan."

"Ah, yes, the captured Ryall manager. How goes the study?"

"It's too early to tell, Admiral. I've tried to convince her that our two species have a great deal in common and, therefore, that it's stupid for us to fight. Sometimes she seems receptive, other times not."

"So you have said in your reports. How long before you become convinced that your task is hopeless?"

"When I've tried everything I can think of, I suppose."

Gower laughed. "A good answer, and one which convinces me that I was correct in asking you here."

"I don't understand, Admiral."

"You are, of course, aware that *Royal Avenger* will not be allowed to make the journey to Earth."

Bethany nodded. "Terrestrial regulations forbid it."

"Unfortunately, true. I will therefore be transferring my flag to *Discovery*."

"You're relieving Richard of his command?"

"Not at all. He commands the cruiser, I command the expedition. The only difference is in the vessel from which that command is exercised. However, transferring my flag to *Discovery* presents me with a problem. As you are undoubtedly aware, my staff is largely drawn from the ranks of Royal Avenger's line officers. Were I to take them with me, I would leave this ship unable to defend itself. That, of course, is unthinkable. Therefore, I've decided to limit the number of *Avenger*'s personnel who will accompany me.

"Among those I will be leaving behind are two officers extremely knowledgeable of Earth history, officers whose expertise I will need during the coming negotiations with the Interstellar Council. It has occurred to me that you could replace that expertise."

"Are you offering me a job, Admiral Gower?"

"I am."

Bethany hesitated. "I'm very flattered, but I'm afraid what you ask is impossible."

"Why impossible, Miss Lindquist?"

"I took an oath to look after the best interests of Earth. I can hardly do that and advise you, too."

Gower regarded her with narrowed eyes for a moment, then sighed. "If there is one thing an officer of the king understands, Miss Lindquist, it is the importance of abiding by one's oaths. I had hoped you would not find your duty to Earth in conflict with your duty to this expedition. However, I won't attempt to dissuade you."

"Thank you for that, sir. Is that the reason you asked me here today?"

"That and one other matter," Gower replied. He reached forward, plucked a computer printout from his desk, and held it out to her. "I issued Fleet Order 703 this morning. I would like you to read and sign it before you leave."

FLEET ORDER:—703
DATE:—8 NOVEMBER 2639

TO:—ALL PERSONNEL
CLASSIFICATION:—*MOST SECRET*

FROM: GOWER, S.F.
      COMMANDING ADMIRAL

SUBJECT: EULYSTA CAMPAIGN

1. NO MEMBER OF THIS EXPEDITION SHALL DIVULGE INFORMATION TO NONEXPEDITION MEMBERS CONCERNING EULYSTA, CORLIS, OR THE EVENTS WHICH TRANSPIRED THERE.

2. ANY VIOLATION OF THIS ORDER WILL BE

REGARDED AS HIGH TREASON AND WILL
BE PUNISHED ACCORDINGLY.

(SIGNED)
S.F. GOWER
ADMIRAL
SANDARIAN SPACE NAVY

"What is this?" Bethany asked after reading the order.

"Just what is appears to be, Miss Lindquist. A classification order regarding the Eulysta campaign. It is specifically aimed at ensuring that the terrestrials do not find out about the astrogation data we obtained there."

"But surely such data must be old news to our hosts, Admiral. Why classify it?"

"Because, Miss Lindquist, I believe the terrestrials are still ignorant of the disposition of stars within the hegemony. If I am correct in that belief, then you are wrong, and that data represents our most valuable commodity. The central government may be willing to pay handsomely for what we have in our data banks. In any event, we hope to use whatever leverage the Ryall astrogation data gives us to obtain assistance in routing the Ryall from Aezer."

"If what you suspect is true, Admiral, that is all the more reason why I can't obey this order. It's my duty to get the information to the Interstellar Council as quickly as possible."

Gower nodded. "Captain Drake thought that might be your attitude."

"Richard knew you were going to ask me to sign this?" Bethany asked as she waved the printout at Gower.

"He was aware that I was going to speak to you of it."

"Why that—"

"Please, Miss Lindquist," Gower continued, cutting off the tirade before it had a chance to get started. "It isn't as though we were asking that your lips be sealed forever. Only long enough for us to be given the chance to exploit this knowledge which we bought at the cost of a number of lives."

"I'm sorry, Admiral Gower, but I am pledged to Earth's service regardless of my personal feelings in that matter. I will not sign this order."

Gower leaned back in his seat and regarded her through steepled fingers. When finally he spoke, it was more in sorrow than anger. "In that case, Miss Lindquist, I cannot allow you to leave this ship. You will stay here—in the brig, if necessary—until after *Discovery* and *City of Alexandria* have left for the Goddard–Sol foldpoint."

"You wouldn't dare lock me up!"

Gower's icy calm contrasted sharply with Bethany's fury. "I *would* dare. I have my own duty to perform, and I will perform it even if I must face court-martial when I return home."

"Richard will never stand for this. My uncle has a treaty with the Altan Parliament! Besides, he gave me his word that I wouldn't be muzzled."

"I do not represent the Altan Parliament, Miss Lindquist. Nor do I think Captain Drake will fight me on this. He also has his duty, which at the moment requires that he obey my orders. Should he choose not to, he will be proclaimed a mutineer. Hardly seems worth it considering our argument merely concerns the timing of our revelation to the terrestrials."

"You're saying that you *will* tell them?" Bethany asked.

"For what it is worth, I give you my word. When we've gotten what we came to get, or when it becomes clear that is not possible, I will hand them the astrogation data personally."

Bethany glowered at him for long seconds before snapping. "What is it you want me to agree to?"

"Merely that you will not divulge our secret without permission from either myself or Captain Drake. Do you agree?"

"I agree under protest. However, I plan to lodge a formal protest with Parliament when we return home."

"I understand completely," Gower said, nodding. He

extracted a pen from its zero-gravity holder on top of his desk and handed it to Bethany. "Please sign in the space provided."

Discovery's main viewscreen showed a string of three golden ship symbols and the hazy red ellipsoid that marked the position of the Goddard–Sol foldpoint. The symbols were strung out in line astern formation, with small glowing legends beside each denoting velocity and acceleration vectors as well as the time of arrival at the foldpoint boundary. Other symbols arrayed around the foldpoint displayed the positions of the two dozen orbital fortresses that guarded the gateway to Earth.

"Are those necessary?" Drake asked from his command chair, gesturing to the violet fortress symbols.

"We hope not," Gregory Oldfield said from the observer's seat beside Drake. Normally Bethany would have been seated there, but she hadn't spoken to Drake since her return from *Royal Avenger* more than a week earlier. After hearing Admiral Gower's report of the meeting, he wasn't surprised.

Drake watched the first of the golden markers cross over the boundary of the foldpoint. As it did so, the ship symbol began to blink rapidly.

"Communicator, put through a call to Admiral Ryerson aboard *Teddy Roosevelt*, please."

"Aye aye, sir."

An auxiliary screen cleared to show Ryerson's features. "How do you want to handle this, Admiral?"

"Just the way we planned it, Captain. We'll go through first to alert the defenses on the other side. Give us five minutes, then follow in *Discovery*. Five minutes after that, *City of Alexandria* will come through. Make sure that you begin your identity and password broadcast before you jump. Remember, that password is the only thing protecting you from the automatic defense mechanisms."

"Identity and password. Will do, sir."

As soon as Ryerson broke the connection, Drake turned to his communications officer. "Status check. All departments, Mr. Haydn."

"Yes, sir."

The roll call of department heads began almost immediately. "Environmental Control, ready to jump... Engineering, ready to jump... Combat Control, ready to jump... Astrogation, ready to jump... Fleet commander, ready to jump..." That last was from Admiral Gower, who had chosen to observe the jump from the combat control center—just in case. After half a minute the roll call reached the bridge and moved smoothly from Communication to Astrogation to commanding officer. He finished the roll with the call: "Captain, ready to jump!"

"The ship is buttoned up and ready to jump, Captain!" his executive officer reported.

"Very well, Mr. Marchant."

"Captain, sensors! *Teddy Roosevelt*'s jumpfield is building now."

"Switch main viewscreen to outside view, Mr. Haydn."

"Outside view, Captain."

The schematic diagram on the screen faded away, to be replaced by a black starfield. As Drake watched, the stars moved out radially from the center of the screen as the magnification increased. A tiny foreshortened cylinder appeared in the center of the view and quickly grew until it nearly filled the screen. Drake watched as the telltale waviness that marked a fully charged jumpfield obscured the Earth fleet blastship. Then, in the blink of an eye, the behemoth was gone, with only a few faint stars to mark where she had been.

"*Teddy Roosevelt* has jumped, Captain."

"Very good, Mr. Haydn. Mr. Cristobal, start the countdown clock. We jump in five minutes."

"Aye aye, Captain. The clock has started."

"Are the recordings ready, Communicator?"

"Ready, sir."

"Start them now. I want you to monitor them continuously and notify me immediately if there is any kind of breakdown."

"Yes, sir."

Drake watched the red numerals on the countdown

clock wind slowly down. When the clock still showed two minutes to go, he keyed for Bethany's stateroom. She answered on the second buzz.

"Well, it looks like this is it," he said.

"I guess it does," she replied stiffly.

"Are you watching your screen?"

She nodded.

"Turn to Channel Two. I'll have Sol put up on the screen as soon as we arrive on the other side."

"Thank you for your courtesy, Richard," she said, then abruptly broke the connection.

Drake turned back to the countdown clock. There was now less than a minute to go.

"It's all yours, Mr. Cristobal."

"Thank you, Captain. Generators are at full power, and the jumpfield is building. Thirty seconds to jump. Stand by. Fifteen . . . ten . . . five . . . four . . . three . . . two . . . one . . . Jump!"

CHAPTER 21

"Put the system primary up on the screen, Mr. Cristobal!"

"Coming up now, Captain."

A few seconds passed before the screen flashed once and a yellow-white disk lay centered in the field of view. The only features on the star's surface were half a dozen sunspots trailing one another across an incandescent plasma sea. Even though large enough to swallow a hundred planets the size of Alta, the spots were minor imperfections when judged against the whole disk of the star.

"We're waiting on confirmation, Mr. Cristobal," Drake said after a dozen seconds passed in silence.

"Uh, sorry, sir. I was just rechecking my data. It's Sol all right. The spectrum matches to ten significant places."

"Very well. Mr Haydn, pipe this view into Communications Channel Two. Then switch the main screen to the tactical display."

"Aye aye, Captain!"

The screen changed again, this time to a schematic diagram of the space in the vicinity of the Sol–Goddard foldpoint. As the screen came alight, it began to fill with symbols that quickly painted a picture of the foldpoint defenses. There were several low whistles on *Discovery*'s bridge as their extent became apparent. They had started out formidable and were getting more so with each passing second.

Radar and infrared sensors had quickly detected thousands of objects scattered throughout the volume of space occupied by the foldpoint. Each was the size of a small scout ship and was constructed of an open framework of girders, fuel tanks, and an oversize photon drive. The nearest such was less than a thousand kilometers from *Discovery*, and after a visual examination, the technician manning the threat console tentatively identified it as a high-acceleration orbital mine.

Just beyond the foldpoint's periphery floated two hundred orbital fortresses. Telescopic examination of the closest showed it to be bristling with heavy lasers, antimatter projectors, missile launchers, and various ports that were presumably used to sortie manned interceptors. Interspersed among the offensive weaponry were long- and short-range sensors, heat radiators, communications gear, and a number of less identifiable mechanisms. Judging by the amount of quiescent energy the orbital fortress spilled to space, it was more than a match for any normal fleet of warships.

If the line of orbital fortresses weren't enough, longrange sensors detected three formations of warships maintaining stations at various distances from the foldpoint. Each fleet was positioned to interdict the most direct route to Earth, and each appeared to be composed primarily of blastships and heavy cruisers.

Drake keyed for the technician manning the countermeasures console in the combat control center. "What's the E-M spectrum like, Mr. Benson?"

The technician's lined features split into a wide grin. "You could come close to frying an egg on our hull, Captain, the radar beams are so thick out there! I have identified 1312 separate sources of E-M radiation in the vicinity so far—everything from search and fire-control radars to ranging lasers and communications beams."

"Let me know if that changes."

"Aye aye, sir."

"Mr. Cristobal. Where's *Teddy Roosevelt*?"

"Ten thousand kilometers off our beam, sir. Almost due galactic north. She has gone to one-tenth gee and appears to be maneuvering for rendezvous."

"How long until *Alexandria* comes through?"

"Another two minutes, twelve seconds, sir."

"All sensors at high gain?"

"Yes, sir. High gain and recording."

"Very well. Stand by to report her arrival."

The countdown chronometer ticked off the remaining minutes and seconds. When the proper time had elapsed, the converted liner flashed into existence some six thousand kilometers in front of *Discovery*'s bow.

"Message from *Teddy Roosevelt*, Captain," the communicator said immediately after *Alexandria*'s arrival.

"Put him on, Mr. Haydn."

"Channel Three, sir."

Drake turned to where Admiral Ryerson's features were visible on an auxiliary screen. "Yes, sir?"

"You have been cleared to enter the Solar system, Captain. Please move your ships to the main traffic corridor as previously instructed."

"Will do, sir."

Ryerson glanced away from the screen pickup, then back again. "We calculate rendezvous in forty minutes."

"See you soon. And Drake?"

"Yes, sir?"

"Welcome home!"

Varlan of the Scented Waters lay in front of the viewscreen in her cabin and stared at the bright double world centered therein. Both displayed the tiny half-moon shapes that showed them to be closer to the system primary than was the human warship in which Varlan was held prisoner. The larger of the two planets was a dazzling blue-white in color, while the smaller satellite appeared to be a dull gray-white. Varlan gazed at the two worlds and pondered recent events.

When Bethany of the Lindquists had first begun their daily interviews, Varlan had seen them as a good way to

stave off the boredom of captivity. They had been intellectual exercises in which she had attempted to unravel
the mystery of why humans act the way they do. And
since Bethany of the Lindquists was effectively the only
human Varlan ever saw, the interviews quickly became
an exercise in understanding why Bethany behaved the
way she did.

Prime among the many riddles that Bethany posed for
Varlan was her steadfast refusal to see the logical paradox in her idea that cooperation between intelligent species was not only possible but desirable. At first Varlan
had thought to educate Bethany concerning this obvious
blind spot. She had done this by recounting the many
hard lessons her species had learned during their long
competition with the swift eaters. However, Bethany
had remained as optimistic as ever. Varlan, in turn—
concerned that Bethany might react badly if her cher-
ished delusion were challenged too directly—had
softened her verbal opposition. She had even conceded
that cooperation between species was theoretically possible, if highly unlikely in practice.

It had all seemed a harmless enough way to humor
her jailer while also providing the intellectual stimulation
she needed to keep her own fears in check. Varlan had
always considered herself a rational modern thinker and
had never believed the ancient superstitions of her race.
Still, the entry of the human ships into the Evil Star had
made her apprehensive and troubled her sleep. She had
often dreamed of being chased by gaping-jawed swifts
with razorlike teeth.

Eventually, the human fleet had moved out of the Evil
Star and Varlan's mood had improved. With the return to
normal space, she had scanned the new black sky for
many hundreds of heartbeats. Although her knowledge
of astronomy was no better than the average Ryall's, she
hoped to determine whether the human ship had returned to the hegemony. Unfortunately, those few con-
stellations which she was able to recognize seemed
oddly skewed, an indication that they were far distant
from any of the systems familiar to the Ryall manager.

It had been in this period that Bethany of the Lindquists had been particularly excited during their daily interviews. When Varlan had asked the reason for her mood, Bethany replied that the ship had entered the Goddard star system. The name, Bethany had informed her, was that of a famous human philosopher/priest of the past.

There followed many days in which interesting events had taken place, including the arrival of several very large human warships. From her solitary prison in *Discovery*'s habitat ring, Varlan monitored the comings and goings by counting the number of times spin gravity was removed from the ship. She had also judged the progress of events by the changes in Bethany's moods. Toward the end of the period, the human female had seemed distracted and uncharacteristically silent.

"Is something wrong, Bethany of the Lindquists?" Varlan had asked.

"It's nothing," Bethany responded. "I'm mad at Admiral Gower and Richard. I'll get over it."

At Varlan's urging, Bethany had gone on to explain that Gower had asked her to do something that implied dishonor to the Clan of the Lindquists. Bethany had complied under pressure and was now unhappy for having done so. Curious, Varlan had asked the nature of the implied dishonor, but Bethany refused to explain further. As for why her displeasure with Gower also applied to Bethany's mate to be, Varlan had no clue, and Bethany seemed unable to explain.

After ten minutes spent trying to understand, Varlan said, "I'm afraid that I do not comprehend mammalian mating practices well enough to comment, Bethany. I must tell you that egg laying would seem to be a much simpler method of procreation."

Bethany made the gesture with her lips that Varlan knew to be the human equivalent of a smile. "You may well be right."

There had followed a long period in which the aft bulkhead was the deck rather than the curved outer hull. This, Varlan knew, meant that the ship was under power. She passed the time viewing films from the human entertainment library and thinking about what she had learned. At the end of several days, *Discovery* underwent a series of acceleration changes, then jumped to yet another star system.

During the interview session immediately following the jump between stars, Bethany once again showed all the symptoms of excitement. She spoke rapidly, moved her hands in short, jerky motions, and paced the room.

"What is wrong?" Varlan asked. "Have you and Richard ceased your hostilities?"

Bethany shook her head. "I'm still giving him the *cold shoulder.*" The translator had failed to render any interpretation of the last two words. "But I'm finding it harder and harder. He's sent me flowers every day and twice invited me to dinner in his cabin. I suppose I'll have to forgive him sooner or later."

"You don't seem unhappy."

Bethany grinned. "Far from it! I saw Earth today through the big telescope."

"Earth?" Varlan asked.

"Our destination, the place we started for when we began this expedition."

"Was this 'Earth' a famous human like 'Goddard'?"

"No, of course not," Bethany replied with a laugh. "Earth is the central world of human space."

"The seat of your government?"

Bethany nodded.

"It must have been colonized quite a long time ago to have achieved such power," Varlan observed.

Bethany laughed again. "You don't understand. Earth isn't a colony. It's the mother world, the place where humans first evolved."

Bethany had left shortly thereafter, leaving Varlan alone to consider the implications of this new bit of information. Of all the lessons the Ryall had learned during their long competition with the swifts, the most important was the need to seek out and destroy the viper's nest. For sixty circuits of the Ryall home world about its star, warriors of the hegemony had sought to do just that. They had failed utterly. Yet, the much sought after home world of the humans lay a mere two interstellar jumps beyond the Evil Star—easy striking distance for a strong warfleet!

Suddenly, Varlan knew her destiny. She must somehow get this vital information back to Those Who Rule. She watched the blue-white and gray-white orbs and considered how such a feat might be accomplished.

Bethany Lindquist turned over in her bed, raised herself to one elbow, and rearranged her pillow for the sixth time. Rolling over onto her stomach, she tried to blank the whirling thoughts from her mind. After five fruitless minutes in which she willed herself not to think—and thought ever more actively as a result—she lifted her head and opened her eyes to search for the chronometer on the nightstand. The red numerals glared back at her: 01:37. Sighing, she sat up, swung bare feet down onto the carpeted deck, and stood erect. Working from memory in the darkened cabin, she groped for her robe, slipped into its silky embrace, then pulled it tight about her. She moved to the door and pushed it open. A rectangle of blue light from the corridor spilled across her. She stepped out into the corridor, closed the cabin door behind her, and padded softly in the direction of the wardroom. As she moved through the deserted ship, she pondered the reasons why she was having trouble sleeping.

The first, of course, was the fact that they would enter Earth parking orbit the following day. All through their journey from the Sol–Goddard foldpoint, Bethany had spent hours watching Earth grow larger on the screen. She had watched it transformed from an indistinct blur to a living world. She had noted Earth's similarity to Alta, then reminded herself that the correlation was, by definition, the other way around.

She had stared at the impossibly thin line of Earth's atmosphere and thought of the thousands of generations that had lived beneath its protective blanket of air. She had peered down at vast expanses of ocean and remembered all the pictures she'd seen of coral reefs, sunken ships, and icebergs the size of mountains. She had stared in wonder at the familiar shapes of continents that she had never expected to see in person. Considering the excitement she felt at having finally arrived, it was no wonder that she was having trouble sleeping.

The second matter that was keeping Bethany awake was the breakthrough that she had made with Varlan earlier in the day. The session had started out like any other, with the centaur discussing Ryall philosophy. Then they had continued a discussion that had begun with their first interview on Corlis: comparing the attitudes of humans and Ryall toward their offspring. Bethany had been discussing the love of human parents for their children, and Varlan had replied that the Ryall felt similarly about their own offspring.

"But you can't know who your children are!" Bethany had said.

"Of course not. When the time comes to lay my eggs, instinct takes over. I dig a hole in warm sand, deposit the eggs, and then cover them over. I have very little memory of the event afterward. If I wished to know my own hatchlings—a desire which my people consider to be perverted—I would require the assistance of another to mark my nest and to keep watch until the eggs hatched. However, it is not necessary to know one's parents in Ryall society. The hatchlings are brought up collectively and are loved every bit as much as your human offspring."

"See, our two species have something in common, after all," Bethany replied.

Varlan was silent for a long time. Finally, she spoke softly and carefully. "Perhaps you are right, Bethany of the Lindquists. Perhaps we are more alike than I first believed."

There had followed a long discussion in which Varlan admitted that she could have been wrong about the inevitability of conflict between species. Bethany had called a halt shortly thereafter to give the alien concept time to mature in the Ryall's mind.

Bethany was still thinking about Varlan as she reached the small galley that adjoined the wardroom, the refrigerator of which was kept well stocked for the benefit of midwatch crewmen. Bethany had intended to warm a bulb of milk to take back to her cabin. She hadn't expected to find anyone in the galley so late and was therefore surprised to discover Greg Oldfield seated at the small serving table in front of a plate of cold cuts and cheese.

"Evening, Miss Lindquist," the first secretary said, looking up from carving a piece off the end of a long yellow cheese.

"Good, evening, Mr. Oldfield."

"Please, I'm Greg to my friends."

"And I'm Bethany to mine, Greg."

"Join me in a snack, Bethany?"

"No, thank you. I just came down for a drink of milk."

"Sounds good. Mind making me one, too?"

"Warm or cold?"

"Cold, please."

Bethany moved to the refrigerator, dispensed two drinking bulbs, then slipped one into the warmer. A minute later, she was seated across the table from Oldfield.

"Couldn't sleep?" the terrestrial diplomat asked.

"No. I guess I'm just too excited about tomorrow."

"Big day for you people, I imagine."

"My family has waited six generations for what will take place tomorrow," Bethany said. "Yes, I would say that it will be a big day!"

"I've been meaning to ask you about that," Oldfield replied. "Mind telling me how it is that you happen to be the representative of the terrestrial ambassador to Alta?"

Bethany recounted the story of Granville Whitlow and his compulsion to maintain a terrestrial presence on Alta after the failure of the foldpoint. She told him of the deal Whitlow had made to transfer control of the three Grand Fleet battle cruisers to the newly formed colonial navy. She told of the generations of Whitlows who had kept the dream alive for more than a century. When she finished, the first secretary sat and gazed at Bethany with a new respect.

"I had no idea. I will have to bring this matter to the attention of my superiors when we land. Such loyalty should be rewarded."

"All I want is to deliver my uncle's dispatches to the proper people."

"You'll deliver them to the coordinator himself if I have anything to say about it."

Discovery's Control Room Number One was crowded. In addition to Richard Drake and the full bridge duty crew, Admiral Gower, First Secretary Oldfield, and Bethany Lindquist were all present for the final approach. In order to accommodate the admiral and first secretary, Drake had ordered two temporary acceleration couches installed. The additional couches made the control room crowded and somewhat obscured Drake's field of view. He had gladly accepted those inconveniences, however, because the arrangement left the permanent observer's couch free for Bethany.

"I can watch the approach from my stateroom," she had answered when he first invited her to observe the proceedings from the bridge.

"You'll do nothing of the sort. We started this voyage together, and by God, we're going to finish it the same way!"

"Yes, Richard," she'd replied meekly. Later, when she arrived on the bridge, her lingering feelings of pique had been quickly submerged by the excitement of the occasion. She had even managed to be civil to Admiral Gower when he arrived to take his station.

The main viewscreen had been focused on the swelling Earth for the past several hours. The only time it had been diverted was when the battle cruiser swept in past the orbit of Luna. The moon was near enough to appear larger than the Earth at the moment of closest approach. Sol was low behind the satellite, a celestial arrangement that plunged the near face into shadow. The darkness was broken only by the carpets of silver lights that marked the positions of the satellite's underground cities.

The fleet continued inward. As each ship fell toward Earth, it retarded its hyperbolic velocity by throwing a stream of photons forward along its path at the speed of light. Thus balanced on cones of light, each ship decelerated at a constant one-half gravity. *Teddy Roosevelt* led the procession, followed by *Discovery*, with *City of Alexandria* bringing up the rear.

As *Discovery* fell deeper into Earth–Luna space, sensor operators began to issue ever more frequent warnings of impending close encounters with objects in orbit about the planet. After a heart-pounding few seconds, each report would be declared a close approach rather than a possible collision, and Drake would begin to breath again. Eventually, sensor operators reported that *Teddy Roosevelt* was decelerating rapidly for final approach.

"Stand by for our own transition to final power," Argos Cristobal said from his station upon hearing the report.

"You have the conn, Mr. Cristobal," Drake replied.

"Aye aye, sir. Engines to full power in fifteen seconds. Ten...five...three...two...one. Power!"

Drake felt himself pulled deeper into his acceleration couch. After several minutes, *Discovery*'s maneuvering computer sensed that conditions were right for a thousand-kilometer-high circular orbit about the planet. Electronic orders flashed from the bridge to the engine spaces in the cruiser's central cylinder, and the flow of power to the photon engines was disrupted.

Suddenly, weight evaporated around Drake. The residual springiness of the acceleration couch padding threw him gently forward into his restraining harness, where he oscillated for a few cycles before coming to rest. There followed several seconds of silence, finally broken by Greg Oldfield's cheery voice.

"Welcome to Earth, people. Welcome home!"

CHAPTER 22

Earth, as viewed from the vantage point of low orbit, may possibly be the most beautiful sight in the universe. Certainly there are planets that are larger and more gaudy, and others that are surrounded by truly impressive ring structures or multiple hurtling moons. There are even worlds in the terrestrial classification that sport brighter blues, greener greens, and whites the color of new-fallen snow. Despite this, Earth is still the most beautiful to human eyes. For on no other world can one gaze down at the cradle of the human race. Nowhere else does the approach of darkness throw into stark relief the outline of a five-thousand-year-old pyramid or highlight the twisting form of a stone wall a thousand kilometers long. On no other world can a spacefaring traveler see the primitive concrete and steel structures whence his ancestors first reached upward toward the stars.

To the Altans especially, surveying the world of their forefathers from on high brought with it a feeling of reverence and quiet joy. Even so, most of *Discovery*'s crew had had their fill of orbital sightseeing by the end of the second day. They were anxious to get their feet on solid ground, to breath deeply of air untainted by recycling units, to partake of the only environment in the universe for which human beings are perfectly adapted.

Discovery and *City of Alexandria* were in orbit for more than forty hours before Greg Oldfield announced that a ground-to-orbit craft would be up to transport the official negotiating team the following day. When asked the reason for the delay, he blamed difficulties in arranging a proper welcoming ceremony. Admiral Gower wondered aloud to Richard Drake whether the reason wasn't more basic—namely, that the terrestrials had yet to establish a policy regarding their newly rediscovered colonies.

The list of those who would be the first to go down to the surface had been in preparation since the truncated Helldiver Fleet had left Goddard. From *Discovery*, the negotiating team would consist of Admiral Gower, Richard Drake, Phillip Walkirk, and half a dozen assistants and advisers. Richard Drake's assistant would be Argos Cristobal, *Discovery*'s astrogator. Cristobal had made a thorough study of the captured Ryall astrogation data and would be a valuable man to have along when a deal was struck with the Interstellar Council. *City of Alexandria*'s contribution to the team would include Stanislaw Barrett, Count Husanic, their two assistants, six scientists, and two economists. Bethany Lindquist would also accompany the party in her capacity as her uncle's representative, as would First Secretary Oldfield, who had been assigned as their terrestrial liaison officer.

Upon entering the shuttle the next day, Richard Drake made sure that he and Bethany occupied adjoining acceleration couches. They spoke very little during the transfer craft's stop at *City of Alexandria*. Finally, after they had departed the liner and begun the long fall toward Earth, Drake turned to Bethany. "What say we declare a truce for the duration?"

"I don't know what you're talking about, Richard," she replied stiffly.

"You know damned well what I'm talking about, my love. You're still mad because Admiral Gower threatened to throw you in the brig."

"Don't I have a right to be mad?"

"You did at the time," he replied. "However, that was ten days ago. Gower did what he had to do, and you made the best bargain you could. You should have come to grips with it by now. This pouting is childish."

Drake noted the signs of a building explosion and was surprised when it didn't come. Instead, Bethany leaned back in her acceleration couch and regarded him more calmly than she had in days. "I'm not mad at Admiral Gower anymore. As you say, he did what he had to do."

"Then who are you mad at?"

"You."

"Me? What did I do?"

"You sent me over there without so much as a hint of what Gower was planning."

Drake glanced in the direction of Greg Oldfield. The first secretary was seated three rows in front of them on the opposite side of the fuselage. He was engaged in animated conversation with his seat mate and seemed oblivious to everyone around him. Even so, Drake lowered his voice to a whisper that was nearly masked by the hypersonic keening outside the hull.

"Damn it, I couldn't warn you. I had my orders. Besides, Gower was absolutely correct in asking you what he did. That data is ours. If we're to give it to the terrestrials, then we have a right to get a fair price in return."

"What makes you think you'll need it?" Bethany asked, matching Drake's whisper. "How do you know they won't give us everything we ask for? Maybe there's no need for us to hold the data for ransom."

Drake shrugged. "In which case, we'll give it to them without hesitation."

"And if we can't agree on a plan to drive the Ryall from Aezer?"

"Then we'll work something out. No one is arguing that what we know is too important to be kept a secret any longer than necessary."

She looked at him sharply. "Do you really mean that, Richard?"

"I do."

She smiled. "In that case, you're forgiven."

"Care to seal that with a kiss?"

She smiled. "If that is the proper protocol."

"Believe me, it is."

They embraced for long seconds, totally oblivious to the dozen or so people seated behind them. They then sat back to watch the Mother of Men unfold beneath them.

Outside the window, the lights of central Asia sparkled amid the ghostly glow of plasma dancing around the window frame. The racing shuttle overtook the terminator, and night turned quickly into day. Shortly after the coming of the sun, a chain of islands appeared in the midst of a vast blue ocean. To the east of the islands, huge squares of blue-green water marked the position of several midocean farms.

A few minutes later, a coastline emerged from the haze in front of them. Drake knew from having studied the shuttle's flight path that he was looking at the western coast of the North American continent. The shuttle made landfall just above a large bay surrounded by an even larger city.

The shuttle banked right and turned toward a far-off smudge of light brown on the horizon. Ten minutes later, the smudge had grown into a large desert in the center of which lay a sprawling spaceport. As the craft swept over the spaceport, it banked sharply and began to lose altitude. There followed a series of maneuvers that brought the ground up with astonishing rapidity. Then the brown of the desert turned to the dirty black of tarmac, and the shuttle touched down with the double squeal of tires that had marked returns to Earth for half a thousand years.

As soon as the shuttle had slowed sufficiently to pull off the runway, Greg Oldfield climbed to his feet and moved to the front of the cabin before turning to face the others. "Welcome to Mohave Spaceport. There will be a short ceremony inside the terminal. Afterward, we will board an aircraft for Mexico City. In the meantime, sit back and enjoy the view. We'll be at the terminal in another few minutes."

Ciudad de México (Mexico City) was the largest metropolis Bethany Lindquist had ever seen. From her room in one of the towers that dominated the skyline she could look out across the city toward the twin volcanoes Istacíhuatl and Popocatepetl. Closer, but no less imposing, was the man-made mountain that served as headquarters for the Council for the Promotion of Interstellar Trade and Cooperation.

Bethany smiled as she remembered the shock of first seeing those archaic words chiseled into the marble lintel over the main entrance to what was, in reality, the de facto capital of human space. She had always known that "the central government" had begun life as a mercantile association. The events by which the association had first acquired the trappings of a supranational body—and later, of a sovereign government—were legend. Still, seeing it with one's own eyes drove home the point far more effectively than reading about it on a computer screen.

Bethany had been in Mexico City three days. The first day had included an appearance in front of a full session of the Interstellar Council. She and her fellow colonists had sat in the central rotunda of the council chamber while speaker after speaker rose to praise their visitors from the lost systems of the Antares Cluster. Yet, after half an hour of listening to the unrelenting praise, Bethany began to notice that the speeches were rife with high-sounding words but noticeably lacking in concrete proposals.

After the general session, the managers of the Helldiver Expedition had been taken somewhere else to meet the powers that be. Bethany had tried to have herself included in the group, but Admiral Gower had refused, pointing out not unkindly that she was a self-professed agent for the other side.

Therefore, while the military men, scientists, and economists all went off to meet their various counterparts, Bethany sought out the library at the *Universidad de México*. There she scanned summaries of the

history of human space since the Ryall capture of
Aezer. She was disheartened to discover that not much
had changed since the Sandarians had been cut off
from the rest of human space. The war with the Ryall
still ground on with no end in sight, and the military
situation had, if anything, deteriorated noticeably.

Nor was that her only disturbing discovery. For two
hours she had scanned issues of Mexico City newsfaxes
dating back to the days of the Antares Supernova. Her
historian's eye had picked up a distressing pattern, one
that a nonprofessional could easily miss.

When news of the Ryall depredations had first
reached Earth, a great war fever had broken out. This
had been followed by the expenditure of vast sums of
money to build up humanity's capabilities for both offense and defense. In a decade or less, human space
had been organized into a smoothly functioning mechanism for the prosecution of interstellar war. It had been
in this period that the Solar system's foldpoint defenses
had first been constructed, as had similar defenses in
nearly every system within three foldspace transitions
of Ryall space. And for three generations humanity had
worked tirelessly to defeat the Ryall.

Then, forty years earlier, the first cracks had appeared in humanity's resolve. The initial indications of
faltering will had come when the press ceased talking
about winning the war and became preoccupied with
"containing the centaurs." Over the next two decades,
offensive operations came virtually to a standstill, and
even more resources were diverted to foldpoint defenses. Toward the end of the period, even defensive appropriations began to have difficulty making it through
the council.

About the time the Ryall took Aezer, large groups of
dissenters began to make their presence felt. The first
system to openly defy the council on a war-related issue
had been Scuyler's Star. The Scuylerians had declared
themselves neutral in the fight and had refused to supply
their quota of ships for the annual fleet levy. The rebel-
lion had been put down by the Grand Fleet, which had
occupied Scuyler in a bloodless operation that had nev-

ertheless sent a strong message to other would-be paci-
fists.

The pacifist movement had gone underground. Not
surprisingly, one of the strongest centers of the movement was Earth herself. For the average terrestrial, the
war was far away. At their closest, the centaurs were
four foldspace transitions distant. To reach the Solar
system they would have to fight their way through a
dozen fleets and four sets of foldpoint defenses. As a
result of this insulating barrier of multiple defensive
lines, the average terrestrial saw no good reason for his
taxes to be used protecting "a few colony worlds who
should do more to protect themselves." This attitude
was especially apparent in the actions of some of the
major nation-states—which stubbornly maintained the
fiction that they were the Interstellar Council's equals.
Over the past decade, most governments had passed
nonbinding resolutions calling for a reduction in war
appropriations.

Bethany was mildly depressed when she returned to
her hotel. It was a familiar feeling, brought on by a too-
concentrated dose of history taken in too little time. For
history, like news, is mostly bad. Bethany had learned
the wisdom of that old Chinese curse, "May you live in
interesting times!" during her first year as an undergraduate at Homeport University. She had often considered
that only a historian could truly appreciate the subtle
depth of the sentiment.

Upon reaching her room, she discovered a message
informing her that she had been invited on a tour of
Mexico City and that if she wished to accept, a guide
would be waiting for her in the lobby of her hotel at
0700 hours the following morning. The guide turned out
to be a perky blonde by the name of Ryssa Blenham,
who was also the daughter of the second coordinator
for the Interstellar Council. Over breakfast, Bethany
learned that Ryssa was from Galleria, which lay at the
opposite end of human space from Alta. The two
women spent the morning touring garish museums,
stolid sixteenth-century churches, and various monu-
ments to Mexico City's past. At each monument, Beth-

any reflected on the fact that each stone figure or bronze plaque represented an instant of blood and pain —be it the result of earthquake, revolution, or war. At noon, Ryssa guided her to one of the open-air cafés that adorned both sides of a wide boulevard. The two women ate a light lunch of gazpacho and salad and talked about their respective childhoods. Inevitably, the conversation turned to Bethany's position with the Helldiver Expedition.

"I understand that you are a diplomat," Ryssa said.

Bethany, who was in the process of sipping wine from a glass, laughed. "Only in the broadest sense of the word, Ryssa." She went on to explain her family's history and her own appointment as official representative of the hereditary terrestrial ambassador to Alta. She ended by explaining that she was on Earth to deliver the accumulated dispatches of the Homeport embassy to someone in the diplomatic service of the Interstellar Council.

"But these dispatches are over a century old, are they not?" Ryssa asked.

Bethany nodded. "Some of them."

"They must contain many secrets, then, to be important after all this time."

"On the contrary, most are mundane day-to-day matters. Annual accountings of terrestrial property on Alta, summaries of embassy political activity, lists of passport expirations and renewals, corrections to immigration records, marriage records, that sort of thing."

"But surely you didn't go to all this trouble merely to bring routine reports to the council! If it is as you say, who will want to read the stuff?"

Bethany shrugged. "I doubt anyone will. Except for my uncle's cover letter, it's all pretty dry reading."

Ryssa shook her head. "Then it seems to me that you have come a long way for nothing."

Bethany leaned back in her chair and regarded her hostess with narrowed eyes. There was something about the question that made her uncomfortable, and Bethany struggled for the proper words to explain.

"It isn't the contents of my uncle's dispatches that are

important, Ryssa. Rather, it's the principle they represent. Granville Whitlow took an oath to look after Earth's interests on Alta. He spent his life upholding that oath. His descendants have done the same for six generations. The dispatches I carry are the product of those six lives. When I deliver them into the hands of the proper authorities, I will, in effect, be saying that those lives counted for something!"

"It sounds as though it is very important to you."

"It is. *Very* important."

"In that case, perhaps I can speak to my father of this."

The next morning Bethany received a call from a pleasant young woman with a Spanish accent notifying her that she had an appointment with the second coordinator of the Interstellar Council at 1000 hours, and "would that be convenient for Señorita Lindquist?" After assuring her caller that she would be there, Bethany spent the rest of the morning preparing for the audience.

Sir Joshua Blenham, senior delegate to the Interstellar Council from Galleria, Socata IV, was a large bear of a man with a bushy mustache and wrinkles around the eyes. He had a tendency to boom when he talked but immediately made Bethany feel at ease. In addition to Blenham, there were three other men in the office. She recognized two of them as being functionaries who had taken Richard Drake and the other Helldiver leaders away after the general audience on the first day. The third man was a stranger to her.

"Miss Bethany Lindquist, may I present Raoul Letterer, Alphonse Grast, and Kelton Dalwood?" Blenham said as he indicated the three in turn. "I won't bore you with their overlong titles or what they do. Frankly, our administrative organization is such that it is sometimes difficult even for us to understand. However, let us say that they are involved in the question of assisting your colony and that of the Sandarians. Gentlemen, Miss Lindquist is a terrestrial loyalist."

"So I understand from First Secretary Oldfield's report," Letterier said. "Frankly, Miss Lindquist, I am amazed that people such as you and your uncle still exist on Alta."

"Why, Mr. Letterier?"

"It has been a long time since the Antares Supernova. To be frank, we very nearly had forgotten about you. We had assumed that you would have forgotten about us. To find colonists still loyal to the council is amazing."

"You misunderstand," Bethany replied. "My uncle isn't loyal to this particular Interstellar Council any more than you are loyal to whatever council ruled during the year Granville Whitlow left Earth for Alta. My uncle is loyal to the idea of Earth."

"You are correct, Miss Lindquist. I don't understand."

"On Alta, gentlemen, Earth is a legend. It's a fairyland place where the cities are paved with gold and justice always triumphs. Its leaders are the wisest, its courts the fairest, its freedoms the greatest in the whole galaxy. It's an ideal which all other people must strive to live up to. *That* is the Earth to which my uncle gives his loyalty."

"You seem to be implying that we don't measure up," Blenham replied.

"I spent some time in the university library the day before yesterday. From what I saw, I'm not sure that you do."

"Surely *you* didn't expect this world to be the fairyland place which you describe," Letterier said.

"No," Bethany agreed. "But I didn't expect to find a planet apathetic about the Ryall threat, either."

"And is that what you think you have found?"

"I came away from my studies with that strong impression, sir."

"Well then, perhaps we can convince you otherwise," Blenham said. "In the meantime, I understand that you have some dispatches for me. Do you have them with you?"

"Yes, sir," Bethany replied. She reached into her pouch and retrieved the record tile on which had been recorded the administrative details of 127 years of embassy operations. She handed it to Blenham.

The coordinator held the tile between thumb and forefinger and studied the play of colors from the hologram interference patterns before placing the tile on his desk. At a signal from the coordinator, all four men rose to their feet. Puzzled, Bethany did likewise.

Blenham came around the desk with a small case in his hands. He stopped in front of Bethany and removed something from the case. Clearing his throat, Blenham said formally, "Bethany Lindquist, by the power vested in me by the Interstellar Council, and on behalf of Ambassador Clarence Whitlow, Chief of Mission, Valeria IV, I bestow on you the order of Terra, with all the rights and privileges pertaining thereto. I further thank you on behalf of the council for your loyalty and that of your family for these many years of unheralded service."

Bethany found her eyes filling with moisture as Blenham lifted the gold medal with its rainbow-colored ribbon over her head. He then kissed her on both cheeks, and each of the others present shook her hand solemnly.

"What, nothing to say?" Blenham asked when he had finished.

"I thank you for my uncle," Bethany replied with a sniff. "This"— she gestured toward the medal —"will make all the years of ridicule worth it."

Letterier grinned. "You may not know it, Miss Lindquist, but a stipend of 100,000 stellars a year goes with that bit of metal you have around your neck. Your uncle is a rich man."

"Can we get on with it, Sir Joshua?" the man who had been introduced as Alphonse Grast asked from where he had retaken his seat.

"You are so impatient, Alphonse," Blenham replied with a sigh. "However, I suppose we do have a schedule to maintain. Miss Lindquist, if you are agreeable, Mr. Grast would like to ask you a few questions."

"What sort of questions?" Bethany asked as she returned to the chair in which she had been sitting.

"I am a member of the Grand Fleet general staff, Miss Lindquist. I hold the rank of commodore in that service, and I am assigned to military intelligence. I would appreciate it if you would answer some questions for me."

"Of course, if I'm able."

Grast gazed levelly into her eyes. "Please tell us how it is that you have a Ryall prisoner onboard your ship!"

"She's lying!"

Sir Joshua Blenham, who thirty seconds earlier had escorted Bethany Lindquist to his office door and then directed his secretary to see her safely out of the building, turned and regarded Commodore Grast with a look of distaste. "Must you always be so direct in your assertions, Alphonse? Here our guest has barely departed, and already you are casting aspersions on her character."

"I merely state fact, Coordinator. They are all lying to us. We need no expert in voice stress analysis to tell us that. Did you see the way she tensed up when we mentioned the Ryall prisoner onboard their flagship. From the way she flinched, you would think I had jabbed her with a pin."

"I have to agree, Sir Joshua," Raoul Letterier said. "I was watching the young lady quite closely. Her whole body tensed when Alphonse asked her about the Ryall."

"Perhaps that was because of this research she claims to be doing," Blenham replied. "What about that, Mr. Dalwood?"

The man who had been introduced as Kelton Dalwood was in reality a technician trained in analyzing voice stress patterns and inferring things from them—sometimes quite important things. While the other three men argued, he had been going over the recordings he had been making surreptitiously while Bethany talked. At Blenham's question, he looked up.

"Beg your pardon, Coordinator?"

"The question, Mr. Dalwood, is whether Miss Lindquist is hypersensitive about this research she claims to be conducting on the Ryall aboard their ship."

"No, sir. Her level of stress was relatively low during the period when she was explaining her research. It appears to be the fact that we know about this particular Ryall which has her spooked."

"Can you infer the reason for that, Technician?" Grast asked.

"No, sir. There weren't sufficient questions asked to determine that."

"Let us not confine our discussions to the girl, gentlemen," Letterier said. "Do you have any explanation for this anomalous reading that we seem to be getting from all of the colonists, Mr. Dalwood?"

"No, sir. All I can tell you is that their level of tension soars right off the scale when we ask about either their trip through the nebula or the Ryall."

"My God! You don't suppose the Ryall know this trick for diving into exploding stars, do you?" Letterier asked.

"Unlikely," Commodore Grast replied. "If they did, we would have found ourselves under attack in half a dozen systems across human space."

"Could it be this antiradiation gizmo they are trying to protect?"

The voice stress technician shook his head. "We've tested half a dozen of them now, and they show a very straightforward reaction when someone asks questions about their antiradiation device. They tell the questioner that they would love to give it to us but that formal agreements will have to be signed first. Their reaction is that of enlightened self-interest, not the subliminal guilt which first made us suspicious that they are hiding something."

"Well, gentlemen, we won't very well discover that sitting in this office," Blenham replied. "What say we continue listening to what they tell us and keep our ears tuned to this apparent mystery. In the meantime, perhaps Miss Lindquist will take us up on our offer to help in her Ryall research."

Grast nodded with satisfaction. "If we can just get the

beast in our own interrogation chambers we'll be able to learn everything it knows."

"In the meantime, let us continue to treat our guests as guests. Perhaps they will eventually tell us their secret of their own accord."

"And if they do not?" Raoul Letterier asked.

"Then we will have to find another way, won't we?"

CHAPTER 23

Richard Drake had been in Mexico City for two days and had so far seen little more than the interiors of conference rooms. The negotiating team had broken up into individuals or working groups immediately following their reception by the full Interstellar Council.

The diplomatic/political working group consisted of Stan Barrett, Count Husanic, and their two assistants. The four diplomats accompanied First Secretary Old-field to the Colonial Department, where they discussed the details of reestablishing diplomatic relations with their counterparts. The conferences had touched on such matters as diplomatic recognition, travel documentation, quarantine restrictions, and reciprocal trade agreements.

The scientists had mostly gone off on their own or in the company of one or two terrestrial colleagues. Their assigned task was to become familiar with the technical developments that had taken place since Sandar's isolation from the rest of human space. Most had chosen various libraries around the city in which to perform their research. Boris Alvarez, whose task it was to determine the strides that had been made in deciphering captured Ryall technology, was one of a small group who had chosen the library at the University of Mexico for their labors. After a briefing by university librarians concerning information retrieval procedures, Alvarez had allowed himself to be led to one of the large study areas. As he was passing a bank of information terminals, he found Bethany Lindquist comfortably ensconced in one of the small study cubicles.

"I see that we are research partners once again," he'd said as he paused beside her.

Startled by the interruption, Bethany had looked up, seen who it was, then smiled. "Hello, Boris. What brings you here?"

"Just trying to get current in my field," he replied. "And you?"

"The same. I'm studying history from a terrestrial point of view."

"That could take quite some time."

"Not at the rate I'm scanning. I've clocked myself at just under a decade every ten minutes. I haven't crammed like this since my days as an undergraduate."

"Are you learning anything?"

"I'm learning *something*! However, it's too early to figure out precisely what."

"Well, I had best get to it myself. Good hunting."

"You too, Boris!"

Like the civilians, the Altan and Sandarian naval officers had formed a working group with their terrestrial counterparts. Where the diplomatic working group had been whisked upstairs in the council building, the military people were transported across town to the foothills of the Serranía del Ajusco mountains. There they found Grand Fleet Headquarters, a glass skyscraper whose proportions rivaled those of the mountain range beyond.

The first meeting was devoted to mutual orientation. On the colonists' side, both Drake and Gower made presentations concerning the naval strength of their respective star systems. In addition, Admiral Gower gave a detailed review of Sandarian operations against the Ryall and a candid assessment of the Battle of Sandar, which the colonists had very nearly lost. Questions by Admiral Ryerson and Grand Admiral Belton, Grand Fleet chief of staff, kept the session going until well after the normal time for the noon meal.

Following a quick snack in the senior officers' dining room, it was the terrestrials' turn to orient the Altans and Sandarians. The task fell to a Commodore Muñoz, a small man with a speaking voice that tended to lapse into a nasal monotone. Muñoz began his review of the military situation in human space by giving an overview of the relative strengths, battle tactics, and strategies used by human and Ryall fleets over the past century. He then began a detailed analysis of Grand Fleet operations during the seventeen years since the fall of Aezer.

Four hours later, Drake felt as though his head were going to burst from its load of new information. Still, despite the immensity of the subject matter, one overall impression had stood out starkly in the mass of details. *Homo sapiens* and *Centaurus sapiens* were locked in a struggle to the death, a struggle that the centaurs were winning.

When Antares exploded, it had linked human and Ryall space through three star systems—Aezer, Constantine, and Klamath. In one other system, Napier, shock wave focusing had temporarily created a fourth foldline link between the two realms. Unfortunately for all concerned, the temporary foldpoint in the Napier system had lasted long enough for the two races to become aware of each other's existence and for the first Ryall attacks to be launched against New Providence.

The two decades that followed had seen a steady increase in the number of Ryall attacks against human space. The assaults had triggered a massive human defense effort in which foldpoints were fortified, vast numbers of warships constructed, and the economy of human space put on a war footing. Those early years had also seen a series of large-scale offensive operations launched against the centaurs. However, despite some early successes, the Grand Fleet and its auxiliaries had failed to halt the Ryall encroachment into human territory. The best they could do was slow the centaur advance.

Constantine had been the first system lost to the Ryall, and along with it, a prime world colonized only thirty years earlier. The survivors had fled to the adjoining star system of Hallowell. There the Grand Fleet had fought a pitched battle to protect the Hallowell–Constantine foldpoint against a determined Ryall thrust. When the Ryall attack failed, both sides settled down to fortify their respective sides of the foldline link. The inherent advantage that each foldpoint gave to its own set of defenders had produced a stalemate that had lasted more than fifty years.

The second system to be lost to the Ryall had been Aezer. That, of course, had brought about Sandar's isolation and triggered five bloody attempts at regaining the system—three by the Sandarians and two others by the Grand Fleet.

Drake had no need to ask about the battle for the third system, Klamath. He had seen evidence of how the fight was going when *Conqueror* fell into the Val system.

As Drake sat and listened to the litany of failures on which Commodore Muñoz was attempting to place the best possible face, he suddenly realized that here was confirmation that the terrestrials were ignorant of the true nature of the Ryall hegemony. Had they known that Ryall space occupied a single compact foldspace cluster, it would not have been necessary to postulate a Ryall force that, in Drake's opinion, was 300 percent too large.

Nor had all the reverses come on the battlefield. It was inevitable that the long, unsuccessful war would also take its toll on the home front. Unable to dislodge their enemies from any of the gateway systems to Ryall space and faced with an erosion of public support for the war, the Grand Fleet had adopted a defensive strategy. They began to place more and more emphasis on foldpoint defenses, less and less on taking the battle to the Ryall.

It was a quiet and depressed group of Altan and Sandarian military men who returned to their hotel that evening. For unlike the terrestrials, to whom the situation had seemed a natural, lifelong evolution, the Altans and Sandarians had been hit with it in a single blow. Worse, they knew the underlying reason for humanity's troubles lay in the Ryalls' seeming ability to be everywhere at once. And unlike the terrestrials, they recognized the danger that ability posed to the future existence of the human race.

The following morning's meeting was held in the same conference room, but with a larger audience. Following introductions, Admiral Belton turned the meeting over to Admiral Gower, who explained that Altan and Sandarian strategists had been working on a plan to break the Aezer blockade. He concluded by saying, "With your permission, Admiral Belton, I will turn the floor over to my chief strategist, Commander Sir Garrett Foster. He will explain in detail what we have in mind."

Foster was a typical product of the Sandarian military academy—a stern-faced, taciturn man with a quiet voice that nonetheless had the strength of command to it. He strode to the holoscreen at the front of the conference room and turned to face the audience.

"Good afternoon, sirs. I would like to begin today by reviewing the current situation in the Antares Cluster. If I may have the lights down, please." The overhead lights dimmed, and the holoscreen came to light. In its depths was a foldspace topology chart showing the overall structure of the Antares Foldspace Cluster. "You will note from the chart that there is but a single conventional postnova sequence of foldspace transitions between Hellsgate and human space. Anyone wishing to travel from Sandar to Sol must first transition between the Hellsgate, Aezer, Hermes, Sacata, Carswell, and Vega systems. Upon reaching Vega, of course, it is a simple matter for a ship to reach Sol.

"Unfortunately, the Ryall cut the lifeline between Sandar and human space seventeen years ago. They did this when they took control of the Aezer system and established their blockade there. Since that time, both of our forces have attempted to break the blockade without success." Foster gazed out over his audience. "What do you suppose would have happened if we had been able to coordinate those attacks?"

"That is hardly relevant, Commander," Admiral Ryerson replied. "With the sole link between us cut, we had no way of communicating our plans to you."

"True enough, Admiral," Foster replied, turning back to the foldspace chart. "More than true, in fact. It is one of basic principles of the universe that all communications, save those which travel via foldline link, are limited to the speed of light. Had we of Sandar sent you a radio message detailing our plans to attack Aezer, that message would still be on its way a couple of centuries hence. The same had you attempted to send us a similar message. Without communication, there can be no coordination; without coordination, no hope of victory.

"That is what the Ryall did to us when they captured Aezer. By destroying our ability to act in concert, the centaurs ensured that they would never face simultaneous attacks on the Aezer foldpoints. This leaves them free to concentrate their entire force at whichever foldpoint comes under attack and to shift it quickly to the opposite side of the system should the need arise. Up until now, however, the chance of both foldpoints coming under attack at the same time has been too low for them to worry about."

Foster gazed at the assembled Grand Fleet officers and let the meaning of what he was saying sink in. When he continued, he had a grim little smile on his face. "I am here to tell you that things have changed, gentlemen. Obviously, or else I wouldn't *be here* to tell you!

"What has changed is the fact that we and the Altans have developed an antiradiation field that allows our ships to penetrate the Antares Nebula. In so doing, we have bypassed the Ryall blockade of Aezer and reestablished communication with the rest of human space. In so doing, we have also provided a means to drive the Ryall from the Aezer system. This time we *can* coordinate the date and hour of our attacks against Aezer."

"Are you suggesting a simultaneous assault at both ends of the Aezer system?" Admiral Ryerson asked.

"No, sir," Foster responded. "A simultaneous attack would mean that both of our forces would engage fold-point defenses that are at full strength. No, we have something more subtle in mind. You see, the Ryall know that they've hurt Sandar badly. They've bled us during each of our attacks on Aezer, and again at the Battle of Sandar. It is the belief of the Sandarian general staff that the Ryall commander in the Aezer system has effectively written us off as a serious threat. It pains me to tell you that he is very nearly correct in that assessment.

"We propose, therefore, that the Grand Fleet send a battle group through the nebula to Hellsgate. There they will be joined by Altan and Sandarian naval forces. At a prearranged time, a second battle group will launch a diversionary attack against Aezer from the Hermes system. This attack will be designed to draw Ryall forces away from the Aezer–Hellsgate fold-point and toward Aezer–Hermes. Then, at the moment we judge the defenses to be at their weakest, the battle group in the Hellsgate system will attack the Aezer–Hellsgate foldpoint and destroy whatever defenses remain.

"As quickly as the attacking force is able to break free of the foldpoint, it will divide into two groups. The first group will race to the third foldpoint in the Aezer system, the one leading back into Ryall space. There they will attempt to destroy all Ryall reinforcements as they materialize. The second group will cross the system and engage the Aezer–Hermes defenses from behind, thus clearing the foldpoint for entry by the Hermes battle group. Once we've occupied Aezer in strength, we should be able to hold the system against anything the centaurs can throw at us."

"An interesting plan," Admiral Ryerson said. "Have you subjected it to rigorous analysis?"

"We have," Foster replied. "We estimate an 85 percent chance of success if we use two battle groups in the attack, 97 percent if we use three."

"We'll have to check your data."

"Of course," Admiral Gower replied from his place beside Drake.

For the next six hours, the conference discussed the myriad details that would have to be worked out for such an attack to succeed. There was the matter of outfitting one or two battle groups with antiradiation fields and of the support ships that would be required. There was the operation's impact on Grand Fleet operations in the rest of human space. And finally, there was the cost to be considered. As the sun disappeared behind the nearby mountains, sending tongues of azure shadow leaping across fleet headquarters, Admiral Belton called a halt to the discussions. "We've done enough for today, people. Major Krael, how long to convert this proposal into a feasibility plan and program it into your computers?"

"Twelve to sixteen hours, sir," Belton's chief of analysis said. "We should have preliminary results by the day after tomorrow."

"Then I propose that we reconvene at that time. Is that agreeable to you, Admiral Gower?"

"It is."

"Very well. I hereby declare this meeting to be adjourned!"

CHAPTER 24

Richard Drake's third full day on Earth began with a meeting of the various Helldiver working groups to discuss what each had discovered since their reception by the Interstellar Council. The meeting took place in the ballroom of the hotel where the delegation was staying. There had been some talk of choosing another site to make electronic eavesdropping more difficult, but the state of the technology was such that countermeasures of that kind were largely ineffective. And since they lacked the equipment to make the meeting room truly "bug-proof," Admiral Gower saw no reason not to let convenience control the choice.

By and large, the reports were encouraging. Count Husanic, speaking for the diplomatic/political working group, announced that the council leaders had shown considerable interest in reestablishing relations with the lost colonies of Alta and Sandar. Indeed, if the cause of reunification had a problem, it was probably with the Altan Parliament and the Sandarian Royal Council. For in the years since Sandar's isolation, the Interstellar Council had significantly increased the cost of membership in the community of human-occupied planets. Current war taxes alone amounted to a full 10 percent of a planet's gross output. Additionally, each planet was required to raise and maintain a full squadron of ships for incorporation into the Grand Fleet.

One of the agreements discussed by the diplomats had been a protocol concerning the exchange of technology. The terrestrials had been quick to emphasize that the signing of such an agreement would require the immediate surrender of all data pertaining to the antiradiation field. In return, the I.C. would give Alta and Sandar full rights to all data classified as militarily sensitive.

Another tentative agreement called for the Altan and Sandarian high commands to turn over all intelligence information concerning the Ryall to the Grand Fleet. Upon hearing the proposal, Admiral Gower wondered aloud whether the terrestrials had any particular intelligence data in mind. He didn't say so aloud, but his tone made it clear that his question was really: "Do they know about the Ryall astrogation data?" Count Husanic assured him that the sharing of intelligence data was merely one of many prerequisites to representation of the Interstellar Council.

Following Count Husanic's report, Richard Drake reviewed the progress of the military working group and emphasized the fact that their plan to free the Aezer system was being evaluated by Grand Fleet experts even as they spoke. Finally, several scientists summarized the results of their studies. None had come across any startling new developments, but several commented that they were dismayed by the emphasis that the terrestrials placed on defensive research versus offensive. "If you ask me," one said, "they are trying to dig themselves a hole and pull it in after them."

The meeting broke up shortly after noon. Richard Drake, with nothing pending, decided that the time had come to see the sights of Mexico City. He stopped in the hotel gift shop, which was almost as large as a Homeport department store, and purchased what the saleslady assured him was a typical leisure outfit in the current style. He changed from his uniform, made sure that he had plenty of pesos, and took the lift to the lobby. There he found Bethany waiting for one of the lifts to arrive and take her upstairs.

"Hello, stranger!"

Bethany glanced at the obvious local type in the chartreuse kilt and lime-green shirt, looked away, then looked back again with wide eyes as she recognized the familiar face. "Richard! I was beginning to wonder if you had been swallowed up in a chasm somewhere. Where did you get that outfit?"

"Like it?" he asked, posturing to show off what—to Altan eyes, at least—appeared to be a caricature of bad taste. "The lady assured me that I would blend right in."

"In a neon jungle, maybe," she replied, laughing. "Have you eaten yet?"

"Is that an invitation to lunch, my love?"

"It is."

"Then I accept. And no, I haven't eaten yet."

"Fine. Let's go up to my room so I can change."

"I'm right behind you."

Drake waited in the bedroom while Bethany slipped into what he thought of as another "native costume"—a mauve skirt and blouse with dark purple boots and a matching shoulder bag.

"I see we shop in the same store," she said as she slipped into his arms and tilted her head up for a kiss.

"Or take advice from the same saleswoman," he said just before planting his lips on hers. They stayed that way for long seconds before breaking the embrace. He indicated the double bed with a tilt of his head. "Care to delay lunch?"

"It's tempting," she replied, "but I've had a big morning and I'm famished."

"Then lunch it is. Do you know someplace besides the hotel restaurant where we can eat?"

"I do. Come on, we'll find a cab."

The restaurant was on top of one of the tall buildings downtown. It was decorated to appear as a forest clearing, with the tables interspersed among tall trees. A small, gurgling stream ran through the dining area at a slant. A small wooden bridge crossed the stream where it bisected the main walkway.

"Nice," Drake said as he glanced around. "How do you know about this place?"

"Ryssa told me about it."

"Who's Ryssa?"

"My guide. She's also the daughter of the second co-ordinator."

Drake whistled. "Sounds like you've been getting the VIP treatment."

She nodded. At that moment, a waiter appeared, handed them two ornate, gilt-edged menus, and took their drink orders.

"Tell me about your morning," Drake said.

"Beg your pardon?" Bethany replied absentmindedly as she attempted to read the indecipherable Spanish of the menu.

"You said you had a big morning back at the hotel. Tell me about it."

"Not much to tell, Richard. I met Ryssa's father, and he gave me this." Bethany reached into her shoulder bag, retrieved a small rectangular box, opened it, and handed it to Drake. Inside was a golden medallion suspended from a multicolored ribbon.

"Beautiful. What is it?"

"Merely the Order of Terra, the highest medal that can be awarded to someone in the diplomatic service. They presented it to me so that I can give it to Uncle Clarence."

"You've delivered your dispatches!"

Bethany nodded.

"Well, I say this calls for a drink." Drake signaled their waiter and asked that their order be changed to champagne. When the glasses arrived, they held their drinks aloft while Drake proposed a toast. "To duties fulfilled and promises yet to keep."

Bethany put her drink down on the white tablecloth. "That was very poetic, Richard. What did it mean?"

"You don't remember!" he accused.

"Remember what?"

"A certain night two years ago. We were walking in

the garden of the Sandarian Royal Palace, looking at all
the flowers..."

"I remember, silly! That was the night you proposed
to me."

"And you said?"

"I said yes."

"I beg to differ, my love. You said, 'Yes, as soon as I
deliver my uncle's dispatches to Earth.' Remember?"

"Of course I remember."

"You've delivered your dispatches. So, how about
it?"

"You want to get married? *Now?*"

"Why not now?"

"Come to think of it," Bethany replied, "I can't think
of any reason why we shouldn't."

"Good! Let's find someone who can tell us about the
local customs. Where do you suppose we should look?"

"There's no need," Bethany replied. "I asked Ryssa
about local marriage customs yesterday."

"Oh?" Drake asked, his eyebrows rising.

Bethany turned red. "I don't know how the subject
came up. It just did. The first thing I knew, Ryssa was
talking about what it takes to get married in Mexico
City."

"I'm not criticizing, merely curious about what she
told you."

"We have to go down to the local hall of records and
take out a license. The cost is one hundred pesos. After
that there is a three-day waiting period, following which
we can be married in either a religious or a civil ceremony."

"You said you wanted to be married in a cathedral.
Any idea where we might find one?"

"Ryssa said that she would be glad to talk to the
priests at *Catedral Metropolitana*. It's mostly used as a
church museum these days, but they occasionally hold
weddings there, too. Since Ryssa's father is the second
coordinator, she doesn't think she'll have much difficulty talking them into allowing us to use the cathedral."

"You *have* been busy, haven't you?" he asked.
When she started to blush again, he reached out and

patted her hand. "Here's the afternoon schedule: We finish lunch, go down to the hall of records, pay our hundred pesos, and then end up back at the hotel. Agreeable to you?"

"Whatever you say, my love."

Later, Bethany rested her head on Drake's chest while he stroked up and down her spine. "I can hardly believe it! Three more days and we'll be husband and wife."

"Shall I get the license out and let you look at it again?"

"No need, Richard. Besides, you know I can't read it anyway."

After lunch they had indeed sought out the Ciudad de México Ministerio de Registrador and recorded their desire to obtain a marriage license. They had been asked to fill out innumerable forms and answer a number of questions put to them by a functionary with a self-important air about him. When the functionary had satisfied himself that all was in order and that the proper fee had been paid, they were issued a marriage license printed in Spanish.

Bethany had called Ryssa from the municipal building where the ministerio was located. The blond woman had smiled broadly at the news and had immediately asked to speak with the lucky man. Drake had moved into the phone pickup's field of view and introduced himself.

"You are a lucky man, Captain Drake. I hope you know that."

"I am well aware of that fact, Miss Blenham."

"I'm Ryssa to my friends, Captain."

"And I'm Richard to mine, Ryssa."

"I'm looking forward to meeting you in the flesh, Richard. I'll call the cathedral immediately and make a reservation. Any particular time?"

"Any time after three days from now," he replied.

"Let's see, your waiting period is up Friday afternoon. Will Saturday morning be acceptable?"

"More than acceptable."

"Then Saturday it is. If I run into a hitch, I'll try for Sunday afternoon between services."

"Fine," Bethany said.

"Have you done any shopping for your trousseau yet?" Ryssa asked.

Bethany laughed. "We only decided to get married an hour ago. I haven't had the time!"

"How about if I stop by your hotel tomorrow morning and we go buy out the town?"

"I don't want to be a bother, Ryssa."

"A bother? My dear, this is the most excitement I've had this year! Why, this is a true-life fairy tale. Just wait until the news media get hold of the story!"

"Uh, we were hoping to keep this out of the press, Ryssa," Drake replied. He had been observing the terrestrial media on the few occasions when he had free time and wasn't sure that he liked what he saw.

"Wish we could, Richard," Ryssa replied. "You entered your names in the registrar's computer, did you not?"

"Yes."

"Then it's already too late. The fax services have already been alerted. Believe me, they have some of the most sophisticated information recall programs on this or any other planet. They probably assigned a reporter to follow up about the time Bethany was punching my number into the phone."

"We didn't know!" Bethany said. "Is there any way we can undo it?"

Ryssa thought a moment. "You can register me as your agent for the affair. That will force them to deal through me. The privacy laws are very strict on such matters."

"How do we do that?"

Ryssa reached out and touched a control somewhere out of sight of the phone pickup. "Do you, Richard Drake and Bethany Lindquist, legal residents of Alta, Valeria IV, assign to one Ryssa Blenham the sole right to act as your personal agent for your upcoming nuptials?"

"We do," Drake replied.

"Bethany has to say it, too!"

"We do," Bethany agreed.

"Then that's taken care of. I'll register with the ministry, and you'll be shielded from inquisitive reporters."

"Thank you, Ryssa."

"You're welcome, Bethany. The best of luck to both of you, and I'll be there at 0700 tomorrow to help you do your shopping. Good-bye, Captain Drake."

"Good-bye, Ryssa."

After they had signed off, they had taken a cab back to the hotel for an afternoon of lovemaking. The sun was just beginning to color the western sky red when Bethany was reminded of something tnat she had been meaning to tell him but that she had forgotten in the excitement.

"Richard."

"Yes, my love?"

"Mind if we discuss business for a bit?"

"If we must," he replied lazily.

She rolled off him and propped herself up on one elbow. "Something happened at the ceremony today that you should know about."

He turned to face her and in so doing mimicked her position. "What?"

"Coordinator Blenham asked me why we had a Ryall prisoner onboard *Discovery*."

Drake blinked and then sat straight up in bed. He was suddenly fully awake and alert. "What did you tell him?"

"That I was engaged in research on Ryall psychology, that Varlan was my subject, and that he would have to talk to either you or Admiral Gower if he wanted more details."

"Did he act as though he knew about a certain item?"

"I don't think so, Richard, but it's difficult to be sure. I think he was merely checking out Greg Oldfield's report of a Ryall aboard our ship. When I explained that the research was confidential, he told me about various psychodrugs which the terrestrials have developed for use on Ryall prisoners. He offered to place specialists at my disposal if I wanted to use them."

"You can't very well accept his offer."

"Why not?"

"Because Varlan knows far too much to risk narco-quiz. I wonder if the offer wasn't a ploy on Blenham's part."

"Then you *do* think that he suspects something?" she asked.

Drake told her about the proposed agreement that required the colonists to share all intelligence information and Count Husanic's theory that it was a mere formality. "Originally, I thought so, too. Now, with your news, I'm not so sure."

"But how *could* they know?"

"That," Drake replied, "is one hell of a good question!"

Sometime during the night each Helldiver delegate received a message in his or her hotel room that the various working group meetings scheduled for the following day had been canceled. In their place there would be a conference in the Hall of Ministers at council headquarters at 1000 hours.

"What's going on?" Bethany asked Drake when he showed her the note that he had found in the message basket of his hotel fax machine.

"I imagine Admiral Belton's people have finished their analysis of our plan for getting Aezer back."

"Is this a good sign or a bad sign?"

He shook his head. "I wish I knew."

"Do you think Admiral Gower would mind if I tagged along?" Bethany asked.

"I thought you and Ryssa were going shopping this morning."

"I'll call and cancel. This is more important."

"In that case, you're invited whether Admiral Gower minds or not. This concerns all of us."

If Gower was surprised when Bethany showed up on Drake's arm at the Hall of Ministers, he didn't show it. The hall was a large, elliptical room dominated by a single conference table. Guides in the livery of the council bureaucracy ushered each newly arrived colonist to a seat, while across the table, the terrestrial attendees were slowly filtering in. Drake nodded to Admirals Belton and Ryerson as he took his seat. Both acknowledged his greeting, but with a curtness that made it impossible for him to prejudge the outcome of the coming conference. Seated two places down from Belton was a civilian whose features bore a strong family resemblance to those of Ryssa Blenham. Drake wasn't surprised when one of the terrestrials addressed the man as "Coordinator Blenham."

Two minutes later the first coordinator entered the hall through a door opposite the one through which the colonists had entered. Drake recognized him from his official portrait, which hung in the lobby of Grand Fleet Headquarters across town. The first coordinator conferred briefly with Blenham and Admiral Belton, then gaveled the meeting to order. As soon as silence had descended in the hall, he faced Stan Barrett and Count Husanic.

"Who will speak for your side, gentlemen? You, Mr. Barrett?"

"I yield to Count Husanic, Coordinator. He will act as Helldiver spokesman."

"Very well. Since this is the first time we have all been assembled in a single spot, I suggest that we each introduce ourselves. For those who do not know me, I am First Coordinator Dolph Gellard, council representative from United Europe, Earth." The introductions continued around the table, with each man or woman giving his or her name and occupation. When the circuit had been completed, Gellard formally announced the purpose of the meeting.

"On Tuesday last, at Grand Fleet Headquarters, Admiral Gower's people presented a plan by which the Ryall might be driven from the Aezer system. Grand Admiral Belton's staff has studied this proposal for the past two days, and the grand admiral informs me that they are now ready to respond. Admiral Belton, the floor is yours!"

Belton spoke to an aide, and suddenly the tapestries that covered the walls on each side of the table slid apart to reveal a pair of holoscreens positioned to give everyone a clear view. Each screen came alight to display the same foldspace topology chart that Commander Foster had used during his presentation to the military working group. Belton quickly explained how Foster had proposed to drive the Ryall from the Aezer star system.

"Now then," he said after completing his summary, "my staff has analyzed this plan, and we are prepared to make our official recommendations to the council. Before doing so, however, I would like to take a few moments to explain some of the factors which have a bearing on our results. We basically utilized the same data as Commander Foster of Admiral Gower's staff, with three exceptions:

"First, in our opinion, Foster's estimate of Ryall force strength in the Aezer system is much too low. Based on the strength which the Ryall displayed at the Battle of Sandar, we believe the Ryall fleet to have a minimum of fifty percent more ships in the system than the Altan–Sandarian data give them credit for. Therefore, and to ensure that we err on the side of conservatism, we assumed twice as many Ryall ships are at Aezer than did Commander Foster.

"Secondly, we believe that the composition of available human forces used in Foster's analysis was not realistic in that he underestimated the number of capital ships available for both the diversionary attack and the primary assault force. This we remedied in our own analyses.

"Finally, we evaluated Foster's numbers concerning the number of Ryall warships which will be drawn away by a diversionary attack on the Aezer–Hermes foldpoint and the time it would take for that foldpoint to be reinforced. In both cases we made minor adjustments to the data before we ran our analyses.

"We then ran a number of worst-case analyses of the Altan–Sandarian plan. We are happy to report that, given our assumptions and even with the modifications I've mentioned, a coordinated assault by the combined Grand Fleet, Altan, and Sandarian forces has a better than eighty percent chance of succeeding. In light of this result, the Grand Fleet is prepared to recommend that the proposed plan be adopted by the full Interstellar Council."

"Thank you, Grand Admiral," Coordinator Gellard replied. "And my congratulations to you, Admiral Gower, for the excellent work by your staff."

"Does that mean that you will go ahead with the operation, Coordinator?"

"It means, Admiral, that you have made it over the first hurdle. There are, however, several other things which need to be considered before we leap too precipitously into the unknown."

"Such as?"

"Specifically, there is the matter of Altan and Sandarian representation on the Interstellar Council. Count Husanic, are your people ready to accept the burdens which come with membership?"

"They are, Coordinator."

"And you, Mr. Barrett? Will the Altan Parliament agree to our terms?"

"I fail to see that we have any choice in the matter, Mr. Coordinator."

"In that case, gentlemen, it would seem that we have cleared the day's second obstacle. Shall we try for three? What does our chief economist say about these two planets rejoining the Community of Man?"

A small man with a permanent stoop rose from his position near the end of the table on the terrestrial side. "Mr. Coordinator, the Office of Economic Evaluation has no objection to these two systems' reintegration into human space. Any economic dislocations which result will be short-lived and easily countered. There will be no need for even such mild measures as limited trade restrictions."

One by one, the first coordinator polled his experts up and down the table. One by one, the experts gave him the green light to proceed with the incorporation of Alta and Sandar into the body politic of human space. While the head of the Department of Manpower Utilization was making his report, Gellard turned and held a whispered conference with an aide. The aide nodded, reached down, and extracted a sheaf of papers from a briefcase out of sight under the table. He handed the papers to the first coordinator, who looked at them carefully. Even from where he was seated, Drake could see the golden flash of an ornate seal that had been attached to the first sheet in the stack.

"Ladies and gentlemen," the coordinator said, following the manpower expert's report, "I hold in my hand the official applications for membership of Alta, Valeria IV, and Sandar, Hellsgate IV, to the Interstellar Council. These papers require only my own signature and that of Second Coordinator Blenham for your applications to go to the full council. However, before we will sign, there is one additional matter which must be resolved. Commodore Grast, will you please come in?"

This last was apparently addressed to thin air. However, a moment later, the door behind the first coordinator opened and an officer Drake had never seen before entered the conference hall. Simultaneously, there was a quiet gasp from Bethany.

"What is it?" Drake asked.

"He's the one who asked me about Varlan," she replied.

The officer scanned the ranks of the colonists with cold eyes for long seconds before speaking. "Good morning, ladies and gentlemen. My name is Alphonse Grast. I am with military intelligence. Although we have never met before—with the single exception of Miss Lindquist—I feel that I know most of you personally. You see, I am the officer assigned to resolve a mystery which first came to our attention when we reviewed certain recordings made by First Secretary Oldfield while your ship was still in the Goddard system.

"During routine voice stress analysis of statements made by Captain Drake, Admiral Gower, Stanislaw Barrett, Count Husanic, and others, it came to our attention that you were displaying symptoms which usually would indicate that you were not telling us the truth. These symptoms are extremely subtle, but over the years we have made a science of detecting and categorizing them—a very *exact* science, I might add.

"Although our curiosity was aroused, we weren't particularly concerned at first. After all, it was to be expected that you would shade the truth a bit to improve your bargaining position. However, as we studied you more and more, the pattern of prevarication began to take on increasingly ominous overtones. To be blunt about it, whenever anyone asked you about your journey through the nebula, or whenever the general subject of the Ryall arose in a conversation, your voice stress patterns suggested that we should not believe what you were telling us. Despite our best efforts, however, we have been unable to figure out the reason for this behavior. Therefore, I ask you now. What is it that you are trying to hide?"

Husanic looked at Barrett, who glanced at Gower and Drake in turn. After half a minute of silence, Count Husanic cleared his throat. "A useful technique, this voice stress analysis. I wish we had known about it earlier."

"It would have done you no good, sir," Grast replied. "The physiological reactions which the technique measures are totally involuntary. You can partially mask them if you understand the principles involved, but no one is a good enough actor to eliminate them completely."

Husanic sighed and looked at Coordinator Gellard. "As Commodore Grast has surmised, we do know something that we have kept from you. Specifically, we are in possession of data vital to the prosecution of the war."

"What data, sir?"

"Extremely valuable data, Mr. Coordinator. Before we divulge what we know, however, we must have your assurance that you will help us against the Ryall."

"You see your applications for membership in the Interstellar Council before you, sir," Gellard replied. "We cannot give you a greater assurance than that. Nor can we act on your application until we know what it is that you know."

"Very well, Mr. Coordinator. I will take you at your

word." Count Husanic turned to face Admiral Gower. "The ball would seem to be in your court, Admiral."

Gower nodded slowly. "I suppose we have gotten what we came for. Ladies and gentlemen, our journey here was not quite as straightforward as we have led you to believe. We did, in fact, take one small detour en route..."

CHAPTER 25

Saturday morning dawned crisp and clear. The rising sun was a golden ball framed by the blue-tinged flanks of the Istacíhuatl and Popocatepetl volcanoes. A gentle wind from the southeast carried with it the smell of pines and the promise of cool weather. Richard Drake stood on the balcony of his hotel room and breathed deeply of the crisp morning air as he surveyed the city. To the north, the sun's rays reflected off the windows of the neo-Aztec megastructures that housed much of the city's population. The vast pyramids fluoresced with orange fire all across their eastern flanks, while on their western slopes, aircraft avoidance beacons still stabbed out into space at a steady rate of one flash each second. Directly below Drake's vantage point, maintenance machines fanned out across one of the city's many greenswards to begin their daily tasks. Halfway to the horizon, a traffic circle was just beginning to fill with vehicles as people got an early start on their Saturday morning errands. As he watched Mexico City come awake on the day he was to be married, Richard Drake was reminded of how much difference forty-eight hours can make in a situation.

The catalyst, of course, had been Admiral Gower's

revelation that the Helldiver Expedition had in its possession astrogation data for the Ryall hegemony. The mood in the Hall of Ministers had changed quickly following the announcement. Terrestrials who moments earlier had stared at their colonial counterparts with expressions of suspicion and distrust were suddenly wide-eyed at the prospect of learning the topology of enemy space. Admiral Gower had barely finished his statement before being deluged with questions about the data. When he refused to say any more, Coordinator Gellard suggested that they finalize the terms under which Alta and Sandar would take their rightful places among the worlds of human space.

It had taken less than a hour for the two sides to reach a tentative agreement. For their part, the terrestrials agreed to start planning for the Aezer campaign immediately. In return, the colonists promised that their first official act as newly inducted members of the Interstellar council would be to turn over all captured data to the council and the Grand Fleet.

A session of the full Interstellar Council was convened later that same afternoon. The sole purpose of the session was to induct Alta and Sandar back into the political organization of human space. With the other Helldiver personnel looking on, Count Husanic and Stan Barrett were each given their charters of responsibility, welcomed formally to the Interstellar Council by Coordinator Gellard, and escorted to their seats by a delegation of senior council representatives. As soon as both were properly seated, they were given a standing ovation by everyone in the hall. At the end of the ceremony, which lasted less than twenty minutes, the council was adjourned by acclamation.

Half an hour later it was the colonists' turn to uphold their part of the bargain. Argos Cristobal found himself in a large lecture hall in front of a holoscreen and a hastily gathered audience of council representatives, Grand Fleet officers, and university professors. Cristobal used a series of foldspace topology charts to explain what the Helldiver Fleet had learned about Ryall space, including the fact that the hegemony occupied a single, closely coupled foldspace cluster. The briefing lasted for more than an hour, with numerous interruptions for questions. It ended finally with the distribution of record tiles containing copies of the captured Ryall data.

That night, Coordinator Gellard hosted a gala in honor of human space's two newest worlds. Midway through his opening remarks, the first coordinator surprised everyone by announcing the pending marriage of Richard Drake and Bethany Lindquist. The crowd, which was already buzzing with news of the day's events, had screamed their approval at the news. The astonished couple fought their way through a crowd of well-wishers to the podium, where Drake stammered out a speech of appreciation in which he somehow managed to invite everyone present to attend the ceremony.

The following two days had been long and busy for Richard and Bethany. Drake had divided his time between assisting Grand Fleet analysts in their planning for the Aezer campaign and fending off Mexico City florists who wanted to provide the flowers for the wedding "at cost." Bethany and Ryssa Blenham had spent all of Thursday shopping for Bethany's trousseau and appearing on afternoon holovision programs. Friday had been spent in getting Bethany's wedding dress fitted and at the beauty parlor. As a result of their schedules, the bride and groom didn't see each other again until Friday evening. The occasion that brought them together was the wedding rehearsal.

Like most Spanish colonial churches, *Catedral Metropolitana* sported twin bell towers and a number of architectural styles—a legacy of the three hundred years required to complete construction. Inside, the wedding party gathered in front of the ornate *Altar del Rey*—the Altar of the King—to receive instruction concerning the following day's ceremony. Admiral Gower was to give the bride away, while Phillip Walkirk had been chosen Drake's best man. Their instructor was a young priest who acted as the assistant to the Archbishop of Mexico City.

A minor hitch developed when the archbishop's assistant discovered that the couple were members of the Church of Alta. He agreed to proceed when a quick comparison of doctrine turned up no beliefs sufficiently unorthodox to block the ceremony and after Ryssa Blenham took him aside to explain the political importance of this particular wedding. The rehearsal had then continued without a problem.

"What's this?" Drake asked as they were leaving and came to a high scaffold toward the back of the cathedral on which several holocameras and long-range microphones were mounted.

"I told you that people would be interested in your wedding," Ryssa replied. "They're going to beam the ceremony over one of the auxiliary entertainment channels. They expect a couple of million people to watch tomorrow—not a large number compared to a grand network hookup, but not bad for a simple wedding."

"I'm beginning to wonder just how *simple* this wedding is going to be," Drake had replied.

Ryssa laughed. "Never let it be said that we don't show a visitor a good time!"

The rest of Friday evening had been taken up by a post-wedding-rehearsal party. When Drake finally returned to his hotel, it was well past midnight. He woke an hour before dawn, showered, shaved, and stepped outside onto the balcony to greet the coming dawn.

"Scared?" Phillip Walkirk asked in a stage whisper. He and Drake were standing in front of the gilt *Altar del Rey*, looking out over the rows of filled pews.

"Frightened to death," Drake whispered back.

As they stood there, they were assaulted by the sound of hundreds of separate conversations. Seating for the event had been by strict protocol order. The front pews were reserved for friends of the bride and groom—at the very least, people who had actually met them. Officials of the Interstellar Council came next, followed by officers of the Mexican government and of the Grand Fleet. Seating for the general public was on a first-come–first-served basis and took up the rear half of the cathedral where the pews disappeared into gloom. The news media hadn't been provided seating. They roamed freely through the aisles with their hand-held cameras. However, out of respect for the solemnity of the event they were attired in the same formal wear as the other guests.

Drake wore his best dress uniform, with the Order of Sandar on his breast. Phillip Walkirk was also in uniform. He wore the dress blues of the Sandarian Navy. Other Altan and Sandarian uniforms were sprinkled throughout the front rows of the cathedral.

Suddenly, the cathedral organ fell silent. It had been softly playing a series of tunes that Drake hadn't recognized. A ripple of expectation swept through the crowd as numerous necks were craned and heads turned to gaze toward the narthex at the rear of the cathedral. There was a flurry of activity at the back of the long central aisle. The priest who had conducted the previous evening's rehearsal strode purposely up the cathedral's right side aisle. He stopped at the control box set back in an alcove. The chandeliers overhead slowly dimmed, and a series of spotlights high in the rafters sprang to light. Particles of dust scintillated in the beams as the central aisle was illuminated with brilliant white light.

The organ stuttered for several notes, then began the sonorous strains of "The Wedding March." There followed a vast noise as five hundred spectators rose to their feet and turned to face the rear. A pair of flower girls stepped off from the back of the cathedral, pacing slowly forward in time to the music, sprinkling rose petals as they came. They were followed by a dozen maids of honor in matching organdy dresses. Then murmurs of appreciation and wishes for a long life arose at the back of the church and slowly moved forward as the bride came into view.

Bethany's gown was of white, iridescent cloth. The bodice shaded from opaque to translucent as it rose from breast to shoulders, and the skirt sparkled with a thousand tiny stars. The white lace veil was supported by a mantilla in the local style. The gown was completed with a train that stretched four meters behind Bethany as she marched into view on Admiral Gower's arm. Drake barely noticed his superior. Like everyone else in the cathedral, he had eyes only for his bride.

The ceremony was in Spanish, since the Archbishop of Mexico City either didn't know or didn't choose to use Standard. After a short ceremony in which the Archbishop asked God's blessings on the congregation, he read a portion of the marriage ceremony in Spanish, then halted to allow the younger priest to translate. Rather than being awkward, Drake found that the stately pauses provided a certain solemnity to the occasion.

"Who giveth this woman to this man?...Do you, Richard Arthur Drake...promise to love, honor, and cherish...in sickness and in health...in good times and in bad...so long as you both shall live?"

"I do."

"Do you, Bethany Patricia Lindquist...promise to love, honor, and obey...in sickness and in health...in good times and in bad...so long as you both shall live?"

"I do."

"By the power vested in me by His Holiness, by the officials of Ciudad de México, and Estados Unidos Méxicanos...and in the name of the Father, the Son, and the Holy Spirit...I now pronounce you man and wife.

"You may kiss the bride!"

"I don't want this to end!"

Bethany was lying beside Drake on the beach at Acapulco, soaking up the rays of a sun she had never really expected to see in her lifetime. Despite the season—early winter—and the cool temperature, the rays warmed her back and suffused her with a feeling of total well-being.

"Neither do I," her new husband said as he worked suntan lotion into her skin. They were alone, and Bethany had removed the halter top of her swimming suit to develop an even tan. Every third stroke, Drake would let his hand drop down her side to the swell of her breast. The barely perceptible shiver that ran through her body told him that she was enjoying the attention.

Their honeymoon had been everything both of them had hoped for. They had spent their nights in passionate lovemaking and their days laying in the cool water of Acapulco Bay. One day they would skin-dive along the rocky shore, and the next they would take a sailboat out into the Sea of Cortez. And on some days they would merely swim and lie in the sand. During the evenings they would take in the varied nightlife of a city that had been a tourist attraction for nearly seven hundred years.

Almost as much fun for Bethany were the Acapulco shops. Twice she had taken Drake on buying sprees, spending money freely until he'd begun to worry about the bills coming due.

"How do you propose to pay for all of this?" he'd asked, gesturing to the packages she had loaded him down with.

"Ryssa said there was a considerable sum of cash in the wedding gifts. I was going to use that. And if we run short, I can always tap the stipend that accompanied the Order of Terra," she informed him cheerfully.

"That money belongs to your uncle!"

"I've got enough saved up in the Bank of Homeport to make it good once we get home. And then, of course, there's your own fabulous salary as a naval oficer, my dear husband!"

Drake's response had been a half-hearted attempt at strangling his bride. Throughout its history, the Altan Space Navy had been forced to operate on a shoestring. Even though the Ryall threat had changed that, the pay scales hadn't been revised upward since Drake's first year out of the naval academy.

For an entire week they were just two people in love. They ate together, slept together, showered together, and made love together. By mutual consent, neither turned on the holovision set in their bungalow, looked at a newsfax, or consciously listened to other people's conversations. It was as though the rest of the universe had faded to unreality and only the two honeymooners mattered in the scheme of things.

On the seventh day, Drake found himself on the beach, rubbing suntan lotion into his wife's back. After long consideration, he reluctantly punctured the cocoon with which they had surrounded themselves. "We ought to be thinking about a return to Mexico City, you know."

"Must we, Richard?" she asked lazily.

"I'm afraid so. Admiral Gower isn't going to let me lie on the beach forever. Not while he's doing all the work of liaison with the Interstellar Council."

"I would think a little work would be good for him."

Drake laughed as his hands swept once more down her bare back. "That isn't the proper attitude for a Navy wife, my love. Admirals don't work. They *own* people who work."

She was silent for long minutes. So long, in fact, that he thought she might have fallen asleep. Finally, she spoke. "When were you thinking of going back, Richard?"

"Monday morning," he replied. "That way, we will have had eight full days of honeymoon."

She sighed. "I suppose that's more than a lot of other people get in their lives. I'd hoped we could see more of Earth, though."

"There's nothing to keep us from going on tour later," he replied. "It will take at least three months to work out the details for the attack on Aezer."

Bethany sighed. "There will always be an attack to plan, won't there, Richard? Our lives are destined to be filled with battle—preparations for, fighting of, and recovery from."

"I don't know about that," Drake replied. "After all, once we've retrieved Aezer from the centaurs, Alta should be fairly safe. And I won't be able to ride the ships forever, you know. One of these days the flight surgeon will downcheck me for lack of acceleration tolerance. After a few years behind a desk I'll be eligible for retirement."

Bethany snorted. "What will you do in retirement?"

"We could always move to West Continent and start a farm."

There was a long silence, broken only by the sound of the waves pounding the shore. Finally, Bethany said, "Do you know what I sometimes find myself thinking of, Richard?"

"Yours truly, I hope."

She laughed. "That too. But sometimes I remember how beautiful it was on Corlis. That valley where the Ryall had their mine and smelter must have been something to see before they stripped it of vegetation. Now, if I were to go in for homesteading, that's the place I'd like to do it."

"Too bad Corlis is in Ryall space."

"Yes, too bad," she replied. Bethany had been resting face down on a beach towel. She suddenly reached under herself, held her halter in position, and sat up. Twisting to turn her back to her husband, she asked him to snap her top. He took his time about it and allowed his hands to roam lovingly as he did so. When he had finished, Bethany turned to face him. "Are we really going back to Mexico City on Monday?"

He nodded. "I think it's best."

"In that case, I want to talk to Coordinator Blenham as soon as we get back."

"What about?"

"He offered to lend me an interrogator for Varlan, remember? Now that the secret is out, I think I'll take him up on it."

"Why, for God's sake?"

"Because I think I was making progress with her on our trip from Goddard to Sol, but I can't really be sure. I want to give her a shot of truth drug to find out what she *really* thinks."

"What if she's been converted to our way of thinking?"

"Then there's hope that this war can end someday," Bethany replied. "Who knows, maybe we can actually make peace with the damned beasties!"

"And if not?"

"Then I suppose we'll have to kill them all."

They walked the beach and talked until after sunset, returning to their bungalow only when the air became too cool for comfort. Drake was the first to see the message with the red "urgent" stamp in the wire basket next to the phone.

"What is it?" Bethany asked as Drake tore open the outer envelope and retrieved the message flimsy inside. He read it through quickly.

"It's from Admiral Gower. I'm sorry, love, but we have to leave tonight."

"Why? What's happened?"

"Gower thinks there is some sort of trouble with the negotiations. The terrestrials have been acting noncommittal for the past couple of days. There's a rumor going around the capital that the Interstellar Council may be on the verge of rejecting the plan to attack Aezer!"

CHAPTER 26

Phillip Walkirk met the newlyweds at the Mexico City airport. It was nearly midnight, and the terminal was empty of everyone except late-night travelers.

"What's happened?" Drake asked as soon as he and Bethany had disembarked from the short-haul airliner that had transported them south from Acapulco.

"We're not exactly sure, Captain. Things were going well until last Wednesday. We were holding daily conferences with the Grand Fleet, making real progress in planning the Aezer assault. Then I was sent up to Washington to answer technical questions about the antiradiation field. When I returned yesterday, I found our whole delegation concerned that the terrestrials no longer seem interested in our problem. It's nothing you can put your finger on. They just aren't acting as aggressively as they had been. Also, several of the upper-level people have missed recent planning sessions."

"That hardly seems reason enough to start worrying that they'll go back on their word," Drake replied.

"Yes, sir. That's exactly what I said. But there are other indications of a problem, too. Stan Barrett and

Count Husanic have overheard conversations on the floor of the council."

"What conversations?"

"Vaguely disturbing references to Alta and Sandar. Whenever Barrett or Husanic try to ask anyone about it, that person always turns evasive. Also, the other representatives have taken to giving them looks."

"Looks?"

"Count Husanic describes them as the sort you would expect if you were suffering from a terminal disease and everyone but you knew about it."

"Can't Husanic clear this up with Coordinator Gellard?" Bethany asked.

"He's tried to get an appointment with the first coordinator for two days running," the prince replied. "So far, official word is that Gellard's schedule is filled up through the end of next week."

"Grand Admiral Belton?" Drake asked.

"Unavailable."

"How about Admiral Ryerson?"

"He's gone back up to *Teddy Roosevelt*. I've suggested that Captain Marston take the landing boat over to see him—the two ships are still only about a hundred kilometers apart in orbit—but Marston can't get permission to board the blastship. They're having 'maintenance problems.' Also, Ryerson is too busy to come to the screen."

Drake considered Phillip's words, then nodded. "Sounds like someone passed the word to place us on the pariah list."

"Yes, sir. That's what Admiral Gower thinks, too. It's his opinion that something has happened to cause the terrestrials to rethink our proposal, that they are still arguing about it among themselves, and that they don't want to talk to us until they've formulated policy."

"What about the second coordinator?" Bethany asked.

"Blenham?" Phillip Walkirk replied. "I don't think anyone has tried him yet. I doubt whether it would do any good considering all the other people who are 'unavailable.'"

"Maybe I should try," Bethany mused. "I still have his offer to help with Varlan's interrogation. I can use that as the excuse to get in to see him, then try to pump him for information."

"Are you willing to do that?" Drake asked. "After all, you are still officially on their side, you know."

She shook her head. "Not since I became Mrs. Richard Drake, citizen of Alta."

"Then that's what we'll do," Drake said. The three of them hurried to the baggage claim area and from there to the taxi stand in front of the terminal building. They were back at the delegation's hotel twenty minutes later.

"Mrs. Drake to see you, Coordinator. I told her that she would need an appointment during the regular work week, but she's very insistent."

Sir Joshua Blenham looked up from the report he was reading and frowned in the direction of his secretary. It was Sunday morning, and outside Blenham's floor-to-ceiling window, the Mexican capital was its usual sleepy self. It would get busy later in the day when weekend shoppers flooded the downtown malls. At the moment, however, everyone was either in church or else watching the European football championships on the holocube.

"Mrs. Drake? I'm sorry, but I don't know any Mrs. Drake."

"Have you forgotten that you attended her wedding last week?"

"Oh, Bethany Lindquist Drake! Why didn't you say so?"

"I believe that is precisely what I said, Coordinator."

"So you did! Please, send her in."

A minute later, Bethany walked through the door of the second coordinator's office. Blenham rose and crossed the distance between them in long strides. "Good morning, my dear. What brings you here on a Sunday morning?"

"I called your home, Coordinator. Ryssa told me that you were working today."

"Unfortunately, yes. The paperwork has been piling up around here all week. I thought I would get some filing done. But forgive my manners. Come in, have a seat! I'll see if Marisa can find us some hot coffee."

Bethany sat on the couch Blenham had indicated but refused the offer of refreshment. She'd tried Earth coffee when she first arrived and hadn't cared for the bitter brew. The aftertaste made her wonder what Alta's founding fathers had seen in the stuff.

"You are looking well," Blenham said once he too had settled on the couch. "I would say that married life agrees with you."

"It agrees with me very well, Coordinator. I only wish we could have stayed on the beach at least another week. Two would have been even better."

"Why didn't you?"

Bethany told him of the message that Richard had received in Acapulco and of Phillip Walkirk's comments when he picked them up at the airport the previous evening. "The entire Helldiver delegation is getting very concerned, sir. We are all hoping that someone in authority could explain what's happening to us."

Blenham looked uncomfortable for a moment. "I wish I could help, Bethany, but I'm not presently at liberty to tell you any more than you already know. As you have surmised, we've run into a problem. Our experts are trying to find their way around it. When they do, you will be told."

"Why not tell us now? Maybe we can help."

"I'm sorry, but I have my orders. I can say nothing more."

"I understand, Coordinator."

Blenham smiled wanly. "I doubt that you do, Mrs. Drake, but I admire your diplomacy for saying so. Is there anything else I can do for you?"

"Yes, sir. I would like to accept your offer of help with Varlan, that is, if it's still open."

"Of course! What is it that you would like?"

"Could you lend me one of your interrogation experts? I want to test Varlan to see how sincere she has been lately."

"Where will this interrogation take place?"

"Onboard *Discovery*, if that is all right with you."

"Suits me just fine. When would you like to do it?"

"As soon as possible."

"How about the day after tomorrow?"

"That will be fine."

"Very well, I will arrange it. And Bethany—"

"Yes, sir?"

"Try not to worry. Things will work themselves out presently."

Three days after Drake's return to Mexico City, the embargo on information was suddenly lifted when Drake, Admiral Gower, Stan Barrett, and Count Husanic were summoned to a meeting with the first coordinator.

"What do you suppose this means?" Drake asked Gower when the admiral showed him the invitation.

"I don't know," Gower replied. "Except for what little information your wife brought back from the second coordinator, we've been completely in the dark."

At the mention of his wife, Drake felt a pang of loneliness. Bethany's departure for orbit the previous evening was the first time the two of them had been apart since the wedding.

The four men arrived at the first coordinator's office on the top floor of council headquarters at the appointed hour. There they found the first coordinator, Second Coordinator Blenham, Grand Admiral Belton, and Admiral Ryerson waiting for them. There were handshakes all around as the eight settled into place around a small conference table. Coordinator Gellard began the meeting by thanking them for coming so promptly.

"You have to admit that you have a way of piquing a person's curiosity, Mr. Coordinator," Husanic replied.

"I must explain our recent behavior, Count Husanic. Approximately one week ago, Admiral Belton's experts stumbled onto something with potentially far-reaching consequences. We needed time to review the implications before we confronted you directly. I'm afraid our clumsiness in handling the matter was caused by an unauthorized leak on the floor of the Interstellar Council. Unfortunately, the man who started the rumors is a council representative, so there is very little we can do about his transgression. Still, he has caused you people considerable mental anguish, and for that I apologize on behalf of all of us. We should have acted differently."

"Apology accepted," Husanic replied. "Now, sir, can we get to whatever it is that is bothering you?"

"'If it were done...'twere well it were done quickly!'" the second coordinator quoted.

"Admiral Belton," the first coordinator said. "Will you please explain to our guests?"

"Yes, sir," Belton replied. The admiral got to his feet and walked over to a bookcase that covered an entire wall of the first coordinator's office. He manipulated a control, and several things began to happen simultaneously. The window behind the coordinator's desk turned opaque while a section of the bookcase swung forward to reveal a wall-mounted holoscreen. The screen came alight to reveal a foldspace map of the Ryall hegemony. The map had been color-coded to show the various interconnecting paths between Ryall stars.

"The data which you gentlemen provided has been a godsend," the admiral began, gesturing toward the foldspace topology chart. "In the nearly two weeks since we received this new information, our analysts have been working round the clock to incorporate it into our strategic and tactical doctrines. In order to accomplish this, we have been reanalyzing practically every engagement we've ever fought with the Ryall. In so doing, we have understood things which have puzzled us for the better part of a century. In short, gentlemen, we have been learning the advantages which the Spica Foldspace Cluster confers on the Ryall.

"The most important advantage which our enemies derive from the cluster comes from its unusually high connectivity quotient. This close coupling of the Ryall stars manifests itself in a number of ways, most of them bad from our point of view. As has already been noted by Captain Drake and others, the Spica Cluster allows the Ryall to utilize their forces much more effectively than can we. In other words, they are able to do the same job with far fewer ships."

"Do you have any quantitative figures on that?" Gower asked.

Belton nodded. "We think the factor is approximately two point seven. For the nonmilitary men among us, that means that 100 Ryall starships can do the work of 270 human ships."

A low whistle emanated from somewhere on Drake's left. He wasn't sure, but he thought it came from Stan Barrett.

Belton continued. "Nor is force multiplication the only manifestation of a high connectivity quotient. For with their short travel times, the Ryall have no need to defend in depth. They can concentrate their forces in those systems where they dispute with us. Should we open up a new front anywhere else, it's a relatively easy matter for them to rush forces to the new battle zone.

"Lastly, of course, there is the advantage which their tightly bound foldspace cluster confers on their industrial capabilities. The short travel distances and times, plus the numerous opportunities for transshipment, allow their planetary economies to be integrated with one another, whereas our own worlds' economies are only loosely bound together. With their low transportation costs, Ryall worlds can afford to specialize.

"We see this in the Ryall system of Carratyl, whose primary activity is the production of agricultural products for the rest of the hegemony. Presumably, there are Ryall worlds which specialize in the production of starships, and still others who are heavy- or light-industry specialists."

"So far, Admiral," Drake said, "you haven't said anything we didn't already know."

"Quite true, Captain. I have been discussing the strategic consequences of the fact that the Ryall hegemony occupies the Spica Foldspace Cluster. These are fairly obvious to anyone who cares to think about them. Now, let us turn to the tactical advantages, which aren't so easily determined."

Belton picked up a screen control and punched a number into its keypad. The Spica foldspace topology chart disappeared, to be replaced by one showing the relationship of the Hellsgate, Aezer, and Hermes systems, including all the foldpoints of each.

"Let us consider our battle plan for breaking the Ryall blockade of Aezer," Belton continued. "A Grand Fleet battle group will launch a diversionary attack against the Aezer–Hermes foldpoint in the hope that the Ryall commander will choose to strip his Aezer–Hellsgate defenses to provide reinforcements. Some forty hours later, a mixed force of Grand Fleet, Sandarian, and Altan starships will launch an all-out assault against the weakened Aezer–Hellsgate foldpoint. Once Aezer–Hellsgate is open, our ships will race to blockade the foldpoint leading back to Ryall space in order to cut off the flow of Ryall reinforcements and to attack the Aezer–Hermes defenses from behind."

Belton turned to face Gower and Drake. "It's a good plan, gentlemen. It has the elegance of simplicity and just the right touch of genius. Unfortunately, it has one minor defect. It won't work!"

There was a long pause in which Drake looked at Gower, and then both men locked eyes with their respective diplomatic representatives. Finally, Gower cleared his throat. "I fail to see a flaw in our thinking, Admiral Belton."

"The flaw," Belton replied, "is in the assumption that the Ryall will denude the Aezer–Hellsgate defenses in response to a threat against Aezer–Hermes. That seemed a logical assumption two weeks ago when you first presented your plan to us. However, now that we understand the hegemony's topology, we no longer believe the Ryall will choose to reinforce from within the Aezer system.

"Rather, we believe the Ryall commander will call for

reinforcements from the home worlds, which means that our force attacking from Hellsgate will be thrown against full-strength foldpoint defenses."

"The Ryall won't have time to get ships from the heart of Ryall space," Admiral Gower replied.

"I wish that were true," Belton responded. "However, we have simulated it a hundred times using a hundred different scenarios. Like us, the Ryall use communications relays between their front lines and their home worlds. It will take them less than eight hours to get word of the initial attack back into the heart of Ryall space. Even if we launched simultaneous assaults against both foldpoints and were able to punch through without unacceptable losses, by the time we reached the third Aezer foldpoint, we'd find it boiling with reinforcements."

The silence was even longer this time. Coordinator Gellard was the first to speak. When he did so, there was great sadness in his voice. "I'm sorry, gentlemen, but under the circumstances, we will have to withdraw our support from the plan to attack Aezer."

"*You're abandoning us?*"

"Not abandoning you, Captain Drake. Your worlds are members of the Interstellar Council, and we will treat them as such. We cannot, however, commit our forces to an attack we know will fail. Sorry."

"Forgive me if I appear confused, Mr. Coordinator," Admiral Gower replied in an icy voice. "You will not help us dislodge the Ryall from Aezer, but you are not abandoning us. What, precisely, does that mean?"

"We are proposing," Gellard said, "that you recognize reality. The truth is that both Alta and Sandar are in an untenable position and will not survive another twenty years of blockade."

"What other choice do we have?"

"We propose that you consider the possibility of evacuating your worlds. We will, of course, help transport your populations to other planets in human space."

CHAPTER 27

Bethany Drake lay in the acceleration couch and watched *Discovery* grow gradually larger in the bulkhead-mounted viewscreen. Beside her, a psychotechnician named Kirsten Moldare did the same. The two were the sole passengers aboard the small ground-to-orbit shuttle that had lifted out of Mohave Spaceport an hour previously, bound for low orbit.

"You came through an exploded star *in that*?" Kirsten asked as she gestured toward the screen where the Altan battle cruiser lay silhouetted against a black backdrop.

Bethany nodded. "More than once."

"My God, it must be at least a century old!"

"Closer to a century and a half. But *Discovery*'s been well cared for, so I think you'll find her a sound ship." Bethany pretended not to notice when her companion gulped conspicuously. Obviously, Kirsten had just remembered that she would soon board that antique in the center of the screen.

Coordinator Blenham had moved quickly to accommodate Bethany's request for a trained interrogator. One call to Grand Fleet Headquarters had resulted in Lieutenant Kirsten Moldare, Doctor of Alien Psychology, being assigned to assist in the examination of Varlan's motives.

The shuttle's approach and entry into the battle cruiser's hangar bay was accomplished without difficulty. The usual air rush and swirling expansion fog announced their safe arrival. Rorqual Marchant greeted the two women as they exited the forward air lock.

"Welcome back aboard, Bethany. And congratulations on your marriage! The captain couldn't have made a better choice."

"Did you have a chance to see the ceremony, Commander Marchant?" Bethany asked.

"Everyone onboard saw it, and they've been playing the recording ever since. *City of Alexandria*, too."

"Please thank the crew for their lovely wedding present." Ryssa Blenham had purchased a figurine of the Aztec goddess of fertility on behalf of the *Discovery*'s crew and had presented it to Richard and Bethany at the reception that had followed their wedding.

"You can thank them yourself. I've taken the liberty of scheduling lunch in the crew's mess. I hope you don't mind."

"I'm honored!" Bethany turned to indicate her companion. "Commander Rorqual Marchant, I would like to present Lieutenant Kirsten Moldare of the Grand Fleet. Kirsten, Commander Marchant, *Discovery*'s executive officer."

"Welcome aboard, Lieutenant."

"Thank you, Commander."

"Is there anything I can do to assist you while you're aboard *Discovery*?"

"You can restore spin gravity as quickly as possible, Commander. I'm an alien psychologist, not a line officer. My stomach has been trying to crawl up my backbone ever since we made orbit."

"You'll be feeling better in about fifteen minutes," Marchant replied.

Bethany helped Kirsten to Drake's office to await the promised return of a comfortable level of ship's spin. While they waited, the two women discussed the coming interview.

"None of this will hurt Varlan, will it?" Bethany asked.

Kirsten shook her head. "The suppressant I will be using has been judged pharmacologically safe for Ryall biochemistry. As for the possibility of the subject injuring herself, I will take care of that by administering an immobilizer."

"She isn't likely to become violent, is she?"

"Such reactions are quite common, Mrs. Drake. You must understand that the drug suppresses her higher mentation without affecting her emotions. Once she is under, Varlan will act very like a human being under the influence of a powerful psychodrug. Left unhindered in her movements, she could well injure either herself or us."

"What if she refuses to submit willingly? She's strong as two men, you know."

"I doubt that will be a problem. The Ryall are fairly stoic creatures once they know something is inevitable." Kirsten swallowed, lifted a hand, and patted her midsection. "I would say Commander Marchant has been as good as his word. Gravity seems to be restored."

Bethany nodded. "We're up to approximately one-tenth standard. It will get stronger rather quickly now."

"It's already enough to keep my stomach from doing flip-flops. Shall we go meet our subject?"

Bethany led Kirsten to the stateroom that had been converted into Varlan's quarters. She nodded to the Marine on duty in the corridor outside, then entered the cabin.

"Greetings, Bethany of the Lindquists!" Varlan's high-pitched whistle sang out as she caught sight of her visitors.

"Hello, Varlan. Miss me?"

"Very much. I observed your mating ritual on my entertainment screen. The symbolism seemed quite complex. I would like to speak of it at some future time."

"I'd be more than happy to talk to you, Varlan. Has the crew been treating you well?"

"They feed me regularly, but I miss our daily discussions."

Bethany nodded. "You aren't alone in that. Varlan, I would like you to meet Kirsten Moldare. She works for Those Who Rule on Earth. Kirsten, I have the honor to present Varlan of the Scented Waters, manager of the Corlis Mineral Extraction Complex and my friend."

"Greetings, Varlan," the psychologist replied, mimicking the Ryall gesture of obeisance as she did so. "It is an honor for one such as myself to meet so accomplished a member of the Great Race."

Varlan put her earflaps full up and regarded this new human with one obsidian eye. "Greetings, Kirsten of the Moldares. I, too, am honored that you would take the time to greet me. May I ask your purpose in doing so?"

"Bethany has told me of your conversations with her. I have spoken to a number of your fellows and have found none with your great wisdom."

"It is true that Bethany has caused me to look deeply into my own soul," the Ryall replied.

"It is always difficult to grasp concepts that are alien to normal thought patterns," Kirsten said. "That you have succeeded in doing so reflects credit on the Clan of the Scented Waters."

"I thank the daughter of the Moldares for her kind words."

"I would ask a favor of you, Varlan."

"What favor?"

"I am one who studies your admirable species as a profession."

"You are an interrogator of captives?"

"Yes," Kirsten answered with more honesty than she would have used with a human being.

"And you wish to interrogate me?"

"I wish to study more deeply the wisdom which led you to your new insight. I have a drug which will aid in the examination."

"Drug?" Varlan asked. The translator signaled the sudden alarm which the Ryall felt by increasing its volume.

"It will make your limbs heavy and possibly cause your eyes to feel hot. You will not be harmed in any way."

Varlan folded her ears tight against her head and turned to face Bethany. "Is this *your* wish, Bethany of the Lindquists?"

"It would be most helpful, Varlan."

The Ryall hesitated for long seconds, then made the gesture that signified reluctant acceptance of a situation.

"Please assume a resting position," Kirsten ordered.

Varlan tucked her six legs up under her torso and wrapped her tail close in as she sank slowly to the carpeted deck. Kirsten extracted a hypodermic gun from her medkit and walked to where the Ryall lay. Kneeling, she ran her fingers across Varlan's back, searching the Ryall's dorsal spine for a particular vertebra. When she found it, she pressed the hypodermic to the joint and injected a dose of the drug.

"The drug will take a moment to become effective, Varlan. Do not be frightened by the sensations. They are harmless."

The two women watched carefully as the Ryall's head began to wobble, then slowly slipped downward to the deck. Less than a minute after the injection, the Ryall lay stretched out like a sleeping dragon. Only her eyes showed that she was awake and aware.

"How do you feel?" Kirsten asked from her position beside the prone centaur.

"Sleepy, but not sleepy," the translator box around the Ryall's neck responded. The computer's diction was as clear as ever, but Bethany thought she detected an imprecision in the Ryall's own speech pattern. She commented on it to Kirsten.

"That's normal," the psychologist replied. She used a small box to check the Ryall's heart rate, temperature, and respiration, then nodded with satisfaction. "She's definitely under. Start out simply, as we discussed."

Bethany slid down next to the prone form on the deck, making it easier for Varlan to see her. "What is your full name, please?"

"I am Varlan of the Scented Waters Clan."

"And your home world?"

"Beautiful Darthan!"

"And what was your position on Corlis?"

"I was the manager of the mineral extraction facility."

"Do you know who I am?"

"You are Bethany of the Lindquists, human and my jailer."

"Am I nothing else to you?"

"You relieve my boredom and teach me about your species, which my kind call 'monsters.'"

"Surely you don't think that I am a monster, Varlan."

The Ryall didn't answer. Kirsten gestured that Bethany should repeat the question, which she did. There was another long delay in which Bethany noted that Varlan's breathing shifted from a slow, rhythmic motion to a fast, shallow pant. Whatever control the drug had over her wasn't complete. Somewhere beneath that gray-green hide stretched over the pear-shaped skull, a battle raged. Then, suddenly, it was as though a barrier had given way somewhere in the Ryall's mind. Varlan began to emit a long squeal of sound nearly too fast for the translator to keep up.

"You are worse than a monster! Your species is the spawn of the Evil Star who would gorge yourselves on our hatchlings if we gave you the chance. You are creatures who must be destroyed, even though your destruction be the work of a thousand generations!"

The aircraft from Mohave Spaceport delivered a thoroughly dejected Bethany Drake into the arms of her husband some sixteen hours later.

"How did it go?" he asked after a kiss of greeting. The question was purely rhetorical. He could see from her expression how it had gone.

"Oh, Richard, it was horrible!" she sobbed. "You can't imagine how much Varlan hates us."

"And her conversion to our point of view?"

"All a sham. She had some vague plan about getting Earth's location to the Ryall High Command. Here I thought I was making real progress, and all the time she was planning an attack on Earth."

Drake drew his wife into his arms and held her. They stood that way for long minutes, oblivious to the looks of passersby. Finally, Bethany sniffed, lifted her head from his shoulder, and forced a smile. "And how was your day, my husband?"

"Compared to yours?" he asked. "Not good. I'll tell you about it when we get back to the hotel."

Later, in the privacy of their room, he recounted the session in the first coordinator's office. She listened in growing horror as he related the terrestrials' final conclusion.

"*Evacuation?* They can't be serious!"

"I'm afraid they're damned serious," Drake replied. "They've written off both Val and Hellsgate. Their strategy simulators give us no chance of dislodging the Ryall from Aezer."

"Then we'll resupply through the nebula."

Drake shook his head. "They checked that, too. The supply effort needed to hold off the Ryall would divert too many resources from the rest of human space. It would never be authorized."

"And yet, they are willing to undertake the more massive task of evacuating two entire star systems through the nebula. Where are they going to get *those* ships?"

"You don't need all that many, my love. I've seen their figures."

"We're talking *six billion* people, Richard. Four billion Sandarians and two billion of us. What with our belongings, it would take every starship in human space."

"They aren't talking about belongings. They plan to use cold sleep and stack the evacuees like cordwood. You can pack a lot of people in one of the big colony ships if you don't have to worry about minor things like eating, breathing, and elbow room."

"Surely they won't make us abandon everything, Richard. They can't be that cruel."

"The offer is to evacuate people, period! No dogs, no cats, no potted plants, no paintings, no possessions of

any kind. Considering that you go into a cold-sleep tank
nude, we may not even have the clothes off our backs
when we arrive wherever it is they decide to resettle us.
That is the other bit of good news. We won't be sent to a
single world. They want to disperse us throughout
human space."

"You told them no, of course."

He grinned. "We told them, *'Hell, no!'* "

"Good. What did they say to that?"

"They suggested that we avoid hasty judgments and
think about it awhile. They reminded us that we either
evacuate now or prepare to be overrun by the Ryall
sometime in the next twenty years."

"Surely there has to be another choice!" Bethany
said.

"If there is, I haven't thought of it."

She let her hand steal into his. They sat quietly for
long minutes while she tried to adjust to this new shock.
Finally, she turned to Drake. "What are we going to do,
Richard?"

He smiled the smile of one who has been pushed past
his limit. "I don't know about you, my beautiful wife,
but I think I'm going to get drunk! Care to join me?"

She shrugged. "Why not? I don't see how it can make
things worse than they already are!"

The binge proved to be a bust. Drake had finished
one drink and started another when he decided that
alcohol wasn't the answer. He looked up to discover
that his wife had not even finished her first. By mutual
consent, they retired to the balcony and sat side by
side on the chaise longue as they looked out over the
city.

The sun had long since set, leaving the lights of Mexico City a carpet of glittering jewels strewn across the
ancient lake bed where, more than eleven hundred years
earlier, Hernán Cortés had defeated the Aztec priest-
king Moctezuma II. Overhead, the stars were washed
out by the glow from the city until only the brightest
were visible. Still, Drake tried to trace the constella-
tions, gazing off to the south in the hope of spotting a

red-orange spark in the sky. After awhile, Bethany joined him.

"Is that it?" she asked, pointing out a star on the horizon where the Sierra Nevada mountains formed a black wall.

Drake shook his head. "Wrong direction. That's east. That's probably Mars you're looking at. I'm not sure that Antares is visible in Earth's northern hemisphere at this time of year, anyway."

Bethany snuggled close. "It doesn't matter. We couldn't see home, anyway."

Drake nuzzled her hair and smiled. "Remember the first time we met?"

"At Mrs. Mortridge's party? How can I forget? You were telling everyone about the *Conqueror* mission, and that man made that silly comment about how surprising it was that some of the dead spacers were women . . ."

"Whereupon you jumped in with both feet to set him straight about the history of women in space!"

She grinned. "Uncle Clarence always says that I have a tendency toward preachiness. Were you mad at me for interrupting your story?"

"Far from it. I had told that same tale a dozen times or more. You were a breath of fresh air. Besides, you were the most beautiful thing I had ever seen."

Bethany sighed. "And I thought you were particularly dashing in your uniform. I was flattered that you even bothered to talk to me."

They lapsed into silence again for long minutes. Finally, Bethany said, "Do you know what I'll miss the most if we're forced to evacuate, Richard?"

"We're not going to be."

"I know that," she answered. "But if we *were* going to abandon our homes, do you know what I would miss the most?"

"What?"

"The smell of the air after a spring rain in the highlands when the xanthro bushes all bloom at once."

Drake nodded. The heavy odor of the xanthro seeds was much favored as a perfume on Alta. Before the nova, extract of xanthro had been a major export industry for the planet.

"I think I'd miss hiking up Clearether Peak the most," Drake replied. "It's a struggle getting to the top, but once there you can see three hundred kilometers in every direction."

"Sounds like fun."

"I'll take you there—" Drake had been about to say that the two of them would climb Clearether someday. He stopped himself when he realized that the opportunity might never present itself.

Bethany had no difficulty following his interrupted train of thought. Tears welled up in her eyes.

"Damn it, Richard, it just isn't fair!"

"What isn't?"

"This whole situation. Here we are talking about losing our homes to the Ryall, and for what? Are we less intelligent than they are? Are they better warriors? Do they build better ships? No, on all counts! We're losing this damned war because the wrong damned star chose the wrong damned time to end its life. Why couldn't it have been Spica that exploded? Where would the Ryall have been then?" Bethany had sensed her husband's body suddenly go tense next to her. She turned and studied his expression, which was that of someone deep in thought. "Richard, what's wrong?"

"Nothing's wrong," he said after several seconds of silence. He sat up in the lounger, swung his legs over the side, and stood up. "I just had a weird thought."

"What?"

"Best that I don't get your hopes up just yet," he said before taking long strides toward the telephone screen inside.

Bethany followed, curious. "Who are you calling?"

"Grand Fleet Headquarters."

"Why?"

"I need access to one of their tactical simulators. I doubt my idea will stand up to analysis. And even if it turns out to be theoretically possible, it may not be practical."

"I don't understand, Richard."

He looked at her and grinned. "Neither do I—yet! But when I do, we may find that the Ryall aren't in nearly as impregnable a position as we think. In fact, the Antares Supernova may well have been the worst thing that ever happened to them!"

CHAPTER 28

Another meeting was convened in the first coordinator's office two days later. As before, the Interstellar Council was represented by Coordinators Gellard and Blenham; the Grand Fleet, by Admirals Belton and Ryerson; and the colonists, by Admiral Gower, Stan Barrett, and Count Husanic. Also present was Bethany Drake, who was now representing only herself. The only person missing from the gathering was Richard Drake, at whose instigation it had been arranged.

"Where is the good captain, Mrs. Drake?" Coordinator Blenham asked as he checked his wrist chronometer. It was already five minutes past the scheduled starting time, and Blenham was anxious to be done in time for his 1400 appointment.

"He'll be here," Bethany replied. "He's coming from Grand Fleet Headquarters and may have been delayed in traffic."

Coordinator Gellard turned to Belton. "What is Captain Drake doing at headquarters, Admiral?"

"We granted him access to our big strategic simulator two nights ago, Coordinator. He's been engaged in some sort of theoretical study ever since."

"What sort of study, Admiral?"

"Unknown, sir. Drake has everything under a personal security code that blocks everyone else from getting access to his project. Whatever he's doing is costing considerable computer time. There have been complaints from other users."

Gellard turned to Gower. "What do you know of this, Admiral?"

"Nothing," Admiral Gower responded. "I haven't been in contact with Captain Drake since our last conference in this office. As you can well imagine, none of us have felt like socializing lately."

"Mrs. Drake?"

Bethany shook her head slowly. "Sorry, Coordinator. All I know is that we were sitting on our balcony the night before last when he jumped up, called a taxi, and headed off into the night for Grand Fleet H.Q. Except for the call where he asked me to set up this meeting, I haven't seen or talked to him since."

Gellard opened his mouth to say something but was cut off by the brief chime of his desk intercom. He leaned forward and pressed a control. "Yes?"

"Captain Drake is here to see you, Coordinator."

"Send him in."

A moment later, the door opened and Richard Drake entered the office. Two days of continuous effort punctuated only by brief catnaps and hurriedly eaten snacks had transformed him. There were dark circles under his red-rimmed eyes, his cheeks were sunken, and his normally immaculate uniform looked as though it had been slept in. Despite the evidence of fatigue and lack of sleep, he strode purposefully across the office to stand in front of the first coordinator's desk.

Gellard gazed up at Drake. "When your wife asked for this meeting, Captain, I granted it because I thought you colonists had come to your senses regarding this Aezer matter. Now I find out that you've been utilizing expensive Grand Fleet equipment for a project which even your commanding officer knows nothing about. What is going on here?"

"I will be most happy to answer that question if I may borrow your holoscreen, Coordinator."

Gellard nodded. "By all means!"

Drake moved to the bookcase and touched the same control that he'd seen Admiral Ryerson use three days earlier. Once again the bookcase swung away from the wall to reveal the holoscreen behind it. Drake reached into an inner pocket and extracted a record tile, which he inserted into a slot next to the screen. He turned to face his audience.

"Gentlemen, three days ago you presented the results of a Grand Fleet analysis concerning the Altan–Sandarian plan to drive the Ryall from the Aezer star system. At that time you pointed out that the plan's basic assumption—that the Ryall would strip the Aezer–Hellsgate foldpoint defenses to reinforce Aezer–Hermes—was incorrect. By utilizing the astrogation data which we provided, you proved that the fast communications and travel times within the hegemony made it likely that the centaurs would reinforce directly from their home stars. Since such reinforcement makes a diversionary attack worse than useless, you recommended that the attack not be carried out as planned.

"Now, the obvious solution to such a predicament would be a strategy of simultaneous large-scale attacks against both foldpoints. Unfortunately, your analysis proved once again that such a tactic has little chance of working. The problem is that we would not be able to seize the system quickly enough to prevent the Ryall reinforcements from entering it. In such a situation, superior Ryall mobility would likely allow them to overpower any of our ships that survived the initial assault.

"Finally, you recommended that we accept the fact that our situation is hopeless and abandon our homes while there is still time to do so."

"Everyone in this room is well aware of recent events, Captain Drake. What is your point?"

"I am merely reminding you, Coordinator, that as things stand, no course of action appears likely to break the Ryall stranglehold on the Aezer system. I propose that we accept this unpleasant fact and look elsewhere for the solution to our dilemma. When solving a problem, gentlemen, it is always useful to step back a bit and look to fundamentals.

"Several weeks ago, Coordinator, I sat in Grand Fleet Headquarters and listened to your chief strategist attempt to explain away the obvious fact that humanity has been losing ground to the Ryall for much of the past century. What I heard was that the Ryall have more ships and a larger resource base than we do. Yet the Ryall data we captured show this not to be true. The Ryall fleet is *not* larger than our fleet. Their ships are no better equipped. Indeed, the Ryall hegemony is substantially smaller than human space, and Ryall warriors are neither smarter, more tenacious, nor braver than human warriors." Drake paused in his recitation and looked at his audience. "So why, gentlemen, are we still losing this war?"

"They have Spica," Coordinator Blenham said.

"Correct! At the risk of disagreeing with the poet, the fault lies not in ourselves but in our stars. The Ryall are the beneficiaries of a simple accident of nature. They inhabit the Spica Foldspace Cluster."

Drake turned abruptly and activated the control that brought the holoscreen to life. In the screen's pseudo-depth was a diagram very like the one Drake had developed that first night he'd learned the Ryall secret. Scintillating in the blackness of space lay all the stars of human space and the Ryall hegemony. Each star was color-coded and had a tiny line connecting it to its neighbors.

"Here we see the problem displayed in a form which is relatively easy to understand. Where we humans are spread along the spiral arm in a collection of stars only barely related to one another, the Ryall inhabit a compact ball of stars, each tied closely to Spica. As Admiral Belton explained in our last meeting, the advantages of this arrangement include substantially faster communications between systems, a more efficient utilization of natural resources, and a degree of industrial integration which our own worlds can only dream about. While none of these factors is decisive in and of itself, taken in toto, they give the Ryall an advantage that we find nearly impossible to overcome."

Drake stabbed out with a finger and pointed to the star that was at the center of the ball of red threads that permeated the Ryall portion of the screen. "If we are ever to win this war, we will have to counter the advantages which the Ryall derive from their foldspace cluster."

"And how do you propose to do that, Captain?" Blenham asked.

Drake grinned. "Quite easily, Coordinator. All we need do is capture and hold Spica!"

There was a sudden silence from each of the listeners. Even Bethany was surprised to the point of speechlessness. Finally, Admiral Belton came alive. He looked from the screen to Drake and back again.

"Captain, I hope you don't take offense at my next remark. Whether you do or not, however, I must ask it. *Are you drunk, or just plain crazy?*"

"Neither, Admiral. It can be done. I know because I've spent the past two days proving that it can be done!"

"If you can't dislodge the Ryall from Aezer, how the hell do you propose securing the central star of their whole damned hegemony? For Christ's sake, how do you propose getting to Spica in the first place?"

"By using the back door, Admiral. Specifically, the transition sequence will be Antares, Eulysta, Carratyl, Spica."

"They'll slaughter you before you get halfway there."

"No, they won't. Remember, the entire Ryall fleet is centered in the Aezer, Constantine, and Klamath systems. Eulysta, being one of their interior stars, is virtually uninhabited. Even if they are rebuilding the Corlis Complex, there won't be more than half a dozen commercial starships in the system. As for Carratyl, it's a backwater agricultural system with a single naval base and no foldpoint defenses at all. If we can only get to the Carratyl–Spica foldpoint before the alarm is spread throughout the hegemony, we'll be able to pour an overwhelming force of ships into Spica before they'll be able to react."

"Let's say we succeed in capturing Spica," Belton said. "What's to stop the whole damned Ryall navy from pouncing on us immediately thereafter?"

"Nothing, Admiral. In fact, you can expect them to do just that. But remember our own problems in attempting to break the Ryall blockade of Aezer. By capturing Spica, we turn the existing tactical equation on its ear. This time it will be the human forces which possess interior lines of communication, superior coordination, and mobility. For once, it will be the Ryall who will have to fight blind. They will be forced to feed their fleets through the various foldpoints piecemeal, and we will destroy them the same way."

"How long do you think we can hold eight separate foldpoints against determined attack?" Ryerson asked.

"As long as necessary, sir. Our assault force will hold only long enough for us to bring up orbital fortresses. We will get those by stripping some of the foldpoint defenses here in human space. Once the fortresses are in place, we will be able to hold Spica as well as we hold our own systems."

"Hold it for how long?"

"Until they either learn civility or run out of ships."

"That could take the better part of a thousand years!"

"I don't think so, sir. You see, the centaurs' great advantage is also their Achilles' heel. The hegemony depends on fast, inexpensive star travel. Their industrial base is highly integrated, with each world specializing in what it does best. The moment we succeed in blocking the hub system of their foldspace cluster, their industrial machine begins to fall apart. If we maintain our choke hold long enough, the hegemony will suffer a catastrophic economic collapse. Once that happens, their ability to wage war will be gone. We can then capture their home systems one at a time. We'll force them back to their home worlds until they learn to accept our right to exist."

Coordinator Gellard turned to Gower. "You have

been very quiet during all of this, Admiral. What do you think of this fantastic scheme?"

"I'm not sure what to make of it, Coordinator," Gower replied. "It certainly has the virtue of originality. Also, I find that I like it much better than your suggestion that we abandon Alta and Sandar to the Ryall. Still, it's a big step."

"Too big a step, I fear," Gellard replied. "The council will never take such a gamble."

Drake, who had been living on stimulants for two days, listened to the cavalier rejection of his plan and fought back rising anger.

"The council doesn't have any choice in the matter." Drake turned to his wife. "Tell him what Varlan told you!"

Bethany recounted her interview with the Ryall prisoner and her disappointment at learning that Varlan's seeming conversion had been a sham. She told them of the Ryall's half-formed hope that someday she would be able to get the information of Earth's location to the Ryall high command.

"Don't you see?" Drake asked when Bethany had finished. "If they ever discover Earth's location, they mean to destroy it! That is the choice which faces the council. Either we go after Spica now that we know their secret, or else they come after Earth as soon as they learn ours. Which will it be?"

The coordinator was silent for long seconds. Bethany's revelation had obviously had an impact on him. Nearly a minute passed before a troubled man looked at Drake and nodded slowly. "I'll see that your plan is brought before the council. What they will do with it, I cannot predict."

EPILOGUE

Richard Drake was working at his desk aboard Alta's newest blastship, *Conquerer II*, when his communications screen beeped for attention. He keyed acceptance and found himself face to face with the chief communications officer.

"What is it, Mr. Haydn?"

"We've just received a Priority One Flash from Earth, Admiral. It's in code and addressed to all ships and command centers."

"Put it on my screen."

A moment later, random alphanumeric groups began to scroll up Drake's screen. He input his personal authorization code, and the groupings were instantly transformed into sentences. Drake scanned the message with a growing sense of excitement.

****MOST SECRET****MOST SECRET****
****MOST SECRET****

FROM: COMMANDER—SPICA ASSAULT
        FORCE

TO: COMMANDING OFFICERS, ALL SHIPS
AND COMMAND CENTERS

DATE: 17 JULY 2642 (U.C.)

SUBJECT: BATTLE ORDERS

MESSAGE BEGINS:

1. AT 1314 STANDARD, THIS DATE, GUARD
FORCE—ANTARES REPORTED THE PENE-
TRATION BY A SINGLE RYALL CRAFT INTO
THE NEBULA FROM EULYSTA.

2. THE SUBJECT CRAFT WAS ENGAGED
AND DESTROYED BEFORE IT COULD RE-
TURN TO ITS BASE.

3. PURSUANT TO STANDING ORDERS RE-
GARDING A RYALL PENETRATION OF THE
NEBULA, ALL SHIPS WILL PROCEED IM-
MEDIATELY TO THEIR JUMP-OFF POINTS.

4. FLEET RENDEZVOUS WILL TAKE PLACE
AT THE ANTARES—EULYSTA FOLDPOINT,
0100 HOURS, 25 AUGUST 2642 (U.C.).

5. EULYSTA ASSAULT WILL BEGIN AT 0900
HOURS, 25 AUGUST 2642.

6. GOOD LUCK AND GODSPEED TO YOU
ALL!

BELTON, G.T.
COMMANDING ADMIRAL
SPICA ASSAULT FORCE

MESSAGE ENDS.

****MOST SECRET****MOST SECRET****
****MOST SECRET****

Drake finished the message and turned to Moriet
Haydn. "Notify all captains, first officers, and astrogators that there will be an officers' briefing aboard the
flagship in two hours. Then get me Mrs. Drake. She

should be at the university. If not, try my home."

"Yes, sir," the communicator replied crisply. "Are we on, Admiral?"

Drake nodded. "We're on!"

While he waited, Drake leaned back in his chair and thought of all the things yet to be done before the three dozen starships of the Altan contingent would be truly ready for battle. The fleet hadn't been scheduled to launch for another six weeks. Launching this early would create a multitude of problems, not the least of which would be the need to complete numerous maintenance tasks while under boost. Still, it could have been far worse. Had the centaurs penetrated the nebula a year earlier, they would have found humanity ill prepared for the confrontation.

"Your wife is on the line, Admiral."

"Thank you, Mr. Haydn. Secure this channel, please."

"Secured, sir."

Drake felt his heart stutter as Bethany's features flashed on the screen. It had been two months since he'd last been home, and even the pace at which he'd been driving himself couldn't completely mask his loneliness.

"What's the matter, Richard?" Bethany asked, her voice and expression showing her apprehension at the unexpected call.

"We just got word that the Ryall have crashed the nebula."

Bethany emitted a quick gasp. "How many ships?"

"Just one. The guard force took care of it."

"How do you suppose they figured it out?"

He shrugged. "Could have been anything. Maybe we didn't cover our tracks well enough back on Corlis. Or maybe some Ryall genius asked the same questions we did once we realized *Conqueror* had come through the nebula. It won't do them any good, though. They lost their ship and will be wondering if they've misplaced a decimal point in their calculations. By the time they're ready to try again, we'll be all over them."

"When are you leaving?"

"First units depart parking orbit in six hours."

"I wish you didn't have to go so soon," she said, her voice suddenly cracking with emotion.

"I'm glad the time has finally come," he replied. "We've delayed too long as it is. We should have launched six months ago. I'm just sorry I won't be here for the birth of our son."

"I'll forgive you this one time," she replied with a forced laugh. "After all, what you're doing is more important than what I'll be doing."

He shook his head. "Never more important, my love. Merely more pressing. Anyway, I'll be back before the little hellion's first birthday."

"Promise?"

"I promise."

There was a long delay in which Drake saw tears appear in Bethany's eyes. His own eyes felt damp as well. Finally, she whispered, "I love you, Richard."

Drake reached out and touched the face of the screen as if to stroke her cheek. "I love you, too, my darling. I'm sorry, but I've got to go. I've a staff conference to prepare for. I'll call you again this same time tomorrow and every day until we jump for Napier."

"I'll be waiting," she replied.

He blew her a kiss, then broke the circuit. After a minute, he called up an external view and watched the line of ships that trailed *Conqueror II* in its orbit. First came *Discovery*, now under Rorqual Marchant's command. Beyond the battle cruiser were her sister ships, *Dagger* and *Dreadnought*. And beyond these, the newer ships faded out of sight in an unbroken chain. The two years since the Helldiver Expedition's return from Earth had been busy ones for Alta's shipyards.

As he watched his trailing armada, Drake's gaze was attracted to the glint of a particularly bright spark in the upper portion of his screen. He didn't have to consult his ephemeris to know what star he was looking at. Even though the Antares Supernova had grown progressively dimmer as Alta fell ever deeper into the expanding bubble of nova light, the nova was still the brightest star in Alta's sky.

Somehow that seemed fitting. For beyond that incandescent beacon, two great fleets would soon vie for control of the galaxy. It would be a fierce battle and one whose outcome was far from certain. No one knew better than Drake the risks the Spica campaign represented for humanity's future. It was a single throw of the dice on which had been bet the survival of two intelligent species. Despite the enormity of the wager, however, there was no reasonable alternative for humankind. For nearly a century, the Ryall had been slowly winning their war of attrition against the worlds of human space. Unless the geography of foldspace could be changed in the near future, the situation could only end in Earth's destruction and humanity's defeat.

The attack on Spica would give humankind a chance to put right the damage caused by the Antares Nova—*a fighting chance*. Down through the ages, that was all human beings had ever asked for. It was all they had ever needed.

ABOUT THE AUTHOR

Michael McCollum was born in Phoenix, Arizona, in 1946 and is a graduate of Arizona State University, where he majored in aerospace propulsion and minored in nuclear engineering. He has been employed as an aerospace engineer since graduation and has worked on nearly every military and civilian aircraft in production today. At various times in his career, Mr. McCollum has also worked on the precursor to the Space Shuttle Main Engine, a nuclear valve to replace the one that failed at Three Mile Island, and a variety of guided missiles.

He began writing in 1974 and has been a regular contributor to *Analog Science Fiction*. He has also appeared in *Isaac Asimov's* and *Amazing*. *Antares Passage* is his fifth novel for Del Rey.

He is married to a lovely lady by the name of Catherine and is the father of three children: Robert, Michael, and Elizabeth.